THE SUPERNATURAL TALES OF THOMAS HARDY

Edited by Peter Haining

W. Foulsham & Co. Ltd.

London · New York · Toronto · Cape Town · Sydney

'A story dealing with the supernatural should never be explained away in the unfortunate manner of Mrs Radcliffe.'

THOMAS HARDY
(1840–1928)

'At mothy curfew-tide – they've a way of whispering to me.' A sketch by Thomas Hardy himself illustrating his fascination with the supernatural

W. Foulsham & Company Limited
Yeovil Road, Slough, Berkshire, SL1 4JH

ISBN 0–572–01489–9

Printed in Great Britain by St. Edmundsbury Press,
Bury St. Edmunds, Suffolk.

CONTENTS

A master of the macabre – Thomas Hardy photographed by Walter Thomas

INTRODUCTION

Thomas Hardy's life-long fascination with the supernatural and his utilisation of the theme in his novels and short stories is one of the less appreciated elements of this great writer's work. Although he remains to this day one of the most widely read of all literary authors – in 1987, for instance, he toppled Charles Dickens as the most popular novelist among the examiners who choose the texts to be studied in schools, with seven titles to Dickens' five – his contribution to the supernatural genre tends to be overlooked amidst the wealth of his 'realistic' stories. Yet, as I hope this long-overdue volume will prove, he was also a master of the tale of mystery and the macabre and of the 40-odd short stories he wrote during his career, over a third of these feature the supernatural in one form or another.

I must confess that I was not aware of the full extent of Hardy's contribution to the genre until some years ago when I began to follow up an intriguing episode in one of his most famous novels, *Tess of the D'Urbervilles* published in 1891. The incident I am referring to concerns Tess and the Phantom Coach of the D'Urbervilles which appears in Chapter XXXIII. It caught my interest the moment I read it, and not only prompted me to try and discover the basis of the legend – if, indeed, there *was* any truth in it – but also whether phantoms and the supernatural in general were topics that Hardy had referred to elsewhere in his work.

I quickly came to realise that not only was he as intrigued by the whole subject as I am myself, but that he had drawn liberally on the local traditions and superstitions of the West Country as the basis for several of his other books and a substantial number of his short stories. The supernatural, I discovered, had first surfaced in one of his earliest novels, *Desperate Remedies* (1871) – which, on reading, I found to be firmly rooted in the Gothic school of fiction – followed by *The Return of the Native* (1878) and the aforementioned *Tess*, and was a continuing element in his short tales from 'What The Shepherd Saw' written in 1881 right through to his very last piece of prose, 'A Changed Man' published in 1900. After that, it was still to be found as a continuing thread in the poetry which he turned to as his sole means of expression after the Church, some critics and even members of the public attacked what they saw as the pessimism and even anti-Christian feeling in his later books.

It is, I think, worth quoting the episode from *Tess* because it is so representative of Hardy's interest in the subject as well as being typical of the absorbing and unique manner in which he presented it for his readers – a style now the envy of many a writer in the supernatural genre. The legend of the ghostly coach is related to Tess by Angel Clare, the man with whom she falls in love.

> 'I tremble at many things.' (Tess says) 'It is all so serious, Angel. Among other things I seem to have seen this carriage before, to be very well acquainted with it. It is very odd – I must have seen it in a dream.'

'Oh – you have heard the legend of the D'Urberville Coach – that well-known superstition of this county about your family when they were very popular here; and this lumbering old thing reminds you of it.'

'I have never heard of it to my knowledge,' said she. 'What is the legend – may I know it?'

'Well, I would rather not tell it in detail just now. A certain D'Urberville of the sixteenth or seventeenth century committed a dreadful crime in his family coach; and since that time members of the family see or hear the old coach whenever – But I'll tell you another day – it is rather gloomy. Evidently some dim knowledge of it has been brought back to your mind by the sight of this venerable caravan.'

'I don't remember hearing it before,' she murmured. 'Is it when we are going to die, Angel, that members of my family see it, or is it when we have committed a crime?'

'Now, Tess!'

He silenced her by a kiss.

Enquiry has revealed that like so much Hardy wrote, there is a solid basis of fact in this legend. The original vehicle which the author heard about and incorporated into his story was said to be associated with the Turberville family of Dorset and ran from their ancestral seat at Woodbridge Manor to a point near Bere Regis. Catching sight of it was believed to presage a death in the family.

When or how Hardy heard this folk tale we do not know, but we have this assurance from one of his letters to the famous nineteenth century folklorist, Edward Clodd, dated 1894, about all such instances in his work: 'I may say, once for all, that every superstition, custom, etc., described in my novels may be depended on as true records of the same, whatever merit they may have as such, and are not inventions of mine.'

There seems little doubt that he was picking up scraps of information about the supernatural right from his childhood – a point which Ruth Firor has helped put into perspective in her excellent study, *Folkways in Thomas Hardy* (1962):

'Hardy, like Æschylus, had a temperamental leaning towards the use of premonitions, omens, ghosts and prophecies. He was born and spent the impressionable years of boyhood and young manhood among a people who still thought in a primitive way, upon whose lips an ancient dialect still lived, and in whose hearts lingered the dark, inexplicable fears of prehistoric man. Hardy grew up in this atmosphere; though always above it by reason of a cultivated mother, the forces of a formal education, and a widening acquaintance with the world outside of Wessex, he was nonetheless a part of his own community and gloried in the fact. Hardy's intimate knowledge of folklore and folk-custom had an almost incalculable influence upon his art.'

Accepting these facts, then, is it any wonder that the supernatural should feature so largely in his work? It would surely be a surprise if it had *not*! And let me just clarify the point here and now that by 'supernatural' I am using the word in its broadest sense, incorporating all that is weird, mysterious, macabre, inexplicable and even horrific. All of these elements you will find richly displayed in the stories which follow.

Thomas Hardy, who was born in 1840 in High Bockhampton in the Dorset parish of Stinsford, admitted that as a child he was 'imaginative, dreamy, credulous of vague mysteries.' Still, though, his stonemason father who was the leader of the church choir, instilled in him a love of music and saw him well schooled both locally and in Dorchester until he was 16. From there he began to train for that most practical of professions, architecture, leaving for London when he was 22. Yet despite all the attractions of the big city, still the lure of rural life and country traditions filled his mind – expressed in poetry and his early prose tales – until eventually the success of his novel, *Far From The Madding Crowd*, in 1874, drew him back to his native heath.

Through all of these years and beyond, though, he dreamed of experiencing the kind of strange events that filled local gossip. And, occasionally, he came very close to them, as an entry in his diary for February 28, 1883 indicates:

'Passed a lonely old house, formerly an inn. The road contractor now living there showed us into the stable, and drew our attention to the furthest stall. When the place was an inn, he said, it was the haunt of smugglers, and in a quarrel there one night a man was killed in that stall. If an old horse is put there on certain nights, at about two in the morning (when the smuggler died) the horse cries like a child, and on entering you find him in a lather of sweat.'

Not surprisingly, the thing Thomas Hardy most wanted was to actually see a ghost *himself*. Though, by now, he was generally thought of by his admirers as the epitomy of the man of reason, he confessed in one letter written in 1916 that this was not really the truth.

'You must not,' he said, 'think me a hard-headed rationalist for all this. Half my time – particularly when writing verse – I "believe" (in the modern sense of the word) not only in the things Bergson believes in, but in spectres, mysterious voices, intuitions, omens, dreams, haunted places, etc., etc.'

In time his desire for some confirmation about the supernatural became almost an obsession, and he informed one of his friends, William Archer, that he would 'give ten years of my life to see a ghost.' Remarkably, this request was granted – though we have no way of knowing whether the price was extracted! – if we are to believe another of his friends, Sir Sydney Cockerell. He tells us in his book, *Friends of a Lifetime* (1940) that Hardy saw a man dressed in clothes at least a century old in Stinsford Churchyard on Christmas Eve 1919.

'The ghost said, "A green Christmas,"' Sir Sydney writes. 'T.H. replied, "I like a green Christmas." Then the ghost went into the church, T. followed, to see who this strange man in 18th Century dress might be – and found no one.'

According to this same authority, Hardy later decided the phantom must have been that of his grandfather, who was buried in the churchyard. (Hardy, of course, buried his first wife in this churchyard, and though his own ashes were placed in Poets' Corner in Westminster Abbey – next to those of Dickens – before cremation, his heart was removed and this was laid to rest in Stinsford.)

Such evidence, and there is more of the same kind, serves to show just some of the reasons why Hardy was so interested in the supernatural and gave it such vivid expression – particularly in his short stories. I have heard it claimed that some of Thomas Hardy's finest efforts in fiction are to be found among his short stories, and on the evidence of the tales herein this is a claim not easy to dispute.

The eighteen items which form this collection have been drawn from a variety of sources, newspapers, magazines and books, all of which are detailed in the prefaces to each story. Some are earlier or alternative versions of the more easily obtainable stories, while all are presented in chronological order to show the development of Hardy's art in this particular genre.

In all of the stories, Hardy can be seen as a writer who brilliantly combines both the traditional and the modern, and whereas much of the fiction written in the last century has now been confined to the oblivion it deserves, his earns enthusiastic new readers with each passing generation. For though they undeniably present a world that has disappeared, there is much that is timeless in them, too. If that were not so, then why do we still enjoy the ghost story in an age when science endeavours to deny that such things exist? I am sure that as long as mankind acknowledges the darker recesses of his soul, then the supernatural stories of Thomas Hardy will have something to communicate to each and every one of us.

PETER HAINING
Boxford, Suffolk.
March 1988.

WHAT THE SHEPHERD SAW

Thomas Hardy wrote his first story of terror and the supernatural in the autumn of 1881 and as it was set at Christmas, it was published, most appropriately, in the Christmas number of *The Illustrated London News*. The tale concerns a shepherd boy, Bill Mills, who is the unobserved eyewitness to a brutal murder, and it is very much in the time honoured tradition of the Gothic horror story, right down to its location close to a group of Druid's stones. Hardy was very interested in the numerous ancient stone monuments to be found in his part of England, particularly the inherent mystery which is so much a part of them all, and they were to feature again in several of his later stories and novels. As Ruth Firor has commented on this story, 'All Druid Stones, of course, are favourite haunts of ghosts, and the trilithon on Marlbury Down is no exception.'

Marlbury Downs where the drama is enacted is, in fact, Marlborough Downs in Wiltshire, and Shakeforest Towers has been identified as Clatford Hall, a manor house on Clatford Down not far from the town of Marlborough. Close by is the Druidical trilithon of the tale known far and wide as the 'Devil's Den'. 'What The Shepherd Saw' is an impressive and chilling story by any standards, and once Hardy had proved to himself that he could work in the undeniably demanding genre of the supernatural, it is small wonder that he should have returned to the theme again and again.

WHAT THE SHEPHERD SAW

FIRST NIGHT

The genial Justice of the Peace – now, alas, no more – who made himself responsible for the facts of this story, used to begin in the good old-fashioned way with a bright moonlight night and a mysterious figure, an excellent stroke for an opening, even to this day, if well followed up.

The Christmas moon (he would say) was showing her cold face to the upland, the upland reflecting the radiance in frost-sparkles so minute as only to be discernible by an eye near at hand. This eye, he said, was the eye of a shepherd lad, young for his occupation, who stood within a wheeled hut of the kind commonly in use among sheep-keepers during the early lambing season, and was abstractedly looking through the loophole at the scene without.

The spot was called Lambing Corner, and it was a sheltered portion of that wide expanse of rough pasture land known as the

Marlbury Downs, which you directly traverse when following the turnpike-road across Mid-Wessex from London, through Aldbrickham, in the direction of Bath and Bristol. Here, where the hut stood, the land was high and dry, open, except to the north, and commanding an undulating view for miles. On the north side grew a tall belt of coarse furze, with enormous stalks, a clump of the same standing detached in front of the general mass. The clump was hollow, and the interior had been ingeniously taken advantage of as a position for the before-mentioned hut, which was thus completely screened from winds, and almost invisible, except through the narrow approach. But the furze twigs had been cut away from the two little windows of the hut, that the occupier might keep his eye on his sheep.

In the rear, the shelter afforded by the belt of furze bushes was artificially improved by an inclosure of upright stakes, interwoven with boughs of the same prickly vegetation, and within the inclosure lay a renowned Marlbury-Down breeding flock of eight hundred ewes.

To the south, in the direction of the young shepherd's idle gaze, there rose one conspicuous object above the uniform moonlit plateau, and only one. It was a Druidical trilithon, consisting of three oblong stones in the form of a doorway, two on end, and one across as a lintel. Each stone had been worn, scratched, washed, nibbled, split, and otherwise attacked by ten thousand different weathers; but now the blocks looked shapely and little the worse for wear, so beautifully were they silvered over by the light of the moon. The ruin was locally called the Devil's Door.

An old shepherd presently entered the hut from the direction of the ewes, and looked around in the gloom. 'Be ye sleepy?' he asked in cross accents of the boy.

The lad replied rather timidly in the negative.

'Then,' said the shepherd, 'I'll get me home-along, and rest for a few hours. There's nothing to be done here now as I can see. The ewes can want no more tending till daybreak – 'tis beyond the bounds of reason that they can. But as the order is that one of us must bide, I'll leave 'ee, d'ye hear. You can sleep by day, and I can't. And you can be down to my house in ten minutes if anything should happen. I can't afford 'ee candle; but, as 'tis Christmas week, and the time that folks have hollerdays, you can enjoy yerself by falling asleep a bit in the chair instead of biding awake all the time. But mind, not longer at once than while the shade of the Devil's Door moves a couple of spans, for you must keep an eye upon the ewes.'

The boy made no definite reply, and the old man, stirring the fire in the stove with his crook-stem, closed the door upon his companion and vanished.

As this had been more or less the course of events every night since the season's lambing had set in, the boy was not at all surprised at the charge, and amused himself for some time by lighting straws at the stove. He then went out to the ewes and new-born lambs, re-entered, sat down, and finally fell asleep. This was his customary manner of performing his watch, for though special permission for naps had this week been accorded, he had, as a matter of fact, done the same thing on every preceding night, sleeping often till awakened by a smack on the shoulder at three or four in the morning from the crook-stem of the old man.

It might have been about eleven o'clock when he awoke. He was so surprised at awaking without, apparently, being called or struck, that on second thoughts he assumed that somebody must have called him in spite of appearances, and looked out of the hut window towards the sheep. They all lay as quiet as when he had visited them, very little bleating being audible, and no human soul disturbing the scene. He next looked from the opposite window, and here the case was different. The frost-facets glistened under the moon as before; an occasional furze bush showed as a dark spot on the same; and in the foreground stood the ghostly form of the trilithon. But in front of the trilithon stood a man.

That he was not the shepherd or any one of the farm labourers was apparent in a moment's observation, his dress being a dark suit, and his figure of slender build and graceful carriage. He walked backwards and forwards in front of the trilithon.

The shepherd lad had hardly done speculating on the strangeness of the unknown's presence here at such an hour, when he saw a second figure crossing the open sward towards the locality of the trilithon and furze clump that screened the hut. This second personage was a woman; and immediately on sight of her the male stranger hastened forward, meeting her just in front of the hut window. Before she seemed to be aware of his intention he clasped her in his arms.

The lady released herself and drew back with some dignity.

'You have come, Harriet – bless you for it!' he exclaimed fervently.

'But not for this,' she answered, in offended accents. And then, more good-naturedly, 'I have come, Fred, because you entreated me so! What can have been the object of your writing such a letter? I feared I might be doing you grievous ill by staying away. How did you come here?'

'I walked all the way from my father's.'

'Well, what is it? How have you lived since we last met?'

'But roughly; you might have known that without asking. I have seen many lands and many faces since I last walked these downs, but I have only thought of you.'

'Is it only to tell me this that you have summoned me so strangely?'

A passing breeze blew away the murmur of the reply and several succeeding sentences, till the man's voice again became audible in the words, 'Harriet – truth between us two! I have heard that the Duke does not treat you too well.'

'He is warm-tempered, but he is a good husband.'

'He speaks roughly to you, and sometimes even threatens to lock you out of doors.'

'Only once, Fred! On my honour, only once. The Duke is a fairly good husband, I repeat. But you deserve punishment for this night's trick of drawing me out. What does it mean?'

'Harriet, dearest, is this fair or honest? Is it not notorious that your life with him is a sad one – that, in spite of the sweetness of your temper, the sourness of his embitters your days? I have come to know if I can help you. You are a Duchess, and I am Fred

Ogbourne; but it is not impossible that I may be able to help you. . . . By God! the sweetness of that tongue ought to keep him civil, especially when there is added to it the sweetness of that face!'

'Captain Ogbourne!' she exclaimed, with an emphasis of playful fear. 'How can such a comrade of my youth behave to me as you do? Don't speak so, and stare at me so! Is this really all you have to say? I see I ought not to have come. 'Twas thoughtlessly done.'

Another breeze broke the thread of discourse for a time.

'Very well. I perceive you are dead and lost to me,' he could next be heard to say; '"Captain Ogbourne" proves that. As I once loved you I love you now, Harriet, without one jot of abatement; but you are not the woman you were – you once were honest towards me; and now you conceal your heart in made-up speeches. Let it be; I can never see you again.'

'You need not say that in such a tragedy tone, you silly. You may see me in an ordinary way – why should you not? But, of course, not in such a way as this. I should not have come now, if it had not happened that the Duke is away from home, so that there is nobody to check my erratic impulses.'

'When does he return?'

'The day after tomorrow, or the day after that.'

'Then meet me again tomorrow night.'

'No, Fred, I cannot.'

'If you cannot tomorrow night, you can the night after; one of the two before he comes please bestow on me. Now, your hand upon it! Tomorrow or next night you will see me to bid me farewell!' He seized the Dutchess's hand.

'No, but Fred – let go my hand! What do you mean by holding me so? If it be love to forget all respect to a woman's present position in thinking of her past, then yours may be so, Frederick. It is not kind and gentle of you to induce me to come to this place for pity of you, and then to hold me tight here.'

'But see me once more! I have come two thousand miles to ask it.'

'O, I must not! There will be slanders – Heaven knows what! I cannot meet you. For the sake of old times don't ask it.'

'Then own two things to me; that you did love me once, and that your husband is unkind to you often enough now to make you think of the time when you cared for me.'

'Yes – I own them both,' she answered faintly. 'But owning such as that tells against me; and I swear the inference is not true.'

'Don't say that; for you have come – let me think the reason of your coming what I like to think it. It can do you no harm. Come once more!'

He still held her hand and waist. 'Very well, then,' she said. 'Thus far you shall persuade me. I will meet you tomorrow night or the night after. Now, let me go.'

He released her, and they parted. The Duchess ran rapidly down the hill towards the outlying mansion of Shakeforest Towers, and when he had watched her out of sight, he turned and strode off in the opposite direction. All then was silent and empty as before.

Yet it was only for a moment. When they had quite departed,

another shape appeared upon the scene. He came from behind the trilithon. He was a man of stouter build than the first, and wore the boots and spurs of a horseman. Two things were at once obvious from this phenomenon: that he had watched the interview between the Captain and the Duchess; and that, though he probably had seen every movement of the couple, including the embrace, he had been too remote to hear the reluctant words of the lady's conversation – or, indeed, any words at all – so that the meeting must have exhibited itself to his eye as the assignation of a pair of well-agreed lovers. But it was necessary that several years should elapse before the shepherd boy was old enough to reason out this.

The third individual stood still for a moment, as if deep in meditation. He crossed over to where the lady and gentleman had stood, and looked at the ground; then he too turned and went away in a third direction, as widely divergent as possible from those taken by the two interlocutors. His course was towards the highway; and a few minutes afterwards the trot of a horse might have been heard upon its frosty surface, lessening till it died away upon the ear.

The boy remained in the hut, confronting the trilithon as if he expected yet more actors on the scene, but nobody else appeared. How long he stood with his little face against the loophole he hardly knew; but he was rudely awakened from his reverie by a punch in his back, and in the feel of it he familiarly recognized the stem of the old shepherd's crook.

'Blame thy young eyes and limbs, Bill Mills – now you have let the fire out, and you know I want it kept in! I thought something would go wrong with 'ee up here, and I couldn't bide in bed no more than thistledown on the wind, that I could not! Well, what's happened, fie upon 'ee?'

'Nothing.'

'Ewes all as I left 'em?'

'Yes.'

'Any lambs want bringing in?'

'No.'

The shepherd relit the fire, and went out among the sheep with a lantern, for the moon was getting low. Soon he came in again.

'Blame it all – thou'st say that nothing have happened; when one ewe have twinned and is like to go off, and another is dying for want of half an eye of looking to! I told 'ee, Bill Mills, if anything went wrong to come down and call me; and this is how you have done it.'

'You said I could go to sleep for a hollerday, and I did.'

'Don't you speak to your betters like that, young man, or you'll come to the gallows-tree! You didn't sleep all the time, or you wouldn't have been peeping out of that there hole! Now you can go home, and be up here again by breakfast-time. I be an old man, and there's old men that deserve well of the world; but no – I must rest how I can!'

The elder shepherd then lay down inside the hut, and the boy went down the hill to the hamlet where he dwelt.

SECOND NIGHT

When the next night drew on the actions of the boy were almost enough to show that he was thinking of the meeting he had witnessed, and of the promise wrung from the lady that she would come there again. As far as the sheep-tending arrangements were concerned, tonight was but a repetition of the foregoing one. Between ten and eleven o'clock the old shepherd withdrew as usual for what sleep at home he might chance to get without interruption, making up the other necessary hours of rest at some time during the day: the boy was left alone.

The frost was the same as on the night before, except perhaps that it was a little more severe. The moon shone as usual, except that it was three quarters of an hour later in its course; and the boy's condition was much the same, except that he felt no sleepiness whatever. He felt, too, rather afraid; but upon the whole he preferred witnessing an assignation of strangers to running the risk of being discovered absent by the old shepherd.

It was before the distant clock of Shakeforest Towers had struck eleven that he observed the opening of the second act of this midnight drama. It consisted in the appearance of neither lover nor Duchess, but of the third figure – the stout man, booted and spurred – who came up from the easterly direction in which he had retreated the night before. He walked once round the trilithon, and next advanced towards the clump concealing the hut, the moonlight shining full upon his face and revealing him to be the Duke. Fear seized upon the shepherd boy: the Duke was Jove himself to the rural population, whom to offend was starvation, homelessness, and death, and whom to look at was to be mentally scathed and dumbfoundered. He closed the stove, so that not a spark of light appeared, and hastily buried himself in the straw that lay in a corner.

The Duke came close to the clump of furze and stood by the spot where his wife and the Captain had held their dialogue; he examined the furze as if searching for a hiding-place, and in doing so discovered the hut. The latter he walked round and then looked inside; finding it to all seeming empty, he entered, closing the door behind him and taking his place at the little circular window against which the boy's face had been pressed just before.

The Duke had not adopted his measures too rapidly, if his object were concealment. Almost as soon as he had stationed himself there eleven o'clock struck, and the slender young man who had previously graced the scene promptly reappeared from the north quarter of the down. The spot of assignation having, by the accident of his running forward on the foregoing night, removed itself from the Devil's Door to the clump of furze, he instinctively came thither, and waited for the Duchess where he had met her before.

But a fearful surprise was in store for him tonight, as well as for the trembling juvenile. At his appearance the Duke breathed more and more quickly, his breathings being distinctly audible to the crouching boy. The young man had hardly paused when the alert nobleman softly opened the door of the hut, and, stepping round the furze, came full upon Captain Fred.

'You have dishonoured her, and you shall die the death you deserve!' came to the shepherd's ears, in a harsh, hollow whisper through the boarding of the hut.

The apathetic and taciturn boy was excited enough to run the risk of rising and looking from the window, but he could see nothing for the intervening furze boughs, both the men having gone round to the side. What took place in the few following moments he never exactly knew. He discerned portion of a shadow in quick muscular movement; then there was the fall of something on the grass; then there was stillness.

Two or three minutes later the Duke became visible round the corner of the hut, dragging by the collar the now inert body of the second man. The Duke dragged him across the open space towards the trilithon. Behind this ruin was a hollow, irregular spot, overgrown with furze and stunted thorns, and riddled by the old holes of badgers, its former inhabitants, who had now died out or departed. The Duke vanished into this depression with his burden, reappearing after the lapse of a few seconds. When he came forth he dragged nothing behind him.

He returned to the side of the hut, cleansed something on the grass, and again put himself on the watch, though not as before, inside the hut, but without, on the shady side. 'Now for the second!' he said.

It was plain, even to the unsophisticated boy, that he now awaited the other person of the appointment – his wife, the Duchess – for what purpose it was terrible to think. He seemed to be a man of such determined temper that he would scarcely hesitate in carrying out a course of revenge to the bitter end. Moreover – though it was what the shepherd did not perceive – this was all the more probable, in that the moody Duke was labouring under the exaggerated impression which the sight of the meeting in dumb show had conveyed.

The jealous watcher waited long, but he waited in vain. From within the hut the boy could hear his occasional exclamations of surprise, as if he were almost disappointed at the failure of his assumption that his guilty Duchess would surely keep the tryst. Sometimes he stepped from the shade of the furze into the moonlight, and held up his watch to learn the time.

About half-past eleven he seemed to give up expecting her. He then went a second time to the hollow behind the trilithon, remaining there nearly a quarter of an hour. From this place he proceeded quickly over a shoulder of the declivity, a little to the left, presently returning on horseback, which proved that his horse had been tethered in some secret place down there. Crossing anew the down between the hut and the trilithon, and scanning the precincts as if finally to assure himself that she had not come, he rode slowly downwards in the direction of Shakeforest Towers.

The juvenile shepherd thought of what lay in the hollow yonder; and no fear of the crook-stem of his superior officer was potent enough to detain him longer on that hill alone. Any live company, even the most terrible, was better than the company of the dead; so, running with the speed of a hare in the direction pursued by the horseman, he overtook the revengeful Duke at the second descent (where the great western road crossed before you came to the old park entrance on that side – now closed up and the lodge cleared away, though at the time it was wondered why, being considered the most convenient gate of all).

Once within the sound of the horse's footsteps, Bill Mills felt comparatively comfortable; for, though in awe of the Duke because of his position, he had no moral repugnance to his companionship on account of the grisly deed he had committed, considering that powerful nobleman to have a right to do what he chose on his own lands. The Duke rode steadily on beneath his ancestral trees, the hoofs of his horse sending up a smart sound now that he had reached the hard road of the drive, and soon drew near the front door of his house, surmounted by parapets with square-cut battlements that cast a notched shade upon the gravelled terrace. These outlines were quite familiar to little Bill Mills, though nothing within their boundary had ever been seen by him.

When the rider approached the mansion a small turret door was quickly opened and a woman came out. As soon as she saw the horseman's outlines she ran forward into the moonlight to meet him.

'Ah dear – and are you come?' she said. 'I heard Hero's tread just when you rode over the hill, and I knew it in a moment. I would have come further if I had been aware—'

'Glad to see me, eh?'

'How can you ask that?'

'Well; it is a lovely night for meetings.'

'Yes, it is a lovely night.'

The Duke dismounted and stood by her side. 'Why should you have been listening at this time of night, and yet not expecting me?' he asked.

'Why, indeed! There is a strange story attached to that, which I must tell you at once. But why did you come a night sooner than you said you would come? I am rather sorry – I really am!' (shaking her head playfully) 'for as a surprise to you I had ordered a bonfire to be built, which was to be lighted on your arrival tomorrow; and now it is wasted. You can see the outline of it just out there.'

The Duke looked across to a spot of rising glade, and saw the faggots in a heap. He then bent his eyes with a bland and puzzled air on the ground, 'What is this strange story you have to tell me that kept you awake?' he murmured.

'It is this – and it is really rather serious. My cousin Fred Ogbourne – Captain Ogbourne as he is now – was in his boyhood a great admirer of mine, as I think I have told you, though I was six years his senior. In strict truth, he was absurdly fond of me.'

'You have never told me of that before.'

'Then it was your sister I told – yes, it was. Well, you know I have not seen him for many years, and naturally I had quite forgotten his admiration of me in old times. But guess my surprise when the day before yesterday, I received a mysterious note bearing no address, and found on opening it that it came from him. The contents frightened me out of my wits. He had returned from Canada to his father's house, and conjured me by all he could think of to meet him at once. But I think I can repeat the exact words, though I will show it to you when we get indoors.'

'MY DEAR COUSIN HARRIET,' the note said, 'After this long absence you will be surprised at my sudden reappearance, and more by what I am going to ask. But if my life and future are of any concern to you at all, I beg that you will grant my request. What I require of you, is, dear Harriet, that you meet me about eleven tonight by the Druid stones on Marlbury Downs, about a mile or more from your house. I cannot say more, except to entreat you to come. I will explain all when you are there. The one thing is, I want to see you. Come alone. Believe me, I would not ask this if my happiness did not hang upon it – God knows how entirely! I am too agitated to say more – Yours.

FRED.'

'That was all of it. Now, of course, I ought not to have gone, as it turned out, but that I did not think of then. I remembered his impetuous temper, and feared that something grievous was impending over his head, while he had not a friend in the world to help him, or any one except myself to whom he would care to make his trouble known. So I wrapped myself up and went to Marlbury Downs at the time he had named. Don't you think I was courageous?'

'Very.'

'When I got there – but shall we not walk on; it is getting cold?' The Duke, however, did not move. 'When I got there he came, of course, as a full grown man and officer, and not as the lad that I had known him. When I saw him I was sorry I had come. I can hardly tell you how he behaved. What he wanted I don't know even now; it seemed to be no more than the mere meeting with me. He held me by the hand and waist – O so tight – and would not let me go till I had promised to meet him again. His manner was so strange and passionate that I was afraid of him in such a lonely place, and I promised to come. Then I escaped – then I ran home – and that's all. When the time drew on this evening for the appointment – which, of course, I never intended to keep – I felt uneasy, lest when he found I meant to disappoint him he would come on to the house; and that's why I could not sleep. But you are so silent!'

'I have had a long journey.'

'Then let us get into the house. Why did you come alone and unattended like this?'

'It was my humour.'

After a moment's silence, during which they moved on, she said, 'I have thought of something which I hardly like to suggest to you. He said that if I failed to come tonight he would wait again tomorrow night. Now, shall we tomorrow night go to the hill together – just to see if he is there; and if he is, read him a lesson on his foolishness in nourishing this old passion, and sending for me so oddly, instead of coming to the house?'

'Why should we see if he's there?' said her husband moodily.

'Because I think we ought to do something in it. Poor Fred! He would listen to you if you reasoned with him, and set our positions in their true light before him. It would be no more than Christian kindness to a man who unquestionably is very miserable from some cause or other. His head seems quite turned.'

By this time they had reached the door, rung the bell, and

waited. All the house seemed to be asleep; but soon a man came to them, the horse was taken away, and the Duke and Duchess went in.

THIRD NIGHT

There was no help for it. Bill Mills was obliged to stay on duty, in the old shepherd's absence, this evening as before, or give up his post and living. He thought as bravely as he could of what lay behind the Devil's Door, but with no great success, and was therefore in a measure relieved, even if awe-striken, when he saw the forms of the Duke and Duchess strolling across the frosted greensward. The Duchess was a few yards in front of her husband and tripped on lightly.

'I tell you he has not thought it worth while to come again!' the Duke insisted, as he stood still, reluctant to walk further.

'He is more likely to come and wait all night; and it would be harsh treatment to let him do it a second time.'

'He is not here; so turn and come home.'

'He seems not to be here, certainly; I wonder if anything has happened to him. If it has, I shall never forgive myself!'

The Duke, uneasily, 'O, no. He has some other engagement.'

'That is very unlikely.'

'Or perhaps he has found the distance too far.'

'Nor is that probable.'

'Then he may have thought better of it.'

'Yes, he may have thought better of it; if, indeed, he is not here all the time – somewhere in the hollow behind the Devil's Door. Let us go and see; it will serve him right to surprise him.'

'O, he's not there.'

'He may be lying very quiet because of you,' she said archly.

'O, no – not because of me!'

'Come, then. I declare, dearest, you lag like an unwilling school-boy tonight and there's no responsiveness in you! You are jealous of that poor lad, and it is quite absurd of you.'

'I'll come! I'll come! Say no more, Harriet!' And they crossed over the green.

Wondering what they would do, the young shepherd left the hut, and doubled behind the belt of furze, intending to stand near the trilithon unperceived. But, in crossing the few yards of open ground he was for a moment exposed to view.

'Ah, I see him at last!' said the Duchess.

'See him!' said the Duke. 'Where?'

'By the Devil's Door; don't you notice a figure there? Ah, my poor lover-cousin, won't you catch it now?' And she laughed half-pityingly. 'But what's the matter?' she asked, turning to her husband.

'It is not he!' said the Duke hoarsely. 'It can't be he!'

'No, it is not he. It is too small for him. It is a boy.'

'Ah, I thought so! Boy, come here.'

The youthful shepherd advanced with apprehension.

'What are you doing here?'

'Keeping sheep, your Grace.'

'Ah, you know me! Do you keep sheep here every night?'

'Off and on, my Lord Duke.'

'And what have you seen here tonight or last night?' inquired the Duchess. 'Any person waiting or walking about?'

The boy was silent.

'He has seen nothing,' interrupted her husband, his eyes so forbiddingly fixed on the boy that they seemed to shine like points of fire. 'Come, let us go. The air is too keen to stand in long.'

When they were gone the boy retreated to the hut and sheep, less fearful now than at first – familiarity with the situation having gradually overpowered his thoughts of the buried man. But he was not to be left alone long. When an interval had elapsed of about sufficient length for walking to and from Shakeforest Towers, there appeared from that direction the heavy form of the Duke. He now came alone.

The nobleman, on his part, seemed to have eyes no less sharp than the boy's, for he instantly recognized the latter among the ewes, and came straight towards him.

'Are you the shepherd lad I spoke to a short time ago?'

'I be, my Lord Duke.'

'Now listen to me. Her Grace asked you what you had seen this last night or two up here, and you made no reply. I now ask the same thing, and you need not be afraid to answer. Have you seen anything strange these nights you have been watching here?'

'My Lord Duke, I be a poor heedless boy, and what I see I don't bear in mind.'

'I ask you again,' said the Duke, coming nearer, 'have you seen anything strange these nights you have been watching here?'

'O, my Lord Duke! I be but the under-shepherd boy, and my father he was but your humble Grace's hedger, and my mother only the cinder-woman in the back-yard! I fall asleep when left alone, and I see nothing at all!'

The Duke grasped the boy by the shoulder, and, directly impending over him, stared down into his face, 'Did you see anything strange done here last night, I say?'

'O, my Lord Duke, have mercy, and don't stab me!' cried the shepherd, falling on his knees. 'I have never seen you walking here, or riding here, or lying-in-wait for a man, or dragging a heavy load!'

'H'm!' said his interrogator, grimly, relaxing his hold. 'It is well to know that you have never seen those things. Now, which would you rather – *see me do those things now*, or keep a secret all your life?'

'Keep a secret, my Lord Duke!'

'Sure you are able?'

'O, your Grace, try me!'

'Very well. And now, how do you like sheep-keeping?'

'Not at all. 'Tis lonely work for them that think of spirits, and I'm badly used.'

'I believe you. You are too young for it. I must do something to make you more comfortable. You shall change this smock-frock for a real cloth jacket, and your thick boots for polished shoes. And you shall be taught what you have never yet heard of, and be put to school, and have bats and balls for the holidays, and be made a man of. But you must never say you have been a shepherd boy, and watched on the hills at night, for shepherd boys are not liked in good company.'

'Trust me, my Lord Duke.'

'The very moment you forget yourself, and speak of your shepherd days – this year, next year, in school, out of school, or riding in your carriage twenty years hence – at that moment my help will be withdrawn, and smash down you come to shepherding forthwith. You have parents, I think you say?'

'A widowed mother only, my Lord Duke.'

'I'll provide for her, and make a comfortable woman of her, until you speak of – what?'

'Of my shepherd days, and what I saw here.'

'Good. If you do speak of it?'

'Smash down she comes to widowing forthwith!'

'That's well – very well. But it's not enough. Come here.' He took the boy across to the trilithon, and made him kneel down.

'Now, this was once a holy place,' resumed the Duke. 'An altar stood here, erected to a venerable family of gods, who were known and talked of long before the God we know now. So that an oath sworn here is doubly an oath. Say this after me: "May all the host above – angels and archangels, and principalities and powers – punish me; may I be tormented wherever I am – in the house or in the garden, in the fields or in the roads, in church or in chapel, at home or abroad, on land or at sea; may I be afflicted in eating and in drinking, in growing up and in growing old, in living and dying, inwardly and outwardly, and for always, if I ever speak of my life as a shepherd boy, or of what I have seen done on this Marlbury Down. So be it, and so let it be. Amen and amen." Now kiss the stone.'

The trembling boy repeated the words, and kissed the stone, as desired.

The Duke led him off by the hand. That night the junior shepherd slept in Shakeforest Towers, and the next day he was sent away for tuition to a remote village. Thence he went to a preparatory establishment, and in due course to a public school.

Fourth Night

On a winter evening many years subsequent to the above-mentioned occurrences, the *ci-devant* shepherd sat in a well-furnished office in the north wing of Shakeforest Towers in the guise of an ordinary educated man of business. He appeared at this time as a person of thirty-eight or forty, though actually he was several years younger. A worn and restless glance of the eye now and then, when he lifted his head to search for some letter or paper which had been mislaid, seemed to denote that his was not a mind so thoroughly at ease as his surroundings might have led an observer to expect. His pallor, too, was remarkable for a countryman. He was professedly engaged in writing, but he shaped not a word. He had sat there only a few minutes, when, laying down his pen and pushing back his chair, he rested a hand uneasily on each of the chair-arms and looked on the floor.

Soon he arose and left the room. His course was along a passage which ended in a central octagonal hall; crossing this he knocked at a door. A faint, though deep, voice told him to come in. The room he entered was the library, and it was tenanted by a single person only – his patron the Duke.

During this long interval of years the Duke had lost all his heaviness of build. He was, indeed, almost a skeleton; his white hair was thin, and his hands were nearly transparent. 'Oh – Mills?' he murmured. 'Sit down. What is it?'

'Nothing new, your Grace. Nobody to speak of has written, and nobody has called.'

'Ah – what then? You looked concerned.'

'Old times have come to life, owing to something waking them.'

'Old times be cursed – which old times are they?'

'That Christmas week twenty-two years ago, when the late Duchess's cousin Frederick implored her to meet him on Marlbury Downs. I saw the meeting – it was just such a night as this – and I, as you know, saw more. She met him once, but not the second time.'

'Mills, shall I recall some words to you – the words of an oath taken on that hill by a shepherd boy?'

'It is unnecessary. He has strenuously kept that oath and promise. Since that night no sound of his shepherd life has crossed his lips – even to yourself. But do you wish to hear more, or do you not, your Grace?'

'I wish to hear no more,' said the Duke sullenly.

'Very well; let it be so. But a time seems coming – may be quite near at hand – when, in spite of my lips, that episode will allow itself to go undivulged no longer.'

'I wish to hear no more!' repeated the Duke.

'You need be under no fear of treachery from me,' said the steward, somewhat bitterly. 'I am a man to whom you have been kind – no patron could have been kinder. You have clothed and educated me; have installed me here; and I am not unmindful. But what of it – has your Grace gained much by my stanchness? I think not. There was great excitement about Captain Ogbourne's disappearance, but I spoke not a word. And his body has never been found. For twenty-two years I have wondered what you did with him. Now I know. A circumstance that occurred this afternoon recalled the time to me most forcibly. To make it certain to myself that all was not a dream, I went up there with a spade; I searched, and saw enough to know that something decays there in a closed badger's hole.'

'Mills, do you think the Duchess guessed?'

'She never did, I am sure, to the day of her death.'

'Did you leave all as you found it on the hill?'

'I did.'

'What made you think of going up there this particular afternoon?'

'What your Grace says you don't wish to be told.'

The Duke was silent; and the stillness of the evening was so marked that there reached their ears from the outer air the sound of a tolling bell.

'What is that bell tolling for?' asked the nobleman.

'For what I came to tell you of, your Grace.'

'You torment me – it is your way!' said the Duke querulously. 'Who's dead in the village?'

'The oldest man – the old shepherd.'

'Dead at last – how old is he?'

'Ninety-four.'

'And I am only seventy. I have four-and-twenty years to the good!'

'I served under that old man when I kept sheep on Marlbury Downs. And he was on the hill that second night, when I first exchanged words with your Grace. He was on the hill *all the time*; but I did not know he was there – nor did you.'

'Ah!' said the Duke, starting up. 'Go on – I yield the point – you may tell!'

'I heard this afternoon that he was at the point of death. It was that which set me thinking of that past time – and induced me to search on the hill for what I have told you. Coming back I heard that he wished to see the Vicar to confess to him a secret he had kept for more than twenty years – "out of respect to my Lord the Duke" – something that he had seen committed on Marlbury Downs when returning to the flock on a December night twenty-two years ago. I have thought it over. He had left me in charge that evening; but he was in the habit of coming back suddenly, lest I should have fallen asleep. That night I saw nothing of him, though he had promised to return. He must have returned, and – found reason to keep in hiding. It is all plain. The next thing is that the Vicar went to him two hours ago. Further than that I have not heard.'

'It is quite enough. I will see the Vicar at daybreak tomorrow.'

'What to do?'

'Stop his tongue for four-and-twenty years – till I am dead at ninety-four, like the shepherd.'

'Your Grace – while you impose silence on me, I will not speak, even though my neck should pay the penalty. I promised to be yours, and I am yours. But is this persistence of any avail?'

'I'll stop his tongue, I say!' cried the Duke with some of his old rugged force. 'Now, you go home to bed, Mills, and leave me to manage him.'

The interview ended, and the steward withdrew. The night, as he had said, was just such an one as the night of twenty-two years before, and the events of the evening destroyed in him all regard for the season as one of cheerfulness and goodwill. He went off to his own house on the further verge of the park, where he led a lonely life, scarcely calling any man friend. At eleven he prepared to retire to bed – but did not retire. He sat down and reflected. Twelve o'clock struck; he looked out at the colourless moon, and, prompted by he knew not what, put on his hat and emerged into the air. Here William Mills strolled on and on, till he reached the top of Marlbury Downs, a spot he had not visited at this hour of the night during the whole score-and-odd years.

He placed himself, as nearly as he could guess, on the spot where the shepherd's hut had stood. No lambing was in progress there now, and the old shepherd who had used him so roughly had ceased from his labours that very day. But the trilithon stood up white as ever; and, crossing the intervening sward, the steward fancifully placed his mouth against the stone. Restless and self-reproachful as he was, he could not resist a smile as he thought of the terrifying oath of compact, sealed by a kiss upon the stones of a Pagan temple. But he had kept his word, rather as a promise than as a formal vow, with much wordly advantage to himself, though not much happiness; till increase of years had bred reactionary feelings which led him to receive the news of tonight with emotions akin to relief.

While leaning against the Devil's Door and thinking on these things, he became conscious that he was not the only inhabitant of the down. A figure in white was moving across his front with long, noiseless strides. Mills stood motionless, and when the form drew quite near he perceived it to be that of the Duke himself in his nightshirt – apparently walking in his sleep. Not to alarm the old man, Mills clung close to the shadow of the stone. The Duke went straight on into the hollow. There he knelt down, and began scratching the earth with his hands like a badger. After a few minutes he arose, sighed heavily, and retraced his steps as he had come.

Fearing that he might harm himself, yet unwilling to arouse him, the steward followed noiselessly. The Duke kept on his path unerringly, entered the park, and made for the house, where he let himself in by a window that stood open – the one probably by which he had come out. Mills softly closed the window behind his patron, and then retired homeward to await the revelations of the morning, deeming it unnecessary to alarm the house.

However, he felt uneasy during the remainder of the night, no less on account of the Duke's personal condition than because of that which was imminent next day. Early in the morning he called at Shakeforest Towers. The blinds were down, and there was something singular upon the porter's face when he opened the door. The steward inquired for the Duke.

The man's voice was subdued as he replied: 'Sir, I am sorry to say that his Grace is dead! He left his room some time in the night, and wandered about nobody knows where. On returning to the upper floor he lost his balance and fell downstairs.'

The steward told the tale of the Down before the Vicar had spoken. Mills had always intended to do so after the death of the Duke. The consequences to himself he underwent cheerfully; but his life was not prolonged. He died, a farmer at the Cape, when still somewhat under forty-nine years of age.

The splendid Marlbury breeding flock is as renowned as ever, and, to the eye, seems the same in every particular that it was in earlier times; but the animals which composed it on the occasion of the events gathered from the Justice are divided by many ovine generations from its members now. Lambing Corner has long since ceased to be used for lambing purposes, though the name still lingers on as the appellation of the spot. This abandonment of site may be partly owing to the removal of the high furze bushes which lent such convenient shelter at that date. Partly, too, it may be due to another circumstance. For it is said by present shepherds in that district that during the nights of Christmas week flitting shapes are seen in the open space around the trilithon, together with the gleam of a weapon, and the shadow of a man dragging a burden into the hollow. But of these things there is no certain testimony.

THE THREE STRANGERS

'What The Shepherd Saw' has been described as a precursor of this second story, 'The Three Strangers', and indeed its mixture of the inexplicable and the grim shows how Hardy's skill at handling such themes had developed in less than two years. It, too, had been written late in the year of 1882 and was then first published in *Longman's Magazine* in March 1883.

'The Three Strangers' is to most intents and purposes a mystery story, with the reader as eye-witness to the coming and going of three men at a remote shepherd's cottage where a happy christening party is taking place. One of the strangers proves to be the local hangman on his way to perform the execution of a sheep stealer at Casterbridge. The revellers instinctively withdraw from this 'grim figure' – as Hardy describes him – some of them seeming to take him for the Devil himself. The two other visitors are key figures in the story, too, but it would spoil the reader's enjoyment of it if I were to reveal anything further about them here. Hardy placed this story at the start of his collection, *Wessex Tales* when it was issued in 1888, and in 1895 it was dramatised as 'The Three Wayfarers'. It was also selected for special praise by Herbert A. Wise and Phyllis Fraser in their prestigious anthology, *Great Tales of Terror and the Supernatural* (1947) when they described it as 'probably Hardy's best story.' It is certainly a tale that remains long in the memory and is an outstanding description of mounting tension.

THE THREE STRANGERS

Among the few features of agricultural England which retain an appearance but little modified by the lapse of centuries may be reckoned the high, grassy, and furzy downs, coombs, or ewe-leases, as they are indifferently called, that fill a large area of certain counties in the south and south-west. If any mark of human occupation is met with hereon, it usually takes the form of the solitary cottage of some shepherd.

Fifty years ago such a lonely cottage stood on such a down, and may possibly be standing there now. In spite of its loneliness, however, the spot, by actual measurement, was not more than five miles from a county-town. Yet that affected it little. Five miles of irregular upland, during the long inimical seasons, with their sleets, snows, rains, and mists afford withdrawing space enough to isolate a Timon or a Nebuchadnezzar; much less, in fair weather, to please that less repellent tribe, the poets, philosophers, artists, and others who 'conceive and meditate of pleasant things.'

Some old earthen camp or barrow, some clump of trees, at least some starved fragments of ancient hedge is usually taken advantage of in the erection of these forlorn dwellings. But, in the present case, such a kind of shelter had been disregarded. Higher Crowstairs, as the house was called, stood quite detached and undefended. The only reason for its precise situation seemed to be the crossing of two footpaths at right angles hard by, which may have crossed there and thus for a good five hundred years. Hence the house was exposed to the elements on all sides. But, though the wind up here blew unmistakably when it did blow, and the rain hit hard whenever it fell, the various weathers of the winter season were not quite so formidable on the coomb as they were imagined to be by dwellers on low ground. The raw rimes were not so pernicious as in the hollows, and the frosts were scarcely so severe. When the shepherd and his family who tenanted the house were pitied for their sufferings from the exposure, they said that upon the whole they were less inconvenienced by 'wuzzes and flames' (hoarses and phlegms) than when they had lived by the stream of a snug neighbouring valley.

The night of 28th March 182–, was precisely one of the nights that were wont to call forth these expressions of commiseration. The level rainstorm smote walls, slopes, and hedges like the cloth-yard shafts of Senlac and Crecy. Such sheep and outdoor animals as had no shelter stood with their buttocks to the winds; while the tails of little birds trying to roost on some scraggy thorn were blown inside-out like umbrellas. The gable-end of the cottage was stained with wet, and the eavesdroppings flapped against the wall. Yet never was commiseration for the shepherd more misplaced. For that cheerful rustic was entertaining a large party in glorification of the christening of his second girl.

The guests had arrived before the rain began to fall, and they were all now assembled in the chief or living room of the dwelling. A glance into the apartment at eight o'clock on this eventful evening would have resulted in the opinion that it was as cosy and comfortable a nook as could be wished for in boisterous weather. The calling of its inhabitant was proclaimed by a number of highly polished sheep crooks without stems that were hung ornamentally over the fireplace, the curl of each shining crook varying from the antiquated type engraved in the patriarchal pictures of old family Bibles to the most approved fashion of the last local sheep-fair. The room was lighted by half a dozen candles having wicks only a trifle smaller than the grease which enveloped them, in candlesticks that were never used but at high-days, holy-days, and family feasts. The lights were scattered about the room, two of them standing on the chimney-piece. This position of candles was in itself significant. Candles on the chimney-piece always meant a party.

On the hearth, in front of a back-brand to give substance, blazed a fire of thorns, that crackled 'like the laughter of the fool.'

Nineteen persons were gathered here. Of these, five women, wearing gowns of various bright hues, sat in chairs along the wall; girls shy and not shy filled the window-bench; four men, including Charley Jake the hedge-carpenter, Elijah New the parish-clerk, and

John Pitcher, a neighbouring dairyman, the shepherd's father-in-law, lolled in the settle; a young man and maid, who were blushing over tentative *pourparlers* on a life companionship, sat beneath the corner-cupboard; and an elderly engaged man of fifty or upward moved restlessly about from spots where his betrothed was not to the spot where she was. Enjoyment was pretty general, and so much the more prevailed in being unhampered by conventional restrictions. Absolute confidence in each other's good opinion begat perfect ease, while the finishing stroke of manner, amounting to a truly princely serenity, was lent to the majority by the absence of any expression or trait denoting that they wished to get on in the world, enlarge their minds, or do any eclipsing thing whatever – which nowadays so generally nips the bloom and *bonhomie* of all except the two extremes of the social scale.

Shepherd Fennel had married well, his wife being a dairyman's daughter from a vale at a distance, who brought fifty guineas in her pocket – and kept them there, till they should be required for ministering to the needs of a coming family. This frugal woman had been somewhat exercised as to the character that should be given to the gathering. A sit-still party had its advantages; but an undisturbed position of ease in chairs and settles was apt to lead on the men to such an unconscionable deal of toping that they would sometimes fairly drink the house dry. A dancing-party was the alternative; but this, while avoiding the foregoing objection on the score of good drink, had a counterbalancing disadvantage in the matter of good victuals, the ravenous appetites engendered by the exercise causing immense havoc in the buttery. Shepherdess Fennel fell back upon the intermediate plan of mingling short dances with short periods of talk and singing, so as to hinder any ungovernable rage in either. But this scheme was entirely confined to her own gentle mind: the shepherd himself was in the mood to exhibit the most reckless phases of hospitality.

The fiddler was a boy of those parts, about twelve years of age, who had a wonderful dexterity in jigs and reels, though his fingers were so small and short as to necessitate a constant shifting for the high notes, from which he scrambled back to the first position with sounds not of unmixed purity of tone. At seven the shrill tweedle-dee of this youngster had begun, accompanied by a booming groundbass from Elijah New, the parish clerk, who had thoughtfully brought with him his favourite musical instrument, the serpent. Dancing was instantaneous, Mrs Fennel privately enjoining the players on no account to let the dance exceed the length of a quarter of an hour.

But Elijah and the boy, in the excitement of their position, quite forgot the injunction. Moreover, Oliver Giles, a man of seventeen, one of the dancers, who was enamoured of his partner, a fair girl of thirty-three rolling years, had recklessly handed a new crownpiece to the musicians, as a bribe to keep going as long as they had muscle and wind. Mrs Fennel, seeing the steam begin to generate on the countenances of her guests, crossed over and touched the fiddler's elbow and put her hand on the serpent's mouth. But they took no notice, and fearing she might lose her character of genial hostess if she were to interfere too markedly, she retired and sat down helpless. And so the dance whizzed on with cumulative fury, the performers moving in their planet-like courses, direct and retrograde, from apogee to perigee, till the hand of the well-kicked clock at the bottom of the room had travelled over the circumference of an hour.

While these cheerful events were in course of enactment within Fennel's pastoral dwelling, an incident having considerable bearing on the party had occurred in the gloomy night without. Mrs Fennel's concern about the growing fierceness of the dance corresponded in point of time with the ascent of a human figure to the solitary hill of Higher Crowstairs from the direction of the distant town. This personage strode on through the rain without a pause, following the little-worn path which, farther on in its course, skirted the shepherd's cottage.

It was nearly the time of full moon, and on this account, though the sky was lined with a uniform sheet of dripping cloud, ordinary objects out of doors were readily visible. The sad, wan light revealed the lonely pedestrian to be a man of supple frame; his gait suggested that he had somewhat passed the period of perfect and instinctive agility, though not so far as to be otherwise than rapid of motion when occasion required. At a rough guess, he might have been about forty years of age. He appeared tall, but a recruiting sergeant, or other person accustomed to the judging of men's heights by the eye, would have discerned that this was chiefly owing to his gauntness, and that he was not more than five-feet-eight or nine.

Notwithstanding the regularity of his tread, there was caution in it, as in that of one who mentally feels his way; and despite the fact that it was not a black coat nor a dark garment of any sort that he wore, there was something about him which suggested that he naturally belonged to the black-coated tribes of men. His clothes were of fustian, and his boots hobnailed, yet in his progress he showed not the mud-accustomed bearing of hobnailed and fustianed peasantry.

By the time that he had arrived abreast of the shepherd's premises the rain came down, or rather came along, with yet more determined violence. The outskirts of the little settlement partially broke the force of wind and rain, and this induced him to stand still. The most salient of the shepherd's domestic erections was an empty sty at the forward corner of his hedgeless garden, for in these latitudes the principle of masking the homelier features of your establishment by a conventional frontage was unknown. The traveller's eye was attracted to this small building by the pallid shine of the wet slates that covered it. He turned aside, and, finding it empty, stood under the pent-roof for shelter.

While he stood, the boom of the serpent within the adjacent house, and the lesser strains of the fiddler, reached the spot as an accompaniment to the surging hiss of the flying rain on the sod, its louder beating on the cabbage-leaves of the garden, on the eight or ten beehives just discernible by the path, and its dripping from the eaves into a row of buckets and pans that had been placed under the walls of the cottage. For at Higher Crowstairs, as at all such elevated domiciles, the grand difficulty of housekeeping was an insufficiency of water; and a casual rainfall was utilized by turning out, as catchers, every utensil that the house contained. Some queer stories might be told of the contrivances for economy in suds and dishwaters that are absolutely necessitated in upland habitations during the droughts of summer. But at this season there were no such exigencies; a mere acceptance of what the skies bestowed was sufficient for an abundant store.

At last the notes of the serpent ceased and the house was silent. This cessation of activity aroused the solitary pedestrian from the reverie into which he had elapsed, and, emerging from the shed, with an apparently new intention, he walked up the path to the house-door. Arrived here, his first act was to kneel down on a large stone beside the row of vessels, and to drink a copious draught from one of them. Having quenched his thirst, he rose and lifted his hand to knock, but paused with his eye upon the panel. Since the dark surface of the wood revealed absolutely nothing, it was evident that he must be mentally looking through the door, as if he wished to measure thereby all the possibilities that a house of this sort might include, and how they might bear upon the question of his entry.

In his indecision he turned and surveyed the scene around. Not a soul was anywhere visible. The garden path stretched downward from his feet, gleaming like the track of a snail; the roof of the little well (mostly dry), the well-cover, the top rail of the garden-gate, were varnished with the same dull liquid glaze; while, far away in the vale, a faint whiteness of more than usual extent showed that the rivers were high in the meads. Beyond all this winked a few bleared lamplights through the beating drops – lights that denoted the situation of the county-town from which he had appeared to come. The absence of all notes of life in that direction seemed to clinch his intentions, and he knocked at the door.

Within, a desultory chat had taken the place of movement and musical sound. The hedge-carpenter was suggesting a song to the company, which nobody just then was inclined to undertake, so that the knock afforded a not unwelcome diversion.

'Walk in!' said the shepherd promptly.

The latch clicked upward, and out of the night our pedestrian appeared upon the door-mat. The shepherd arose, snuffed two of the nearest candles, and turned to look at him.

Their light disclosed that the stranger was dark in complexion and not unprepossessing as to feature. His hat, which for a moment he did not remove, hung low over his eyes, without concealing that they were large, open, and determined, moving with a flash rather than a glance round the room. He seemed pleased with his survey, and, baring his shaggy head, said, in a rich, deep voice: 'The rain is so heavy, friends, that I ask leave to come in and rest awhile.'

'To be sure, Stranger,' said the shepherd. 'And faith, you've been lucky in choosing your time, for we are having a bit of a fling for a glad cause – though, to be sure, a man could hardly wish that glad cause to happen more than once a year.'

'Nor less,' spoke up a woman. 'For 'tis best to get your family over and done with, as soon as you can, so as to be all the earlier out of the fag o't.'

'And what may be this glad cause?' asked the stranger.

'A birth and christening,' said the shepherd.

The stranger hoped his host might not be made unhappy either by too many or too few of such episodes and, being invited by a gesture to a pull at the mug, he readily acquiesced. His manner, which, before entering, had been so dubious, was now altogether that of a careless and candid man.

'Late to be traipsing athwart this coomb – hey?' said the engaged man of fifty.

'Late it is, Master, as you say. – I'll take a seat in the chimney corner, if you have nothing to urge against it, Ma'am; for I am a little moist on the side that was next the rain.'

Mrs Shepherd Fennel assented, and made room for the self-invited comer, who, having got completely inside the chimney corner, stretched out his legs and arms with the expansiveness of a person quite at home.

'Yes, I am rather cracked in the vamp,' he said freely, seeing that the eyes of the shepherd's wife fell upon his boots, 'and I am not well fitted either. I have had some rough times lately, and have been forced to pick up what I can get in the way of wearing, but I must find a suit better fit for working-days when I reach home.'

'One of hereabouts?' she inquired.

'Not quite that – farther up the country.'

'I thought so. And so be I; and by your tongue you come from my neighbourhood.'

'But you would hardly have heard of me,' he said quickly. 'My time would be long before yours, Ma'am, you see.'

This testimony to the youthfulness of his hostess had the effect of stopping her cross-examination.

'There is only one thing more wanted to make me happy,' continued the newcomer, 'and that is a little baccy, which I am sorry to say I am out of.'

'I'll fill your pipe,' said the shepherd.

'I must ask you to lend me a pipe likewise.'

'A smoker, and no pipe about 'ee?'

'I have dropped it somewhere on the road.'

The shepherd filled and handed him a new clay pipe, saying, as he did so, 'Hand me your baccy-box – I'll fill that too, now I am about it.'

The man went through the movement of searching his pockets.

'Lost that too?' said his entertainer, with some surprise.

'I am afraid so,' said the man with some confusion. 'Give it to me in a screw of paper.' Lighting his pipe at the candle with a suction that drew the whole flame into the bowl, he resettled himself in the corner and bent his looks upon the faint steam from his damp legs, as if he wished to say no more.

Meanwhile the general body of guests had been taking little notice of this visitor by reason of an absorbing discussion in which they were engaged with the band about a tune for the next dance. The matter being settled, they were about to stand up when an interruption came in the shape of another knock at the door.

At sound of the same the man in the chimney corner took up the poker and began stirring the brands as if doing it thoroughly were the one aim of his existence; and a second time the shepherd said, 'Walk in!' In a moment another man stood upon the straw-woven door-mat. He too was a stranger.

This individual was one of a type radically different from the first. There was more of the commonplace in his manner, and a certain jovial cosmopolitanism sat upon his features. He was several years older than the first arrival, his hair being slightly frosted, his eyebrows bristly, and his whiskers cut back from his cheeks. His face was rather full and flabby, and yet it was not altogether a face without power. A few grog-blossoms marked the neighbourhood of his nose. He flung back his long drab greatcoat, revealing that beneath it he wore a suit of cinder-grey shade throughout, large heavy seals, of some metal or other that would take a polish, dangling from his fob as his only personal ornament. Shaking the water drops from his low-crowned glazed hat, he said, 'I must ask for a few minutes' shelter, comrades, or I shall be wetted to my skin before I get to Casterbridge.'

'Make yourself at home, Master,' said the shepherd, perhaps a trifle less heartily than on the first occasion. Not that Fennel had the least tinge of niggardliness in his composition; but the room was far from large, spare chairs were not numerous, and damp companions were not altogether desirable at close quarters for the women and girls in their bright-coloured gowns.

However, the second comer, after taking off his greatcoat, and hanging his hat on a nail in one of the ceiling-beams as if he had been specially invited to put it there, advanced and sat down at the table. This had been pushed so closely into the chimney corner, to give all available room to the dancers, that its inner edge grazed the elbow of the man who had ensconced himself by the fire; and thus the two strangers were brought into close companionship. They nodded to each other by way of breaking the ice of unacquaintance, and the first stranger handed his neighbour the family mug – a huge vessel of brown ware, having its upper edge worn away like a threshold by the rub of whole generations of thirsty lips that had gone the way of all flesh, and bearing the following inscription burnt upon its rotund side in yellow letters:

THERE IS NO FUN
UNTIL i CUM

The other man, nothing loth, raised the mug to his lips, and drank on, and on, and on – till a curious blueness overspread the countenance of the shepherd's wife, who had regarded with no little surprise the first stranger's free offer to the second of what did not belong to him to dispense.

'I knew it!' said the toper to the shepherd with much satisfaction. 'When I walked up your garden before coming in, and saw the hives all of a row, I said to myself, "Where there's bees there's honey, and where there's honey there's mead." But mead of such a truly comfortable sort as this I really didn't expect to meet in my older days.' He took yet another pull at the mug, till it assumed an ominous elevation.

'Glad you enjoy it!' said the shepherd warmly.

'It is goodish mead,' assented Mrs Fennel, with an absence of enthusiasm which seemed to say that it was possible to buy praise for one's cellar at too heavy a price. 'It is trouble enough to make – and really I hardly think we shall make any more. For honey sells well, and we ourselves can make shift with a drop o'small mead and metheglin for common use from the comb-washings.'

'Oh, but you'll never have the heart!' reproachfully cried the stranger in cinder-grey, after taking up the mug a third time and setting it down empty. 'I love mead, when 'tis old like this, a I love to go to church o' Sundays, or to relieve the needy any day of the week.'

'Ha, ha, ha!' said the man in the chimney corner, who, in spite of the taciturnity induced by the pipe of tobacco, could not or would not refrain from this slight testimony to his comrade's humour.

Now the old mead of those days, brewed of the purest first-year or maiden honey, four pounds to the gallon – with its due complement of white of eggs, cinnamon, ginger, cloves, mace, rosemary, yeast, and processes of working, bottling, and cellaring – tasted remarkably strong; but it did not taste so strong as it actually was. Hence, presently, the stranger in cinder-grey at the table, moved by its creeping influence, unbuttoned his waistcoat, threw himself back in his chair, spread his legs, and made his presence felt in various ways.

'Well, well, as I say,' he resumed, 'I am going to Casterbridge, and to Casterbridge I must go. I should have been almost there by this time; but the rain drove me into your dwelling, and I'm not sorry for it.'

'You don't live in Casterbridge?' said the shepherd.

'Not as yet; though I shortly mean to move there.'

'Going to set up in trade, perhaps?'

'No, no,' said the shepherd's wife. 'It is easy to see that the gentleman is rich, and don't want to work at anything.'

The cinder-grey stranger paused, as if to consider whether he would accept that definition of himself. He presently rejected it by answering. 'Rich is not quite the word for me, Dame. I do work, and I must work. And even if I only get to Casterbridge by midnight I must begin work there at eight to-morrow morning. Yes, het or wet, blow or snow, famine or sword, my day's work tomorrow must be done.'

'Poor man! Then, in spite o' seeming, you be worse off than we,' replied the shepherd's wife.

''Tis the nature of my trade, men and maidens. 'Tis the nature of my trade more than my poverty. . . . But really and truly I must up and off, or I shan't get a lodging in the town.' However, the speaker did not move, and directly added, 'There's time for one more draught of friendship before I go; and I'd perform it at once if the mug were not dry.'

'Here's a mug o'small,' said Mrs Fennel. 'Small, we call it, though to be sure 'tis only the first wash o' the combs.'

'No,' said the stranger, disdainfully. 'I won't spoil your first kindness by partaking o' your second.'

'Certainly not,' broke in Fennel. 'We don't increase and multiply every day, and I'll fill the mug again.' He went away to the dark place under the stairs where the barrel stood. The shepherdess followed him.

'Why should you do this?' she said, reproachfully, as soon as they were alone. 'He's emptied it once, though it held enough for ten people; and now he's not contented wi' the small, but must needs call for more o' the strong! And a stranger unbeknown to any of us. For my part, I don't like the look o' the man at all.'

'But he's in the house, my honey; and 'tis a wet night, and a christening. Daze it, what's a cup of mead more or less? There'll be plenty more next bee-burning.'

'Very well – this time, then,' she answered, looking wistfully at the barrel. 'But what is the man's calling, and where is he one of, that he could come in and join us like this?'

'I don't know. I'll ask him again.'

The catastrophe of having the mug drained dry at one pull by the stranger in cinder-grey was effectually guarded against this time by Mrs Fennel. She poured out his allowance in a small cup, keeping the large one at a discreet distance from him. When he had tossed off his portion the shepherd renewed his inquiry about the stranger's occupation.

The latter did not immediately reply, and the man in the chimney corner, with sudden demonstrativeness, said, 'Anybody may know my trade – I'm a wheelwright.'

'A very good trade for these parts,' said the shepherd.

'And anybody may know mine – if they've the sense to find it out,' said the stranger in cinder-grey.

'You may generally tell what a man is by his claws,' observed the hedge-carpenter, looking at his own hands. 'My fingers be as full of thorns as an old pincushion is of pins.'

The hands of the man in the chimney corner instinctively sought the shade, and he gazed into the fire as he resumed his pipe. The man at the table took up the hedge-carpenter's remark, and added smartly, 'True; but the oddity of my trade is that, instead of setting a mark upon me, it sets a mark upon my customers.'

No observation being offered by anybody in elucidation of this enigma, the shepherd's wife once more called for a song. The same obstacle's presented themselves as at the former time – one had no voice, another had forgotten the first verse. The stranger at the table, whose soul had now risen to a good working temperature, relieved the difficulty by exclaiming that, to start the company, he would sing himself. Thrusting one thumb into the armhole of his waistcoat, he waved the other hand in the air, and, with an extemporizing gaze at the shining sheep-crooks above the mantelpiece, began:

O my trade it is the rarest one,
Simple shepherds all –
My trade is a sight to see:
For my customers I tie, and take them up on high,
And waft 'em to a far countree!

The room was silent when he had finished the verse – with one exception, that of the man in the chimney corner, who at the singer's word, 'Chorus!' joined him in a deep bass voice of musical relish:

And waft 'em to a far countree!

Oliver Giles, John Pitcher the dairyman, the parish-clerk, the engaged man of fifty, the row of young women against the wall, seemed lost in thought not of the gayest kind. The shepherd looked meditatively on the ground, the shepherdess gazed keenly at the singer, and with some suspicion; she was doubting whether this stranger were merely singing an old song from recollection, or was composing one there and then for the occasion. All were as perplexed at the obscure revelation as the guests at Belshazzar's Feast, except the man in the chimney corner, who quietly said, 'Second verse, Stranger,' and smoked on.

The singer thoroughly moistened himself from his lips inward, and went on with the next stanza as requested:

My tools are but common ones,
Simple shepherds all –
My tools are no sight to see:
A little hempen string, and a post whereon to swing,
Are implements enough for me!

Shepherd Fennel glanced round. There was no longer any doubt that the stranger was answering his question rhythmically. The guests one and all started back with suppressed exclamations. The young woman engaged to the man of fifty fainted half-way, and would have proceeded, but finding him wanting in alacrity for catching her she sat down trembling.

'Oh, he's the –!' whispered the people in the background, mentioning the name of an ominous public officer. 'He's come to do it! 'Tis to be at Casterbridge jail tomorrow – the man for sheep stealing – the poor clockmaker we heard of, who used to live away at Shottsford and had no work to do – Timothy Summers, whose family were a-starving, and so he went out of Shottsford by the highroad, and took a sheep in open daylight, defying the farmer and the farmer's wife and the farmer's lad, and every man jack among 'em. He' (and they nodded toward the stranger of the deadly trade) 'is come from up the country to do it because there's not enough to do in his own county-town, and he's got the place here, now our own country-man's dead; he's going to live in the same cottage under the prison wall.'

The stranger in cinder-grey took no notice of this whispered string of observations, but again wetted his lips. Seeing that his friend in the chimney corner was the only one who reciprocated his joviality in any way, he held out his cup towards that appreciative comrade, who also held out his own. They clinked together, the eyes of the rest of the room hanging upon the singer's actions. He parted his lips for the third verse; but at that moment another knock was audible upon the door. This time the knock was faint and hesitating.

The company seemed scared; the shepherd looked with consternation towards the entrance, and it was with some effort that he resisted his alarmed wife's deprecatory glance, and uttered for the third time the welcoming words, 'Walk in!'

The door was gently opened, and another man stood upon the mat. He, like those who had preceded him, was a stranger. This time it was a short, small personage, of fair complexion, and dressed in a decent suit of dark clothes.

'Can you tell me the way to –?' he began: when, gazing round the room to observe the nature of the company among whom he had fallen, his eyes lighted on the stranger in cinder-grey. It was just at the instant when the latter, who had thrown his mind into his song with such a will that he scarcely heeded the interruption, silenced all whispers and inquiries by bursting into his third verse:

To-morrow is my working day,
Simple shepherds all –
To-morrow is a working day for me:
For the farmer's sheep is slain, and the lad who did it ta'en,
And on his soul may God ha' merc-y!

The stranger in the chimney corner, waving cups with the singer so heartily that his mead splashed over on the hearth, repeated in his bass voice as before:

And on his soul may God ha' merc-y!

All this time the third stranger had been standing in the doorway. Finding now that he did not come forward or go on speaking, the guests particularly regarded him. They noticed to their surprise that he stood before them the picture of abject terror – his knees trembling, his hand shaking so violently that the door latch by which he supported himself rattled audibly: his white lips were parted, and his eyes fixed on the merry officer of justice in the middle of the room. A moment more and he had turned, closed the door, and fled.

'What a man can it be?' said the shepherd.

The rest, between the awfulness of their late discovery and the odd conduct of this third visitor, looked as if they knew not what to think, and said nothing. Instinctively they withdrew farther and farther from the grim gentleman in their midst, whom some of them seemed to take for the Prince of Darkness himself, till they formed a remote circle, an empty space of floor being left between them and him –

. . . circulas, cujus centrum diabolus.

The room was so silent – though there were more than twenty people in it – that nothing could be heard but the patter of the rain against the window-shutters, accompanied by the occasional hiss of a stray drop that fell down the chimney into the fire, and the steady puffing of the man in the corner, who had now resumed his pipe of long clay.

The stillness was unexpectedly broken. The distant sound of a gun reverberated through the air – apparently from the direction of the county-town.

'Be jiggered!' cried the stranger who had sung the song, jumping up.

'What does that mean?' asked several.

'A prisoner escaped from the jail – that's what it means.'

All listened. The sound was repeated, and none of them spoke but the man in the chimney corner, who said quietly, 'I've often been told that in this county they fire a gun at such times; but I never heard it till now.'

'I wonder if it is *my* man?' murmured the personage in cinder-grey.

'Surely it is!' said the shepherd involuntarily. 'And surely we've zeed him! That little man who looked in at the door by now, and quivered like a leaf when he zeed ye and heard your song!'

'His teeth chattered, and the breath went out of his body,' said the dairyman.

'And his heart seemed to sink within him like a stone,' said Oliver Giles.

'And he bolted as if he'd been shot at,' said the hedge-carpenter.

'True – his teeth chattered, and his heart seemed to sink; and he bolted as if he'd been shot at,' slowly summed up the man in the chimney corner.

'I didn't notice it,' remarked the hangman.

'We were all a-wondering what made him run off in such a fright,' faltered one of the women against the wall, 'and now 'tis explained!'

The firing of the alarm-gun went on at intervals, low and sullenly, and their suspicions became a certainty. The sinister gentleman in the cinder-grey roused himself. 'Is there a constable here?' he asked, in thick tones. 'If so, let him step forward.'

The engaged man of fifty stepped quavering out from the wall, his betrothed beginning to sob on the back of the chair.

'You are a sworn constable?'

'I be, Sir.'

'Then pursue the criminal at once, with assistance, and bring him back here. He can't have gone far.'

'I will, Sir, I will – when I've got my staff. I'll go home and get it, and come sharp here, and start in a body.'

'Staff! – never mind your staff; the man'll be gone!'

'But I can't do nothing without my staff – can I, William, and John, and Charles Jake? No; for there's the king's royal crown a-painted on en in yaller and gold, and the lion and the unicorn, so as when I raise en up and hit my prisoner, 'tis made a lawful blow thereby. I wouldn't 'tempt to take up a man without my staff – no, not. If I hadn't the law to gie me courage, why, instead o' my taking up him he might take up me!'

'Now, I'm a king's man myself, and can give you authority enough for this,' said the formidable officer in grey. 'Now then, all of ye, be ready. Have ye any lanterns?'

'Yes – have ye any lanterns? – I demand it!' said the constable.

'And the rest of you able-bodied—'

'Able-bodied men – yes – the rest of ye!' said the constable.

'Have you some good stout staves and pitchforks—'

'Staves and pitchforks – in the name o' the law! And take 'em in yer hands and go in quest, and do as we in authority tell ye!'

Thus aroused, the men prepared to give chase. The evidence was, indeed, though circumstantial, so convincing, that but little argument was needed to show the shepherd's guests that after what they had seen it would look very much like connivance if they did not instantly pursue the unhappy third stranger, who could not as yet have gone more than a few hundred yards over such uneven country.

A shepherd is always well provided with lanterns; and, lighting these hastily, and with hurdle-staves in their hands, they poured out of the door, taking a direction along the crest of the hill, away from the town, the rain having fortunately a little abated.

Disturbed by the noise, or possibly by unpleasant dreams of her baptism, the child who had been christened began to cry heartbrokenly in the room overhead. These notes of grief came down through the chinks of the floor to the ears of the women below, who jumped up one by one, and seemed glad of the excuse to ascend and comfort the baby, for the incidents of the last half-hour greatly oppressed them. Thus in the space of two or three minutes the room on the ground floor was deserted quite.

But it was not for long. Hardly had the sound of footsteps died away when a man returned round the corner of the house from the direction the pursuers had taken. Peeping in at the door and seeing nobody there, he entered leisurely. It was the stranger of the chimney corner, who had gone out with the rest. The motive of his return was shown by his helping himself to a cut piece of skimmer-cake that lay on a ledge beside where he had sat, and which he had apparently forgotten to take with him. He also poured out half a cup more mead from the quantity that remained, ravenously eating and drinking these as he stood. He had not finished when another figure came in just as quietly – his friend in cinder-grey.

'Oh – you here?' said the latter, smiling. 'I thought you had gone to help in the capture.' And this speaker also revealed the object of his return by looking solicitously round for the fascinating mug of old mead.

'And I thought you had gone,' said the other, continuing his skimmer-cake with some effort.

'Well, on second thoughts, I felt there were enough without me,' said the first confidentially, 'and such a night as it is, too. Besides, 'tis the business o' the Government to take care of its criminals – not mine.'

'True; so it is. And I felt as you did, that there were enough without me.'

'I don't want to break my limbs running over the humps and hollows of this wild country.'

'Nor I neither, between you and me.'

'These shepherd-people are used to it – simple-minded souls, you know, stirred up to anything in a moment. They'll have him ready for me before the morning, and no trouble to me at all.'

'They'll have him, and we shall have saved ourselves all labour in the matter.'

'True, true. Well, my way is to Casterbridge; and 'tis as much as my legs will do to take me that far. Going the same way?'

'No, I am sorry to say! I have to get home over there' (he nodded indefinitely to the right), 'and I feel as you do, that it is quite enough for my legs to do before bedtime.'

The other had by this time finished the mead in the mug, after which, shaking hands heartily at the door, and wishing each other well, they went their several ways.

In the meantime the company of pursuers had reached the end of the hog's-back elevation which dominated this part of the down. They had decided on no particular plan of action; and, finding that the man of the baleful trade was no longer in their company, they seemed quite unable to form any such plan now. They descended in all directions down the hill, and straightway several of the party fell into the snare set by Nature for all misguided midnight ramblers over this part of the cretaceous formation. The 'lanchets,' or flint slopes, which belted the escarpment at intervals of a dozen yards, took the less cautious ones unawares, and losing their footing on the rubbly steep they slid sharply downward, the lanterns rolling from their hands to the bottom, and there lying on their sides till the horn was scorched through.

When they had again gathered themselves together, the shepherd, as the man who knew the country best, took the lead, and guided them round these treacherous inclines. The lanterns, which seemed rather to dazzle their eyes and warn the fugitive than to assist them in the exploration, were extinguished, due silence was observed; and in this more rational order they plunged into the vale. It was a grassy, briery, moist defile, affording some shelter to any person who had sought it; but the party perambulated it in vain, and ascended on the other side. Here they wandered apart, and after an interval closed together again to report progress. At the second time of closing in they found themselves near a lonely ash, the single tree on this part of the coomb, probably sown there by a passing bird some fifty years before. And here, standing a little to one side of the trunk, as motionless as the trunk itself, appeared the man they were in quest of, his outline being well defined against the sky beyond. The band noiselessly drew up and faced him.

'Your money or your life!' said the constable sternly to the still figure.

'No, no,' whispered John Pitcher. ''Tisn't our side ought to say that. That's the doctrine of vagabonds like him, and we be on the side of the law.'

'Well, well,' replied the constable, impatiently; 'I must say something, mustn't I? and if you had all the weight o' this undertaking upon your mind, perhaps you'd say the wrong thing, too! – Prisoner at the bar, surrender in the name of the Father – the Crown, I mane!'

The man under the tree seemed now to notice them for the first time, and, giving them no opportunity whatever for exhibiting their courage, he strolled slowly towards them. He was, indeed, the little man, the third stranger; but his trepidation had in a great measure gone.

'Well, travellers,' he said, 'did I hear you speak to me?'

'You did; you've got to come and be our prisoner at once!' said the constable. 'We arrest 'ee on the charge of not biding in Casterbridge jail in a decent proper manner to be hung to-morrow morning. Neighbours, do your duty, and seize the culpet!'

On hearing the charge, the man seemed enlightened, and, saying not another word, resigned himself with preternatural civility to the search-party, who, with their staves in their hands, surrounded him on all sides, and marched him back towards the shepherd's cottage.

It was eleven o'clock by the time they arrived. The light shining from the open door, a sound of men's voices within, proclaimed to them as they approached the house that some new events had arisen in their absence. On entering they discovered the shepherd's living-room to be invaded by two officers from Casterbridge jail, and a well-known magistrate who lived at the nearest country-seat, intelligence of the escape having become generally circulated.

'Gentlemen,' said the constable, 'I have brought back your man – not without risk and danger; but every one must do his duty! He is inside this circle of able-bodied persons, who have lent me useful aid, considering their ignorance of Crown work. – Men, bring forward your prisoner!' And the third stranger was led to the light.

'Who is this?' said one of the officials.

'The man,' said the constable.

'Certainly not,' said the turnkey; and the first corroborated his statement.

'But how can it be otherwise?' asked the constable. 'Or why was he so terrified at sight o' the singing instrument of the law who sat there?' Here he related the strange behaviour of the third stranger on entering the house during the hangman's song.

'Can't understand it,' said the officer coolly. 'All I know is that it is not the condemned man. He's quite a different character from this one; a gauntish fellow, with dark hair and eyes, rather good-looking, and with a musical bass voice that if you heard it once you'd never mistake as long as you lived.'

'Why, souls – 'twas the man in the chimney corner!'

'Hey – what?' said the magistrate, coming forward after inquiring particulars from the shepherd in the background. 'Haven't you got the man after all?'

'Well, Sir,' said the constable, 'he's the man we were in search of, that's true; and yet he's not the man we were in search of. For the man we were in search of was not the man we wanted, Sir, if you understand my everyday way; for 'twas the man in the chimney corner!'

'A pretty kettle of fish altogether!' said the magistrate. 'You had better start for the other man at once.'

The prisoner now spoke for the first time. The mention of the man in the chimney corner seemed to have moved him as nothing else could do. 'Sir,' he said, stepping forward to the magistrate, 'take no more trouble about me. The time is come when I may as well speak. I have done nothing; my crime is that the condemned man is my brother. Early this afternoon I left home at Shottsford to tramp it all the way to Casterbridge jail to bid him farewell. I was benighted, and called here to rest and ask the way. When I opened the door I saw before me the very man, my brother, that I thought to see in the condemned cell at Casterbridge. He was in this chimney corner; and jammed close to him, so that he could not have got out if he had tried, was the executioner who'd come to take his life, singing a song about it and not knowing that it was his victim who was close by, joining in to save appearances. My brother looked a glance of agony at me, and I know he meant, "Don't reveal what you see; my life depends on it." I was so terror-struck that I could hardly stand, and, not knowing what I did, I turned and hurried away.'

The narrator's manner and tone had the stamp of truth, and his story made a great impression on all around. 'And do you know where your brother is at the present time?' asked the magistrate.

'I do not. I have never seen him since I closed this door.'

'I can testify to that, for we've been between ye ever since,' said the constable.

'Where does he think to fly to? – what is his occupation?'

'He's a watch-and-clock-maker, Sir.'

''A said 'a was a wheelwright – a wicked rogue,' said the constable.

'The wheels of clocks and watches he meant, no doubt,' said Shepherd Fennel. 'I thought his hands were palish for's trade.'

'Well, it appears to me that nothing can be gained by retaining this poor man in custody,' said the magistrate; 'your business lies with the other unquestionably.'

And so the little man was released off-hand; but he looked nothing the less sad on that account, it being beyond the power of magistrate or constable to raze out the written troubles in his brain, for they concerned another whom he regarded with more solicitude than himself. When this was done, and the man had gone his way, the night was found to be so far advanced that it was deemed useless to renew the search before the next morning.

Next day, accordingly, the quest for the clever sheep-stealer became general and keen, to all appearance at least. But the intended punishment was cruelly disproportioned to the transgression, and the sympathy of a great many country-folk in that district was strongly on the side of the fugitive. Moreover, his marvellous coolness and daring in hob-and-nobbing with the hangman, under the unprecedented circumstances of the shepherd's party, won their admiration. So that it may be questioned if all those who ostensibly made themselves so busy in exploring woods and fields and lanes were quite so thorough when it came to the private examination of their own lofts and outhouses. Stories were afloat of a mysterious figure being occasionally seen in some old overgrown trackway or other, remote from turnpike roads, but when a search was instituted in any of these suspected quarters nobody was found. Thus the days and weeks passed without tidings.

In brief, the bass-voiced man of the chimney corner was never recaptured. Some said that he went across the sea, others that he did not, but buried himself in the depths of a populous city. At any rate, the gentleman in cinder-grey never did his morning's work at Casterbridge, nor met anywhere at all, for business purposes, the genial comrade with whom he had passed an hour of relaxation in the lonely house on the coomb.

The grass has long been green on the graves of Shepherd Fennel and his frugal wife; the guests who made up the christening party have mainly followed their entertainers to the tomb; the baby in whose honour they all had met is a matron in the sere and yellow leaf. But the arrival of the three strangers at the shepherd's that night, and the details connected therewith, is a story as well-known as ever in the country about Higher Crowstairs.

The Romantic Adventures of a Milkmaid

Once again, there is a natural progession between the story of 'The Three Strangers' and 'The Romantic Adventures of a Milkmaid' which Thomas Hardy wrote during the winter of 1882–3 and published in *The Graphic* in its Summer Number 1883. Here the central character, Baron von Xanten, who supernaturally grants the wish of the young milkmaid, Margery Tucker, to go to the Yeomanry Ball, is still more of a Mephistophelian figure than the hangman and actually able to exert magical powers over the young girl. As Ruth Firor has written, 'All through the story runs the suggestion that the Baron is not quite what he seems to be; how else explain the coal-black horses which draw his coach, the whole equipage vanishing mysteriously from sight as if by a stroke of black art?' And she adds even more pointedly, 'Upon his disappearance, the Baron became the centre of a group of dark legends, hinting that he was a limb of the Devil, if not the Evil One himself.'

In truth, 'The Romantic Adventures of a Milkmaid' is quite unlike anything else that Hardy wrote, and its strange mixture of realism and the supernaturally-romantic has caused it to be described as 'a fairy tale for adults.' Evelyn Hardy in her *Thomas Hardy: A Critical Study* (1954) has also said that the story of the mysterious Baron with his ghostly chariot drawn by black phantom horses is yet another instance of Hardy's 'fascination with the black-and-white characters of ballad and folklore.' The parallels between this story and Hardy's famous novel, *Tess of the D'Urbervilles*, which he began writing in 1888 and issued in 1891 are also obvious . . .

The Romantic Adventures of a Milkmaid

I

It was half-past four o'clock (by the testimony of the land-surveyor, my authority for the particulars of this story, a gentleman with the faintest curve of humour on his lips); it was half-past four o'clock on a May morning in the eighteen-forties. A dense white fog hung over the Valley of the Exe, ending against the hills on either side.

But though nothing in the vale could be seen from higher ground, notes of differing kinds gave pretty clear indications that bustling life was going on there. This audible presence and visual absence of an active scene had a peculiar effect above the fog level. Nature had laid a white hand over the creatures ensconced within the vale, as a hand might be laid over a nest of chirping birds.

The noises that ascended through the pallid coverlid were perturbed lowings, mingled with human voices in sharps and flats, and the bark of a dog. These, followed by the slamming of a gate, explained as well as eyesight could have done, to any inhabitant of the district, that Dairyman Tucker's under-milker was driving the cows from the meads into the stalls. When a rougher accent joined in the vociferations of man and beast, it would have been realized that the dairy-farmer himself had come out to meet the cows, pail in hand, and white pinafore on; and when, moreover, some women's voices joined in the chorus, that the cows were stalled and proceedings about to commence.

A hush followed, the atmosphere being so stagnant that the milk could be heard buzzing into the pails, together with occasional words of the milkmaids and men.

'Don't ye bide about long upon the road, Margery. You can be back again by skimming-time.'

The rough voice of Dairyman Tucker was the vehicle of this remark. The barton-gate slammed again, and in two or three minutes a something became visible, rising out of the fog in that quarter.

The shape revealed itself as that of a woman having a young and agile gait. The colours and other details of her dress were then disclosed – a bright pink cotton frock (because winter was over); a small woollen shawl of shepherd's plaid (because summer was not come); a white handkerchief tied over her head-gear, because it was so foggy, so damp, and so early; and a straw bonnet and ribbons peeping from under the handkerchief, because it was likely to be a sunny May day.

Her face was of the hereditary type among families down in these parts: sweet in expression, perfect in hue, and somewhat irregular in feature. Her eyes were of a liquid brown. On her arm she carried a withy basket, in which lay several butter-rolls in a nest of wet cabbage-leaves. She was the 'Margery' who had been told not to 'bide about long upon the road.'

She went on her way across the fields, sometimes above the fog, sometimes below it, not much perplexed by its presence except when the track was so indefinite that it ceased to be a guide to the next stile. The dampness was such that innumerable earthworms lay in couples across the path till, startled even by her light tread, they withdrew suddenly into their holes. She kept clear of all trees. Why was that? There was no danger of lightning on such a morning as this. But though the roads were dry the fog had gathered in the boughs, causing them to set up such a dripping as would go clean through the protecting handkerchief like bullets, and spoil the ribbons beneath. The beech and ash were particularly shunned, for they dripped more maliciously than any. It was an instance of woman's keen appreciativeness of Nature's moods and peculiarities: a man crossing those fields might hardly have perceived that the trees dripped at all.

In less than an hour she had traversed a distance of four miles, and arrived at a latticed cottage in a secluded spot. An elderly woman, scarce awake, answered her knocking. Margery delivered up the butter, and said, 'How is granny this morning? I can't stay to go up to her, but tell her I have returned what we owed her.'

Her grandmother was no worse than usual: and receiving back the empty basket the girl proceeded to carry out some intention which had not been included in her orders. Instead of returning to the light labours of skimming-time, she hastened on, her direction being towards a little neighbouring town. Before, however, Margery had proceeded far, she met the postman, laden to the neck with letter-bags, of which he had not yet deposited one.

'Are the shops open yet, Samuel?' she said.

'O no,' replied that stooping pedestrian, not waiting to stand upright. 'They won't be open yet this hour, except the saddler and ironmonger and little tacker-haired machine-man for the farm folk. They downs their shutters at half-past six, then the baker's at half-past seven, then the draper's at eight.'

'O, the draper's at eight.' It was plain that Margery had wanted the draper's.

The postman turned up a side-path, and the young girl, as though deciding within herself that if she could not go shopping at once she might as well get back for the skimming, retraced her steps.

The public road home from this point was easy but devious. By far the nearest way was by getting over a fence, and crossing the private grounds of a picturesque old country-house, whose chimneys were just visible through the trees. As the house had been shut up for many months, the girl decided to take the straight cut. She pushed her way through the laurel bushes, sheltering her bonnet with the shawl as an additional safeguard, scrambled over an inner boundary, went along through more shrubberies, and stood ready to emerge upon the open lawn. Before doing so she looked around in the wary manner of a poacher. It was not the first time that she had broken fence in her life; but somehow, and all of a sudden, she had felt herself too near womanhood to indulge in such practices with freedom. However, she moved forth, and the house-front stared her in the face, at this higher level unobscured by fog.

It was a building of the medium size, and unpretending, the façade being of stone; and of the Italian elevation made familiar by Inigo Jones and his school. There was a doorway to the lawn, standing at the head of a flight of steps. The shutters of the house were closed, and the blinds of the bedrooms drawn down. Her perception of the fact that no crusty caretaker could see her from the windows led her at once to slacken her pace, and stroll through the flower-beds coolly. A house unblinded is a possible spy, and must be treated accordingly; a house with the shutters together is an insensate heap of stone and mortar, to be faced with indifference.

On the other side of the house the greensward rose to an eminence, whereon stood one of those curious summer shelters sometimes erected on exposed points of view, called an all-the-year-round. In the present case it consisted of four walls radiating from a centre like the arms of a turnstile, with seats in each angle, so that whencesoever the wind came, it was always possible to find a screened corner from which to observe the landscape.

The milkmaid's trackless course led her up the hill and past this erection. At ease as to being watched and scolded as an intruder, her mind flew to other matters; till, at the moment when she was not a yard from the shelter, she heard a foot or feet scraping on the gravel behind it. Some one was in the all-the-year-round, apparently occupying the seat on the other side; as was proved when, on turning, she saw an elbow, a man's elbow, projecting over the edge.

Now the young woman did not much like the idea of going down the hill under the eyes of this person, which she would have to do if she went on, for as an intruder she was liable to be called back and questioned upon her business there. Accordingly she crept softly up and sat in the seat behind, intending to remain there until her companion should leave.

This he by no means seemed in a hurry to do. What could possibly have brought him there, what could detain him there, at six o'clock on a morning of mist when there was nothing to be seen or enjoyed of the vale beneath, puzzled her not a little. But he remained quite still, and Margery grew impatient. She discerned the track of his feet in the dewy grass, forming a line from the house steps, which announced that he was an inhabitant and not a chance passer-by. At last she peeped round.

II

A fine-framed dark-mustachioed gentleman, in dressing-gown and slippers, was sitting there in the damp without a hat on. With one hand he was tightly grasping his forehead, the other hung over his knee. The attitude bespoke with sufficient clearness a mental condition of anguish. He was quite a different being from any of the men to whom her eyes were accustomed. She had never seen mustachios before, for they were not worn by civilians in Lower Wessex at this date. His hands and his face were white – to her view deadly white – and he heeded nothing outside his own existence. There he remained as motionless as the bushes around him; indeed, he scarcely seemed to breathe.

Having imprudently advanced thus far, Margery's wish was to get back again in the same unseen manner; but in moving her foot for the purpose it grated on the gravel. He started up with an air of bewilderment, and slipped something into the pocket of his dressing-gown. She was almost certain that it was a pistol. The pair stood looking blankly at each other.

'My Gott, who are you?' he asked sternly, and with not altogether an English articulation. 'What do you do here?'

Margery had already begun to be frightened at her boldness in invading the lawn and pleasure-seat. The house had a master, and she had not known of it. 'My name is Margaret Tucker, sir,' she said meekly. 'My father is Dairyman Tucker. We live at Silverthorn Dairyhouse.'

'What were you doing here at this hour of the morning?'

She told him, even to the fact that she had climbed over the fence.

'And what made you peep round at me?'

'I saw your elbow, sir; and I wondered what you were doing?'

'And what was I doing?'

'Nothing. You had one hand on your forehead and the other on your knee. I do hope you are not ill, sir, or in deep trouble?' Margery had sufficient tact to say nothing about the pistol.

'What difference would it make to you if I were ill or in trouble? You don't know me.'

She returned no answer, feeling that she might have taken a liberty in expressing sympathy. But, looking furtively up at him, she discerned to her surprise that he seemed affected by her humane wish, simply as it had been expressed. She had scarcely conceived that such a tall dark man could know what gentle feelings were.

'Well, I am much obliged to you for caring how I am,' said he with a faint smile and an affected lightness of manner, which, even to her, only rendered more apparent the gloom beneath. 'I have not slept this past night. I suffer from sleeplessness. Probably you do not.'

Margery laughed a little, and he glanced with interest at the comely picture she presented; her fresh face, brown hair, candid eyes, unpractised manner, country dress, pink hands, empty wicker-basket, and the handkerchief over her bonnet.

'Well,' he said, after his scrutiny, 'I need hardly have asked such a question of one who is Nature's own image. . . . Ah, but, my good little friend,' he added, recurring to his bitter tone and sitting wearily down, 'you don't know what great clouds can hang over some people's lives, and what cowards some men are in face of them. To escape themselves they travel, take picturesque houses, and engage in country sports. But here it is so dreary, and the fog was horrible this morning!'

'Why, this is only the pride of the morning!' said Margery. 'By-and-by it will be a beautiful day.'

She was going on her way forthwith; but he detained her – detained her with words, talking on every innocent little subject he could think of. He had an object in keeping her there more serious than his words would imply. It was as if he feared to be left alone.

While they still stood, the misty figure of the postman, whom Margery had left a quarter of an hour earlier to follow his sinuous course, crossed the grounds below them on his way to the house. Signifying to Margery by a wave of his hand that she was to step back out of sight, in the hinder angle of the shelter, the gentleman beckoned to the postman to bring the bag to where he stood. The man did so, and again resumed his journey.

The stranger unlocked the bag and threw it on the seat, having taken one letter from within. This he read attentively, and his countenance changed.

The change was almost phantasmagorial, as if the sun had burst through the fog upon that face: it became clear, bright, almost radiant. Yet it was but a change that may take place in the commonest human being, provided his countenance be not too wooden, or his artifice have not grown to second nature. He turned to Margery, who was again edging off, and, seizing her hand, appeared as though he were about to embrace her. Checking his impulse, he said, 'My guardian child – my good friend – you have saved me!'

'What from?' she ventured to ask.

'That you may never know.'

She thought of the weapon, and guessed that the letter he had just received had effected this change in his mood, but made no observation till he went on to say, 'What did you tell me was your name, dear girl?'

She repeated her name.

'Margaret Tucker.' He stooped, and pressed her hand. 'Sit down for a moment – one moment,' he said, pointing to the end of the seat, and taking the extremest further end for himself, not to discompose her. She sat down.

'It is to ask a question,' he went on, 'and there must be confidence between us. You have saved me from an act of madness! What can I do for you?'

'Nothing, sir.'

'Nothing?'

'Father is very well off, and we don't want anything.'

'But there must be some service I can render, some kindness, some votive offering which I could make, and so imprint on your memory as long as you live that I am not an ungrateful man?'

'Why should you be grateful to me, sir?'

He shook his head. 'Some things are best left unspoken. Now think. What would you like to have best in the world?'

Margery made a pretence of reflecting – then fell to reflecting seriously; but the negative was ultimately as undisturbed as ever: she could not decide on anything she would like best in the world; it was too difficult, too sudden.

'Very well – don't hurry yourself. Think it over all day. I ride this afternoon. You live – where?'

'Silverthorn Dairyhouse.'

'I will ride that way homeward this evening. Do you consider by eight o'clock what little article, what little treat, you would most like of any.'

'I will, sir,' said Margery, now warming up to the idea. 'Where shall I meet you? Or will you call at the house, sir?'

'Ah – no. I should not wish the circumstances known out of which our acquaintance rose. It would be more proper – but no.'

Margery, too, seemed rather anxious that he should not call. 'I could come out, sir,' she said. 'My father is odd-tempered, and perhaps—'

It was agreed that she should look over a stile at the top of her father's garden, and that he should ride along a bridle-path outside, to receive her answer. 'Margery,' said the gentleman in conclusion, 'now that you have discovered me under ghastly conditions, are you going to reveal them, and make me an object for the gossip of the curious?'

'No, no, sir!' she replied earnestly. 'Why should I do that?'

'You will never tell?'

'Never, never will I tell what has happened here this morning.'

'Neither to your father, nor to your friends, nor to anyone?'

'To no one at all,' she said.

'It is sufficient,' he answered. 'You mean what you say, my dear maiden. Now you want to leave me. Goodbye!'

She descended the hill, walking with some awkwardness; for she felt the stranger's eyes were upon her till the fog had enveloped her from his gaze. She took no notice now of the dripping from the trees; she was lost in thought on other things. Had she saved this handsome, melancholy, sleepless, foreign gentleman who had had a trouble on his mind till the letter came? What had he been going to do? Margery could guess that he had meditated death at his own hand. Strange as the incident had been in itself, to her it had seemed stranger even than it was. Contrasting colours heighten each other by being juxtaposed; it is the same with contrasting lives.

Reaching the opposite side of the park there appeared before her for the third time that little old man, the foot-post. As the turnpike-road ran, the postman's beat was twelve miles a day; six miles out from the town, and six miles back at night. But what with zigzags, devious ways, offsets to country seats, curves to farms, looped courses, and triangles to outlying hamlets, the ground actually covered by him was nearer one-and-twenty miles. Hence it was that Margery, who had come straight, was still abreast of him, despite her long pause.

The weighty sense that she was mixed up in a tragical secret with an unknown and handsome stranger prevented her joining very readily in chat with the postman for some time. But a keen interest in her adventure caused her to respond at once when the bowed man of mails said, 'You hit athwart the grounds of Mount Lodge, Miss Margery, or you wouldn't ha' met me here. Well, somebody hev took the old place at last.'

In acknowledging her route Margery brought herself to ask who the new gentleman might be.

'Guide the girl's heart! What! don't she know? And yet how should ye – he's only just a-come. – Well, nominal, he's a fishing gentleman, come for the summer only. But, more to the subject, he's a foreign noble that's lived in England so long as to be without any true country: some of his letters call him Baron, some Squire, so that 'a must be born to something that can't be earned by elbow-grease and Christian conduct. He was out this morning a-watching the fog. "Postman," 'a said, "good-morning: give me the bag." O, yes, 'a's a civil genteel nobleman enough.'

'Took the house for fishing, did he?'

'That's what they say, and as it can be for nothing else I suppose it's true. But, in final, his health's not good, 'a b'lieve; he's been living too rithe. The London smoke got into his wyndpipe, till 'a couldn't eat. However, I shouldn't mind having the run of his kitchen.'

'And what is his name?'

'Ah – there you have me! 'Tis a name no man's tongue can tell, or even woman's, except by pen-and-ink and good scholarship. It begins with X, and who, without the machinery of a clock in's inside, can speak that? But here 'tis – from his letters.' The postman with his walking-stick wrote upon the ground:

III

The day, as she had prognosticated, turned out fine; for weather-wisdom was imbibed with their milk-sops by the children of the Exe Vale. The impending meeting excited Margery, and she performed her duties in her father's house with mechanical unconsciousness.

Milking, skimming, cheesemaking were done. Her father was asleep in the settle, the milkmen and maids were gone home to their cottages, and the clock showed a quarter to eight. She dressed herself with care, went to the top of the garden, and looked over the stile. The view was eastward, and a great moon hung before her in a sky which had not a cloud. Nothing was moving except on the minutest scale, and she remained leaning over, the nighthawk sounding his croud from the bough of an isolated tree on the open hill-side.

Here Margery waited till the appointed time had passed by three-quarters of an hour; but no Baron came. She had been full of an idea, and her heart sank with disappointment. Then at last the pacing of a horse became audible on the soft path without, leading up from the watermeads, simultaneously with which she beheld the form of the stranger, riding home, as he had said.

The moonlight so flooded her face as to make her very conspicuous in the garden-gap. 'Ah, my maiden – what is your name – Margery!' he said. 'How came you here? But of course I remember – we were to meet. And it was to be at eight – *proh pudor!* – I have kept you waiting!'

'It doesn't matter, sir. I've thought of something.'

'Thought of something?'

'Yes, sir. You said this morning that I was to think what I would like best in the world, and I have made up my mind.'

'I did say so – to be sure I did,' he replied, collecting his thoughts. 'I remember to have had good reason for gratitude to you.' He placed his hand to his brow, and in a minute alighted, and came up to her with the bridle in his hand. 'I was to give you a treat or present, and you could not think of one. Now you have done so. Let me hear what it is, and I'll be as good as my word.'

'To go to the Yeomanry Ball that's to be given this month.'

'The Yeomanry Ball – Yeomanry Ball?' he murmured, as if, of all requests in the world, this was what he had least expected. 'Where is what you call the Yeomanry Ball?'

'At Exonbury.'

'Have you ever been to it before?'

'No, sir.'

'Or to any ball?'

'No.'

'But did I not say a gift – a present?'

'Or a treat?'

'Ah, yes, or a treat,' he echoed, with the air of one who finds himself in a slight fix. 'But with whom would you propose to go?'

'I don't know. I have not thought of that yet.'

'You have no friend who could take you, even if I got you an invitation?'

Margery looked at the moon. 'No one who can dance,' she said; adding, with hesitation, 'I was thinking that perhaps—'

'But, my dear Margery,' he said, stopping her, as if he half-divined what her simple dream of a cavalier had been; 'it is very odd that you can think of nothing else than going to a Yeomanry Ball. Think again. You are sure there is nothing else?'

'Quite sure, sir,' she decisively answered. At first nobody would have noticed in that pretty young face any sign of decision; yet it was discoverable. The mouth, though soft, was firm in line; the eyebrows were distinct, and extended near to each other. 'I have thought of it all day,' she continued, sadly. 'Still, sir, if you are sorry you offered me anything, I can let you off.'

'Sorry? – Certainly not, Margery,' he said, rather nettled. 'I'll show you that whatever hopes I have raised in your breast I am honourable enough to gratify. If it lies in my power,' he added with sudden firmness, 'you *shall* go to the Yeomanry Ball. In what building is it to be held?'

'In the Assembly Rooms.'

'And would you be likely to be recognized there? Do you know many people?'

'Not many, sir. None, I may say. I know nobody who goes to balls.'

'Ah, well; you must go, since you wish it; and if there is no other way of getting over the difficulty of having nobody to take you, I'll take you myself. Would you like me to do so? I can dance.'

'O yes, sir; I know that, and I thought you might offer to do it. But would you bring me back again?'

'Of course I'll bring you back. But, by-the-bye, can *you* dance?'

'Yes.'

'What?'

'Reels, and jigs, and country-dances like the New-Rigged-Ship, and Follow-my-Lover, and Haste-to-the-Wedding, and the College Hornpipe, and the Favourite Quickstep, and Captain White's dance.'

'A very good list – a very good! but unluckily I fear they don't dance any of those now. But if you have the instinct we may soon cure your ignorance. Let me see you dance a moment.'

She stood out into the garden-path, the stile being still between them, and seizing a side of her skirt with each hand, performed the movements which are even yet far from uncommon in the dances of the villagers of merry England. But her motions, though graceful, were not precisely those which appear in the figures of a modern ballroom.

'Well, my good friend, it is a very pretty sight,' he said, warming up to the proceedings. 'But you dance too well – you dance all over your person – and that's too thorough a way for the present day. I should say it was exactly how they danced in the time of your poet Chaucer; but as people don't dance like it now, we must consider. First I must inquire more about this ball, and then I must see you again.'

'If it is a great trouble to you, sir, I—'

'O no, no. I will think it over. So far so good.'

The Baron mentioned an evening and an hour when he would be passing that way again; then mounted his horse and rode away.

On the next occasion, which was just when the sun was changing places with the moon as an illuminator of Silverthorn Dairy, she found him at the spot before her, and unencumbered by a horse. The melancholy that had so weighed him down at their first interview, and had been perceptible at their second, had quite disappeared. He pressed her right hand between both his own across the stile.

'My good maiden, Gott bless you!' said he warmly. 'I cannot help thinking of that morning! I was too much over-shadowed at first to take in the whole force of it. You do not know all; but your presence was a miraculous intervention. Now to more cheerful matters. I have a great deal to tell – that is, if your wish about the ball be still the same?'

'O yes, sir – if you don't object.'

'Never think of my objecting. What I have found out is something which simplifies matters amazingly. In addition to your Yeomanry Ball at Exonbury, there is also to be one in the next county about the same time. This ball is not to be held at the Town Hall of the county-town as usual, but at Lord Toneborough's, who is colonel of the regiment, and who, I suppose, wishes to please the yeomen because his brother is going to stand for the county. Now I find I could take you there very well, and the great advantage of that ball over the Yeomanry Ball in this county is, that there you would be absolutely unknown, and I also. But do you prefer your own neighbourhood?'

'O no, sir. It is a ball I long to see – I don't know what it is like; it does not matter where.'

'Good. Then I shall be able to make much more of you there, where there is no possibility of recognition. That being settled, the next thing is the dancing. Now reels and such things do not do. For think of this – there is a new dance at Almack's and everywhere else, over which the world has gone crazy.'

'How dreadful!'

'Ah – but that is a mere expression – gone mad. It is really an ancient Scythian dance; but, such is the power of fashion, that, having once been adopted by Society, this dance has made the tour of the Continent in one season.'

'What is its name, sir?'

'The polka. Young people, who always dance, are ecstatic about it, and old people, who have not danced for years, have begun to dance again on its account. All share the excitement. It arrived in London only some few months ago – it is now all over the country. Now this is your opportunity, my good Margery. To learn this one dance, will be enough. They will dance scarce anything else at that ball. While, to crown all, it is the easiest dance in the world, and as I know it quite well I can practise you in the step. Suppose we try?'

Margery showed some hesitation before crossing the stile: it was a Rubicon in more ways than one. But the curious reverence which was stealing over her for all that this stranger said and did was too much for prudence. She crossed the stile.

Withdrawing with her to a nook where two high hedges met, and where the grass was elastic and dry, he lightly rested his arm on her waist, and practised with her the new step of fascination. Instead of music he whispered numbers, and she, as may be supposed, showed no slight aptness in following his instructions. Thus they moved round together, the moon-shadows from the twigs racing over their forms as they turned.

The interview lasted about half-an-hour. Then he somewhat abruptly handed her over the stile and stood looking at her from the other side.

'Well,' he murmured, 'what has come to pass is strange! My whole business after this will be to recover my right mind!'

Margery always declared that there seemed to be some power in the stranger that was more than human, something magical and compulsory, when he seized her and gently trotted her round. But lingering emotions may have led her memory to play pranks with the scene, and her vivid imagination at that youthful age must be taken into account in believing her. However, there is no doubt that the stranger, whoever he might be, and whatever his powers, taught her the elements of modern dancing at a certain interview by moonlight at the top of her father's garden, as was proved by her possession of knowledge on the subject that could have been acquired in no other way.

His was of the first rank of commanding figures, she was one of the most agile of milkmaids, and to casual view it would have seemed all of a piece with Nature's doings that things should go on thus. But there was another side to the case; and whether the strange gentleman were a wild olive tree, or not, it was questionable if the acquaintance would lead to happiness. 'A fleeting romance and a possible calamity': thus it might have been summed up by the practical.

Margery was in Paradise; and yet she was not at this date distinctly in love with the stranger. What she felt was something more mysterious, more of the nature of veneration. As he looked at her across the stile she spoke timidly, on a subject which had apparently occupied her long.

'I ought to have a ball-dress, ought I not, sir?'

'Certainly. And you shall have a ball-dress.'

'Really?'

'No doubt of it. I won't do things by halves for my best friend. I have thought of the ball-dress, and of other things also.'

'And is my dancing good enough?'

'Quite – quite.' He paused, lapsed into thought, and looked at her. 'Margery,' he said, 'do you trust yourself unreservedly to me?'

'O yes, sir,' she replied brightly; 'if I am not too much trouble: if I am good enough to be seen in your society.'

The Baron laughed in a peculiar way. 'Really, I think you may assume as much as that. – However, to business. The ball is on the twenty-fifth, that is next Thursday week; and the only difficulty about the dress is the size. Suppose you lend me this?' And he touched her on the shoulder to signify a tight little jacket she wore.

Margery was all obedience. She took it off and handed it to him. The Baron rolled and compressed it with all his force till it was about as large as an apple-dumpling, and put it into his pocket.

'The next thing,' he said, 'is about getting the consent of your friends to your going. Have you thought of this?'

'There is only my father. I can tell him I am invited to a party, and I don't think he'll mind. Though I would rather not tell him.'

'But it strikes me that you must inform him something of what you intend. I would strongly advise you to do so.' He spoke as if rather perplexed as to the probable custom of the English peasantry in such matters, and added, 'However, it is for you to decide. I know nothing of the circumstances. As to getting to the ball, the plan I have arranged is this. The direction to Lord Toneborough's being the other way from my house, you must meet me at Three-Walks-End in Chillington Wood, two miles or more from here. You know the place? Good. By meeting there we shall save five or six miles of journey – a consideration, as it is a long way. Now, for the last time: are you still firm in your wish for this particular treat and no other? It is not too late to give it up. Cannot you think of something else – something better – some useful household articles you require?'

Margery's countenance, which before had been beaming with expectation, lost its brightness: her lips became close, and her voice broken. 'You have offered to take me, and now—'

'No, no, no,' he said, patting her cheek. 'We will not think of anything else. You shall go.'

IV

But whether the Baron, in naming such a distant spot for the rendezvous, was in hope she might fail him, and so relieve him after all of his undertaking, cannot be said; though it might have been strongly suspected from his manner that he had no great zest for the responsibility of escorting her.

But he little knew the firmness of the young woman he had to deal with. She was one of those soft natures whose power of adhesiveness to an acquired idea seems to be one of the special attributes of that softness. To go to a ball with this mysterious personage of romance was her ardent desire and aim; and none the less in that she trembled with fear and excitement at her position in so aiming. She felt the deepest awe, tenderness, and humility towards the Baron of the strange name; and yet she was prepared to stick to her point.

Thus it was that the afternoon of the eventful day found Margery trudging her way up the slopes from the vale to the place of appointment. She walked to the music of innumerable birds, which increased as she drew away from the open meads towards the groves. She had overcome all difficulties. After thinking out the question of telling or not telling her father, she had decided that to tell him was to be forbidden to go. Her contrivance therefore was this: to leave home this evening on a visit to her invalid grandmother, who lived not far from the Baron's house; but not to arrive at her grandmother's till breakfast-time next morning. Who would suspect an intercalated experience of twelve hours with the Baron at a ball? That this piece of deception was indefensible she afterwards owned readily enough; but she did not stop to think of it then.

It was sunset within Chillington Wood by the time she reached Three-Walks-End – the converging point of radiating trackways, now floored with a carpet of matted grass, which had never known other scythes than the teeth of rabbits and hares. The twitter overhead had ceased, except from a few braver and larger birds, including the cuckoo, who did not fear night at this pleasant time of year. Nobody seemed to be on the spot when she first drew near, but no sooner did Margery stand at the intersection of the roads than a slight crashing became audible, and her patron appeared. He was so transfigured in dress that she scarcely knew him. Under a light great-coat, which was flung open, instead of his ordinary clothes he wore a suit of thin black cloth, an open waistcoat with a frill all down his shirt-front, a white tie, shining boots, no thicker than a glove, a coat that made him look like a bird, and a hat that seemed as if it would open and shut like an accordion.

'I am dressed for the ball – nothing worse,' he said, drily smiling. 'So will you be soon.'

'Why did you choose this place for our meeting, sir?' she asked, looking around and acquiring confidence.

'Why did I choose it? Well, because in riding past one day I observed a large hollow tree close by here, and it occurred to me when I was last with you that this would be useful for our purpose. Have you told your father?'

'I have not yet told him, sir.'

'That's very bad of you, Margery. How have you arranged it, then?'

She briefly related her plan, on which he made no comment, but, taking her by the hand as if she were a little child, he led her through the undergrowth to a spot where the trees were older, and standing at wider distances. Among them was the tree he had spoken of – an elm; huge, hollow, distorted, and headless, with a rift in its side.

'Now go inside,' he said, 'before it gets any darker. You will find there everything you want. At any rate, if you do not you must do without it. I'll keep watch; and don't be longer than you can help to be.'

'What am I to do, sir?' asked the puzzled maiden.

'Go inside, and you will see. When you are ready wave your handkerchief at that hole.'

She stooped into the opening. The cavity within the tree formed a lofty circular apartment, four or five feet in diameter, to which daylight entered at the top, and also through a round hole about six feet from the ground, marking the spot at which a limb had been amputated in the tree's prime. The decayed wood of cinnamon-brown, forming the inner surface of the tree, and the warm evening glow, reflected in at the top, suffused the cavity with a faint mellow radiance.

But Margery had hardly given herself time to heed these things. Her eye had been caught by objects of quite another quality. A large white oblong paper box lay against the inside of the tree; over it, on a splinter, hung a small oval looking-glass.

Margery seized the idea in a moment. She pressed through the rift into the tree, lifted the cover of the box, and, behold, there was disclosed within a lovely white apparition in a somewhat flattened state. It was the ball-dress.

This marvel of art was, briefly, a sort of heavenly cobweb. It was a gossamer texture of precious manufacture, artistically festooned in a dozen flounces or more.

Margery lifted it, and could hardly refrain from kissing it. Had anyone told her before this moment that such a dress could exist, she would have said, 'No; it's impossible!' She drew back, went forward, flushed, laughed, raised her hands. To say that the maker of that dress had been an individual of talent was simply understatement: he was a genius, and she sunned herself in the rays of his creation.

She then remembered that her friend without had told her to make haste, and she spasmodically proceeded to array herself. In removing the dress she found satin slippers, gloves, a handkerchief nearly all lace, a fan, and even flowers for the hair. 'O, how could he think of it!' she said, clasping her hands and almost crying with agitation. 'And the glass – how good of him!'

Everything was so well prepared, that to clothe herself in these garments was a matter of ease. In a quarter of an hour she was ready, even to shoes and gloves. But what led her more than anything else into admiration of the Baron's foresight was the discovery that there were half-a-dozen pairs each of shoes and gloves, of varying sizes, out of which she selected a fit.

Margery glanced at herself in the mirror, or at as much as she could see of herself: the image presented was superb. Then she hastily rolled up her old dress, put it in the box, and thrust the latter on a ledge as high as she could reach. Standing on tiptoe, she waved the handkerchief through the upper aperture, and bent to the rift to go out.

But what a trouble stared her in the face. The dress was so airy, so fantastical, and so extensive, that to get out in her new clothes by the rift which had admitted her in her old ones was an impossibility. She heard the Baron's steps crackling over the dead sticks and leaves.

'O, sir!' she began in despair.

'What – can't you dress yourself?' he inquired from the back of the trunk.

'Yes; but I can't get out of this dreadful tree!'

He came round to the opening, stooped, and looked in. 'It is obvious that you cannot,' he said, taking in her compass at a glance; and adding to himself, 'Charming! who would have thought that clothes could do so much! – Wait a minute, my little maid; I have it!' he said more loudly.

With all his might he kicked at the sides of the rift, and by that means broke away several pieces of the rotten touchwood. But, being thinly armed about the feet, he abandoned that process, and went for a fallen branch which lay near. By using the large end as a lever, he tore away pieces of the wooden shell which enshrouded Margery and all her loveliness, till the aperture was large enough for her to pass without tearing her dress. She breathed her relief: the silly girl had begun to fear that she would not get to the ball after all.

He carefully wrapped round her a cloak he had brought with him: it was hooded, and of a length which covered her to the heels.

'The carriage is waiting down the other path,' he said, and gave her his arm. A short trudge over the soft dry leaves brought them to the place indicated. There stood the brougham, the horses, the coachman, all as still as if they were growing on the spot, like the trees. Margery's eyes rose with some timidity to the coachman's figure.

'You need not mind him,' said the Baron. 'He is a foreigner, and heeds nothing.'

In the space of a short minute she was handed inside; the Baron buttoned up his overcoat, and surprised her by mounting with the coachman. The carriage moved off silently over the long grass of the vista, the shadows deepening to black as they proceeded. Darker and darker grew the night as they rolled on; the neighbourhood familiar to Margery was soon left behind, and she had not the remotest idea of the direction they were taking. The stars blinked out, the coachman lit his lamps, and they bowled on again.

In the course of an hour and a half they arrived at a small town, where they pulled up at the chief inn and changed horses; all being done so readily that their advent had plainly been expected. The journey was resumed immediately. Her companion never descended to speak to her; whenever she looked out there he sat upright on his perch, with the mien of a person who had a difficult duty to perform, and who meant to perform it properly at all costs. But Margery could not help feeling a certain dread at her situation – almost, indeed, a wish that she had not come. Once or twice she thought, 'Suppose he is a wicked man, who is taking me off to a foreign country, and will never bring me home again.'

But her characteristic persistence in an original idea sustained her against these misgivings except at odd moments. One incident in particular had given her confidence in her escort: she had seen a tear in his eye when she expressed her sorrow for his troubles. He may have divined that her thoughts would take an uneasy turn, for when they stopped for a moment in ascending a hill he came to the window. 'Are you tired, Margery?' he asked kindly.

'No, sir.'

'Are you afraid?'

'N – no, sir. But it is a long way.'

'We are almost there,' he answered. 'And now, Margery,' he said in a lower tone, 'I must tell you a secret. I have obtained this invitation in a peculiar way. I thought it best for your sake not to come in my own name, and this is how I have managed. A man in this county, for whom I have lately done a service, one whom I can trust, and who is personally as unknown here as you and I, has (privately) transferred his card of invitation to me. So that we go under his name. I explain this that you may not say anything imprudent by accident. Keep your ears open and be cautious.' Having said this the Baron retreated again to his place.

'Then he is a wicked man after all!' she said to herself; 'for he is going under a false name.' But she soon had the temerity not to mind it: wickedness of that sort was the one ingredient required just now to finish him off as a hero in her eyes.

They descended a hill, passed a lodge, then up an avenue; and presently there beamed upon them the light from other carriages, drawn up in a file, which moved on by degrees; and at last they halted before a large arched doorway, round which a group of people stood.

'We are among the latest arrivals, on account of the distance,' said the Baron, reappearing. 'But never mind; there are three hours at least for your enjoyment.'

The steps were promptly flung down, and they alighted. The steam from the flanks of their swarthy steeds, as they seemed to her, ascended to the parapet of the porch, and from their nostrils the hot breath jetted forth like smoke out of volcanoes, attracting the attention of all.

V

The bewildered Margery was led by the Baron up the steps to the interior of the house, whence the sounds of music and dancing were already proceeding. The tones were strange. At every fourth beat a deep and mighty note throbbed through the air, reaching Margery's soul with all the force of a blow.

'What is that powerful tune, sir – I have never heard anything like it?' she said.

'The Drum Polka,' answered the Baron. 'The strange dance I spoke of and that we practised – introduced from my country and other parts of the Continent.'

Her surprise was not lessened when, at the entrance to the ballroom, she heard the names of her conductor and herself announced as 'Mr and Miss Brown.'

However, nobody seemed to take any notice of the announcement, the room beyond being in a perfect turmoil of gaiety, and Margery's consternation at sailing under false colours subsided. At the same moment she observed awaiting them a handsome, dark-haired, rather *petite* lady in cream-coloured satin. 'Who is she?' asked Margery of the Baron.

'She is the lady of the mansion,' he whispered. 'She is the wife of a peer of the realm, the daughter of a marquis, has five Christian names; and hardly ever speaks to commoners, except for political purposes.'

'How divine – what joy to be here!' murmured Margery, as she contemplated the diamonds that flashed from the head of her ladyship, who was just inside the ballroom door, in front of a litle gilded chair, upon which she sat in the intervals between one arrival and another. She had come down from London at great inconvenience to herself, openly to promote this entertainment.

As Mr and Miss Brown expressed absolutely no meaning to Lady Toneborough (for there were three Browns already present in this rather mixed assembly), and as there was possibly a slight awkwardness in poor Margery's manner, Lady Toneborough touched their hands lightly with the tips of her long gloves, said, 'How d'ye do,' and turned round for more comers.

'Ah, if she only knew we were a rich Baron and his friend, and not Mr and Miss Brown at all, she wouldn't receive us like that, would she?' whispered Margery confidentially.

'Indeed, she wouldn't!' drily said the Baron. 'Now let us drop into the dance at once; some of the people here, you see, dance much worse than you.'

Almost before she was aware she had obeyed his mysterious influence, by giving him one hand, placing the other upon his shoulder, and swinging with him round the room to the steps she had learnt on the sward.

At the first gaze the apartment had seemed to her to be floored with black ice; the figures of the dancers appearing upon it upside down. At last she realized that it was highly-polished oak, but she was none the less afraid to move.

'I am afraid of falling down,' she said.

'Lean on me; you will soon get used to it,' he replied. 'You have no nails in your shoes now, dear.'

His words, like all his words to her, were quite true. She found it amazingly easy in a brief space of time. The floor, far from hindering her, was a positive assistance to one of her natural agility and litheness. Moreover, her marvellous dress of twelve flounces inspired her as nothing else could have done. Externally a new creature, she was prompted to new deeds. To feel as well-dressed as the other women around her is to set any woman at her ease, whencesoever she may have come: to feel much better dressed is to add radiance to that ease.

Her prophet's statement on the popularity of the polka at this juncture was amply borne out. It was among the first seasons of its general adoption in country houses; the enthusiasm it excited tonight was beyond description, and scarcely credible to the youth of the present day. A new motive power had been introduced into the world of poesy – the polka, as a counterpoise to the new motive power that had been introduced into the world of prose – steam.

Twenty finished musicians sat in the music gallery at the end, with romantic mop-heads of raven hair, under which their faces and eyes shone like fire under coals.

The nature and object of the ball had led to its being very inclusive. Every rank was there, from the peer to the smallest yeoman, and Margery got on exceedingly well, particularly when the recuperative powers of supper had banished the fatigue of her long drive.

Sometimes she heard people saying, 'Who are they? – brother and sister – father and daughter? And never dancing except with each other – how odd!' But of this she took no notice.

When not dancing the watchful Baron took her through the drawing-rooms and picture-galleries adjoining, which tonight were thrown open like the rest of the house; and there, ensconcing her in some curtained nook, he drew her attention to scrap-books, prints, and albums, and left her to amuse herself with turning them over till the dance in which she was practised should again be called. Margery would much have preferred to roam about during these intervals; but the words of the Baron were law, and as he commanded so she acted. In such alternations the evening winged away; till at last came the gloomy words, 'Margery, our time is up.'

'One more – only onc!' she coaxed, for the longer they stayed the more freely and gaily moved the dance. This entreaty he granted; but on her asking for yet another, he was inexorable. 'No,' he said. 'We have a long way to go.'

Then she bade adieu to the wondrous scene, looking over her shoulder as they withdrew from the hall; and in a few minutes she was cloaked and in the carriage. The Baron mounted to his seat on the box, where she saw him light a cigar; they plunged under the trees, and she leant back, and gave herself up to contemplate the images that filled her brain. The natural result followed: she fell asleep.

She did not awake till they stopped to change horses, when she saw against the stars the Baron sitting as erect as ever. 'He watches like the Angel Gabriel, when all the world is asleep!' she thought.

With the resumption of motion she slept again, and knew no more till he touched her hand and said, 'Our journey is done – we are in Chillington Wood.'

It was almost daylight. Margery scarcely knew herself to be awake till she was out of the carriage and standing beside the Baron, who, having told the coachman to drive on to a certain point indicated, turned to her.

'Now,' he said, smiling, 'run across to the hollow tree; you know where it is. I'll wait as before, while you perform the reverse operation to that you did last night.' She took no heed of the path now, nor regarded whether her pretty slippers became scratched by the brambles or no. A walk of a few steps brought her to the particular tree which she had left about nine hours earlier. It was still gloomy at this spot, the morning not being clear.

She entered the trunk, dislodged the box containing her old clothing, pulled off the satin shoes, and gloves, and dress, and in ten minutes emerged in the cotton gown and shawl of shepherd's plaid.

The Baron was not far off. 'Now you look the milkmaid again,' he said, coming towards her. 'Where is the finery?'

'Packed in the box, sir, as I found it.' She spoke with more humility now. The difference between them was greater than it had been at the ball.

'Good,' he said. 'I must just dispose of it; and then away we go.'

He went back to the tree, Margery following at a little distance. Bringing forth the box, he pulled out the dress as carelessly as if it had been rags. But this was not all. He gathered a few dry sticks, crushed the lovely garment into a loose billowy heap, threw the gloves, fan, and shoes on the top, then struck a light and ruthlessly set fire to the whole.

Margery was agonised. She ran forward; she implored and entreated. 'Please, sir – do spare it – do! My lovely dress – my dear, dear slippers – my fan – it is cruel! Don't burn them, please!'

'Nonsense. We shall have no further use for them if we live a hundred years.'

'But spare a bit of it – one little piece, sir – a scrap of the lace – one bow of the ribbon – the lovely fan – just something!'

But he was as immovable as Rhadamanthus. 'No,' he said, with a stern gaze of his aristocratic eye. 'It is of no use for you to speak like that. The things are my property. I undertook to gratify you in what you might desire because you had saved my life. To go to a ball, you said. You might much more wisely have said anything else, but no; you said, to go to a ball. Very well – I have taken you to a ball. I have brought you back. The clothes were only the means, and I dispose of them my own way. Have I not a right to?'

'Yes, sir,' she said meekly.

He gave the fire a stir, and lace and ribbons, and the twelve flounces, and the embroidery, and all the rest crackled and disappeared. He then put in her hands the butter basket she had brought to take on to her grandmother's, and accompanied her to the edge of the wood, where it merged in the undulating open country in which her granddame dwelt.

'Now, Margery,' he said, 'here we part. I have performed my contract – at some awkwardness, if I was recognized. But never mind that. How do you feel – sleepy?'

'Not at all, sir,' she said.

'That long nap refreshed you, eh? Now you must make me a promise. That if I require your presence at any time, you will come to me. . . . I am a man of more than one mood,' he went on with sudden solemnity; 'and I may have desperate need of you again, to deliver me from that darkness as of Death which sometimes encompasses me. Promise it, Margery – promise it; that, no matter what stands in the way, you will come to me if I require you.'

'I would have if you had not burnt my pretty clothes!' she pouted.

'Ah – ungrateful!'

'Indeed, then, I will promise, sir,' she said from her heart. 'Wherever I am, if I have bodily strength I will come to you.'

He pressed her hand. 'It is a solemn promise,' he replied. 'Now I must go, for you know your way.'

'I shall hardly believe that it has not been all a dream!' she said, with a childish instinct to cry at his withdrawal. 'There will be nothing left of last night – nothing of my dress, nothing of my pleasure, nothing of the place!'

'You shall remember it in this way,' said he. 'We'll cut our initials on this tree as a memorial, so that whenever you walk this path you will see them.'

Then with a knife he inscribed on the smooth bark of a beech tree the letters M. T., and underneath a large X.

'What, have you no Christian name, sir?' she said.

'Yes, but I don't use it. Now, good-bye, my little friend. – What will you do with yourself to-day, when you are gone from me?' he lingered to ask.

'Oh – I shall go to my granny's,' she replied with some gloom; 'and have breakfast, and dinner, and tea with her, I suppose; and in the evening I shall go home to Silverthorn Dairy, and perhaps Jim will come to meet me, and all will be the same as usual.'

'Who is Jim?'

'O, he's nobody – only the young man I've got to marry some day.'

'What! – you engaged to be married? – Why didn't you tell me this before?'

'I – I don't know, sir.'

'What is the young man's name?'

'James Hayward.'

'What is he?'

'A master lime-burner.'

'Engaged to a master lime-burner, and not a word of this to me! Margery, Margery! when shall a straightforward one of your sex be found! Subtle even in your simplicity! What mischief have you caused me to do, through not telling me this? I wouldn't have so endangered anybody's happiness for a thousand pounds. Wicked girl that you were; why didn't you tell me?'

'I thought I'd better not!' said Margery, beginning to be frightened.

'But don't you see and understand that if you are already the property of a young man, and he were to find out this night's excursion, he may be angry with you and part from you for ever? With him already in the field I had no right to take you at all; he undoubtedly ought to have taken you; which really might have been arranged, if you had not deceived me by saying you had nobody.'

Margery's face wore that aspect of woe which comes from the repentant consciousness of having been guilty of an enormity. 'But he wasn't good enough to take me, sir!' she said, almost crying; 'and he isn't absolutely my master until I have married him, is he?'

'That's a subject I cannot go into. However, we must alter our tactics. Instead of advising you, as I did at first, to tell of this experience to your friends, I must now impress on you that it will be best to keep a silent tongue on the matter – perhaps for ever and ever. It may come right some day, and you may be able to say "All's well that ends well." Now, good morning, my friend. Think of Jim, and forget me.'

'Ah, perhaps I can't do that,' she said, with a tear in her eye, and a full throat.

'Well – do your best. I can say no more.'

He turned and retreated into the wood, and Margery, sighing, went on her way.

VI

Between six and seven o'clock in the evening of the same day a young man descended the hills into the valley of the Exe, at a point about midway between Silverthorn and the residence of Margery's grandmother, four miles to the east.

He was a thoroughbred son of the country, as far removed from what is known as the provincial, as the latter is from the out-and-out gentleman of culture. His trousers and waistcoat were of fustian, almost white, but he wore a jacket of old-fashioned blue West-of-England cloth, so well preserved that evidently the article was relegated to a box whenever its owner engaged in such active occupations as he usually pursued. His complexion was fair, almost florid, and he had scarcely any beard.

A novel attraction about this young man, which a glancing stranger would know nothing of, was a rare and curious freshness of atmosphere that appertained to him, to his clothes, to all his belongings, even to the room in which he had been sitting. It might almost have been said that by adding him and his implements to an over-crowded apartment you made it healthful. This resulted from his trade. He was a lime-burner; he handled lime daily; and in return the lime rendered him an incarnation of salubrity. His hair was dry, fair, and frizzled, the latter possibly by the operation of the same caustic agent. He carried as a walking-stick a green sapling, whose growth had been contorted to a corkscrew pattern by a twining honeysuckle.

As he descended to the level ground of the water-meadows he cast his glance westward, with a frequency that revealed him to be in search of some object in the distance. It was rather difficult to do this, the low sunlight dazzling his eyes by glancing from the river away there, and from the 'carriers' (as they were called) in his path – narrow artificial brooks for conducting the water over the grass. His course was something of a zigzag from the necessity of finding points in these carriers convenient for jumping. Thus peering and leaping and winding, he drew near the Exe, the central river of the miles-long mead.

A moving spot became visible to him in the direction of his scrutiny, mixed up with the rays of the same river. The spot got nearer, and revealed itself to be a slight thing of pink cotton and shepherd's plaid, which pursued a path on the brink of the stream. The young man so shaped his trackless course as to impinge on the path a little ahead of this coloured form, and when he drew near her he smiled and reddened. The girl smiled back to him; but her smile had not the life in it that the young man's had shown.

'My dear Margery – here I am!' he said gladly in an undertone, as with a last leap he crossed the last intervening carrier, and stood at her side.

'You've come all the way from the kiln, on purpose to meet me, and you shouldn't have done it,' she reproachfully returned.

'We finished there at four, so it was no trouble; and if it had been – why, I should ha' come.'

A small sigh was the response.

'What, you are not even so glad to see me as you would be to see your dog or cat?' he continued. 'Come, Mis'ess Margery, this is rather hard. But, by George, how tired you dew look! Why, if you'd been up all night your eyes couldn't be more like tea-saucers. You've walked tew far, that's what it is. The weather is getting warm now, and the air of these low-lying meads is not strengthening in summer. I wish you lived up on higher ground with me, beside the kiln. You'd get as strong as a hoss! Well, there; all that will come in time.'

Instead of saying yes, the fair maid repressed another sigh.

'What, won't it, then?' he said.

'I suppose so,' she answered. 'If it is to be, it is.'

'Well said – very well said, my dear.'

'And if it isn't to be, it isn't.'

'What? Who's been putting that into your head? Your grumpy granny, I suppose. However, how is she? Margery, I have been thinking today – in fact, I was thinking it yesterday and all the week – that really we might settle our little business this summer.'

'This summer?' she repeated, with some dismay. 'But the partnership? Remember it was not to be till after that was completed.'

'There I have you!' said he, taking the liberty to pat her shoulder, and the further liberty of advancing his hand behind it to the other. 'The partnership is settled. 'Tis "Vine and Hayward, limeburners," now, and "Richard Vine" no longer. Yes. Cousin Richard has settled it so, for a time at least, and 'tis to be painted on the carts this week – blue letters – yaller ground. I'll hose one of 'em, and drive en round to your door as soon as the paint is dry, to show 'ee how it looks?'

'Oh, I am sure you needn't take that trouble, Jim; I can see it quite well enough in my mind,' replied the young girl – not without a flitting accent of superiority.

'Hullo,' said Jim, taking her by the shoulders, and looking at her hand. 'What dew that bit of incivility mean? Now, Margery, let's sit down here, and have this cleared.' He rapped with his stick upon the rail of a little bridge they were crossing, and seated himself firmly, leaving a place for her.

'But I want to get home-along, dear Jim,' she coaxed.

'Fidgets. Sit down, there's a dear. I want a straightforward answer, if you please. In what month, and on what day of the month, will you marry me?'

'O, Jim,' she said, sitting gingerly on the edge, 'that's too plain-spoken for you yet. Before I look at it in that business light I should have to – to—'

'But your father has settled it long ago, and you said it should be as soon as I became a partner. So, dear, you must not mind a plain man wanting a plain answer. Come, name your time.'

She did not reply at once. What thoughts were passing through her brain during the interval? Not images raised by his words, but whirling figures of men and women in red and white and blue, reflected from a glassy floor, in movements timed by the thrilling beats of the Drum Polka. At last she said slowly, 'Jim, you don't know the world, and what a woman's wants can be.'

'But I can make you comfortable. I am in lodgings as yet, but I can have a house for the asking; and as to furniture, you shall choose of the best for yourself – the very best.'

'The best! Far are you from knowing what that is!' said the little woman. 'There be ornaments such as you never dream of; work-tables that would set you in amaze; silver candlesticks, tea and coffee pots that would dazzle your eyes; tea-cups, and saucers, gilded all over with guinea-gold; heavy velvet curtains, gold clocks, pictures and looking-glasses beyond your very dreams. So don't say I shall have the best.'

'H'm!' said Jim gloomily; and fell into reflection. 'Where did you get those high notions from, Margery?' he presently inquired. 'I'll swear you hadn't got 'em a week ago.' She did not answer, and he added, '*Yew* don't expect to have such things, I hope; deserve them as you may?'

'I was not exactly speaking of what I wanted,' she said severely. 'I said, things a woman *could* want. And since you wish to know what I *can* want to quite satisfy me, I assure you I can want those!'

'You are a pink-and-white conundrum, Margery,' he said; 'and I give you up for tonight. Anybody would think the devil had showed you all the kingdoms of the world since I saw you last!'

She reddened. 'Perhaps he has!' she murmured; then arose, he following her; and they soon reached Margery's home, approaching it from the lower or meadow side – the opposite to that of the garden top, where she had met the Baron.

'You'll come in, won't you, Jim?' she said, with more ceremony than heartiness.

'No – I think not tonight,' he answered. 'I'll consider what you've said.'

'You are very good, Jim,' she returned lightly. 'Good-bye.'

VII

Jim thoughtfully retraced his steps. He was a village character, and he had a villager's simplicity: that is, the simplicity which comes from the lack of a complicated experience. But simple by nature he certainly was not. Among the rank and file of rustics he was quite a Talleyrand, or rather had been one, till he lost a good deal of his self-command by falling in love.

Now, however, that the charming object of his distraction was out of sight, he could deliberate, and measure, and weigh things with some approach of keenness. The substance of his queries was, What change had come over Margery – whence these new notions?

Ponder as he would he could evolve no answer save one, which, eminently unsatisfactory as it was, he felt it would be unreasonable not to accept: that she was simply skittish and ambitious by nature, and would not be hunted into matrimony till he had provided a well-adorned home.

Jim retrod the miles to the kiln, and looked to the fires. The kiln stood in a peculiar, interesting, even impressive spot. It was at the end of a short ravine in a limestone formation, and all around was an open hilly down. The nearest house was that of Jim's cousin and partner, which stood on the outskirts of the down beside the turnpike-road. From this house a little lane wound between the steep escarpments of the ravine till it reached the kiln, which faced down the miniature valley, commanding it as a fort might command a defile.

The idea of a fort in this association owed little to imagination. For on the nibbled green steep above the kiln stood a bygone worn-out specimen of such an erection, huge, impressive, and difficult to scale even now in its decay. It was a British castle or entrenchment, with triple rings of defence, rising roll behind roll, their outlines cutting sharply against the sky, and Jim's kiln nearly undermining their base. When the lime-kiln flared up in the night, which it often did, its fires lit up the front of these ramparts to a great majesty. They were old friends of his, and while keeping up the heat through the long darkness, as it was sometimes his duty to do, he would imagine the dancing lights and shades about the stupendous earthwork to be the forms of those giants who (he supposed) had heaped it up. Often he clambered upon it, and walked about the summit, thinking out the problems connected with his business, his partner, his future, his Margery.

It was what he did this evening, continuing the meditation on the young girl's manner that he had begun upon the road, and still, as then, finding no clue to the change.

While thus engaged he observed a man coming up the ravine to the kiln. Business messages were almost invariably left at the house below, and Jim watched the man with the interest excited by a belief that he had come on a personal matter. On nearer approach Jim recognized him as the gardener at Mount Lodge some miles away. If this meant business, the Baron (of whose arrival Jim had vaguely heard) was a new and unexpected customer.

It meant nothing else, apparently. The man's errand was simply to inform Jim that the Baron required a load of lime for the garden.

'You might have saved yourself trouble by leaving word at Mr Vine's,' said Jim.

'I was to see you personally,' said the gardener, 'and to say that the Baron would like to inquire of you about the different qualities of lime proper for such purposes.'

'Couldn't you tell him yourself?' said Jim.

'He said I was to tell you that,' replied the gardener; 'and it wasn't for me to interfere.'

No motive other than the ostensible one could possibly be conjectured by Jim Hayward at this time; and the next morning he started with great pleasure, in his best business suit of clothes. By eleven o'clock he and his horse and cart had arrived on the Baron's premises, and the lime was deposited where directed; and exceptional spot, just within view of the windows of the south front.

Baron von Xanten, pale and melancholy, was sauntering in the sun on the slope between the house and the all-the-year-round. He looked across to where Jim and the gardener were standing, and the identity of Hayward being established by what he brought, the Baron came down, and the gardener withdrew.

The Baron's first inquiries were, as Jim has been led to suppose they would be, on the exterminating effects of lime upon slugs and snails in its different conditions of slaked and unslaked, ground and in the lump. He appeared to be much interested by Jim's explanations, and eyed the young man closely whenever he had an opportunity.

'And I hope trade is prosperous with you this year.' said the Baron.

'Very, my noble lord,' replied Jim, who, in his uncertainty on the proper method of address, wisely concluded that it was better to err by giving too much honour than by giving too little. 'In short, trade is looking so well that I've become a partner in the firm.'

'Indeed; I am glad to hear it. So now you are settled in life.'

'Well, my lord, I am hardly settled, even now. For I've got to finish it – I mean, to get married.'

'That's an easy matter, compared with the partnership.'

'Now a man might think so, my baron,' said Jim, getting more confidential. 'But the real truth is, 'tis the hardest part of all for me.'

'Your suit prospers, I hope?'

'It don't,' said Jim. 'It don't at all just at present. In short, I can't for the life o' me think what's come over the young woman lately.' And he fell into deep reflection.

Though Jim did not observe it, the Baron's brow became shadowed with self-reproach as he heard those simple words, and his eyes had a look of pity. 'Indeed – since when?' he asked.

'Since yesterday, my noble lord.' Jim spoke meditatively. He was resolving upon a bold stroke. Why not make a confidant of this kind gentleman instead of the parson, as he had intended? The thought was no sooner conceived than acted on. 'My lord,' he resumed, 'I have heard that you are a nobleman of great scope and talent, who has seen more strange countries and characters than I have ever heard of, and know the insides of men well. Therefore I would fain put a question to your noble lordship, if I may so trouble you, and having nobody else in the world who could inform me so trewly.'

'Any advice I can give is at your service, Hayward. What do you wish to know?'

'It is this, my baron. What can I do to bring down a young woman's ambition that's got to such a towering height there's no reaching it or compassing it: how get her to be pleased with me and my station as she used to be when I first knew her?'

'Truly, that's a hard question, my man. What does she aspire to?'

'She's got a craze for fine furniture.'

'How long has she had it?'

'Only just now.'

The Baron seemed still more to experience regret. 'What furniture does she specially covet?' he asked.

'Silver candlesticks, work-tables, looking-glasses, gold tea-things, silver tea-pots, gold clocks, curtains, pictures, and I don't know what all – things I shall never get if I live to be a hundred – not so much that I couldn't raise the money to buy 'em, as that I ought to put it to other uses, or save it for a rainy day.'

'You think the possession of those articles would make her happy?'

'I really think they might, my lord.'

'Good. Open your pocket-book and write as I tell you.'

Jim in some astonishment did as commanded, and elevating his pocket-book against the garden-wall, thoroughly moistened his pencil, and wrote at the Baron's dictation:

'Pair of silver candlesticks: inlaid work-table and work-box: one large mirror: two small ditto: one gilt china tea and coffee service: one silver tea-pot, coffee-pot, sugar-basin, jug, and dozen spoons: French clock: pair of curtains: six large pictures.'

'Now,' said the Baron, 'tear out that leaf and give it to me. Keep a close tongue about this; go home, and don't be surprised at anything that may come to your door.'

'But, my noble lord, you don't mean that your lordship is going to give—'

'Never mind what I am going to do. Only keep your own counsel. I perceive that, though a plain countryman, you are by no means deficient in tact and understanding. If sending these things to you gives me pleasure, why should you object? The fact is, Hayward, I occasionally take an interest in people, and like to do a little for them. I take an interest in you. Now go home, and a week hence invite Marg – the young woman and her father to tea with you. The rest is in your own hands.'

A question often put to Jim in after times was why it had not occurred to him at once that the Baron's liberal conduct must have been dictated by something more personal than sudden spontaneous generosity to him, a stranger. To which Jim always answered that, admitting the existence of such generosity, there had appeared nothing remarkable in the Baron selecting himself as its object. The Baron had told him that he took an interest in him; and self-esteem, even with the most modest, is usually sufficient to override any little difficulty that might occur to an outsider in accounting for a preference. He moreover considered that foreign noblemen, rich and eccentric, might have habits of acting which were quite at variance with those of their English compeers.

So he drove off homeward with a lighter heart than he had known for several days. To have a foreign gentleman take a fancy to him – what a triumph to a plain sort of fellow, who had scarcely expected the Baron to look in his face. It would be a fine story to tell Margery when the Baron gave him liberty to speak out.

Jim lodged at the house of his cousin and partner, Richard Vine, a widower of fifty-odd years. Having failed in the development of a household of direct descendants this tradesman had been glad to let his chambers to his much younger relative, when the latter entered on the business of lime manufacture; and their intimacy had led to a partnership. Jim lived upstairs; his partner lived down, and the furniture of all the rooms was so plain and old-fashioned as to excite the special dislike of Miss Margery Tucker, and even to prejudice her against Jim for tolerating it. Not only were the chairs and tables queer, but, with due regard to the principle that a man's surroundings should bear the impress of that man's life and occupation, the chief ornaments of the dwelling were a curious collection of calcinations, that had been discovered from time to time in the lime-kiln – misshapen ingots of strange substance, some of them like Pompeian remains.

The head of the firm was a quiet-living, narrow-minded, though friendly, man of fifty; and he took a serious interest in Jim's love-suit, frequently inquiring how it progressed, and assuring Jim that if he chose to marry he might have all the upper floor at a low rent, he, Mr Vine, contenting himself entirely with the ground level. It had been so convenient for discussing business matters to have Jim in the same house, that he did not wish any change to be made in consequence of a change in Jim's domestic estate. Margery knew of this wish, and of Jim's concurrent feeling, and did not like the idea at all.

About four days after the young man's interview with the Baron, there drew up in front of Jim's house at noon a waggon laden with cases and packages, large and small. They were all addressed to 'Mr Hayward,' and they had come from the largest furnishing warehouses in that part of England.

Three-quarters of an hour were occupied in getting the cases to Jim's rooms. The wary Jim did not show the amazement he felt at his patron's munificence; and presently the senior partner came into the passage, and wondered what was lumbering upstairs.

'O – it's only some things of mine,' said Jim coolly.

'Bearing upon the coming event – eh?' said his partner.

'Exactly,' replied Jim.

Mr Vine, with some astonishment at the number of cases, shortly after went away to the kiln; whereupon Jim shut himself into his rooms, and there he might have been heard ripping up and opening boxes with a cautious hand, afterwards appearing outside the door with them empty, and carrying them off to the outhouse.

A triumphant look lit up his face when, a little later in the afternoon, he sent into the vale to the dairy, and invited Margery and her father to his house to supper.

She was not unsociable that day, and, her father expressing a hard and fast acceptance of the invitation, she perforce agreed to go with him. Meanwhile at home Jim made himself as mysteriously busy as before in those rooms of his, and when his partner returned he too was asked to join in the supper.

At dusk Hayward went to the door, where he stood till he heard the voices of his guests from the direction of the low grounds, now covered with their frequent fleece of fog. The voices grew more distinct, and then on the white surface of the fog there appeared two trunkless heads, from which bodies and a horse and cart gradually extended as the approaching pair rose towards the house.

When they had entered Jim pressed Margery's hand and conducted her up to his rooms, her father waiting below to say a few words to the senior lime-burner.

'Bless me,' said Jim to her, on entering the sitting-room, 'I quite forgot to get a light beforehand; but I'll have one in a jiffy.'

Margery stood in the middle of the dark room, while Jim struck a match; and then the young girl's eyes were conscious of a burst of light, and the rise into being of a pair of handsome silver candlesticks containing two candles that Jim was in the act of lighting.

'Why – where – you have candlesticks like that?' said Margery. Her eyes flew round the room as the growing candle-flames showed other articles. 'Pictures too – and lovely china – why, I knew nothing of this, I declare.'

'Yes – a few things that came to me by accident,' said Jim in quiet tones.

'And a great gold clock under a glass, and a cupid swinging for a pendulum; and O what a lovely work-table – woods of every colour – and a work-box to match. May I look inside that work-box, Jim? – whose is it?'

'O yes; look at it, of course. It is a poor enough thing, but 'tis mine; and it will belong to the woman I marry, whoever she may be, as well as all the other things here.'

'And the curtains and the looking-glasses: why, I declare I can see myself in a hundred places.'

'That tea-set,' said Jim, placidly pointing to a gorgeous china service and a large silver tea-pot on the side-table, 'I don't use at present, being a bachelor-man; but, says I to myself, "whoever I marry will want some such things for giving her parties; or I can sell 'em" – but I haven't took steps for't yet—'

'Sell 'em – no, I should think not,' said Margery with earnest reproach. 'Why, I hope you wouldn't be so foolish! Why, this is exactly the kind of thing I was thinking of when I told you of the things women could want – of course not meaning myself particularly. I had no idea that you had such valuable—' Margery was unable to speak coherently, so much was she amazed at the wealth of Jim's possessions.

At this moment her father and the lime-burner came upstairs; and to appear womanly and proper to Mr Vine, Margery repressed the remainder of her surprise. As for the two elderly worthies, it was not till they entered the room and sat down that their slower eyes discerned anything brilliant in the appointments. Then one of them stole a glance at some article, and the other at another; but each being unwilling to express his wonder in the presence of his neighbours, they received the objects before them with quite an accustomed air; the lime-burner inwardly trying to conjecture what all this meant, and the dairyman musing that if Jim's business allowed him to accumulate at this rate, the sooner Margery became his wife the better. Margery retreated to the work-table, work-box, and tea-service, which she examined with hushed exclamations.

An entertainment thus surprisingly begun could not fail to progress well. Whenever Margery's crusty old father felt the need of a civil sentence, the flash of Jim's fancy articles inspired him to one; while the lime-burner, having reasoned away his first ominous thought that all this had come out of the firm, also felt proud and blithe.

Jim accompanied his dairy friends part of the way home before they mounted. Her father, finding that Jim wanted to speak to her privately, and that she exhibited some elusiveness, turned to Margery and said, 'Come, come, my lady; no more of this nonsense. You just step behind with that young man, and I and the cart will wait for you.'

Margery, a little scared at her father's peremptoriness, obeyed. It was plain that Jim had won the old man by that night's stroke, if he had not won her.

'I know what you are going to say, Jim,' she began, less ardently now, for she was no longer under the novel influence of the shining silver and glass. 'Well, as you desire it, and as my father desires it, and as I suppose it will be the best course for me, I will fix the day – not this evening, but as soon as I can think it over.'

VIII

Notwithstanding a press of business, Jim went and did his duty in thanking the Baron. The latter saw him in his fishing-tackle room, an apartment littered with every appliance that a votary of the rod could require.

'And when is the wedding-day to be, Hayward?' the Baron asked, after Jim had told him that matters were settled.

'It is not quite certain yet, my noble lord,' said Jim cheerfully. 'But I hope 'twill not be long after the time when God A'mighty christens the little apples.'

'And when is that?'

'St Swithin's – the middle of July. 'Tis to be some time in that month, she tells me.'

When Jim was gone the Baron seemed meditative. He went out, ascended the mount, and entered the weather-screen, where he looked at the seats, as though re-enacting in his fancy the scene of that memorable morning of fog. He turned his eyes to the angle of the shelter, round which Margery had suddenly appeared like a vision, and it was plain that he would not have minded her appearing there then. The juncture had indeed been such an impressive and critical one that she must have seemed rather a heavenly messenger than a passing milkmaid, more especially to a man like the Baron, who, despite the mystery of his origin and life, revealed himself to be a melancholy, emotional character – the Jaques of this forest and stream.

Behind the mount the ground rose yet higher, ascending to a plantation which sheltered the house. The Baron strolled up here, and bent his gaze over the distance. The valley of the Exe lay before him, with its shining river, the brooks that fed it, and the trickling springs that fed the brooks. The situation of Margery's house was visible, though not the house itself; and the Baron gazed that way for an infinitely long time, till, remembering himself, he moved on.

Instead of returning to the house he went along the ridge till he arrived at the verge of Chillington Wood, and in the same desultory manner roamed under the trees, not pausing till he had come to Three-Walks-End, and the hollow elm hard by. He peeped in at the rift. In the soft dry layer of touchwood that floored the hollow Margery's tracks were still visible, as she had made them there when dressing for the ball.

'Little Margery!' murmured the Baron.

In a moment he thought better of this mood, and turned to go home. But behold, a form stood behind him – that of the girl whose name had been on his lips.

She was in utter confusion. 'I – I – did not know you were here, sir!' she began. 'I was out for a little walk.' She could get no further; her eyes filled with tears. That spice of wilfulness, even hardness, which characterized her in Jim's company, magically disappeared in the presence of the Baron.

'Never mind, never mind,' said he, masking under a severe manner whatever he felt. 'The meeting is awkward, and ought not to have occurred, especially if, as I suppose, you are shortly to be married to James Hayward. But it cannot be helped now. You had no idea I was here, of course. Neither had I of seeing you. Remember you cannot be too careful,' continued the Baron, in the same grave tone; 'and I strongly request you as a friend to do your utmost to avoid meetings like this. When you saw me before I turned, why did you not go away?'

'I did not see you, sir. I did not think of seeing you. I was walking this way, and I only looked in to see the tree.'

'That shows you have been thinking of things you should not think of,' returned the Baron. 'Good morning.'

Margery could answer nothing. A browbeaten glance, almost of misery, was all she gave him. He took a slow step away from her; then turned suddenly back and, stooping, impulsively kissed her cheek, taking her as much by surprise as ever a woman was taken in her life.

Immediately after he went off with a flushed face and rapid strides, which he did not check till he was within his own boundaries.

The haymaking season now set in vigorously, and the weir-hatches were all drawn in the meads to drain off the water. The streams ran themselves dry, and there was no longer any difficulty in walking about among them. The Baron could very well witness from the elevations about his house the activity which followed these preliminaries. The white shirt-sleeves of the mowers glistened in the sun, the scythes flashed, voices echoed, snatches of song floated about, and there were glimpses of red waggon-wheels, purple gowns, and many-coloured handkerchiefs.

The Baron had been told that the haymaking was to be followed by the wedding, and had he gone down the vale to the dairy he would have had evidence to that effect. Dairyman Tucker's house was in a whirlpool of bustle, and among other difficulties was that of turning the cheeseroom into a genteel apartment for the time being, and hiding the awkwardness of having to pass though the milk-house to get to the parlour door. These household contrivances appeared to interest Margery much more than the great question of dressing for the ceremony and the ceremony itself. In all relating to that she showed an indescribable backwardness, which later on was well remembered.

'If it were only somebody else, and I was one of the bridesmaids, I really think I should like it better!' she murmured one afternoon.

'Away with thee – that's only your shyness!' said one of the milkmaids.

It is said that about this time the Baron seemed to feel the effects of solitude strongly. Solitude revives the simple instincts of primitive man, and lonely country nooks afford rich soil for wayward emotions. Moreover, idleness waters those unconsidered impulses which a short season of turmoil would stamp out. It is difficult to speak with any exactness of the bearing of such conditions on the mind of the Baron – a man whom so little was ever truly known – but there is no doubt that his mind ran much on Margery as an individual, without reference to her rank or quality, or to the question whether she would marry Jim Hayward that summer. She was the single lovely human thing within his present horizon, for he lived in absolute seclusion; and her image unduly affected him.

But, leaving conjecture, let me state what happened. One Saturday evening, two or three weeks after his accidental meeting with her in the wood, he wrote the note following:—

DEAR MARGERY,—

You must not suppose that, because I spoke somewhat severely to you at our chance encounter by the hollow tree, I have any feeling against you. Far from it. Now, as ever, I have the most grateful sense of your considerate kindness to me on a momentous occasion which shall be nameless.

You solemnly promised to come and see me whenever I should send for you. Can you call for five minutes as soon as possible, and disperse those plaguy glooms from which I am so unfortunate as to suffer? If you refuse I will not answer for the consequences. I shall be in the summer shelter of the mount tomorrow morning at half-past ten. If you come I shall be grateful. I have also something for you.

Yours,

X

In keeping with the tenor of this epistle the desponding, self-oppressed Baron ascended the mount on Sunday morning and sat down. There was nothing here to signify exactly the hour, but before the church bells had begun he heard somebody approaching at the back. The light footstep moved timidly, first to one recess, and then to another; then to the third, where he sat in the shade. Poor Margery stood before him.

She looked worn and weary, and her little shoes and the skirts of her dress were covered with dust. The weather was sultry, the sun being already high and powerful, and rain had not fallen for weeks. The Baron, who walked little, had thought nothing of the effects of this heat and drought in inducing fatigue. A distance which had been but a reasonable exercise on a foggy morning was a drag for Margery now. She was out of breath; and anxiety, even unhappiness, was written on her everywhere.

He rose to his feet and took her hand. He was vexed with himself at sight of her. 'My dear little girl!' he said. 'You are tired – you should not have come.'

'You sent for me, sir; and I was afraid you were ill; and my promise to you was sacred.'

He bent over her, looking upon her downcast face, and still holding her hand; then he dropped it, and took a pace or two backwards.

'It was a whim, nothing more,' he said sadly. 'I wanted to see my little friend, to express good wishes – and to present her with this.' He held forward a small morocco case, and showed her how to open it, disclosing a pretty locket set with pearls. 'It is intended as a wedding present,' he continued. 'To be returned to me again if you do not marry Jim this summer – it is to be this summer, I think?'

'It was, sir.' she said with agitation. 'But it is so no longer. And, therefore, I cannot take this.'

'What do you say?'

'It was to have been today; but now it cannot be.'

'The wedding today – Sunday?' he cried.

'We fixed Sunday not to hinder much time at this busy season of the year,' replied she.

'And have you, then, put it off – surely not?'

'You sent for me, and I have come,' she answered humbly, like an obedient familiar in the employ of some great enchanter. Indeed, the Baron's power over this innocent girl was curiously like enchantment, or mesmeric influence. It was so masterful that the sexual element was almost eliminated. It was that of Prospero over the gentle Ariel. And yet it was probably only that of the cosmopolite over the recluse, of the experienced man over the simple maid.

'You have come – on your wedding day! – O Margery, this is a mistake. Of course, you should not have obeyed me, since, though, I thought your wedding would be soon, I did not know it was today.'

'I promised you, sir; and I would rather keep my promise to you than be married to Jim.'

'That must not be – the feeling is wrong!' he murmured, looking at the distant hills. 'There seems to be a fate in all this; I get out of the frying-pan into the fire. What a recompense to you for your goodness! The fact is, I was out of health and out of spirits, so I – but no more of that. Now instantly to repair this tremendous blunder that we have made – that's the question.'

After a pause, he went on hurriedly, 'Walk down the hill; get into the road. By that time I shall be there with a phaeton. We may get back in time. What time is it now? If not, no doubt the wedding can be tomorrow; so all will come right again. Don't cry, my dear girl. Keep the locket, of course – you'll marry Jim.'

IX

He hastened down towards the stables, and she went on as directed. It seemed as if he must have put in the horse himself, so quickly did he reappear with the phaeton on the open road. Margery silently took her seat, and the Baron seemed cut to the quick with self-reproach as he noticed the listless indifference with which she acted. There was no doubt that in her heart she had preferred obeying the apparently important mandate that morning to becoming Jim's wife; but there was no less doubt that had the Baron left her alone she would quietly have gone to the altar.

He drove along furiously, in a cloud of dust. There was much to contemplate in that peaceful Sunday morning – the windless trees and fields, the shaking sunlight, the pause in human stir. Yet neither of them heeded, and thus they drew near to the dairy. His first expressed intention had been to go indoors with her, but this he abandoned as impolitic in the highest degree.

'You may be soon enough,' he said, springing down, and helping her to follow. 'Tell the truth: say you were sent for to receive a wedding present – that it was a mistake on my part – a mistake on yours; and I think they'll forgive. . . . And, Margery, my last request to you is this: that if I send for you again, you do not come. Promise solemnly, my dear girl, that any such request shall be unheeded.'

Her lips moved, but the promise was not articulated. 'O, sir, I cannot promise it!' she said at last.

'But you must; your salvation may depend on it!' he insisted almost sternly. 'You don't know what I am.'

'Then, sir, I promise,' she replied. 'Now leave me to myself, please, and I'll go indoors and manage matters.'

He turned the horse and drove away, but only for a little distance. Out of sight he pulled rein suddenly. 'Only to go back and propose it to her, and she'd come!' he murmured.

He stood up in the phaeton, and by this means he could see over the hedge. Margery still sat listlessly in the same place; there was not a lovelier flower in the field. 'No,' he said; 'no, no – never!' He reseated himself, and the wheels sped lightly back over the soft dust to Mount Lodge.

Meanwhile Margery had not moved. If the Baron could dissimulate on the side of severity she could dissimulate on the side of calm. He did not know what had been veiled by the quiet promise to manage matters indoors. Rising at length she first turned away from the house; and by-and-by, having apparently forgotten till then that she carried it in her hand, she opened the case and looked at the locket. This seemed to give her courage. She turned, set her face towards the dairy in good earnest, and though her heart faltered when the gates came in sight, she kept on and drew near the door.

On the threshold she stood listening. The house was silent. Decorations were visible in the passage, and also the carefully swept and sanded path to the gate, which she was to have trodden as a bride; but the sparrows hopped over it as if it were abandoned; and all appeared to have been checked at its climacteric, like a clock stopped on the strike. Till this moment of confronting the suspended animation of the scene she had not realized the full shock of the convulsion which her disappearance must have caused. It is quite certain – apart from her own repeated assurances to that effect in later years – that in hastening off that morning to her sudden engagement, Margery had not counted the cost of such an enterprise; while a dim notion that she might get back again in time for the ceremony, if the message meant nothing serious, should also be mentioned in her favour. But, upon the whole, she had obeyed the call with an unreasoning obedience worthy of a disciple in primitive times. A conviction that the Baron's life might depend upon her presence – for she had by this time divined the tragical event she had interrupted on the foggy morning – took from her all will to judge and consider calmly. The simple affairs of her and hers seemed nothing beside the possibility of harm to him.

A well-known step moved on the sanded floor within, and she went forward. That she saw her father's face before her, just within the door, can hardly be said: it was rather Reproach and Rage in a human mask.

'What! ye have dared to come back alive, hussy, to look upon the dupery you have practised on honest people! You've mortified us all; I don't want to see 'ee; I don't want to know anything!' He walked up and down the room, unable to command himself. 'Nothing but being dead could have excused 'ee for not meeting and marrying that man this morning; and yet you have the brazen impudence to stand there as well as ever! What be you here for?'

'I've come back to marry Jim, if he wants me to,' she said faintly. 'And if not – perhaps so much the better. I was sent for this morning early. I thought—' She halted. To say that she had thought a man's death might happen by his own hand, if she did not go to him, would never do. 'I was obliged to go,' she said. 'I had given my word.'

'Why didn't you tell us, then, so that the wedding could be put off, without making fools o' us?'

'Because I was afraid you wouldn't let me go, and I had made up my mind to go.'

'To go where?'

She was silent; till she said, 'I will tell Jim all, and why it was; and if he's any friend of mine he'll excuse me.'

'Not Jim – he's no such fool. Jim had put all ready for you, Jim had called at your house, a-dressed up in his new wedding clothes, and a-smiling like the sun; Jim had told the parson, had got the ringers in tow, and the clerk awaiting; and then – you was *gone*! Then Jim turned as pale as rendlewood, and busted out, "If she don't marry me today," 'a said, "she don't marry me at all! No;

let her look elsewhere for a husband. For tew years I've put up with her haughty tricks and her takings," 'a said. "I've droudged and I've traipsed, I've bought and I've sold, all wi' an eye to her; I've suffered horseflesh," he says – yes, them was his noble words – "but I'll suffer it no longer. She shall go!" "Jim," says I, "you be a man. If she's alive, I commend 'ee; if she's dead, pity my old age." "She isn't dead," says he; "for I've just heard she was seen walking off across the fields this morning, looking all of a scornful triumph." He turned round and went, and the rest o' the neighbours went; and here be I left to the reproach o't.'

'He was too hasty,' murmured Margery. 'For now he's said this I can't marry him tomorrow, as I might ha' done; and perhaps so much the better.'

'You can be so calm about it, can ye? Be my arrangements nothing, then, that you should break 'em up, and say off-hand what wasn't done to-day might ha' been done to-morrow, and such flick-flack? Out o' my sight! I won't hear any more. I won't speak to 'ee any more.'

'I'll go away, and then you'll be sorry!'

'Very well, go. Sorry – not I.'

He turned and stamped his way into the cheeseroom. Margery went upstairs. She too was excited now, and instead of fortifying herself in her bedroom till her father's rage had blown over, as she had often done on lesser occasions, she packed up a bundle of articles, crept down again, and went out of the house. She had a place of refuge in these cases of necessity, and her father knew it, and was less alarmed at seeing her depart than he might otherwise have been. This place was Rook's Gate, the house of her grandmother, who always took Margery's part when that young woman was particularly in the wrong.

The devious way she pursued, to avoid the vicinity of Mount Lodge, was tedious, and she was already weary. But the cottage was a restful place to arrive at, for she was her own mistress there – her grandmother never coming downstairs – and Edy, the woman who lived with and attended her, being a cipher except in muscle and voice. The approach was by a straight open road, bordered by thin lank trees, all sloping away from the south-west wind-quarter, and the scene bore a strange resemblance to certain bits of Dutch landscape which have been imprinted on the world's eye by Hobbema and his school.

Having explained to her granny that the wedding was put off, and that she had come to stay, one of Margery's first acts was carefully to pack up the locket and case, her wedding present from the Baron. The conditions of the gift were unfulfilled, and she wished it to go back instantly. Perhaps, in the intricacies of her bosom, there lurked a greater satisfaction with the reason for returning the present than she would have felt just then with a reason for keeping it.

To send the article was difficult. In the evening she wrapped herself up, searched and found a gauze veil that had been used by her grandmother in past years for hiving swarms of bees, buried her face in it, and sallied forth with a palpitating heart till she drew near the tabernacle of her demi-god, the Baron. She ventured only to the back door, where she handed in the parcel addressed to him, and quickly came away.

Now it seems that during the day the Baron had been unable to learn the result of his attempt to return Margery in time for the event he had interrupted. Wishing, for obvious reasons, to avoid direct inquiry by messenger, and being too unwell to go far himself, he could learn no particulars. He was sitting in thought after a lonely dinner when the parcel intimating failure was brought in. The footman whose curiosity had been excited by the mode of its arrival, peeped through the keyhole after closing the door to learn what the packet meant. Directly the Baron had opened it he thrust out his feet vehemently from his chair, and began cursing his ruinous conduct in bringing about such a disaster, for the return of the locket denoted not only no wedding that day, but none tomorrow, or at any time.

'I have done that innocent woman a great wrong!' he murmured. 'Deprived her of, perhaps, her only opportunity of becoming mistress of a happy home!'

X

A considerable period of inaction followed among all concerned.

Nothing tended to dissipate the obscurity which veiled the life of the Baron. The position he occupied in the minds of the country-folk around was one which combined the mysteriousness of a legendary character with the unobtrusive deeds of a modern gentleman. To this day whoever takes the trouble to go down to Silverthorn in Lower Wessex and make inquiries will find existing there almost a superstitious feeling for the moody, melancholy stranger who resided in the Lodge some forty years ago.

Whence he came, whither he was going were alike unknown. It was said that his mother had been an English lady of noble family who had married a foreigner not unheard of in circles where men pile up 'the cankered heaps of strange-achieved gold' – that he had been born and educated in England, taken abroad, and so on. But the facts of a life in such cases are of little account beside the aspect of a life; and hence, though doubtless the years of his existence contained their share of trite and homely circumstance, the curtain which masked all this was never lifted to gratify such a theatre of spectators as those at Silverthorn. Therein lay his charm. His life was a vignette, of which the central strokes only were drawn with any distinctness, the environment shading away to a blank.

He might have been said to resemble that solitary bird, the heron. The still, lonely stream, was his frequent haunt; on its banks he would stand for hours with his rod, looking into the water, beholding the tawny inhabitants with the eye of a philosopher, and seeming to say, 'Bite or don't bite – it's all the same to me.' He was often mistaken for a ghost by children; and for a pollard willow by men, when, on their way home in the dusk, they saw him motionless by some rushy bank, unobservant of the decline of day.

Why did he come to fish near Silverthorn? That was never explained. As far as was known he had no relatives near; the fishing there was not exceptionally good; the society thereabout was decidedly meagre. That he had committed some folly or hasty act, that he had been wrongfully accused of some crime, thus rendering his seclusion from the world desirable for a while, squared very well with his frequent melancholy. But such as he was there he lived, well supplied with fishing-tackle, and tenant of a furnished house, just suited to the requirements of such an eccentric being as he.

Margery's father, having privately ascertained that she was living with her grandmother, and getting into no harm, refrained from communicating with her, in the hope of seeing her contrite at his door. It had, of course, become known about Silverthorn that at the last moment Margery refused to wed Hayward, by absenting herself from the house. Jim was pitied, yet not pitied much, for it was said that he ought not to have been so eager for a woman who had shown no anxiety for him.

And where was Jim himself? It must not be supposed that that tactician had all this while withdrawn from mortal eye to tear his hair in silent indignation and despair. He had, in truth, merely retired up the lonesome defile between the downs to his smouldering kiln, and the ancient ramparts above it; and there, after his first hours of natural discomposure, he quietly waited for overtures from the possibly repentant Margery. But no overtures arrived, and then he meditated anew on the absorbing problem of her skittishness, and how to set about another campaign for her conquest, notwithstanding his late disastrous failure. Why had he failed? To what was her strange conduct owing? That was the thing which puzzled him.

He had made no advance in solving the riddle when, one morning, a stranger appeared on the down above him, looking as if he had lost his way. The man had a good deal of black hair below his felt hat, and carried under his arm a case containing a musical instrument. Descending to where Jim stood, he asked if there were not a short cut across that way to Tivworthy, where a fête was to be held.

'Well, yes, there is,' said Jim. 'But 'tis an enormous distance for 'ee.'

'O yes,' replied the musician. 'I wish to intercept the carrier on the highway.'

The nearest way was precisely in the direction of Rook's Gate, where Margery, as Jim knew, was staying. Having some time to spare, Jim was strongly impelled to make a kind act to the lost musician a pretext for taking observations in that neighbourhood; and telling his acquaintance that he was going the same way, he started without further ado.

They skirted the long length of meads, and in due time arrived at the back of Rook's Gate, where the path joined the high road. A hedge divided the public way from the cottage garden. Jim drew up at this point and said, 'Your road is straight on: I turn back here.'

But the musician was standing fixed, as if in great perplexity.

Thrusting his hand into his forest of black hair, he murmured, 'Surely it is the same – surely!'

Jim, following the direction of his neighbour's eyes, found them to be fixed on a figure till that moment hidden from himself – Margery Tucker – who was crossing the garden to an opposite gate with a little cheese in her arms, her head thrown back, and her face quite exposed.

'What of her?' said Jim.

'Two months ago I formed one of the band at the Yeomanry Ball given by Lord Toneborough in the next county. I saw that young lady dancing the polka there in robes of gauze and lace. Now I see her carry a cheese!'

'Never!' said Jim incredulously.

'But I do not mistake. I say it is so!'

Jim ridiculed the idea; the bandsman protested, and was about to lose his temper, when Jim gave in with the good-nature of a person who can afford to despise opinions; and the musician went his way.

As he dwindled out of sight Jim began to think more carefully over what he had said. The young man's thoughts grew quite to an excitement, for there came into his mind the Baron's extraordinary kindness in regard to furniture, hitherto accounted for by the assumption that the nobleman had taken a fancy to him. Could it be, among all the amazing things of life, that the Baron was at the bottom of this mischief, and that he had amused himself by taking Margery to a ball?

Doubts and suspicions which distract some lovers to imbecility only served to bring out Jim's great qualities. Where he trusted he was the most trusting fellow in the world; where he doubted he could be guilty of the slyest strategy. Once suspicious, he became one of those subtle, watchful characters who, without integrity, make good thieves; with a little, good jobbers; with a little more, good diplomatists. Jim was honest, and he considered what to do.

Retracing his steps, he peeped again. She had gone in; but she would soon reappear, for it could be seen that she was carrying little new cheeses one by one to a spring-cart and horse tethered outside the gate – her grandmother, though not a regular dairywoman, still managing a few cows by means of a man and maid. With the lightness of a cat Jim crept round to the gate, took a piece of chalk from his pocket, and wrote upon the boarding '*The Baron*.' Then he retreated to the other side of the garden where he had just watched Margery.

In due time she emerged with another little cheese, came on to the garden door, and glanced upon the chalked words which confronted her. She started; the cheese rolled from her arms to the ground, and broke into pieces like a pudding.

She looked fearfully round, her face burning like sunset, and, seeing nobody, stooped to pick up the flaccid lumps. Jim, with a pale face, departed as invisibly as he had come. He had proved the bandsman's tale to be true. On his way back he formed a resolution. It was to beard the lion in his den – to call on the Baron.

Meanwhile Margery had recovered her equanimity, and gathered up the broken cheese. But she could by no means account for the handwriting. Jim was just the sort of fellow to play her such a trick at ordinary times, but she imagined him to be far too incensed against her to do it now; and she suddenly wondered if it were any sort of signal from the Baron himself.

Of him she had lately heard nothing. If ever monotony pervaded a life it pervaded hers at Rook's Gate; and she had begun to despair of any happy change. But it is precisely when the social atmosphere seems stagnant that great events are brewing. Margery's quiet was broken first, as we have seen, by a slight start, only sufficient to make her drop a cheese; and then by a more serious matter.

She was inside the same garden one day when she heard two watermen talking without. The conversation was to the effect that the strange gentleman who had taken Mount Lodge for the season was seriously ill.

'How ill?' cried Margery through the hedge, which screened her from recognition.

'Bad abed,' said one of the watermen.

'Inflammation of the lungs,' said the other.

'Got wet, fishing,' the first chimed in.

Margery could gather no more. An ideal admiration rather than any positive passion existed in her breast for the Baron: she had of late seen too little of him to allow any incipient views of him as a lover to grow to formidable dimensions. It was an extremely romantic feeling, delicate as an aroma, capable of quickening to an active principle, or dying to 'a painless sympathy,' as the case might be.

This news of his illness, coupled with the mysterious chalking on the gate, troubled her, and revived his image much. She took to walking up and down the garden paths, looking into the hearts of flowers, and not thinking what they were. His last request had been that she was not to go to him if he should send for her; and now she asked herself, was the name on the gate a hint to enable her to go without infringing the letter of her promise? Thus unexpectedly had Jim's manoeuvre operated.

Ten days passed. All she could hear of the Baron were the same words, 'Bad abed,' till one afternoon, after a gallop of the physician to the Lodge, the tidings spread like lightning that the Baron was dying.

Margery distressed herself with the question whether she might be permitted to visit him and say her prayers at his bedside; but she feared to venture; and thus eight-and-forty hours slipped away, and the Baron still lived. Despite her shyness and awe of him she had almost made up her mind to call when, just at dusk on that October evening, somebody came to the door and asked for her.

She could see the messenger's head against the low new moon. He was a man-servant. He said he had been all the way to her father's, and had been sent thence to her there. He simply brought a note, and, delivering it into her hands, went away.

'DEAR MARGERY TUCKER,' ran the note – 'They say I am not likely to live, so I want to see you. Be here at eight o'clock this evening. Come quite alone to the side-door, and tap four times softly. My trusty man will admit you.

The occasion is an important one. Prepare yourself for a solemn ceremony, which I wish to have performed while it lies in my power.

'VON XANTEN.'

XI

Margery's face flushed up, and her neck and arms glowed in sympathy. The quickness of youthful imagination, and the assumptiveness of woman's reason, sent her straight as an arrow this thought: 'He wants to marry me!'

She had heard of similar strange proceedings, in which the orange-flower and the sad cypress were intertwined. People sometimes wished on their deathbeds, from motives of esteem, to form a legal tie which they had not cared to establish, as a domestic one during their active life.

For a few minutes Margery could hardly be called excited; she was excitement itself. Between surprise and modesty she blushed and trembled by turns. She became grave, sat down in the solitary room, and looked into the fire. At seven o'clock she rose resolved, and went quite tranquilly upstairs, where she speedily began to dress.

In making this hasty toilet nine-tenths of her care were given to her hands. The summer had left them slightly brown, and she held them up and looked at them with some misgiving, the fourth finger of her left hand more especially. Hot washings and cold washings, certain products from bee and flower known only to country girls, everything she could think of, were used upon those little sunburnt hands, till she persuaded herself that they were really as white as could be wished by a husband with a hundred titles. Her dressing completed, she left word with Edy that she was going for a long walk, and set out in the direction of Mount Lodge.

She no longer tripped like a girl, but walked like a woman. While crossing the park she murmured 'Baroness von Xanten' in a pronunciation of her own. The sound of that title caused her such agitation that she was obliged to pause, with her hand upon her heart.

The house was so closely neighboured by shrubberies on three of its sides that it was not till she had gone nearly round it that she found the little door. The resolution she had been an hour in forming failed her when she stood at the portal. While pausing for courage to tap, a carriage drove up to the front entrance a little way off, and peeping round the corner she saw alight a clergyman, and a gentleman in whom Margery fancied that she recognized a well-known solicitor from the neighbouring town. She had no longer any doubt of the nature of the ceremony proposed. 'It is sudden – but I must obey him!' she murmured: and tapped four times.

The door was opened so quickly that the servant must have been standing immediately inside. She thought him the man who had driven them to the ball – the silent man who could be trusted. Without a word he conducted her up the back staircase, and through a door at the top, into a wide corridor. She was asked to wait in a little dressingroom, where there was a fire, and an old metal-framed looking-glass over the mantelpiece, in which she caught sight of herself. A red spot burnt in each of her cheeks; the rest of her face was pale; and her eyes were like diamonds of the first water.

Before she had been seated many minutes the man came back noiselessly, and she followed him to a door covered by a red and black curtain, which he lifted, and ushered her into a large chamber. A screened light stood on a table before her, and on her left the hangings of a tall, dark, four-post bedstead obstructed her view of the centre of the room. Everything here seemed of such a magnificent type to her eyes that she felt confused, diminished to half her height, half her strength, half her prettiness. The man who had conducted her retired at once, and some one came softly round the angle of the bed-curtains. He held out his hand kindly – rather patronisingly: it was the solicitor whom she knew by sight. This gentleman led her forward, as if she had been a lamb rather than a woman, till the occupant of the bed was revealed.

The Baron's eyes were closed, and her entry had been so noiseless that he did not open them. The pallor of his face nearly matched the white bed-linen, and his dark hair and heavy black moustache were like dashes of ink on a clean page. Near him sat the parson and another gentleman, whom she afterwards learnt to be a London physician; and on the parson whispering a few words the Baron opened his eyes. As soon as he saw her he smiled faintly, and held out his hand.

Margery would have wept for him, if she had not been too overawed and palpitating to do anything. She quite forgot what she had come for, shook hands with him mechanically, and could hardly return an answer to his weak 'Dear Margery, you see how I am – how are you?'

In preparing for marriage she had not calculated on such a scene as this. Her affection for the Baron had too much of the vague in it to afford her trustfulness now. She wished she had not come. On a sign from the Baron the lawyer brought her a chair, and the oppressive silence was broken by the Baron's words.

'I am pulled down to death's door, Margery,' he said; 'and I suppose I soon shall pass through. . . . My peace has been much disturbed in this illness, for just before it attacked me I received – that present you returned, from which, and in other ways, I learnt that you had lost your chance of marriage. . . . Now it was I who did the harm, and you can imagine how the news has affected me. It has worried me all the illness through, and I cannot dismiss my error from my mind. . . . I want to right the wrong I have done you before I die. Margery, you have always obeyed me, and, strange as the request may be, will you obey me now?'

She whispered 'Yes.'

'Well, then,' said the Baron, 'these three gentlemen are here for a special purpose: one helps the body – he's called a physician; another helps the soul – he's a parson; the other helps the understanding – he's a lawyer. They are here partly on my account, and partly on yours.'

The speaker then made a sign to the lawyer, who went out of the door. He came back almost instantly, but not alone. Behind him, dressed up in his best clothes, with a flower in his buttonhole and a bridegroom's air, walked – Jim.

XII

Margery could hardly repress a scream. As for flushing and blushing, she had turned hot and turned pale so many times already during the evening, that there was really now nothing of that sort left for her to do; and she remained in complexion much as before. O, the mockery of it! That secret dream – that sweet word 'Baroness!' – which had sustained her all the way along. Instead of a Baron there stood Jim, white-waistcoated, demure, every hair in place, and, if she mistook not, even a deedy spark in his eye.

Jim's surprising presence on the scene may be briefly accounted for. His resolve to seek an explanation with the Baron at all risks had proved unexpectedly easy: the interview had at once been granted, and then, seeing the crisis at which matters stood, the Baron had generously revealed to Jim the whole of his indebtedness to and knowledge of Margery. The truth of the Baron's statement, the innocent nature as yet of the acquaintanceship, his sorrow for the rupture he had produced, was so evident that, far from having any further doubts of his patron, Jim frankly asked his advice on the next step to be pursued. At this stage the Baron fell ill, and, desiring much to see the two young people united before his death, he had sent anew to Hayward, and proposed the plan which they were now about to attempt – a marriage at the bedside of the sick man by special licence. The influence at Lambeth of some friends of the Baron's, and the charitable bequests of his late mother to several deserving Church funds, were generally supposed to be among the reasons why the application for the licence was not refused.

This, however, is of small consequence. The Baron probably knew, in proposing this method of celebrating the marriage, that his enormous power over her would outweigh any sentimental obstacles which she might set up – inward objections that, without his presence and firmness, might prove too much for her acquiescence. Doubtless he foresaw, too, the advantage of getting her into the house before making the individuality of her husband clear to her mind.

Now, the Baron's conjectures were right as to the event, but wrong as to the motives. Margery was a perfect little dissembler on some occasions, and one of them was when she wished to hide any sudden mortification that might bring her into ridicule. She had no sooner recovered from her first fit of discomfiture than pride bade her suffer anything rather than reveal her absurd disappointment. Hence the scene progressed as follows:

'Come here, Hayward,' said the invalid. Hayward came near. The Baron, holding her hand in one of his own, and her lover's in the other, continued, 'Will you, in spite of your recent vexation with her, marry her now if she does not refuse?'

'I will, sir,' said Jim promptly.

'And Margery, what do you say? It is merely a setting of things right. You have already promised this young man to be his wife, and should, of course, perform your promise. You don't dislike Jim?'

'O no, sir,' she said, in a low, dry voice.

'I like him better than I can tell you,' said the Baron. 'He is an honourable man, and will make you a good husband. You must remember that marriage is a life contract, in which general compatibility of temper and worldly position is of more importance than fleeting passion, which never long survives. Now, will you, at my earnest request, and before I go to the South of Europe to die, agree to make this good man happy? I have expressed your views on the subject, haven't I, Hayward?'

'To a T, sir,' said Jim emphatically, with a motion of raising his hat to his influential ally, till he remembered he had no hat on. 'And, though I could hardly expect Margery to gie in for my asking, I feels she ought to gie in for yours.'

'And you accept him, my little friend?'

'Yes, sir,' she murmured, 'if he'll agree to a thing or two.'

'Doubtless he will – what are they?'

'That I shall not be made to live with him till I am in the mind for it; and that my having him shall be kept unknown for the present.'

'Well, what do you think of it, Hayward?'

'Anything that you or she may wish I'll do, my noble lord,' said Jim.

'Well, her request is not unreasonable, seeing that the proceedings are, on my account, a little hurried. So we'll proceed. You rather expected this, from my allusion to a ceremony in my note, did you not, Margery?'

'Yes, sir,' said she, with an effort.

'Good; I thought so; you looked so little surprised.'

We now leave the scene in the bedroom for a spot not many yards off.

When the carriage seen by Margery at the door was driving up to Mount Lodge it arrested the attention, not only of the young girl, but of a man who had for some time been moving slowly about the opposite lawn, engaged in some operation while he smoked a short pipe. A short observation of his doings would have shown that he was sheltering some delicate plants from an expected frost, and that he was the gardener. When the light at the door fell upon the entering forms of parson and lawyer – the former a stranger, the latter known to him – the gardener walked thoughtfully round the house. Reaching the small side-entrance he was further surprised to see it noiselessly open to a young woman, in whose momentarily illumined features he discerned those of Margery Tucker.

Altogether there was something curious in this. The man returned to the lawn front, and perfunctorily went on putting shelters over certain plants, though his thoughts were plainly otherwise engaged. On the grass his footsteps were noiseless, and the night moreover being still, he could presently hear a murmuring from the bedroom window over his head.

The gardener took from a tree a ladder that he had used in nailing that day, set it under the window, and ascended half-way, hoodwinking his conscience by seizing a nail or two with his hand and testing their twig-supporting powers. He soon heard enough to satisfy him. The words of a church-service in the strange parson's voice were audible in snatches through the blind: they were words he knew to be part of the solemnization of matrimony, such as 'wedded wife,' 'richer for poorer,' and so on; the less familiar parts being a more or less confused sound.

Satisfied that a wedding was in progress there, the gardener did not for a moment dream that one of the contracting parties could be other than the sick Baron. He descended the ladder and again walked round the house, waiting only till he saw Margery emerge from the same little door; when, fearing that he might be discovered, he withdrew in the direction of his own cottage.

This building stood at the lower corner of the garden, and as soon as the gardener entered he was accosted by a handsome woman in a widow's cap, who called him father, and said that supper had been ready for a long time. They sat down, but during the meal the gardener was so abstracted and silent that his daughter put her head winningly to one side and said, 'What is it, father dear?'

'Ah – what is it?' cried the gardener. 'Something that makes very little difference to me, but may be of great account to you, if you play your cards well. *There's been a wedding at the Lodge tonight!*' He related to her, with a caution to secrecy, all that he had heard and seen.

'We are folk that have got to get their living,' he said, 'and such ones mustn't tell tales about their betters – Lord forgive the mockery of the word! – but there's something to be made of it. She's a nice maid; so, Harriet, do you take the first chance you get for honouring her, before others know what has happened. Since this is done so privately it will be kept private for some time – till after his death, no question; when I expect she'll take this house for herself, and blaze out as a widow-lady ten thousand pound strong. You being a widow, she may make you her company-keeper; and so you'll have a home by a little contriving.'

While this conversation progressed at the gardener's Margery was on her way out of the Baron's house. She was, indeed, married. But, as we know, she was not married to the Baron. The ceremony over she seemed but little discomposed, and expressed a wish to return alone as she had come. To this, of course, no objection could be offered under the terms of the agreement, and wishing Jim a frigid good-bye, and the Baron a very quiet farewell, she went out by the door which had admitted her. Once safe and alone in the darkness of the park she burst into tears, which dropped upon the grass as she passed along. In the Baron's room she had seemed scared and helpless; now her reason and emotions returned. The father she got away from the glamour of that room, and the influence of its occupant, the more she became of opinion that she had acted foolishly. She had disobediently left her father's house, to obey him here. She had pleased everybody but herself.

However, thinking was now too late. How she got into her grandmother's house she hardly knew; but without a supper, and without confronting either her relative or Edy, she went to bed.

XIII

On going out into the garden next morning, with a strange sense of being another person than herself, she beheld Jim leaning mutely over the gate.

He nodded. 'Good morning, Margery,' he said civilly.

'Good morning,' said Margery in the same tone.

'I beg your pardon,' he continued. 'But which way was you going this morning?'

'I am not going anywhere just now, thank you. But I shall go to my father's by-and-by with Edy.' She went on with a sigh, 'I have done what he has all along wished, that is, married you; and there's no longer reason for enmity atween him and me.'

'Trew – trew. Well, as I am going the same way, I can give you a lift in the trap, for the distance is long.'

'No, thank you – I am used to walking,' she said.

They remained in silence, the gate between them, till Jim's convictions would apparently allow him to hold his peace no longer. 'This is a bad job!' he murmured.

'It is,' she said, as one whose thoughts have only too readily been indentified. 'How I came to agree to it is more than I can tell!' And tears began rolling down her cheeks.

'The blame is more mine than yours, I suppose,' he returned. 'I ought to have said No, and not backed up the gentleman in carrying out this scheme. 'Twas his own notion entirely, as perhaps you know. I should never have thought of such a plan; but he said you'd be willing, and that it would be all right; and I was too ready to believe him.'

'The thing is, how to remedy it,' said she bitterly. 'I believe, of course, in your promise to keep this private, and not to trouble me by calling.'

'Certainly,' said Jim. 'I don't want to trouble you. As for that, why, my dear Mrs Hayward—'

'Don't Mrs Hayward me!' said Margery sharply. 'I won't be Mrs Hayward!'

Jim paused. 'Well, you are she by law, and that was all I meant,' he said mildly.

'I said I would acknowledge no such thing, and I won't. A thing can't be legal when it's against the wishes of the persons the laws are made to protect. So I beg you not to call me that any more.'

'Very well, Miss Tucker,' said Jim deferentially. 'We can live on exactly as before. We can't marry anybody else, that's true; but beyond that there's no difference, and no harm done. Your father ought to be told, I suppose, even if nobody else is? It will partly reconcile him to you, and make your life smoother.'

Instead of directly replying, Margery exclaimed in a low voice:

'O, it is a mistake – I didn't see it all, owing to not having time to reflect! I agreed, thinking that at least I should get reconciled to father by the step. But perhaps he would as soon have me not married at all as married and parted. I must ha' been enchanted – bewitched – when I gave my consent to this! I only did it to please that dear good dying nobleman – though why he should have wished it so much I can't tell!'

'Nor I neither,' said Jim. 'Yes, we've been fooled into it,

Margery,' he said, with extraordinary gravity. 'He's had his way wi' us, and now we've got to suffer for it. Being a gentleman of patronage, and having bought several loads of lime o' me, and having given me all that splendid furniture, I could hardly refuse—'

'What, did he give you that?'

'Ay, sure – to help me win ye.'

Margery covered her face with her hands; whereupon Jim stood up from the gate and looked critically at her. ''Tis a footy plot between you two men to – snare me!' she exclaimed. 'Why should you have done it – why should he have done it – when I've not deserved to be treated so? He bought the furniture, did he! O, I've been taken in – I've been wronged!' The grief and vexation of finding that long ago, when fondly believing the Baron to have lover-like feelings himself for her, he was still conspiring to favour Jim's suit, was more than she could endure.

Jim with distant courtesy waited, nibbling a straw, till her paroxysm was over. 'One word, Miss Tuck – Mrs – Margery,' he then recommenced gravely. 'You'll find me man enough to respect your wish, and to leave you to yourself – for ever and ever, if that's all. But I've just one word of advice to render 'ee. That is, that before you go to Silverthorn Dairy yourself you let me drive ahead and call on your father. He's friends with me, and he's not friends with you. I can break the news, a little at a time, and I think I can gain his goodwill for you now, even though the wedding be no natural wedding at all. At any count, I can hear what he's got to say about 'ee, and come back here and tell 'ee.'

She nodded a cool assent to this, and he left her strolling about the garden in the sunlight while he went on to reconnoitre as agreed. It must not be supposed that Jim's dutiful echoes of Margery's regret at her precipitate marriage were all gospel; and there is no doubt that his private intention, after telling the dairy-farmer what had happened, was to ask his temporary assent to her caprice, till, in the course of time, she should be reasoned out of her whims and induced to settle down with Jim in a natural manner. He had, it is true, been somewhat nettled by her firm objection to him, and her keen sorrow for what she had done to please another; but he hoped for the best.

But, alas for the astute Jim's calculations! He drove on to the dairy, whose white walls now gleamed in the morning sun; made fast the horse to a ring in the wall, and entered the barton. Before knocking, he perceived the dairyman walking across from a gate in the other direction, as if he had just come in. Jim went over to him. Since the unfortunate incident on the morning of the intended wedding they had merely been on nodding terms, from a sense of awkwardness in their relations.

'What – is that thee?' said Dairyman Tucker, in a voice which unmistakably startled Jim by its abrupt fierceness. 'A pretty fellow thou be'st!'

It was a bad beginning for the young man's life as a son-in-law, and augured ill for the delicate consultation he desired.

'What's the matter?' said Jim.

'Matter! I wish some folks would burn their lime without burning other folks' property along wi' it. You ought to be ashamed of yourself. You call yourself a man, Jim Hayward, and an honest lime-burner, and a respectable, market-keeping Christen, and yet at six o'clock this morning, instead o' being where you ought to ha' been – at your work, there was neither vell or mark o' thee to be seen!'

'Faith, I don't know what you are raving at,' said Jim.

'Why – the sparks from thy couch-heap blew over upon my hay-rick, and the rick's burnt to ashes; and all to come out o' my well-squeezed pocket. I'll tell thee what it is, young man. There's no business in thee. I've known Silverthorn folk, quick and dead, for the last couple-o'-score year, and I've never knew one so three-cunning for harm as thee, my gentleman lime-burner; and I reckon it one o' the luckiest days o' my life when I 'scaped having thee in my family. That maid of mine was right; I was wrong. She seed thee to be a drawlacheting rogue, and 'twas her wisdom to go off that morning and get rid o' thee. I commend her for't, and I'm going to fetch her home tomorrow.'

'You needn't take the trouble. She's coming home-along tonight of her own accord. I have seen her this morning, and she told me so.'

'So much the better. I'll welcome her warm. Nation! I'd sooner see her married to the parish fool than thee. Not you – you don't care for my hay. Tarrying about where you shouldn't be – in bed, no doubt; that's what you was a-doing. Now, don't you darken my doors again, and the sooner you be off my bit 'o ground the better I shall be pleased.'

Jim looked, as he felt, stultified. If the rick had been really destroyed, a little blame certainly attached to him, but he could not understand how it had happened. However, blame or none, it was clear he could not, with any self-respect, declare himself to be this peppery old gaffer's son-in-law in the face of such an attack as this.

For months – almost years – the one transaction that had seemed necessary to compose these two families satisfactorily was Jim's union with Margery. No sooner had it been completed than it appeared on all sides as the gravest mishap for both. Stating coldly that he would discover how much of the accident was to be attributed to his negligence, and pay the damage, he went out of the barton, and returned the way he had come.

Margery had been keeping a look-out for him, particularly wishing him not to enter the house, lest others should see the seriousness of their interview; and as soon as she heard wheels she went to the gate, which was out of view.

'Surely father has been speaking roughly to you!' she said, on seeing his face.

'Not the least doubt that he have,'said Jim.

'But is he still angry with me?'

'Not in the least. He's waiting to welcome 'ee.'

'Ah! because I've married you.'

'Because he thinks you have *not* married me! He's jawed me up hill and down. He hates me; and for your sake I have not explained a word.'

Margery looked towards home with a sad, severe gaze. 'Mr Hayward,' she said, 'we have made a great mistake, and we are in a strange position.'

'True, but I'll tell you what, mistress – I won't stand—' He stopped suddenly. 'Well, well; I've promised!' he quietly added.

'We must suffer for our mistake,' she went on. 'The way to suffer least is to keep our own counsel on what happened last evening, and not to meet. I must now return to my father.'

He inclined his head in indifferent assent, and she went indoors, leaving him there.

XIV

Margery returned home, as she had decided, and resumed her old life at Silverthorn. And seeing her father's animosity towards Jim, she told him not a word of the marriage.

Her inner life, however, was not what it once had been. She had suffered a mental and emotional displacement – a shock, which had set a shade of astonishment on her face as a permanent thing.

Her indignation with the Baron for collusion with Jim, at first bitter, lessened with the lapse of a few weeks, and at length vanished in the interest of some tidings she received one day.

The Baron was not dead, but he was no longer at the Lodge. To the surprise of the physicians, a sufficient improvement had taken place in his condition to permit of his removal before the cold weather came. His desire for removal had been such, indeed, that it was advisable to carry it out at almost any risk. The plan adopted had been to have him borne on men's shoulders in a sort of palanquin to the shore near Idmouth, a distance of several miles, where a yacht lay awaiting him. By this means the noise and jolting of a carriage, along irregular bye-roads, were avoided. The singular procession over the fields took place at night, and was witnessed by but few people, one being a labouring man, who described the scene to Margery. When the seaside was reached a long, narrow gangway was laid from the deck of the yacht to the shore, which was so steep as to allow the yacht to lie quite near. The men, with their burden, ascended by the light of lanterns, the sick man was laid in the cabin, and, as soon as his bearers had returned to the shore, the gangway was removed, a rope was heard skirring over wood in the darkness, the yacht quivered, spread her woven wings to the air, and moved away. Soon she was but a small shapeless phantom upon the wide breast of the sea.

It was said that the yacht was bound for Algiers.

When the inimical autumn and winter weather came on, Margery wondered if he were still alive. The house being shut up, and the servants gone, she had no means of knowing, till, on a particular Saturday, her father drove her to Exonbury market. Here, in attending to his business, he left her to herself for a while. Walking in a quiet street in the professional quarter of the town, she saw coming towards her the solicitor who had been present at the wedding, and who had acted for the Baron in various small local matters during his brief residence at the Lodge.

She reddened to peony hues, averted her eyes, and would have passed him. But he crossed over and barred the pavement, and when she met his glance he was looking with friendly severity at her. The street was quiet, and he said in a low voice, 'How's the husband?'

'I don't know, sir,' said she.

'What – and are your stipulations about secrecy and separate living still in force?'

'They will always be,' she replied decisively. 'Mr Hayward and I agreed on the point, and we have not the slightest wish to change the arrangement.'

'H'm. Then 'tis Miss Tucker to the world; Mrs Hayward to me and one or two others only?'

Margery nodded. Then she nerved herself by an effort, and, though blushing painfully, asked, 'May I put one question, sir? Is the Baron dead?'

'He is dead to you and to all of us. Why should you ask?'

'Because, if he's alive, I am sorry I married James Hayward. If he is dead I do not much mind my marriage.'

'I repeat, he is dead to you,' said the lawyer emphatically. 'I'll tell you all I know. My professional services for him ended with his departure from this country; but I think I should have heard from him if he had been alive still. I have not heard at all: and this, taken in connection with the nature of his illness, leaves no doubt in my mind that he is dead.'

Margery sighed, and thanking the lawyer she left him with a tear for the Baron in her eye. After this incident she became more restful; and the time drew on for her periodical visit to her grandmother.

A few days subsequent to her arrival her aged relative asked her to go with a message to the gardener at Mount Lodge (who still lived on there, keeping the grounds in order for the landlord). Margery hated that direction now, but she went. The Lodge, which she saw over the trees, was to her like a skull from which the warm and living flesh had vanished. It was twilight by the time she reached the cottage at the bottom of the Lodge garden, and, the room being illuminated within, she saw through the window a woman she had never seen before. She was dark, and rather handsome, and when Margery knocked she opened the door. It was the gardener's widowed daughter, who had been advised to make friends with Margery.

She now found her opportunity. Margery's errand was soon completed, the young widow, to her surprise, treating her with preternatural respect, and afterwards offering to accompany her home. Margery was not sorry to have a companion in the gloom, and they walked on together. The widow, Mrs Peach, was demonstrative and confidential, and told Margery all about herself. She had come quite recently to live with her father – during the Baron's illness, in fact – and her husband had been captain of a ketch.

'I saw you one morning, ma'am,' she said. 'But you didn't see me. It was when you were crossing the hill in sight of the Lodge. You looked at it, and sighed. 'Tis the lot of widows to sigh, ma'am, is it not?'

'Widows – yes, I suppose; but what do you mean?'

Mrs Peach lowered her voice. 'I can't say more, ma'am, with proper respect. But there seems to be no question of the poor Baron's death; and though these foreign princes can take (as my poor husband used to tell me) what they call left-handed wives, and leave them behind when they go abroad, widowhood is widowhood, left-handed or right. And really, to be the left-handed wife of a foreign baron is nobler than to be married all round to a common man. You'll excuse my freedom, ma'am; but being a widow myself, I have pitied you from my heart; so young as you are, and having to keep it a secret, and (excusing me) having no money out of his vast riches because 'tis swallowed up by Baroness Number One.'

Now Margery did not understand a word more of this than the bare fact that Mrs Peach suspected her to be the Baron's undowered widow, and such was the milkmaid's nature that she did not deny the widow's impeachment. The latter continued—

'But ah, ma'am, all your troubles are straight backward in your memory – while I have troubles before as well as grief behind.'

'What may they be, Mrs Peach?' inquired Margery, with an air of the Baroness.

The other dropped her voice to revelation tones: 'I have been forgetful enough of my first man to lose my heart to a second!'

'You shouldn't do that – it is wrong. You should control your feelings.'

'But how am I to control my feelings?'

'By going to your dead husband's grave, and things of that sort.'

'Do you go to your dead husband's grave?'

'How can I go to Algiers?'

'Ah – too true! Well, I've tried everything to cure myself – read the words against it, gone to the Table the first Sunday of every month, and all sorts. But, avast, my shipmate! – as my poor man used to say – there 'tis just the same. In short, I've made up my mind to encourage the new one. 'Tis flattering that I, a new-comer, should have been found out by a young man so soon.'

'Who is he?' said Margery listlessly.

'A master lime-burner.'

'A master lime-burner?'

'That's his profession. He's a partner-in-co., doing very well indeed.'

'But what's his name?'

'I don't like to tell you his name, for, though 'tis night, that covers all shame-facedness, my face is as hot as a, 'Talian iron, I declare! Do you just feel it.'

Margery put her hand on Mrs Peach's face, and, sure enough, hot it was. 'Does he come courting?' she asked quickly.

'Well – only in the way of business. He never comes unless lime is wanted in the neighbourhood. He's in the Yeomanry, too, and will look very fine when he comes out in regimentals for drill in May.'

'Oh – in the Yeomanry,' Margery said, with a slight relief. 'Then it can't – is he a young man?'

'Yes, junior partner-in-co.'

The description had an odd resemblance to Jim, of whom Margery had not heard a word for months. He had promised silence and absence, and had fulfilled his promise literally, with a gratuitous addition that was rather amazing, if indeed it were Jim whom the widow loved. One point in the description puzzled

Margery: Jim was not in the Yeomanry, unless, by a surprising development of enterprise, he had entered it recently.

At parting Margery said, with an interest quite tender, 'I should like to see you again, Mrs Peach, and hear of your attachment. When can you call?'

'Oh any time, dear Baroness, I'm sure – if you think I am good enough.'

'Indeed, I do, Mrs Peach. Come as soon as you've seen the lime-burner again.'

XV

Seeing that Jim lived several miles from the widow, Margery was rather surprised, and even felt a slight sinking of the heart, when her new acquaintance appeared at her door so soon as the evening of the following Monday. She asked Margery to walk out with her, which the young woman readily did.

'I am come at once,' said the widow breathlessly, as soon as they were in the lane, 'for it is so exciting that I can't keep it. I must tell it to somebody, if only a bird, or a cat, or a garden snail.'

'What is it?' asked her companion.

'I've pulled grass from my husband's grave to cure it – wove the blades into true lover's knots; took off my shoes upon the sod; but, avast, my shipmate!—'

'Upon the sod – why?'

'To feel the damp earth he's in, and make the sense of it enter my soul. But no. It has swelled to a head; he is going to meet me at the Yeomanry Review.'

'The master lime-burner?'

The widow nodded.

'When is it to be?'

'Tomorrow. He looks so lovely in his accoutrements! He's such a splendid soldier; that was the last straw that kindled my soul to say yes. He's home from Exonbury for a night between the drills,' continued Mrs Peach. 'He goes back tomorrow morning for the Review, and when it's over he's going to meet me. . . . But, guide my heart, there he is!'

Her exclamation had rise in the sudden appearance of a brilliant red uniform through the trees, and the tramp of a horse carrying the wearer thereof. In another half-minute the military gentleman would have turned the corner, and faced them.

'He'd better not see me; he'll think I know too much,' said Margery precipitately. 'I'll go up here.'

The widow, whose thoughts had been of the same cast, seemed much relieved to see Margery disappear in the plantation, in the midst of a spring chorus of birds. Once among the trees, Margery turned her head, and before she could see the rider's person, she recognized the horse as Tony, the lightest of three that Jim and his partner owned, for the purpose of carting out lime to their customers.

Jim, then, had joined the Yeomanry since his estrangement from Margery. A man who had worn the young Queen Victoria's uniform for seven days only could not be expected to look as if it were part of his person, in the manner of long-trained soldiers; but he was a well-formed young fellow, and of an age when few positions come amiss to one who has the capacity to adapt himself to circumstances.

Meeting the blushing Mrs Peach (to whom Margery in her mind sternly denied the right to blush at all), Jim alighted and moved on with her, probably at Mrs Peach's own suggestion; so that what they said, how long they remained together, and how they parted, Margery knew not. She might have known some of these things by waiting; but the presence of Jim had bred in her heart a sudden disgust for the widow, and a general sense of discomfiture. She went away in an opposite direction, turning her head and saying to the unconscious Jim, 'There's a fine rod in pickle for you, my gentleman, if you carry out that pretty scheme!'

Jim's military *coup* had decidedly astonished her. What he might do next she could not conjecture. The idea of his doing anything sufficiently brilliant to arrest her attention would have seemed ludicrous, had not Jim, by entering the Yeomanry, revealed a capacity for dazzling exploits which made it unsafe to predict any limitation to his powers.

Margery was now excited. The daring of the wretched Jim in bursting into scarlet amazed her as much as his doubtful acquaintanceship with the demonstrative Mrs Peach. To go to that Review, to watch the pair, to eclipse Mrs Peach in brilliancy, to meet and pass them in withering contempt – if she only could do it! But, alas! she was a forsaken woman. 'If the Baron were alive, or in England,' she said to herself (for sometimes she thought he might possibly be alive), 'and he were to take me to this Review, wouldn't I show that forward Mrs Peach what a lady is like, and keep among the select company, and not mix with the common people at all!'

It might at first sight be thought that the best course for Margery at this juncture would have been to go to Jim, and nip the intrigue in the bud without further scruple. But her own declaration in after days was that whoever could say that was far from realizing her situation. It was hard to break such ice as divided their two lives now, and to attempt it at that moment was a too humiliating proclamation of defeat. The only plan she could think of – perhaps not a wise one in the circumstances – was to go to the Review herself, and be the gayest there.

A method of doing this with some propriety soon occurred to her. She dared not ask her father, who scorned to waste time in sight-seeing, and whose animosity towards Jim knew no abatement; but she might call on her old acquaintance, Mr Vine, Jim's partner, who would probably be going with the rest of the holiday-folk, and ask if she might accompany him in his spring-trap. She had no sooner perceived the feasibility of this, through her being at her grandmother's, than she decided to meet with the old man early the next morning.

In the meantime Jim and Mrs Peach had walked slowly along the road together, Jim leading the horse, and Mrs Peach informing him that her father, the gardener, was at Jim's village, farther on, and that she had come to meet him. Jim, for reasons of his own, was going to sleep at his partner's that night, and thus their route was the same. The shades of eve closed in upon them as they walked, and by the time they reached the lime-kiln, which it was necessary to pass to get to the village, it was quite dark. Jim stopped at the kiln, to see if matters had progressed rightly in his seven days' absence, and Mrs Peach, who stuck to him like a teazle, stopped also, saying she would wait for her father there.

She held the horse while he ascended to the top of the kiln. Then rejoining her, and not quite knowing what to do, he stood beside her looking at the flames, which tonight burnt up brightly, shining a long way into the dark air, even up to the ramparts of the earthwork above them, and overhead into the bosoms of the clouds.

It was during this proceeding that a carriage, drawn by a pair of dark horses, came along the turnpike-road. The light of the kiln caused the horses to swerve a little, and the occupant of the carriage looked out. He saw the bluish, lightning-like flames from the limestone, rising from the top of the furnace, and hard by the figures of Jim Hayward, the widow, and the horse, standing out with spectral distinctness against the mass of night behind. The scene wore the aspect of some unholy assignation in Pandaemonium, and it was all the more impressive from the fact that both Jim and the woman were quite unconscious of the striking spectacle they presented. The gentleman in the carriage watched them till he was borne out of sight.

Having seen to the kiln, Jim and the widow walked on again, and soon Mrs Peach's father met them, and relieved Jim of the lady. When they had parted, Jim, with an expiration not unlike a breath of relief, went on to Mr Vine's, and, having put the horse into the stable, entered the house. His partner was seated at the table, solacing himself after the labours of the day by luxurious alternations between a long clay pipe and a mug of perry.

'Well,' said Jim eagerly, 'what's the news – how do she take it?'

'Sit down – sit down,' said Vine. ''Tis working well; not but that I deserve something o' thee for the trouble I've had in watching her. The soldiering was a fine move; but the woman is a better – who invented it?'

'I myself,' said Jim modestly.

'Well; jealousy is making her rise like a thunder-storm, and in a day or two you'll have her for the asking, my sonny. What's the next step?'

'The widow is getting rather a weight upon a feller, worse luck,' said Jim. 'But I must keep it up until tomorrow, at any rate. I have promised to see her at the Review, and now the great thing is that Margery should see we a-smiling together – I in my full-dress uniform and clinking arms o' war. 'Twill be a good strong sting, and will end the business, I hope. Couldn't you manage to put the hoss in and drive her there? She'd go if you were to ask her.'

'With all my heart,' said Mr Vine, moistening the end of a new pipe in his perry. 'I can call at her grammer's for her – 'twill be all in my way.'

XVI

Margery duly followed up her intention by arraying herself the next morning in her loveliest guise, and keeping watch for Mr Vine's appearance upon the high road, feeling certain that this would form one in the procession of carts and carriages which set in towards Exonbury that day. Jim had gone by at a very early hour, and she did not see him pass. Her anticipation was verified by the advent of Mr Vine about eleven o'clock, dressed to his highest effort; but Margery was surprised to find that, instead of her having to stop him, he pulled in towards the gate of his own accord. The invitation planned between Jim and the old man on the previous night was now promptly given, and, as may be supposed, as promptly accepted. Such a strange coincidence she had never before known. She was quite ready, and they drove onward at once.

The Review was held on some high ground a little way out of the city, and her conductor suggested that they should put up the horse at the inn, and walk to the field – a plan which pleased her well, for it was more easy to take preliminary observations on foot without being seen herself than when sitting elevated in a vehicle.

They were just in time to secure a good place near the front, and in a few minutes after their arrival the reviewing officer came on the ground. Margery's eye had rapidly run over the troop in which Jim was enrolled, and she discerned him in one of the ranks, looking remarkably new and bright, both as to uniform and countenance. Indeed, if she had not worked herself into such a desperate state of mind she would have felt proud of him then and there. His shapely upright figure was quite noteworthy in the row of rotund yeomen on his right and left; while his charger Tony expressed by his bearing, even more than Jim, that he knew nothing about lime-carts whatever, and everything about trumpets and glory. How Jim could have scrubbed Tony to such shining blackness she could not tell, for the horse in his natural state was ingrained with limedust, that burnt the colour out of his coat as it did out of Jim's hair. Now he pranced martially, and was a warhorse every inch of him.

Having discovered Jim her next search was for Mrs Peach, and, by dint of some oblique glancing, Margery indignantly discovered the widow in the most forward place of all, her head and bright face conspicuously advanced; and , what was more shocking, she had abandoned her mourning for a violet drawn-bonnet and a gay spencer, together with a parasol luxuriously fringed in a way Margery had never before seen. 'Where did she get the money?' said Margery, under her breath. 'And to forget that poor sailor so soon!'

These general reflections were precipitately postponed by her discovering that Jim and the widow were perfectly alive to each other's whereabouts, and in the interchange of telegraphic signs of affection, which on the latter's part took the form of a playful fluttering of her handkerchief or waving of her parasol. Richard Vine had placed Margery in front of him, to protect her from the crowd, as he said, he himself surveying the scene over her bonnet. Margery would have been even more surprised than she was if she had known that Jim was not only aware of Mrs Peach's presence, but also of her own, the treacherous Mr Vine having drawn out his flame-coloured handkerchief and waved it to Jim over the young woman's head as soon as they had taken up their position.

'My partner makes a tidy soldier, eh – Miss Tucker?' said the senior lime-burner. 'It is my belief as a Christian that he's got a party here that he's making signs to – that handsome figure o' fun straight over-right him.'

'Perhaps so,' she said.

'And it's growing warm between 'em if I don't mistake,' continued the merciless Vine.

Margery was silent, biting her lip; and the troops being now set in motion, all signalling ceased for the present between soldier Hayward and his pretended sweetheart.

'Have you a piece of paper that I could make a memorandum on, Mr Vine?' asked Margery.

Vine took out his pocket-book and tore a leaf from it, which he handed her with a pencil.

'Don't move from here – I'll return in a minute,' she continued, with the innocence of a woman who means mischief. And, withdrawing herself to the back, where the grass was clear, she pencilled down the words –

'JIM'S MARRIED.'

Armed with this document she crept into the throng behind the unsuspecting Mrs Peach, slipped the paper into her pocket on the top of her handkerchief, and withdrew unobserved, rejoining Mr. Vine with a bearing of *nonchalance*.

By-and-by the troops were in different order, Jim taking a left-hand position almost close to Mrs Peach. He bent down and said a few words to her. From her manner of nodding assent it was surely some arrangement about a meeting by-and-by when Jim's drill was over, and Margery was more certain of the fact when, the Review having ended, and the people having strolled off to another part of the field where sports were to take place, Mrs Peach tripped away in the direction of the city.

'I'll just say a word to my partner afore he goes off the ground, if you'll spare me a minute,' said the old lime-burner. 'Please stay here till I'm back again.' He edged along the front till he reached Jim.

'How is she?' said the latter.

'In a trimming sweat,' said Mr. Vine. 'And my counsel to 'ee is to carry this larry no further. 'Twill do no good. She's as ready to make friends with 'ee as any wife can be; and more showing off can only do harm.'

'But I must finish off with a spurt,' said Jim. 'And this is how I am going to do it. I have arranged with Mrs Peach that, as soon as we soldiers have entered the town and been dismissed, I'll meet her there. It is really to say good-bye, but she don't know that; and I wanted it to look like a 'lopement to Margery's eyes. When I'm clear of Mrs Peach I'll come back here and make it up with Margery on the spot. But don't say I'm coming, or she may be inclined to throw off again. Just hint to her that I may be meaning to be off to London with the widow.'

The old man still insisted that this was going too far.

'No, no, it isn't,' said Jim. 'I know how to manage her. 'Twill just mellow her heart nicely by the time I come back. I must bring her down real tender, or 'twill all fail.'

His senior reluctantly gave in and returned to Margery. A short time afterwards the Yeomanry band struck up, and Jim with the regiment followed towards Exonbury.

'Yes, yes; they are going to meet,' said Margery to herself, perceiving that Mrs Peach had so timed her departure as to be in the town at Jim's dismounting.

'Now we will go and see the games,' said Mr Vine; 'they are really worth seeing. There's greasy poles, and jumping in sacks, and other trials of the intellect, that nobody ought to miss who wants to be abreast of his generation.'

Margery felt so indignant at the apparent assignation, which seemed about to take place despite her anonymous writing, that she helplessly assented to go anywhere, dropping behind Vine, that he might not see her mood.

Jim followed out his programme with literal exactness. No sooner was the troop dismissed in the city than he sent Tony to stable and joined Mrs Peach, who stood on the edge of the pavement expecting him. But this acquaintance was to end: he meant to part from her for ever and in the quickest time, though civilly; for it was important to be with Margery as soon as possible. He had nearly completed the manoeuvre to his satisfaction when, in drawing her handkerchief from her pocket to wipe the tears from her eyes, Mrs Peach's hand grasped the paper, which she read at once.

'What! is that true?' she said, holding it out to Jim.

Jim started and admitted that it was, beginning an elaborate explanation and apologies. But Mrs Peach was thoroughly roused, and then overcome. 'He's married, he's married!' she said, and swooned, or feigned to swoon, so that Jim was obliged to support her.

'He's married, he's married!' said a boy hard by who watched the scene with interest.

'He's married, he's married!' said a hilarious group of other boys near, with smiles several inches broad, and shining teeth; and so the exclamation echoed down the street.

Jim cursed his ill-luck; the loss of time that this dilemma entailed grew serious; for Mrs Peach was now in such a hysterical state that he could not leave her with any good grace or feeling. It was necessary to take her to a refreshment room, lavish restoratives upon her, and altogether to waste nearly half-an-hour. When she had kept him as long as she chose, she forgave him; and thus at last he got away, his heart swelling with tenderness towards Margery. He at once hurried up the street to effect the reconciliation with her.

'How shall I do it?' he said to himself. 'Why, I'll step round to her side, fish for her hand, draw it through my arm as if I wasn't aware of it. Then she'll look in my face, I shall look in hers, and we shall march off the field triumphant, and the thing will be done without takings or tears.'

He entered the field and went straight as an arrow to the place appointed for the meeting. It was at the back of a refreshment tent outside the mass of spectators, and divided from their view by the tent itself. He turned the corner of the canvas, and there beheld Vine at the indicated spot. But Margery was not with him.

Vine's hat was thrust back into his poll. His face was pale, and his manner bewildered. 'Hullo? what's the matter?' said Jim. 'Where's my Margery?'

'You've carried this footy game too far, my man!' exclaimed Vine, with the air of a friend who has 'always told you so.' 'You ought to have dropped it several days ago, when she would have come to 'ee like a cooing dove. Now this is the end o't!'

'Hey! what, my Margery? Has anything happened, for God's sake?'

'She's gone.'

'Where to?'

'That's more than earthly man can tell! I never see such a thing! 'Twas a stroke o' the black art – as if she were sperrited away. When we got to the games I said – mind, you told me to! – I said, "Jim Hayward thinks o' going off to London with that widow woman" – mind, you told me to! She showed no wonderment, though a' seemed very low. Then she said to me, "I don't like standing here in this slummocky crowd. I shall feel more at home among the gentlepeople." And then she went to where the carriages were drawn up, and near her there was a grand coach, a-blazing with lions and unicorns, and hauled by two coal-black horses. I hardly thought much of it then, and by degrees lost sight of her behind it. Presently the other carriages moved off, and I thought still to see her standing there. But no, she had vanished; and then I saw the grand coach rolling away, and glimpsed Margery in it, beside a fine dark gentleman with black mustachios, and a very pale prince-like face. As soon as the horses got into the hard road they rattled on like hell-and-skimmer, and went out of sight in the dust, and – that's all. If you'd come back a little sooner you'd ha' caught her.'

Jim had turned whiter than his pipeclay. 'O, this is too bad – too bad!' he cried in anguish, striking his brow. 'That paper and that fainting woman kept me so long. Who could have done it? But 'tis my fault. I've stung her too much. I shouldn't have carried it so far.'

'You shouldn't – just what I said,' replied his senior.

'She thinks I've gone off with that cust widow; and to spite me she's gone off with the man! Do you know who that stranger wi' the lions and unicorns is? Why, 'tis that foreigner who calls himself a Baron, and took Mount Lodge for six months last year to make mischief – a villain! O, my Margery – that it should come to this! She's lost, she's ruined! – Which way did they go?'

Jim turned to follow in the direction indicated, when, behold, there stood at his back her father, Dairyman Tucker.

'Now look here, young man,' said Dairyman Tucker. 'I've just heard all that wailing – and straightway will ask 'ee to stop it sharp. 'Tis like your brazen impudence to teave and wail when you be another woman's husband; yes, faith, I seed her a-fainting in yer arms when you wanted to get away from her, and honest folk a-standing round who knew you'd married her, and said so. I heard it, though you didn't see me. "He's married!" says they. Some sly register-office business, no doubt; but sly doings will out. As for Margery – who's to be called higher titles in these parts hencefor'ard – I'm her father, and I say it's all right what' she's done. Don't I know private news, hey? Haven't I just learnt that secret weddings of high people can happen at expected deathbeds by special licence, as well as low people at registrars' offices? And can't husbands come back and claim their own when they choose? Begone, young man, and leave noblemen's wives alone; and I thank God I shall be rid of a numskull!'

Swift words of explanation rose to Jim's lips, but they paused there and died. At that last moment he could not, as Margery's husband, announce Margery's shame and his own, and transform her father's triumph to wretchedness at a blow.

'I – I – must leave here,' he stammered. Going from the place in an opposite course to that of the fugitives, he doubled when out of sight, and in an incredibly short space had entered the town. Here he made inquiries for the emblazoned carriage, and gained from one or two persons a general idea of its route. They thought it had taken the highway to London. Saddling poor Tony before he had half eaten his corn, Jim galloped along the same road.

XVII

Now Jim was quite mistaken in supposing that by leaving the field in a roundabout manner he had deceived Dairyman Tucker as to his object. That astute old man immediately divined that Jim was meaning to track the fugitives, in ignorance (as the dairyman supposed) of their lawful relation. He was soon assured of the fact, for, creeping to a remote angle of the field, he saw Jim hastening into the town. Vowing vengeance on the young lime-burner for his mischievous interference between a nobleman and his secretly-wedded wife, the dairy-farmer determined to balk him.

Tucker had ridden on to the Review ground, so that there was no necessity for him, as there had been for poor Jim, to re-enter the town before starting. The dairyman hastily untied his mare from the row of other horses, mounted, and descended to a bridle-path which would take him him obliquely into the London road a mile or so ahead. The old man's route being along one side of an equilateral triangle, while Jim's was along two sides of the same, the former was at the point of intersection long before Hayward.

Arrived here, the dairyman pulled up and looked around. It was a spot at which the highway forked; the left arm, the more important, led on through Sherton Abbas and Melchester to London; the right to Idmouth and the coast. Nothing was visible on the white track to London; but on the other there appeared the back of a carriage which rapidly ascended a distant hill and vanished under the trees. It was the Baron's who, according to the sworn information of the gardener at Mount Lodge, had made Margery his wife.

The carriage having vanished, the dairyman gazed in the opposite direction, towards Exonbury. Here he beheld Jim in his regimentals, laboriously approaching on Tony's back.

Soon he reached the forking roads, and saw the dairy-man by

the wayside. But Jim did not halt. Then the dairyman practised the greatest duplicity of his life.

'Right along the London road, if you want to catch 'em!' he said.

'Thank' ee, dairyman, thank' ee! cried Jim, his pale face lighting up with gratitude, for he believed that Tucker hd learnt his mistake from Vine, and had come to his assistance. Without drawing rein he diminished along the road not taken by the flying pair. The dairyman rubbed his hands with delight, and returned to the city as the cathedral clock struck five.

Jim pursued his way through the dust, up hill and down hill; but never saw ahead of him the vehicle of his search. That vehicle was passing along a diverging way at a distance of many miles from where he rode. Still he sped onwards, till Tony showed signs of breaking down; and then Jim gathered from inquiries he made that he had come the wrong way. It burst upon his mind that the dairyman, still ignorant of the truth, had misinformed him. Heavier in his heart than words can describe he turned Tony's drooping head, and resolved to drag his way home.

But the horse was now so jaded that it was impossible to proceed far. Having gone about half a mile back he came again to a small roadside hamlet and inn, where he put up Tony for a rest and feed. As for himself, there was no quiet in him. He tried to sit and eat in the inn kitchen; but he could not stay there. He went out, and paced up and down the road.

Standing in sight of the white way by which he had come he beheld advancing towards him the horses and carriage he sought, now black and daemonic against the slanting fires of the western sun.

The why and wherefore of this sudden appearance he did not pause to consider. His resolve to intercept the carriage was instantaneous. He ran forward, and doggedly waiting barred the way to the advancing equipage.

The Baron's coachman shouted, but Jim stood firm as a rock, and on the former attempting to push past him Jim drew his sword, resolving to cut the horses down rather than be displaced. The animals were thrown nearly back upon their haunches, and at this juncture a gentleman looked out of the window. It was the Baron himself.

'Who's there?' he inquired.

'James Hayward!' replied the young man fiercely, 'and he demands his wife.'

The Baron leapt out, and told the coachman to drive back out of sight and wait for him.

'I was hastening to find you,' he said to Jim. 'Your wife is where she ought to be, and where you ought to be also – by your own fireside. Where's the other woman?'

Jim, without replying, looked incredulously into the carriage as it turned. Margery was certainly not there. 'The other woman is nothing to me,' he said bitterly. 'I used her to warm up Margery: I have now done with her. The question I ask, my lord, is, what business had you with Margery today?'

'My business was to help her to regain the husband she had seemingly lost. I saw her; she told me you had eloped by the London road with another. I, who have – mostly – had her happiness at heart, told her I would help her to follow you if she wished. She gladly agreed; we drove after, but could hear no tidings of you in front of us. Then I took her – to your house – and there she awaits you. I promised to send you to her if human effort could do it, and was tracking you for that purpose.'

'Then you've been a-pursuing after me?'

'You and the widow.'

'And I've been pursuing after you and Margery! . . . My noble lord, your actions seem to show that I ought to believe you in this; and when you say you've her happiness at heart, I don't forget that you've formerly proved it to be so. Well, Heaven forbid that I should think wrongfully of you if you don't deserve it! A mystery to me you have always been, my noble lord, and in this business more than in any.'

'I am glad to hear you say no worse. In one hour you'll have proof of my conduct – good and bad. Can I do anything more? Say the word, and I'll try.'

Jim reflected. 'Baron,' he said, 'I am a plain man, and wish only to lead a quiet life with my wife, as a man should. You have great power over her – power to any extent, for good or otherwise. If you command her anything on earth, righteous or questionable, that she'll do. So that, since you ask me if you can do more for me, I'll answer this, you can promise never to see her again. I mean no harm, my lord; but your presence can do no good; you will trouble us. If I return to her, will you for ever stay away?'

'Hayward,' said the Baron, 'I swear to you that I will disturb you and your wife by my presence no more.' And he took Jim's hand and pressed it within his own upon the hilt of Jim's sword.

In relating this incident to the present narrator Jim used to declare that, to his fancy, the ruddy light of the setting sun burned with more than earthly fire on the Baron's face as the words were spoken; and that the ruby flash of his eye in the same light was what he never witnessed before nor since in the eye of mortal man. After this there was nothing more to do or say in that place. Jim accompanied his never-to-be-forgotten acquaintance to the carriage, closed the door after him, waved his hat to him, and from that hour he and the Baron met not again on earth.

A few words will suffice to explain the fortunes of Margery while the foregoing events were in action elsewhere. On leaving her companion Vine she had gone distractedly among the carriages, the rather to escape his observation than of any set purpose. Standing here she thought she heard her name pronounced, and turning, saw her foreign friend, whom she had supposed to be, if not dead, a thousand miles off. He beckoned, and she went close. 'You are ill – you are wretched,' he said, looking keenly in her face. 'Where's your husband?'

She told him her sad suspicion that Jim had run away from her. The Baron reflected, and inquired a few other particulars of her late life. Then he said, 'You and I must find him. Come with me.' At this word of command from the Baron she had entered the carriage as docilely as a child, and there she sat beside him till he chose to speak, which was not till they were some way out of the town, at the forking ways, and the Baron had discovered that Jim was certainly not, as they had supposed, making off from Margery along that particular branch of the fork that led to London.

'To pursue him in this way is useless, I perceive,' he said. 'And the proper course now is that I should take you to his house. That done I will return, and bring him to you if mortal persuasion can do it.'

'I didn't want to go to his house without him, sir,' said she, tremblingly.

'Didn't want to!' he answered. 'Let me remind you, Margery Hayward, that your place is in your husband's house. Till you are there you have no right to criticize his conduct, however wild it may be. Why have you not been there before?'

'I don't know, sir,' she murmured, her tears falling silently upon her hand.

'Don't you think you ought to be there?'

She did not answer.

'Of course you ought.'

Still she did not speak.

The Baron sank into silence, and allowed his eye to rest on her. What thoughts were all at once engaging his mind after those moments of reproof? Margery had given herself into his hands without a remonstrance. Her husband had apparently deserted her. She was absolutely in his power, and they were on the high road.

That his first impulse in inviting her to accompany him had been the legitimate one denoted by his words cannot reasonably be doubted. That his second was otherwise soon became revealed, though not at first to her, for she was too bewildered to notice where they were going. Instead of turning and taking the road to Jim's, the Baron, as if influenced suddenly by her reluctance to return thither if Jim was playing truant, signalled to the coachman to take the branch road to the right, as her father had discerned.

They soon approached the coast near Idmouth. The carriage stopped. Margery awoke from her reverie.

'Where are we?' she said, looking out of the window, with a start. Before her was an inlet of the sea, and in the middle of the inlet rode a yacht, its masts repeating as if from memory the rocking they had practised in their native forest.

'At a little sea-side nook, where my yacht lies at anchor,' he said tentatively. 'Now, Margery, in five minutes we can be aboard, and in half-an-hour we can be sailing away all the world over. Will you come?'

'I cannot decide,' she said, in low tones.

'Why not?'

'Because—'

Then on a sudden Margery seemed to see all contingencies: she became white as a fleece, and a bewildered look came into her eyes. With clasped hands she leant on the Baron.

Baron von Xanten observed her distracted look, averted his face, and coming to a decision opened the carriage door, quickly mounted outside, and in a second or two the carriage left the shore behind, and ascended the road by which it had come.

In about an hour they reached Jim Hayward's home. The Baron alighted, and spoke to her through the window. 'Margery, can you forgive a lover's bad impulse, which I swear was unpremeditated?' he asked. 'If you can, shake my hand.'

She did not do it, but eventually allowed him to help her out of the carriage. He seemed to feel the awkwardness keenly; and seeing it, she said, 'Of course I forgive you, sir, for I felt for a moment as you did. Will you send my husband to me?'

'I will, if any man can,' said he. 'Such penance is milder than I deserve! God bless you and give you happiness! I shall never see you again!' He turned, entered the carriage, and was gone; and having found out Jim's course, came up with him upon the road as described.

In due time the latter reached his lodging at his partner's. The woman who took care of the house in Vine's absence at once told Jim that a lady who had come in a carriage was waiting for him in his sitting-room. Jim proceeded thither with agitation, and beheld, shrinkingly ensconced in the large slippery chair, and surrounded by the brilliant articles that had so long awaited her, his long-estranged wife.

Margery's eyes were round and fear-stricken. She essayed to speak, but Jim, strangely enough, found the readier tongue then. 'Why did I do it, you would ask,' he said. 'I cannot tell. Do you forgive my deception? O Margery – you are my Margery still! But how could you trust yourself in the Baron's hands this afternoon, without knowing him better?'

'He said I was to come, and I went,' she said, as well as she could for tearfulness.

'You obeyed him blindly.'

'I did. But perhaps I was not justified in doing it.'

'I don't know,' said Jim musingly. 'I think he's a good man.' Margery did not explain. And then a sunnier mood succeeded her tremblings and tears, till old Mr Vine came into the house below, and Jim went down to declare that all was well, and sent off his partner to break the news to Margery's father, who as yet remained unenlightened.

The dairyman bore the intelligence of his daughter's untitled state as best he could, and punished her by not coming near her for several weeks, though at last he grumbled his forgiveness, and made up matters with Jim. The handsome Mrs Peach vanished to Plymouth, and found another sailor, not without a reasonable complaint against Jim and Margery both that she had been unfairly used.

As for the mysterious gentleman who had exercised such an influence over their lives, he kept his word, and was a stranger to Lower Wessex thenceforward. Baron or no Baron, Englishman or foreigner, he had shown a genuine interest in Jim, and real sorrow for a certain reckless phase of his acquaintance with Margery. That he had a more tender feeling toward the young girl than he wished her or anyone else to perceive there could be no doubt. That he was strongly tempted at times to adopt other than conventional courses with regard to her is also clear, particularly at that critical hour when she rolled along the high road with him in the carriage, after turning from the fancied pursuit of Jim. But at other times he schooled impassioned sentiments into fair conduct, which even erred on the side of harshness. In after years there was a report that another attempt on his life with a pistol, during one of those fits of moodiness to which he seemed constitutionally liable, had been effectual; but nobody in Silverthorn was in a position to ascertain the truth.

There he is still regarded as one who had something about him magical and unearthly. In his mystery let him remain; for a man, no less than a landscape, who awakens an interest under uncertain lights and touches of unfathomable shade, may cut but a poor figure in a garish noontide shine.

When she heard of his mournful death Margery sat in her nursing-chair, gravely thinking for nearly ten minutes, to the total neglect of her infant in the cradle. Jim, from the other side of the fireplace, said, 'You are sorry enough for him, Margery. I am sure of that.'

'Yes, yes,' she murmured, 'I am sorry.' After a moment she added: 'Now that he's dead I'll make a confession, Jim, that I have never made to a soul. If he had pressed me – which he did not – to go with him when I was in the carriage that night beside his yacht, I would have gone. And I was disappointed that he did not press me.'

'Suppose he were to suddenly appear now, and say in a voice of command, "Margery, come with me!"'

'I believe I should have no power to disobey,' she returned, with a mischievous look. 'He was like a magician to me. I think he was one. He could move me as a loadstone moves a speck of steel. . . . Yet no,' she added, hearing the infant cry, 'he would not move me now. It would be so unfair to baby.'

'Well,' said Jim, with no great concern (for *'la jalousie rétrospective,'* as George Sand calls it, had nearly died out of him), 'however he might move 'ee my love, he'll never come. He swore it to me: and he was a man of his word.'

Ancient Earthworks and What Two Enthusiastic Scientists Found There

As I mentioned earlier, Thomas Hardy was fascinated by ancient stone monuments and for many years belonged to the Dorset Natural History and Antiquarian Field Club. It was almost certainly as a result of digs that he went on with the Club that he was inspired to write the following story of the encounter of two men on a stormy night at the ancient fortress of 'Mai-Dun', in fact Maiden Castle, just two miles from Dorchester and considered perhaps the finest prehistoric earthworks in England. Curiously, the tale was first published in America, in the *Detroit Post* in March 1885, and then revised by Hardy for *The English Illustrated Magazine* of December 1893, from which this version is taken. To Hardy's annoyance, though, the title was shortened to 'Ancient Earthworks at Casterbridge.'

The dramatic setting of the story undoubtedly adds to its impact, as does the intriguing knowledge that the scientist tempted to an indiscretion by his discoveries was based on a Dorchester antiquarian whom Thomas Hardy actually knew! Commenting on the piece, Kristin Brady notes interestingly in her work, *The Short Stories of Thomas Hardy* (1982) that the tale is 'based on the same Gothic subject that often attracted Hawthorne: the scientist who in his eager quest for knowledge loses his moral sense. Hardy's particular handling of the theme reveals, however, more than any insight into such a personality type, his own suspicion of people with the credentials of education.' Another excitable critic has even seen the poor man as a kind of potential mad scientist in the Frankenstein mould!

Ancient Earthworks and What Two Enthusiastic Scientists Found There

At one's every step forward it rises higher against the south sky, with an obtrusive personality that compels the senses to regard it and consider. The eyes may bend in another direction, but never without the consciousness of its heavy, high-shouldered presence at its point of vantage. Across the intervening levels the gale races in a straight line from the fort, as if breathed out of it hitherward. With the shifting of the clouds the faces of the steeps vary in colour and in shade, broad lights appearing where mist and vagueness had prevailed, dissolving in their turn into melancholy gray, which spreads over and eclipses the luminous bluffs. In this so-called immutable spectacle all is change.

Out of the invisible marine region on the other side birds soar suddenly into the air, and hang over the summits of the heights with the careless indifference of long familiarity. Their forms are quite white against the tawny concave of cloud, and the curves they exhibit in their floating signify that they are seagulls which have journeyed inland from expected stress of weather. As the birds rise behind the fort, so do the clouds rise behind the birds, almost, as it seems, stroking with their bagging bosoms the uppermost flyers.

The profile of the whole stupendous ruin, as seen at a distance of a mile eastward, is cleanly cut as that of a marble inlay. It is varied with protuberances, which from hereabouts have the animal aspect of warts, wens, knuckles, and hips. It may, indeed, be likened to an enormous many-limbed organism of an antediluvian time – partaking of the cephalopod in shape – lying lifeless, and covered with a thin green cloth, which hides its substance, while revealing its general contour. This dull green mantle of herbage stretches down towards the levels, where the ploughs have essayed for centuries to creep up near and yet nearer to the base of the castle, but have always stopped short before reaching it. The furrows of these environing attempts show themselves distinctly, bending to the incline as they trench upon it; mounting in steeper curves, till the steepness absolutely baffles them, and their parallel threads show themselves like the striae of waves pausing on the curl. The remarkable place of which these are some of the features is 'Mai-Dun' – 'The Castle of the Great Hill,' said to be the Dunium of Ptolemy, the capital of the Durotriges, which eventually came into Roman occupation, and was finally deserted on their withdrawal from the island.

The evening is followed by a night on which an invisible moon bestows a subdued, yet pervasive light – without radiance, as without blackness. From the spot whereon I am ensconced in a cottage, a mile away, the fort has now ceased to be visible; yet, as by day, to anybody whose thoughts have been engaged with it and its barbarous grandeurs of past time the form asserts its existence behind the night gauzes as persistently as if it had a voice. Moreover the south-west wind continues to feed the intervening arable flats with vapours brought directly from its sides.

The midnight hour for which there has been occasion to wait at length arrives, and I journey towards the stronghold in obedience to a request urged earlier in the day. It concerns an appointment, which I rather regret my decision to keep now that night is come. The route thither is hedgeless and treeless – I need not add deserted. The moonlight is sufficient to disclose the pale riband-like surface of the way as it trails along between the expanses of darker fallow. Though the road passes near the fortress it does not conduct directly to its fronts. As the place is without an inhabitant, so it is without a trackway. So presently leaving the macadamized road to pursue its course elsewhither, I step off upon the fallow, and plod stumblingly across it. The castle looms out of the shade by degrees, like a thing waking up and asking what I want there. It is now so enlarged that its whole shape cannot be taken in at one view. The ploughed ground ends as the rise sharpens, the sloping basement of grass begins, and I climb upward to invade Mai-Dun.

Impressive by day as this largest Ancient-British work in the kingdom undoubtedly is, its impressiveness is much increased now. After standing still and spending a few minutes in adding its age to its size, and its size to its solitude, it becomes appallingly mournful in its growing closeness. A squally wind blows in the face with an impact which proclaims that the vapours of the air sail low tonight. The slope that I so laboriously clamber up the wind skips sportively down. Its track can be discerned even in this light by the undulations of the withered grass-bents – the only produce of this upland summit except moss. Four minutes of ascent, and a vantage-ground of some sort is gained. It is only the crest of the outer rampart. Immediately within this a chasm gapes; its bottom is imperceptible, but its sides slope not too steeply to admit of a sliding descent if cautiously performed. The shady bottom, dark and chilly, is thus gained, and reveals itself as a kind of winding lane, wide enough for a waggon to pass along, floored with rank herbage, and trending away, right and left, into obscurity, between the concentric walls of earth. The towering closeness of these on each hand, their impenetrability, and their ponderousness, are felt as a physical pressure. The way is now up the second of them, which stands steeper and higher than the first. To turn aside, as did Christian's companion, from such a Hill Difficulty, is the more natural tendency; but the way to the interior is upward. There is, no doubt, an entrance of some sort to the fortress; but that must be far off on the other side. It might possibly have been the wiser course to seek for easier ingress there.

However, being here, I ascend the second acclivity. The grass stems – the grey beard of the hill – sway in a mass close to my stooping face. The dead heads of these various grasses – fescues, fox-tails, and ryes – bob and twitch as if pulled by a string underground. From a few thistles a whistling proceeds; and even the moss speaks, in its humble way, under the stress of the blast.

That the summit of the second line of defence has been gained is suddenly made known by a contrasting wind from a new quarter, rushing over with the curve of a cascade. These novel gusts raise a sound from the whole camp or castle, playing upon it bodily as upon a harp. It is with some difficulty that a foothold can be preserved under their sweep. Looking aloft for a moment I perceive that the sky is much more densely overcast than it has been hitherto, and in a few instants a dead lull in the gale ensues with almost preternatural abruptness. I take advantage of this to sidle down the second counterscarp, but by the time the ditch is reached the lull reveals itself to be but the precursor of a storm. It begins with a heave of the whole atmosphere, like the sigh of a weary strong man on turning to re-commence unusual exertion, just as I stand here, in the second fosse. That which now radiates from the sky upon the scene is not so much light as vaporous phosphorescence.

The wind, quickening, abandons the natural direction it has pursued on the open upland, and takes the bearing of the gorge's length, rushing along it helter-skelter, and carrying thick rain upon its back. The rain is followed by hailstones which pour through the defile in battalions – rolling, hopping, ricochetting, snapping, clattering down the shelving banks in an undefinable haze of confusion. The solid sides of the fosse seem to quiver under the drenching onset, though it is practically no more to them than the blows of Thor upon the giant of Jotun-land. It is impossible to proceed further till the storm somewhat abates, and I draw up behind a spur of the inner scarp, where possibly a barricade stood two thousand years ago; and thus await events.

The roar of the storm can be heard travelling the complete circuit of the castle – a measured mile – coming round at intervals like a circumambulating column of infantry. Doubtless such a column has passed this way in its time, but the only columns which enter in these latter days are the columns of sheep and oxen that are sometimes seen here now; while the only semblance of heroic voices heard are the utterances of the many winds which make their passage through these ravines.

The expected lightning radiates round, and a rumbling as from its subterranean vaults – if there are any – fills the castle. The lightning repeats itself, and, coming after the aforesaid thoughts of martial men, it bears a wonderful resemblance to swords moving in combat. It has the very brassy hue of the ancient weapons that here were used. The so sudden entry upon the scene of this metallic flame is as the entry of a presiding exhibitor who unrolls the maps, uncurtains the pictures, unlocks the cabinets, and effects a transformation by merely exposing the materials of his science, unintelligibly cloaked till then. The abrupt configuration of the bluffs and mounds is now for the first time clearly revealed – mounds whereon, doubtless, spears and shields have frequently lain while their owners loosened their sandals and yawned and stretched their arms in the sun. For the first time, too, a glimpse is obtainable of the true entrance used by its occupants of old, some way ahead.

There, where all passage has seemed to be inviolably barred by an almost vertical facade, the ramparts are found to overlap each other like loosely clasped fingers, between which a zigzag path may be followed – a cunning construction that puzzles the uninformed eye. But its cunning, even where not obscured by dilapidation, is now wasted on the solitary forms of a few wild badgers, rabbits, and hares. Men must have often gone out by those gates in the morning to battle with the Roman legions under Vespasian; some to return no more, others to come back at evening, bringing with them the noise of their heroic deeds. But not a page, not a stone, has preserved their fame.

Acoustic perceptions multiply tonight. We can almost hear the stream of years that have borne those deeds away from us. Strange articulations seem to float on the air from that point, the gateway, where the animation in past times must frequently have concentrated itself at hours of coming and going, and general excitement. There arises an ineradicable fancy that they are human voices; if so, they must be the lingering air-borne vibrations of conversations uttered at least fifteen hundred years ago. The attention is attracted from mere nebulous imaginings about yonder spot by a real moving of something close at hand.

I recognise by the now moderate flashes of lightning, which are sheet-like and nearly continuous, the gradual elevation of a small mound of earth. At first no larger than a man's fist it reaches the dimensions of a hat, then sinks a little and is still. It is but the heaving of a mole who chooses such weather as this to work in from some instinct that there will be nobody abroad to molest him. As the fine earth lifts and lifts and falls loosely aside fragments of burnt clay roll out of it – clay that once formed part of cups or other vessels used by the inhabitants of the fortress.

The violence of the storm has been counterbalanced by its transitoriness. From being immersed in well-nigh solid media of cloud and hail shot with lightning, I find myself uncovered of the humid investiture and left bare to the mild gaze of the moon, which sparkles now on every wet grass-blade and frond of moss.

But I am not yet inside the fort, and the delayed ascent of the third and last escarpment is now made. It is steeper than either. The first was a surface to walk up, the second to stagger up, the third can only be ascended on the hands and toes. On the summit obtrudes the first evidence which has been met with in these precincts that the time is really the nineteenth century; it is in the form of a white notice-board on a post, and the wording can just be discerned by the rays of the setting moon:

CAUTION. – Any Person found removing Relics, Skeletons, Stones, Pottery, Tiles, or other Material from this Earthwork, or cutting up the Ground, will be Prosecuted as the Law directs.

Here one observes a difference underfoot from what has gone before: scraps of Roman tile and stone chippings protrude through the grass in meagre quantity, but sufficient to tell clearly that masonry stood on the spot. Before the eye stretches under the moonlight the interior of the fort. So open and so large is it as to be practically an upland plateau, and yet its area lies wholly within the walls of what may be designated as one building. It is a long-violated retreat; all its corner-stones, plinths, and architraves were carried away to build neighbouring villages even before mediaeval or modern history began. Many a squared block which once helped to form a bastion here rests now in broken and diminished shape as part of the chimney-corner of some shepherd's cottage within the distant horizon, and the corner-stones of this heathen altar may form the base-course of some ancient village church.

Yet the very bareness of these inner courts and wards, their condition of mere pasturage, protects what remains of them as no defences could do. Nothing is left visible that the hands can seize on or the weather overturn, and a permanence of general outline at least results, which no other condition could ensure.

The position of the castle on this isolated hill bespeaks deliberate and strategic choice exercised by some remote mind capable of prospective reasoning to a far extent. The natural configuration of the surrounding country and its bearing upon such a stronghold were obviously long considered and viewed mentally before its extensive design was carried into execution. Who was the man that said, 'Let it be built here!' – not on that hill yonder, or on that ridge behind, but on this best spot of all? Whether he were some great one of the Belgae, or of the Durotriges, or the travelling engineer of Britain's united tribes, must for ever remain time's secret; his form cannot be realized, nor his countenance, nor the tongue that he spoke, when he set down his foot with a thud and said, 'Let it be here!'

Within the innermost enclosure, though it is so wide that at a superficial glance the beholder has only a sense of standing on a breezy down, the solitude is rendered yet more solitary by the knowledge that between the benighted sojourner herein and all kindred humanity are those three concentric walls of earth which no being would think of scaling on such a night as this, even were he to hear the most pathetic cries issuing hence that could be uttered by a spectre-chased soul. I reach a central mound or platform – the crown and axis of the whole structure. The view from here by day must be of almost limitless extent. On this raised floor, daïs, or rostrum, harps have probably twanged more or less tuneful notes in celebration of daring, strength, or cruelty; of worship, superstition, love, birth, and death; of simple loving-kindness perhaps never. Many a time must the king or leader have directed his keen eyes hence across the open lands towards the ancient road, the Icening Way, still visible in the distance, on the watch for armed companies approaching either to succour or to attack.

I am startled by a voice pronouncing my name. Past and present have become so confusedly mingled under the associations of the spot that for a time it has escaped my memory that this mound was the place agreed on for the aforesaid appointment. I turn and behold my friend. He stands with a dark lantern in his hand and a spade and light pickaxe over his shoulder. He expresses both delight and surprise that I have come. I tell him I had set out before the bad weather began.

He, to whom neither weather, darkness, nor difficulty seems to have any relation or significance, so entirely is his soul wrapped up in his own deep intentions, asks me to take the lantern and accompany him. I take it and walk by his side. He is a man about sixty, small in figure, with gray old-fashioned whiskers cut to the shape of a pair of crumb-brushes. He is entirely in black broadcloth – or rather, at present, black and brown, for he is bespattered with mud from his heels to the crown of his low hat. He has no consciousness of this – no sense of anything but his purpose, his ardour for which causes his eyes to shine like those of a lynx, and gives his motions all the elasticity of an athlete's.

'Nobody to interrupt us at this time of night!' he chuckles with fierce enjoyment.

We retreat a little way and find a sort of angle, an elevation in the sod, a suggested squareness amid the mass of irregularities around. Here, he tells me, if anywhere, the king's house stood. Three months of measurement and calculation have confirmed him in this conclusion.

He requests me now to open the lantern, which I do, and the light streams out upon the wet sod. At last divining his proceedings I say that I had no idea, in keeping the tryst, that he was going to do more at such an unusual time than meet me for a meditative ramble through the stronghold. I ask him why, having a practicable object, he should have minded interruptions and not have chosen the day? He informs me, quietly pointing to his spade, that it was because his purpose is to dig, then signifying with a grim nod the gaunt notice-post against the sky beyond. I inquire why, as a professed and well-known antiquary with capital letters at the tail of his name, he did not obtain the necessary authority, considering the stringent penalties for this sort of thing; and he chuckles fiercely again with suppressed delight, and says, 'Because they wouldn't have given it!'

He at once begins cutting up the sod, and, as he takes the pickaxe to follow on with, assures me that, penalty or no penalty, honest men or marauders, he is sure of one thing, that we shall not be disturbed at our work till after dawn.

I remember to have heard of men who, in their enthusiasm for some special science, art, or hobby, have quite lost the moral sense which would restrain them from indulging it illegitimately; and I conjecture that here, at last, is an instance of such an one. He probably guesses the way my thoughts travel, for he stands up and solemnly asserts that he has a distinctly justifiable intention in this matter; namely, to uncover, to search, to verify a theory or displace it, and to cover up again. He means to take away nothing – not a grain of sand. In this he says he sees no such monstrous sin. I inquire if this is really a promise to me? He repeats that it is a promise, and resumes digging. My contribution to the labour is that of directing the light constantly upon the hole. When he has reached something more than a foot deep he digs more cautiously, saying that, be it much or little there, it will not lie far below the surface; such things never are deep. A few minutes later the point of the pickaxe clicks upon a stony substance. He draws the implement out as feelingly as if it had entered a man's body. Taking up the spade he shovels with care, and a surface, level as an altar, is presently disclosed. His eyes flash anew; he pulls handfuls of grass and mops the surface clean, finally rubbing it with his handkerchief. Grasping the lantern from my hand he holds it close to the ground, when the rays reveal a complete mosaic – a pavement of minute tesserae of many colours, of intricate pattern, a work of much art, of much time, and of much industry. He exclaims in a shout that he knew it always – that it is not a Celtic stronghold exclusively, if at all, but a Roman; the former people having probably contributed little more than the original framework which the latter took and adapted it till it became the present imposing structure.

I ask, What if it is Roman?

A great deal, according to him. That it proves all the world to be wrong in this great argument, and himself alone to be right! Can I wait while he digs further?

I agree – reluctantly; but he does not notice my reluctance. At an adjoining spot he begins flourishing the tools anew with the skill of a navvy, this venerable scholar with letters after his name. Sometimes he falls on his knees, burrowing with his hands in the manner of a hare, and where his old-fashioned broadcloth touches the sides of the hole it gets plastered with the damp earth. He continually murmurs to himself how important, how very important, this discovery is! He draws out an object; we wash it in the same primitive way by rubbing it with the wet grass, and it proves to be a semi-transparent bottle of iridescent beauty, the sight of which draws groans of luxurious sensibility from the digger. Further and further search brings out utensils, weapons. It is strange indeed that by merely peeling off a wrapper of modern accumulations we have lowered ourselves into an ancient world. Finally a skeleton is uncovered, tall and perfect. He lays it out on the grass, bone to its bone.

My friend says the man must have fallen fighting here, as this is no place of burial. He turns again to the trench, scrapes, feels, till from a corner he draws out a heavy lump – a small image four or five inches high. We clean it as before. It is a statuette, apparently of gold, or, more probably, of bronze-gilt – a figure of Mercury, obviously, its head being surmounted with the petasus or winged hat, the usual accessory of that deity. Further inspection reveals the workmanship to be of the highest finish and detail, and,preserved by the limy earth, to be as fresh in every line as on the day it left the hands of its artificer.

We seem to be standing in the Roman Forum and not on a hill in Wessex. Intent upon this truly valuable relic of the old empire of which even this remote spot was a component part, we do not notice what is going on in the present world till reminded of it by the sudden renewal of the storm. Looking up I perceive that the vast extinguisher of cloud has again settled down upon the fortress-town, as if resting upon the edge of the inner rampart, and shutting out the moon. I turn my back to the tempest, still directing the light across the hole. My companion digs on unconcernedly; he is living two thousand years ago, and despises things of the moments as dreams. But at last he is fairly beaten, and standing up beside me looks round on what he has done. The rays of the lantern pass over the trench to the tall skeleton stretched upon the grass on the other side. The beating rain has washed the bones clean and white, and the forehead, cheek-bones, and two-and-thirty sound teeth of the skull glisten in the candle-shine as they lie.

This storm, like the first, is of the nature of a squall, and it ends as abruptly as the other. We dig no further. My friend says that it is enough – he has proved his point. He replaces the bones in the trench and covers them. The next act of his plan is more than difficult, but is carried out. The treasures are inhumed again in their respective holes: they are not ours. Each deposition seems to cost him a twinge; and at one moment I fancied I saw him slip his hand into his coat pocket.

'We must re-bury them all,' say I.

'Oh yes,' he answers with integrity. 'I was wiping my hand.'

The beauties of the tesselated floor of the governor's house are once again consigned to darkness; the trench is filled up; the sod laid smoothly down; he wipes the perspiration from his forehead with the same handkerchief he had used to mop the skeleton clean; and we make for the eastern gate of the fortress.

Dawn bursts upon us suddenly as we reach the opening. It comes by the lifting and thinning of the clouds that way till we are bathed in a pink light. The direction of his homeward journey is not the same as mine, and we part under the outer slope.

Walking along quickly to restore warmth I muse upon my eccentric friend, and cannot help asking myself this question: Did he really replace the gilded image of the god Mercurius with the rest of the treasures? He seemed to do so; and yet I could not testify to the fact. Probably, however, he was as good as his word.

FIVE YEARS AFTER. – I open the foregoing pages of my diary to add that among the effects of my friend, lately deceased, has been found, carefully preserved, a gilt statuette representing Mercury, labelled 'Debased Roman.' No record is attached to explain how it came into his possession. The figure is bequeathed to the Casterbridge Museum.

MAUMBURY RING AND THE MOCK WIFE

Thomas Hardy's interest in archaelogy was widely known by the turn of the century, and it was this that promoted *The Times* newspaper to get in touch with him in 1908 concerning excavations which had been taking place at Maumbury Ring in Dorchester, and request a report on the findings. Hardy duly obliged – but his account was no mere report of a simple dig. To this, he added information about a 'sinister event' also associated with the ring in which a young woman accused of murder had been burned to death at the stake in the year 1705. Hardy's account was published in *The Times* of October 9, and prompted a flurry of letters from readers, in particular about the death of the teenage wife.

Despite his sensitive nature, Hardy had something of a fascination with murder – a fact which may well have originated from his childhood when he had actually witnessed two hangings. One was that of a woman, whose execution he saw from beside the gallows, and the second, two or three years later, when he peered through a telescope at the figure of a man being hung in front of Dorchester gaol. The story of the young wife who was burned at the stake at Maumbury in 1705 for allegedly poisoning her husband obviously remained fixed in Hardy's mind and later inspired him to write a poem, 'The Mock Wife' which I have included at the end of his essay for any reader who may not be familiar with the 'ghastly story', as Hardy so graphically labelled it.

MAUMBURY RING

The present month sees the last shovelful filled in, the last sod replaced, of the excavations in the well-known amphitheatre at Dorchester, which have been undertaken at the instance of the Dorset Field and Antiquarian Club and others, for the purpose of ascertaining the history and date of the ruins. The experts have scraped their spades and gone home to meditate on the results of their exploration, pending the resumption of the work next spring. Mr St George Gray, of Taunton, has superintended the labour, assisted by Mr Charles Prideaux, an enthusiastic antiquary of the town, who, with disinterested devotion to discovery, has preferred to spend his annual holiday from his professional duties at the bottom of chalk trenches groping for *fibulae* or arrow-heads in a drizzling rain, to idling it away on any other spot in Europe.

As usual, revelations have been made of an unexpected kind. There was a moment when the blood of us onlookers ran cold, and we shivered a shiver that was not occasioned by our wet feet and dripping clothes. For centuries the town, the county, and England generally, novelists, poets, historians, guide-book writers, and what not, had been freely indulging their imaginations in picturing scenes that, they assumed, must have been enacted within those oval slopes; the feats, the contests, animal exhibitions, even gladiatorial combats, before throngs of people

> Who loved the games men played with death,
> Where death must win

– briefly, the Colosseum programme on a smaller scale, But up were thrown from one corner prehistoric implements, chipped flints, horns, and other remains, and a voice announced that the earthworks were of the palaeolithic or neolithic age, and not Roman at all!

This, however, was but a temporary and, it is believed, unnecessary alarm. At other points in the structure, as has been already stated in *The Times*, the level floor of an arena, trodden smooth, and coated with traces of gravel, was discovered with Roman relics and coins on its surface; and at the entrance and in front of the podium, a row of post-holes, apparently for barriers, as square as when they were dug, together with other significant marks, which made it fairly probable that, whatever the place had been before Julius Caesar's landing, it had been used as an amphitheatre at some time during the Roman occupation. The obvious explanation, to those who are not specialists, seems to be that here, as elsewhere, the colonists, to save labour, shaped and adapted to their own use some earthworks already on the spot. This was antecedently likely from the fact that the amphitheatre stands on an elevated site – or, in the enigmatic words of Hutchins, is 'artfully set on the top of a plain,' – and that every similar spot in the neighbourhood has a tumulus or tumuli upon it; or had till some were carted away within living memory.

But this is a matter on which the professional investigators will have their conclusive say when funds are forthcoming to enable them to dig further. For some reason they have hitherto left undisturbed the ground about the southern end of the arena, underneath which the *cavea* or vault for animals is traditionally said to be situated, though it is doubtful if any such vault, supposing it ever to have existed, would have been suffered to remain there, stones being valuable in a chalk district. And if it had been built of chalk blocks the frost and rains of centuries would have pulverized them by this time.

While the antiquaries are musing on the puzzling problems that arise from the confusion of dates in the remains, the mere observer who possesses a smattering of local history, and remembers local traditions that have been recounted by people now dead and gone, may walk round the familiar arena, and consider. And he is not, like the archaists, compelled to restrict his thoughts to the early centuries of our era. The sun has gone down behind the avenue on the Roman Via and modern road that adjoins, and the October moon is rising on the south-east behind the parapet, the two terminations of which by the north entrance jut against the sky like knuckles. The place is now in its normal state of repose and silence, save for the occasional bray of a motorist passing along outside in sublime ignorance of amphitheatrical lore, or the clang of shunting at the nearest railway station. The breeze is not strong enough to stir even the grass-bents with which the slopes are covered, and over which the loiterer's footsteps are quite noiseless.

Like all such taciturn presences, Maumbury is less taciturn by night than by day, which simply means that the episodes and incidents associated therewith come back more readily to the mind in nocturnal hours. First, it recalls to us that, if probably Roman, it is a good deal more. Its history under the rule of the Romans would not extend to a longer period than 200 or 300 years, while it has had a history of 1,600 years since they abandoned this island, through which ages it may have been regarded as a handy place for early English council-gatherings, may have been the scene of many an exciting episode in the life of the Western kingdom. But for century after century it keeps itself closely curtained, except at some moments to be mentioned.

The civil wars of Charles I unscreen it a little, and we vaguely learn that it was used by the artillery when the struggle was in this district, and that certain irregularities in its summit were caused then. The next incident that flashes a light over the contours is Sir Christopher Wren's visit a quarter of a century later. Nobody knows what the inhabitants thought to be the origin of its elliptic banks – differing from others in the vicinity by having no trench around them – until the day came when, according to legend, Wren passed up the adjoining highway on his journey to Portland to select stone for St Paul's Cathedral, and was struck with the sight of the mounds. Possibly he asked some rustic at plough there for information. That all tradition of their use as an amphitheatre had been lost is to be inferred from their popular name, and one can quite understand how readily, as he entered and stood on the summit, a man whose studies had lain so largely in the direction of Roman architecture should have ascribed a Roman origin to the erection. That the offhand guess of a passing architect should have turned out to be true – and it does not at present seem possible to prove the whole construction to be prehistoric – is a remarkable tribute to his insight.

The curtain drops for another 40 years, and then Maumbury was the scene of as sinister an event as any associated with it, because it was a definite event. It is one which darkens its concave to this day. This was the death suffered there on March 21, 1705-06, of a girl who had not yet reached her nineteenth year. Here, at any rate, we touch real flesh and blood, and no longer uncertain visions of possible Romans at their games or barbarians at their sacrifices. The story is a ghastly one, but nevertheless very distinctly a chapter of Maumbury's experiences. This girl was the wife of a grocer in the town, a handsome young woman 'of good natural parts,' and educated 'to a proficiency suitable enough to one of her sex, to which likewise was added dancing.' She was tried and condemned for poisoning her husband, a Mr Thomas Channing, to whom she had been married against her wish by the compulsion of her parents. The present writer has examined more than once a report of her trial, and can find no distinct evidence that the thoughtless, pleasure-loving creature committed the crime, while it contains much to suggest that she did not. Nor is any motive discoverable for such an act. She was allowed to have her former lover or lovers about her by her indulgent and weak-minded husband, who permitted her to go her own ways, give parties, and supplied her with plenty of money. However, at the assizes at the end of July, she was found guilty, after a trial in which the testimony chiefly went to show her careless character before and after marriage. During the three sultry days of its continuance, she, who was soon to become a mother, stood at the bar – then, as may be known, an actual bar of iron – 'by reason of which (runs the account) and her much talking, being quite spent, she moved the Court for the liberty of a glass of water.' She conducted her own defence with the greatest ability, and was complimented thereupon by Judge Price, who tried her, but did not extend his compliment to a merciful summing-up. Maybe that he, like Pontius Pilate, was influenced by the desire of the towns-folk to wreak vengeance on somebody, right or wrong, When sentence was about to be passed, she pleaded her condition; and execution was postponed. Whilst awaiting the birth of her child in the old damp gaol by the river at the bottom of the town, near the White Hart inn, which stands there still, she was placed in the common room for women prisoners and no bed provided for her, no special payment having been made to her gaoler, Mr Knapton, for a separate cell. Someone obtained for her the old tilt of a wagon to screen her from surrounding eyes, and under this she was delivered of a son, in December. After her lying-in, she was attacked with an intermittent fever of a violent and lasting kind, which preyed upon her until she was nearly wasted away. In this state, at the next assizes, on the 8th of March following, the unhappy woman, who now said that she longed for death, but still persisted in her innocence, was again brought to the bar, and her execution fixed for the 21st.

On that day two men were hanged before her turn came, and then, 'the under-sheriff having taken some refreshment,' he proceeded to his biggest and last job with this girl not yet 19, now reduced to a skeleton by the long fever, and already more dead than alive. She was conveyed from the gaol in a cart 'by her father's and husband's house,' so that the course of the procession must have been up High-East-street as far as the Bow, thence down South-street and up the straight old Roman road to the Ring beside it. 'When fixed to the stake she justified her innocence to the very last, and left the world with courage seldom found in her sex. She being first strangled, the fire was kindled about five in the afternoon, and in the sight of many thousands she was consumed to ashes.' There is nothing to show that she was dead before the burning began, and from the use of the word 'strangled' and not 'hanged,' it would seem that she was merely rendered insensible before the fire was lit. An ancestor of the present writer, who witnessed the scene, has handed down the information that 'her heart leapt out' during the burning, and other curious details that cannot be printed here. Was man ever 'slaughtered by his fellow man' during the Roman or barbarian use of this place of games or of sacrifice in circumstances of greater atrocity?

A melodramatic, though less gruesome, exhibition within the arena was that which occurred at the time of the 'No Popery' riots, and was witnessed by this writer when a small child. Highly realistic effigies of the Pope and Cardinal Wiseman were borne in procession From Fordington Hill round the town, followed by a long train of mock priests, monks, and nuns, and preceded by a young man discharging Roman candles, till the same wicked old place was reached, in the centre of which there stood a huge rick of furze, with a gallows above. The figures were slung up, and the fire blazed till they were blown to pieces by fireworks contained within them.

Like its more famous prototype, the Collosseum, this spot of sombre records has also been the scene of Christian worship, but only on one occasion, so far as the writer of these columns is aware, that being the Thanksgiving service for Peace a few years ago. The surplices of the clergy and choristers, as seen against the green grass, the shining brass musical instruments, the enormous chorus of singing voices, formed not the least impressive of the congregated masses that Maumbury Ring has drawn into its midst during its existence of a probable eighteen hundred years in its present shape, and of some possible thousands of years in an earlier form.

The Mock Wife

It's a dark drama, this; and yet I know the house, and date;
That is to say, the where and when John Channing met his fate.
The house was one in High Street, seen of burghers still alive,
The year was some two centuries bygone; seventeen-hundred and five.

And dying was Channing the grocer. All the clocks had struck eleven,
And the watchers saw that ere the dawn his soul would be in Heaven;
When he said on a sudden: 'I should *like* to kiss her before I go, –
For one last time!' They looked at each other and murmured, 'Even so.'

She'd just been haled to prison, his wife; yea, charged with
shaping his death:
By poison, 'twas told; and now he was nearing the moment of his
last breath:
He, witless that his young housemate was suspect of such a crime,
Lay thinking that his pangs were but a malady of the time.

Outside the room they pondered gloomily, wondering what to do,
As still he craved her kiss – the dying man who nothing knew:
'Guilty she may not be,' they said; 'so why should we torture him
In these his last few minutes of life? Yet how indulge his whim?'

And as he begged there piteously for what could not be done,
And the murder-charge had flown about the town to every one,
The friends around him in their trouble thought of a hasty plan,
And straightway set about it. Let denounce them all who can.

'O will you do a kindly deed – it may be a soul to save;
At least, great misery to a man with one foot in the grave?'
Thus they to the buxom woman not unlike his prisoned wife;
'The difference he's past seeing; it will soothe his sinking life.'

Well, the friendly neighbour did it; and he kissed her; held her fast;
Kissed her again and yet again. 'I – knew she'd – come at last! –
Where have you been? – Ah, kept away! – I'm sorry – overtried –
God bless you!' And he loosed her, fell back tiredly, and died.

His wife stood six months after on the scaffold before the crowd,
Ten thousand of them gathered there; fixed, silent, and hard-
browed.
To see her strangled and burnt to dust, as was the verdict then
On women truly judged, or false, of doing to death their men.

Some of them said as they watched her burn: 'I am glad he never
knew,
Since a few hold her as innocent – think such she could not do!
Glad, too, that (as they tell) he thought she kissed him ere he died.'
And they seemed to make no question that the cheat was justified.

A Mere Interlude

To return to the year 1885, Hardy followed the story of the two scientists at 'Mai-Dun' with a tale of horror rather deceptively entitled 'A Mere Incident' which was first published in the *Bolton Weekly Journal* in October of that year and later collected in his final prose volume, *A Changed Man* (1913). Jack Sullivan in *The Encyclopedia of Horror and the Supernatural* (1986), cites this story as an example of one of several tales by Hardy that are overshadowed by the macabre – 'The cold hand of dread grips the heroine of "A Mere Interlude" when she realizes she has been lying in a bed between the drowned corpse of one husband and the living body of another,' he writes.

The story has a number of interesting twists as Baptista Trewthen, on her way to marry one man, on a whim marries a former sweetheart she meets on her journey. But just as dramatically as she met him, so Baptista's new husband is taken from her, and she finds herself haunted by the spectre of her past as she attempts to continue her original plans as if nothing had happened. 'A Mere Incident' is noteworthy as the only story by Hardy to be set on the Isles of Lyonesse, better known as the Scilly Isles. Critic Kristin Brady has also advanced the interesting suggestion that Hardy may have taken the idea for his plot from the *Decameron* story of a woman's first husband arriving to confront her just as she is marrying for a second time.

A Mere Interlude

I

The traveller in school-books, who vouched in dryest tones for the fidelity to fact of the following narrative, used to add a ring of truth to it by opening with a nicety of criticism on the heroine's personality. People were wrong, he declared, when they surmized that Baptista Trewthen was a young woman with scarcely emotions or character. There was nothing in her to love, and nothing to hate – so ran the general opinion. That she showed few positive qualities was true. The colours and tones which changing events paint on the faces of active womankind were looked for in vain upon hers. But still waters run deep; and no crisis had come in the years of her early maidenhood to demonstrate what lay hidden within her, like metal in a mine.

She was the daughter of a small farmer in St Maria's, one of the Isles of Lyonesse beyond Off-Wessex, who had spent a large sum, as there understood, on her education, by sending her to the mainland for two years. At nineteen she was entered at the Training College for Teachers, and at twenty-one nominated to a school in the country, near Tor-upon-Sea, whither she proceeded after the Christmas examination and holidays.

The months passed by from winter to spring and summer, and Baptista applied herself to her new duties as best she could, till an uneventful year had elapsed. Then an air of abstraction pervaded her bearing as she walked to and fro, twice a day, and she showed the traits of a person who had something on her mind. A widow, by name Mrs Wace, in whose house Baptista Trewthen had been provided with a sitting-room and bedroom till the schoolhouse should be built, noticed this change in her youthfful tenant's manner, and at last ventured to press her with a few questions.

'It has nothing to do with the place, nor with you', said Miss Trewthen.

'Then it is the salary?'

'No, nor the salary.'

'Then it is something you have heard from home, my dear.'

Baptista was silent for a few moments. 'It is Mr Heddegan,' she murmured. 'Him they used to call David Heddegan before he got his money.'

'And who is the Mr Heddegan they used to call David?'

'An old bachelor at Giant's Town, St Maria's, with no relations whatever, who lives about a stone's throw from father's. When I was a child he used to take me on his knee and say he'd marry me some day. Now I am a woman the jest has turned earnest, and he is anxious to do it. And father and mother say I can't do better than have him.'

'He's well off?'

'Yes – he's the richest man we know – as a friend and neighbour.'

'How much older did you say he was than yourself?'

'I didn't say. Twenty years at least.'

'And an unpleasant man in the bargain perhaps?'

'No – he's not unpleasant.'

'Well, child, all I can say is that I'd resist any such engagement if it's not palatable to 'ee. You are comfortable here, in my little house, I hope. All the parish like 'ee: and I've never been so cheerful, since my poor husband left me to wear his wings, as I've been with 'ee as my lodger.'

The schoolmistress assured her landlady that she could return the sentiment. 'But here comes my perplexity,' she said. 'I don't like keeping school. Ah, you are surprised – you didn't suspect it. That's because I've concealed my feeling. Well, I simply hate school. I don't care for children – they are unpleasant, troublesome little things, whom nothing would delight so much as to hear that you had fallen down dead. Yet I would even put up with them if it was not for the inspector. For three months before his visit I didn't sleep soundly. And the Committee of Council are always changing the Code, so that you don't know what to teach, and what to leave untaught. I think father and mother are right. They say I shall never excel as a schoolmistress if I dislike the work so, and that therefore I ought to get settled by marrying Mr Heddegan. Between us two, I like him better than school; but I don't like him quite so much as to wish to marry him.'

These conversations, once begun, were continued from day to day; till at length the young girl's elderly friend and landlady threw in her opinion on the side of Miss Trewthen's parents. All things considered, she declared, the uncertainty of the school, the labour, Baptista's natural dislike for teaching, it would be as well to take what fate offered, and make the best of matters by wedding her father's old neighbour and prosperous friend.

The Easter holidays came round, and Baptista went to spend them as usual in her native isle, going by train into Off-Wessex and crossing by packet from Pen-zephyr. When she returned in the middle of April her face wore a more settled aspect.

'Well?' said the expectant Mrs Wace.

'I have agreed to have him as my husband,' said Baptista, in an off-hand way. 'Heaven knows if it will be for the best or not. But I have agreed to do it, and so the matter is settled.'

Mrs Wace commended her; but Baptista did not care to dwell on the subject; so that allusion to it was very infrequent between them. Nevertheless, among other things, she repeated to the widow from time to time in monosyllabic remarks that the wedding was really impending; that it was arranged for the summer, and that she had given notice of leaving the school at the August holidays. Later on she announced more specifically that her marriage was to take place immediately after her return home at the beginning of the month aforesaid.

She now corresponded regularly with Mr Heddegan. Her letters from him were seen, at least on the outside, and in part within, by Mrs Wace. Had she read more of their interiors than the occasional sentences shown her by Baptista she would have perceived that the scratchy, rusty handwriting of Miss Trewthen's betrothed conveyed little more matter than details of their future housekeeping, and his preparations for the same, with innumerable 'my dears' sprinkled in disconnectedly, to show the depth of his affection without the inconveniences of syntax.

II

It was the end of July – dry, too dry, even for the season, the delicate green herbs and vegetables that grew in this favoured end of the kingdom tasting rather of the watering-pot than of the pure fresh moisture from the skies. Baptista's boxes were packed, and one Saturday morning she departed by a waggonette to the station, and thence by train to Pen-zephyr, from which port she was, as usual, to cross the water immediately to her home, and become Mr Heddegan's wife on the Wednesday of the week following.

She might have returned a week sooner. But though the wedding day had loomed so near, and the banns were out, she delayed her departure till this last moment, saying it was not necessary for her to be at home long beforehand. As Mr Heddegan was older than herself, she said, she was to be married in her ordinary summer bonnet and grey silk frock, and there were no preparations to make that had not been amply made by her parents and intended husband.

In due time, after a hot and tedious journey, she reached Pen-zephyr. She here obtained some refreshment, and then went towards the pier, where she learnt to her surprise that the little steamboat plying between the town and the islands had left at eleven o'clock; the usual hour of departure in the afternoon having been forestalled in consequence of the fogs which had for a few days prevailed towards evening, making twilight navigation dangerous.

This being Saturday, there was now no other boat till Tuesday, and it became obvious that here she would have to remain for the three days, unless her friends should think fit to rig out one of the island sailing-boats and come to fetch her – a not very likely contingency, the sea distance being nearly forty miles.

Baptista, however, had been detained in Pen-zephyr on more than one occasion before, either on account of bad weather or some such reason as the present, and she was therefore not in any personal alarm. But, as she was to be married on the following Wednesday, the delay was certainly inconvenient to a more than ordinary degree, since it would leave less than a day's interval between her arrival and the wedding ceremony.

Apart from this awkwardness she did not much mind the accident. It was indeed curious to see how little she minded. Perhaps it would not be too much to say that, although she was going to do the critical deed of her life quite willingly, she experienced an indefinable relief at the postponement of her meeting with Heddegan. But her manner after making discovery of the hindrance was quiet and subdued, even to passivity itself; as was instanced by her having, at the moment of receiving information that the steamer had sailed, replied 'Oh,' so coolly to the porter with her luggage, that he was almost disappointed at her lack of disappointment.

The question now was, should she return again to Mrs Wace, in the village of Lower Wessex, or wait in the town at which she had arrived. She would have preferred to go back, but the distance was too great; moreover, having left the place for good, and somewhat dramatically, to become a bride, a return, even for so short a space, would have been a trifle humiliating.

Leaving, then, her boxes at the station, her next anxiety was to secure a respectable, or rather genteel, lodging in the popular seaside resort confronting her. To this end she looked about the town, in which, though she had passed through it half-a-dozen times, she was practically a stranger.

Baptista found a room to suit her over a fruiterer's shop; where she made herself at home, and set herself in order after her journey. An early cup of tea having revived her spirits she walked out to reconnoitre.

Being a schoolmistress she avoided looking at the schools, and having a sort of trade connection with books, she avoided looking at the booksellers; but wearying of the other shops she inspected the churches; not that for her own part she cared much about ecclesiastical edifices; but tourists looked at them, and so would she – a proceeding for which no one would have credited her with any great originality, such, for instance, as that she subsequently showed herself to possess. The churches soon oppressed her. She tried the Museum, but came out because it seemed lonely and tedious.

Yet the town and the walks in this land of strawberries, these headquarters of early English flowers and fruit, were then, as always, attractive. From the more picturesque streets she went to the town gardens, and the Pier, and the Harbour, and looked at the men at work there, loading and unloading as in the time of the Phoenicians.

'Not Baptista? Yes, Baptista it is!'

The words were uttered behind her. Turning round she gave a start, and became confused, even agitated, for a moment. Then she said in her usual un-demonstrative manner, 'O – is it really you, Charles?'

Without speaking again at once, and with a half-smile, the new-comer glanced her over. There was much criticism, and some resentment – even temper – in his eye.

'I am going home,' continued she. 'But I have missed the boat,'

He scarcely seemed to take in the meaning of this explanation, in the intensity of his critical survey. 'Teaching still? What a fine schoolmistress you make, Baptista, I warrant!' he said with a slight flavour of sarcasm, which was not lost upon her.

'I know I am nothing to brag of,' she replied. 'That's why I have given up.'

'O – given up? You astonish me.'

'I hate the profession.'

'Perhaps that's because I am in it.'

'O no, it isn't. But I am going to enter on another life altogether. I am going to be married next week to Mr David Heddegan.'

The young man – fortified as he was by a natural cynical pride and passionateness – winced at this unexpected reply, notwithstanding.

'Who is Mr David Heddegan?' he asked, as indifferently as lay in his power.

She informed him the bearer of the name was a general merchant of Giant's Town, St Maria's Island – her father's nearest neighbour and oldest friend.

'Then we shan't see anything more of you on the mainland?' inquired the schoolmaster.

'O, I don't know about that,' said Miss Trewthen.

'Here endeth the career of the belle of the boarding school your father was foolish enough to send you to. A 'general merchant's' wife in the Lyonesse Isles. Will you sell pounds of soap and pennyworths of tin tacks, or whole bars of saponaceous matter, and great tenpenny nails?'

'He's not in such a small way as that!' she almost pleaded. 'He owns ships, though they are rather little ones!'

'O, well, it is much the same. Come, let us walk on; it is tedious to stand still. I thought you would be a failure in education,' he continued, when she obeyed him and strolled ahead. 'You never showed power that way. You remind me much of some of those women who think they are sure to be great actresses if they go on the stage, because they have a pretty face, and forget that what we required is acting. But you found your mistake, didn't you?'

'Don't taunt me, Charles.' It was noticeable that the young

schoolmaster's tone caused her no anger or retaliatory passion; far otherwise: there was a tear in her eye. 'How is it you are at Pen-zephyr?' she inquired.

'I don't taunt you. I speak the truth, purely in a friendly way, as I should to any one I wished well. Though for that matter I might have some excuse even for taunting you. Such a terrible hurry as you've been in. I hate a woman who is in such a hurry.'

'How do you mean that?'

'Why – to be somebody's wife or other – anything's wife rather than nobody's. You couldn't wait for me, O, no. Well, thank God, I'm cured of all that!'

'How merciless you are!' she said bitterly. 'Wait for you? What does that mean, Charley? You never showed – anything to wait for – anything special towards me.'

'O come, Baptista dear; come!'

'What I mean is, nothing definite,' she expostulated. 'I suppose you liked me a little; but it seemed to me to be only a pastime on your part, and that you never meant to make an honourable engagement of it.'

'There, that's just it! You girls expect a man to mean business at the first look. No man when he first becomes interested in a woman has any definite scheme of engagement to marry her in his mind, unless he is meaning a vulgar mercenary marriage. However, I *did* at last mean an honourable engagement, as you call it, come to that.'

'But you never said so, and an indefinite courtship soon injures a woman's position and credit, sooner than you think.'

'Baptista, I solemnly declare that in six months I should have asked you to marry me.'

She walked along in silence, looking on the ground, and appearing very uncomfortable. Presently he said, 'Would you have waited for me if you had known?' To this she whispered in a sorrowful whisper,' Yes!'

They went still farther in silence – passing along one of the beautiful walks on the outskirts of the town, yet not observant of scene or situation. Her shoulder and his were close together, and he clasped his fingers round the small of her arm – quite lightly, and without any attempt at impetus; yet the act seemed to say, 'Now I hold you, and my will must be yours.'

Recurring to a previous question of hers he said, 'I have merely run down here for a day or two from school near Trufal, before going off to the north for the rest of my holiday. I have seen my relations at Redrutin quite lately, so I am not going there this time. How little I thought of meeting you! How very different the circumstances would have been if, instead of parting again as we must in half-an-hour or so, possibly for ever, you had been now just going off with me, as my wife, on our honeymoon trip. Ha – ha – well – so humorous is life!'

She stopped suddenly. 'I must go back now – this is altogether too painful, Charley! It is not at all a kind mood you are in today.'

'I don't want to pain you – you know I do not,' he said more gently. 'Only it just exasperates me – this you are going to do. I wish you would not.'

'What?'

'Marry him. There, now I have showed you my true sentiments.'

'I must do it now,' said she.

'Why?' he asked, dropping the off-hand masterful tone he had hitherto spoken in, and becoming earnest; still holding her arm, however, as if she were his chattel to be taken up or put down at will. 'It is never too late to break off a marriage that's distasteful to you. Now I'll say one thing; and it is truth: I wish you would marry me instead of him, even now, at the last moment, though you have served me so badly.'

'O, it is not possible to think of that!' she answered hastily, shaking her head. 'When I get home all will be prepared – it is ready even now – the things for the party, the furniture, Mr Heddegan's new suit, and everything. I should require the courage of a tropical lion to go home there and say I wouldn't carry out my promise!'

'Then go, in Heaven's name! But there would be no necessity for you to go home and face them in that way. If we were to marry, it would have to be at once, instantly; or not at all. I should think your affection not worth the having unless you agreed to come back with me to Trufal this evening, where we could be married by licence on Monday morning. And then no Mr David Heddegan or anybody else could get you away from me.'

'I must go home by the Tuesday boat,' she faltered. 'What would they think if I did not come?'

'You could go home by that boat just the same. All the difference would be that I should go with you. You could leave me on the quay, where I'd have a smoke, while you went and saw your father and mother privately; you could then tell them what you had done, and that I was waiting not far off; that I was a schoolmaster in a fairly good position, and a young man you had known when you were at the Training College. Then I would come boldly forward; and they would see that it could not be altered, and so you wouldn't suffer a lifelong misery by being the wife of a wretched old gaffer you don't like at all. Now, honestly; you do like me best, don't you, Baptista?'

'Yes.'

'Then we will do as I say,'

She did not pronounce a clear affirmative. But that she consented to the novel proposition at some moment or other of that walk was apparent by what occurred a little later.

III

An enterprise of such pith required, indeed, less talking than consideration. The first thing they did in carrying it out was to return to the railway station, where Baptista took from her luggage a small trunk of immediate necessaries which she would in any case have required after missing the boat. That same afternoon they travelled up the line to Trufal.

Charles Stow (as his name was), despite his disdainful indifference to things, was very careful of appearances, and made the journey independently of her though in the same train. He told her where she could get board and lodgings in the city; and with merely a distant nod to her of a provisional kind, went off to his own quarters, and to see about the licence.

On Sunday she saw him in the morning across the nave of the pro-cathedral. In the afternoon they walked together in the fields, where he told her that the licence would be ready next day, and would be available the day after, when the ceremony could be performed as early after eight o'clock as they should choose.

His courtship, thus renewed after an interval of two years, was as impetuous, violent even, as it was short. The next day came and passed, and the final arrangements were made. Their agreement was to get the ceremony over as soon as they possibly could the next morning, so as to go on to Pen-zephyr at once, and reach that place in time for the boat's departure the same day. It was in obedience to Baptista's earnest request that Stow consented thus to make the whole journey to Lyonesse by land and water at one heat, and not break it at Pen-zephyr; she seemed to be oppressed with a dread of lingering anywhere, this great first act of disobedience to her parents once accomplished, with the weight on her mind that her home had to be convulsed by the disclosure of it. To face her difficulties over the water immediately she had created them was, however, a course more desired by Baptista than by her lover; though for once he gave way.

The next morning was bright and warm as those which had preceded it. By six o'clock it seemed nearly noon, as is often the case in that part of England in the summer season. By nine they were husband and wife. They packed up and departed by the earliest train after the service; and on the way discussed at length what she should say on meeting her parents, Charley dictating the turn of each phrase. In her anxiety they had travelled so early that when they reached Pen-zephyr they found there were nearly two hours on their hands before the steamer's time of sailing.

Baptista was extremely reluctant to be seen promenading the streets of the watering-place with her husband till, as above stated, the household at Giant's Town should know the unexpected course of events from her own lips; and it was just possible, if not likely, that some Lyonessian might be prowling about there, or even have come across the sea to look for her. To meet any one to whom she was known, and to have to reply to awkward questions about the strange young man at her side before her well-framed announcement had been delivered at proper time and place, was a thing she could not contemplate with equanimity. So, instead of looking at the shops and harbour, they went along the coast a little way.

The heat of the morning was by this time intense. They clambered up on some cliffs, and while sitting there, looking around at St Michael's Mount and other objects, Charles said to her that he thought he would run down to the beach at their feet, and take just one plunge into the sea.

Baptista did not much like the idea of being left alone; it was gloomy, she said. But he assured her he would not be gone more than a quarter of an hour at the outside, and she passively assented.

Down he went, disappeared, appeared again, and looked back. Then he again proceeded, and vanished, till, as a small waxen object, she saw him emerge from the nook that had screened him, cross the white fringe of foam, and walk into the undulating mass of blue. Once in the water he seemed less inclined to hurry than before; he remained a long time; and, unable either to appreciate his skill or criticize his want of it at that distance, she withdrew her eyes from the spot, and gazed at the still outline of St Michael's – now beautifully toned in grey.

Her anxiety for the hour of departure, and to cope at once with the approaching incidents that she would have to manipulate as best she could, sent her into a reverie. It was now Tuesday; she would reach home in the evening – a very late time they would say; but, as the delay was a pure accident, they would deem her marriage to Mr Heddegan to-morrow still practicable. Then Charles would have to be produced from the background. It was a terrible undertaking to think of, and she almost regretted her temerity in wedding so hastily that morning. The rage of her father would be so crushing; the reproaches of her mother so bitter; and perhaps Charles would answer hotly, and perhaps cause estrangement till death. There had obviously been no alarm about her at St Maria's, or somebody would have sailed across to inquire for her. She had, in a letter written at the beginning of the week, spoken of the hour at which she intended to leave her country schoolhouse; and from this her friends had probably perceived that by such timing she would run a risk of losing the Saturday boat. She had missed it, and as a consequence sat here on the shore as Mrs Charles Stow.

This brought her to the present, and she turned from the outline of St. Michael's Mount to look about for her husband's form. He was, as far as she could discover, no longer in the sea. Then he was dressing. By moving a few steps she could see where his clothes lay. But Charles was not beside them.

Baptista looked back again at the water in bewilderment, as if her senses were the victim of some sleight of hand. Not a speck or spot resembling a man's head or face showed anywhere. By this time she was alarmed, and her alarm intensified when she perceived a little beyond the scene of her husband's bathing a small area of water, the quality of whose surface differed from that of the surrounding expanse as the coarse vegetation of some foul patch in a mead differs from the fine green of the remainder. Elsewhere it looked flexuous, here it looked vermiculated and lumpy, and her marine experiences suggested to her in a moment that two currents met and caused a turmoil at this place.

She descended as hastily as her trembling limbs would allow. The way down was terribly long, and before reaching the heap of clothes it occured to her that, after all, it would be best to run first for help. Hastening along in a lateral direction she proceeded inland till she met a man, and soon afterwards two others. To them she exclaimed, 'I think a gentleman who was bathing is in some danger. I cannot see him as I could. Will you please run and help him, at once, if you will be so kind?'

She did not think of turning to show them the exact spot, indicating it vaguely by the direction of her hand, and still going on her way with the idea of gaining more assistance. When she deemed, in her faintness, that she had carried the alarm far enough, she faced about and dragged herself back again. Before reaching the now dreaded spot she met one of the men.

'We can see nothing at all, Miss,' he declared.

Having gained the beach, she found the tide in, and no sign of Charley's clothes. The other men whom she had besought to come had disappeared, it must have been in some other direction, for she had not met them going away. They, finding nothing, had probably thought her alarm a mere conjecture, and given up the quest.

Baptista sank down upon the stones near at hand. Where Charley had undressed was now sea. There could not be the least doubt that he was drowned, and his body sucked under by the current; while his clothes, lying within high-water mark, had probably been carried away by the rising tide.

She remained in a stupor for some minutes, till a strange sensation succeeded the aforesaid perceptions, mystifying her intelligence, and leaving her physically almost inert. With his personal disappearance, the last three days of her life with him seemed to be swallowed up, also his image, in her mind's eye, waned curiously receded far away, grew stranger and stranger, less and less real. Their meeting and marriage had been so sudden, unpremeditated, adventurous, that she could hardly believe that she had played her part in such a reckless drama. Of all the few hours of her life with Charles, the portion that most insisted in coming back to memory was their fortuitous encounter on the previous Saturday, and those bitter reprimands with which he had begun the attack, as it might be called, which had piqued her to an unexpected consummation.

A sort of cruelty, an imperiousness, even in his warmth, had characterized Charles Stow. As a lover he had ever been a bit of a tyrant; and it might pretty truly have been said that he had stung her into marriage with him last. Still more alien from her life did these reflections operate to make him; and then they would be chased away by an interval of passionate weeping and mad regret. Finally, there returned upon the confused mind of the young wife the recollection that she was on her way homeward, and that the packet would sail in three-quarters of an hour.

Except the parasol in her hand, all she possessed was at the station awaiting her onward journey.

She looked in that direction; and, entering one of those undemonstrative phases so common with her, walked quietly on.

At first she made straight for the railway; but suddenly turning she went to a shop and wrote an anonymous line announcing his death by drowning to the only person she had ever heard Charles mention as a relative. Posting this stealthily, and with a fearful look around her, she seemed to acquire a terror of the late events, pursuing her way to the station as if followed by a spectre.

When she got to the office she asked for the luggage that she had left there on the Saturday as well as the trunk left on the morning just lapsed. All were put in the boat, and she herself followed. Quickly as these things had been done, the whole proceeding, nevertheless, had been almost automatic on Baptista's part, ere she had come to any definite conclusion on her course.

Just before the bell rang she heard a conversation on the pier, which removed the last shade of doubt from her mind, if any had existed, that she was Charles Stow's widow. The sentences were but fragmentary, but she could easily piece them out.

'A man drowned – swam out too far – was a stranger to the place – people in boat – saw him go down – couldn't get there in time.'

The news was little more definite than this as yet; though it may as well be stated once for all that the statement was true. Charley, with the over-confidence of his nature, had ventured out too far for his strength, and succumbed in the absence of assistance, his lifeless body being at that moment suspended in the transparent mid-depths of the bay. His clothes, however, had merely been gently lifted by the rising tide, and floated into a nook hard by, where they lay out of sight of the passers-by till a day or two after.

IV

In ten minutes they were steaming out of the harbour for their voyage of four or five hours, at whose ending she would have to tell her strange story.

As Pen-zephyr and all its environing scenes disappeared behind Mousehole and St Clement's Isle, Baptista's ephemeral, meteor-like husband impressed her yet more as a fantasy. She was still in such a trance-like state that she had been an hour on the little packet-boat before she became aware of the agitating fact that Mr Heddegan was on board with her. Involuntarily she slipped from her left hand the symbol of her wifehood.

'Hee-hee! Well, the truth is, I wouldn't interrupt 'ee. "I reckon she don't see me, or won't see me," I said, "and what's the hurry? She'll see enough o' me soon!" I hope ye be well, mee deer?'

He was a hale, well-conditioned man of about five and fifty, of the complexion common to those whose lives are passed on the bluffs and beaches of an ocean isle. He extended the four quarters of his face in a genial smile, and his hand for a grasp of the same magnitude. She gave her own in surprised docility, and he continued:

'I couldn't help coming across to meet 'ee. What an unfortunate thing you missing the boat and not coming Saturday! They meant to have warned 'ee that the time was changed, but forgot it at the last moment. The truth is that I should have informed 'ee myself, but I was that busy finishing up a job last week, so as to have this week free, that I trusted to your father for attending to these little things. However, so plain and quiet as it is all to be, it really do not matter so much as it might otherwise have done, and I hope ye haven't been greatly put out. Now, if you'd sooner that I should not be seen talking to 'ee – if 'ee feel shy at all before strangers – just say. I'll leave 'ee to yourself till we get home.'

'Thank you much. I am indeed a little tired, Mr Heddegan.'

He nodded urbane acquiescence, strolled away immediately, and minutely inspected the surface of the funnel, till some female passengers of Giant's Town tittered at what they must have thought a rebuff – for the approaching wedding was known to many on St Maria's Island, though to nobody elsewhere. Baptista coloured at their satire, and called him back, and forced herself to commune with him in at least a mechanically friendly manner.

The opening event had been thus different from her expectation, and she had adumbrated no act to meet it. Taken aback she passively allowed circumstances to pilot her along; and so the voyage was made.

It was near dusk when they touched the pier of Giant's Town, where several friends and neighbours stood awaiting them. Her father had a lantern in his hand. Her mother, too, was there, reproachfully glad that the delay had at last ended so simply. Mrs Trewthen and her daughter went together along the Giant's Walk, or promenade, to the house, rather in advance of her husband and Mr Heddegan, who talked in loud tones which reached the women over their shoulders.

Some would have called Mrs Trewthen a good mother; but though well meaning she was maladroit, and her intentions missed their mark. This might have been partly attributable to the slight deafness from which she suffered. Now, as usual, the chief utterances came from her lips.

'Ah, yes, I'm so glad, my child, that you've got over safe. It is all ready, and everything so well arranged, that nothing but misfortune could hinder you settling as, with God's grace, becomes 'ee. Close to your mother's door a'most, 'twill be a great blessing, I'm sure; and I was very glad to find from your letters that you'd held your word sacred. That's right – make your word your bond always. Mrs Wace seems to be a sensible woman. I hope the Lord will do for her as he's doing for you no long time hence. And how did 'ee get over the terrible journey from Tor-upon-Sea to Pen-zephyr? Once you'd done with the railway, of course, you seemed quite at home. Well, Baptista, conduct yourself seemly, and all will be well.'

Thus admonished, Baptista entered the house, her father and Mr Heddegan immediately at her back. Her mother had been so didactic that she had felt herself absolutely unable to broach the subjects in the centre of her mind.

The familiar room, with the dark ceiling, the well-spread table, the old chairs, had never before spoken so eloquently of the times ere she knew or had heard of Charley Stow. She went upstairs to take off her things, her mother remaining below to complete the disposition of the supper, and attend to the preparation of tomorrow's meal, altogether composing such an array of pies, from pies of fish to pies of turnips, as was never heard of outside the Western Duchy. Baptista, once alone, sat down and did nothing; and was called before she had taken off her bonnet.

'I'm coming,' she cried, jumping up, and speedily disapparelling herself, brushed her hair with a few touches and went down.

Two or three of Mr Heddegan's and her father's friends had dropped in, and expressed their sympathy for the delay she had been subjected to. The meal was a most merry one except to Baptista. She had desired privacy, and there was none; and to break the news was already a greater difficulty than it had been at first. Everything around her, animate and inanimate, great and small, insisted that she had come home to be married; and she could not get a chance to say nay.

One or two people sang songs, as overtures to the melody of the morrow, till at length bedtime came, and they all withdrew, her mother having retired a little earlier. When Baptista found herself again alone in her bedroom the case stood as before: she had come home with much to say, and she had said nothing.

It was now growing clear even to herself that Charles being dead, she had not determination sufficient within her to break tidings which, had he been alive, would have imperatively announced themselves. And thus with the stroke of midnight came the turning of the scale; her story should remain untold. It was not that upon the whole she thought it best not to attempt to tell it; but that she could not undertake so explosive a matter. To stop the wedding now would cause a convulsion in Giant's Town little short of volcanic. Weakened, tired, and terrified as she had been by the day's adventures, she could not make herself the author of such a catastrophe. But how refuse Heddegan without telling? It really seemed to her as if her marriage with Mr Heddegan were about to take place as if nothing had intervened.

Morning came. The events of the previous days were cut off from her present existence by scene and sentiment more completely than ever. Charles Stow had grown to be a special being of whom, owing to his character, she entertained rather fearful than loving memory. Baptista could hear when she awoke that her parents were already moving about downstairs. But she did not rise till her mother's rather rough voice resounded up the staircase as it had done on the preceding evening.

'Baptista! Come, time to be stirring! The man will be here, by Heaven's blessing, in three-quarters of an hour. He has looked in already for a minute or two – and says he's going to the church to see if things be well forward.'

Baptista arose, looked out of the window, and took the easy course. When she emerged from the regions above she was arrayed in her new silk frock and best stockings, wearing a linen jacket over the former for breakfasting, and her common slippers over the latter, not to spoil the new ones on the rough precincts of the dwelling.

It is unnecessary to dwell at any great length on this part of the morning's proceedings. She revealed nothing; and married Heddegan, as she had given her word to do, on that appointed August day.

V

Mr. Heddegan forgave the coldness of his bride's manner during and after the wedding ceremony, full well aware that there had been considerable reluctance on her part to acquiesce in this neighbourly arrangement, and, as a philosopher of long standing, holding that whatever Baptista's attitude now, the conditions would probably be much the same six months hence as those which ruled among other married couples.

An absolutely unexpected shock was given to Baptista's listless mind about an hour after the wedding service. They had nearly finished the mid-day dinner when the now husband said to her father. 'We think of starting about two. And the breeze being so fair we shall bring up inside Pen-zephyr new pier about six at least.'

'What – are we going to Pen-zephyr?' said Baptista. 'I don't know anything of it.'

'Didn't you tell her?' asked her father of Heddegan.

It transpired that, owing to the delay in her arrival, this proposal too, among other things, had in the hurry not been mentioned to her, except some time ago as a general suggestion that they would go somewhere. Heddegan had imagined that any trip would be pleasant, and one to the mainland the pleasantest of all.

She looked so distressed at the announcement that her husband willingly offered to give it up, though he had not had a holiday off the island for a whole year. Then she pondered on the inconvenience of staying at Giant's Town, where all the inhabitants were bonded, by the circumstances of their situation, into a sort of family party, which permitted and encouraged on such occasions as these oral criticism that was apt to disturb the equanimity of newly married girls, and would especially worry Baptista in her strange situation. Hence, unexpectedly, she agreed not to disorganize her husband's plans for the wedding jaunt, and it was settled that, as originally intended, they should proceed in a neighbour's sailing boat to the metropolis of the district.

In this way they arrived at Pen-zephyr without difficulty or mishap. Bidding adieu to Jenkin and his man, who had sailed them over, they strolled arm in arm off the pier, Baptista silent, cold, and obedient. Heddegan had arranged to take her as far as Plymouth before their return, but to go no further than where they had landed that day. Their first business was to find an inn; and in this they had unexpected difficulty, since for some reason or other – possibly the fine weather – many of the nearest at hand were full of tourists and commercial travellers. He led her on till he reached a tavern which, though comparatively unpretending, stood in as attractive a spot as any in the town; and this, somewhat to their surprise after their previous experience, they found apparently empty. The considerate old man, thinking that Baptista was educated to artistic notions, though he himself was deficient in them, had decided that it was most desirable to have, on such an occasion as the present, an apartment with 'a good view' (the expression being one he had often heard in use among tourists); and he therefore asked for a favourite room on the first floor, from which a bow-window protruded, for the express purpose of affording such an outlook.

The landlady, after some hesitation, said she was sorry that particular apartment was engaged; the next one, however, or any other in the house, was unoccupied.

'The gentleman who has the best one will give it up tomorrow, and then you can change into it,' she added, as Mr Heddegan hesitated about taking the adjoining and less commanding one.

'We shall be gone tomorrow, and shan't want it,' he said.

Wishing not to lose customers, the landlady earnestly continued that since he was bent on having the best room, perhaps the other gentleman would not object to move at once into the one they despised, since, though nothing could be seen from the window, the room was equally large.

'Well if he doesn't care for a view,' said Mr. Heddegan, with the air of a highly artistic man who did.

'O no – I am sure he doesn't,' she said. 'I can promise that you shall have the room you want. If you would not object to go for a walk for half an hour, I could have it ready, and your things in it, and a nice tea laid in the bow-window by the time you come back?'

This proposal was deemed satisfactory by the fussy old tradesman, and they went out. Baptista nervously conducted him in an opposite direction to her walk of the former day in other company, showing on her wan face, had he obseved it, how much she was beginning to regret her sacrificial step for mending matters that morning.

She took advantage of a moment when her husband's back was turned to inquire casually in a shop if anything had been heard of the gentleman who was sucked down in the eddy while bathing.

The shopman said, 'Yes, his body has been washed ashore,' and had just handed Baptista a newspaper on which she discerned the heading, 'A Schoolmaster drowned while bathing,' when her husband turned to join her. She might have pursued the subject without raising suspicion; but it was more than flesh and blood could do, and completing a small purchase almost ran out of the shop.

'What is your terrible hurry, mee deer?' said Heddegan, hastening after.

'I don't know – I don't want to stay in shops,' she gasped.

'And we won't,' he said. 'They are suffocating this weather. Let's go back and have some tay!'

They found the much desired apartment awaiting their entry. It was a sort of combination bed and sitting-room, and the table was prettily spread with high tea in the bow-window, a bunch of flowers in the midst, and a best-parlour chair on each side. Here they shared the meal by the ruddy light of the vanishing sun. But though the view had been engaged, regardless of expense, exclusively for Baptista's pleasure, she did not direct any keen attention out of the window. Her gaze as often fell on the floor and walls of the room as elsewhere, and on the table as much as on either, beholding nothing at all.

But there was a change. Opposite her seat was the door, upon which her eyes presently became riveted like those of a little bird upon a snake. For, on a peg at the back of the door, there hung a hat; such a hat – surely, from its peculiar make, the actual hat – that had been worn by Charles. Conviction grew to certainty when she saw a railway ticket sticking up from the band. Charles had put the ticket there – she had noticed the act.

Her teeth almost chattered; she murmured something incoherent. Her husband jumped up and said, 'You are not well! What is it? What shall I get 'ee?'

'Smelling salts!' she said, quickly and desperately; 'at that chemist's shop you were in just now,'

He jumped up like the anxious old man that he was, caught up his own hat from a back table, and without observing the other hastened out and downstairs.

Left alone she gazed and gazed at the back of the door, then spasmodically rang the bell. An honest-looking country maidservant appeared in response.

'A hat!' murmured Baptista, pointing with her finger. 'It does not belong to us.'

'O yes, I'll take it away,' said the young woman with some hurry 'It belongs to the other gentleman.'

She spoke with a certain awkwardness, and took the hat out of the room. Baptista had recovered her outward composure. 'The other gentleman?' she said. 'Where is the other gentleman?'

'He's in the next room, ma'am. He removed out of this to oblige 'ee.'

'How can you say so? I should hear him if he were there,' said Baptista, sufficiently recovered to argue down an apparent untruth.

'He's there,' said the girl, hardily.

'Then it is strange that he makes no noise,' said Mrs. Heddegan, convicting the girl of falsity by a look.

'He makes no noise; but it is not strange,' said the servant.

All at once a dread took possession of the bride's heart, like a cold hand laid thereon; for it flashed upon her that there was a possibility of reconciling the girl's statement with her own knowledge of facts.

'Why does he make no noise?' she weakly said.

The waiting-maid was silent, and looked at her questioner. 'If I tell you, ma'am, you won't tell missis?' she whispered.

Baptista promised.

'Because he's a-lying dead!' said the girl. 'He's the schoolmaster that was drownded yesterday.'

'O!' said the bride, covering her eyes. 'Then he was in this room till just now?'

'Yes,' said the maid, thinking the young lady's agitation natural enough. 'And I told missis that I thought she oughtn't to have done it, because I don't hold it right to keep visitors so much in the dark where death's concerned; but she said the gentleman didn't die of anything infectious; she was a poor, honest, innkeeper's wife, she says, who had to get her living by making hay while the sun sheened. And owing to the drownded gentleman being brought here, she said, it kept so many people away that we were empty, though all the other houses were full. So when your good man set his mind upon the room, and she would have lost good paying folk if he'd not had it, it wasn't to be supposed, she said, that she'd let anything stand in the way. Ye won't say that I've told ye, please, m'm? All the linen has been changed, and as the inquest won't be till to-morrow, after you are gone, she thought you wouldn't know a word of it, being strangers here.'

The returning footsteps of her husband broke off further narration. Baptista waved her hand, for she could not speak. The waiting-maid quickly withdrew, and Mr Heddegan entered with the smelling salts and other nostrums.

'Any better?' he questioned.

'I don't like the hotel,' she exclaimed, almost simultaneously. 'I can't bear it – it doesn't suit me!'

'Is that all that's the matter?' he returned pettishly (this being the first time of his showing such a mood). 'Upon my heart and life such trifling is trying to any man's temper, Baptista! Sending me about from here to yond, and then when I come back saying 'ee don't like the place that I have sunk so much money and words to get for 'ee. 'Od dang it all, 'tis enough to – But I won't say any more at present, mee dear, though it is just too much to expect to turn out of the house now. We shan't get another quiet place at this time of the evening – every other inn in the town is bustling with rackety folk of one sort and t'other, while here 'tis as quiet as the grave – the country, I would say. So bide still, d'ye hear, and tomorrow we shall be out of the town altogether – as early as you like.'

The obstinacy of age had, in short, overmastered its complaisance, and the young woman said no more. The simple course of telling him that in the adjoining room lay a corpse which had lately occupied their own might, it would have seemed, have been an effectual one without further disclosure, but to allude to *that* subject, however it was disguised, was more than Heddegan's young wife had strength for. Horror broke her down. In the contingency one thing only presented itself to her paralyzed regard – that here she was doomed to abide, in a hideous contiguity to the dead husband and the living, and her conjecture did, in fact, bear itself out. That night she lay between the two men she had married – Heddegan on the one hand, and on the other through the partition against which the bed stood, Charles Stow.

VI

Kindly time had withdrawn the foregoing event three days from the present of Baptista Heddegan. It was ten o'clock in the morning; she had been ill, not in an ordinary or definite sense, but in a state of cold stupefaction, from which it was difficult to arouse her so much as to say a few sentences. When questioned she had replied that she was pretty well.

Their trip, as such, had been something of a failure. They had gone on as far as Falmouth, but here he had given way to her entreaties to return home. This they could not very well do without repassing through Pen-zephyr, at which place they had now again arrived.

In the train she had seen a weekly local paper, and read there a paragraph detailing the inquest on Charles. It was added that the funeral was to take place at his native town of Redrutin on Friday.

After reading this she had shown no reluctance to enter the fatal neighbourhood of the tragedy, only stipulating that they should take their rest at a different lodging from the first; and now comparatively braced up and calm – indeed a cooler creature altogether than when last in the town, she said to David that she wanted to walk out for a while, as they had plenty of time on their hands.

'To a shop as usual, I suppose, mee dear?'

'Partly for shopping,' she said. 'And it will be best for you, dear, to stay in after trotting about so much, and have a good rest while I am gone.'

He assented; and Baptista sallied forth. As she had stated, her first visit was made to a shop, a draper's. Without the exercise of much choice she purchased a black bonnet and veil, also a black stuff gown; a black mantle she already wore. These articles were made up into a parcel which, in spite of the saleswoman's offers, her customer said she would take with her. Bearing it on her arm she turned to the railway, and at the station got a ticket for Redrutin.

Thus it appeared that, on her recovery from the paralyzed mood of the former day, while she had resolved not to blast utterly the happiness of her present husband by revealing the history of the departed one, she had also determined to indulge a certain odd, inconsequent, feminine sentiment of decency, to the small extent to which it could do no harm to any person. At Redrutin she emerged from the railway carriage in the black attire purchased at the shop, having during the transit made the change in the empty compartment she had chosen. The other clothes were now in the bandbox and parcel. Leaving these at the cloak-room she proceeded onward, and after a wary survey reached the side of a hill whence a view of the burial ground could be obtained.

It was now a little before two o'clock. While Baptista waited a funeral procession ascended the road. Baptista hastened across, and by the time the procession entered the cemetery gates she had unobtrusively joined it.

In addition to the schoolmaster's own relatives (not a few), the paragraph in the newspapers of his death by drowning had drawn together many neighbours, acquaintances, and onlookers. Among them she passed unnoticed, and with a quiet step pursued the winding path to the chapel, and afterwards thence to the grave. When all was over, and the relatives and idlers had withdrawn, she stepped to the edge of the chasm. From beneath her mantle she drew a little bunch of forget-me-nots, and dropped them in upon the coffin. In a few minutes she also turned and went away from the cemetery. By five o'clock she was again in Pen-zephyr.

'You have been a mortal long time!' said her husband, crossly. 'I allowed you an hour at most, mee dear.'

'It occupied me longer,' said she.

'Well – I reckon it is wasting words to complain. Hang it, ye look so tired and wisht that I can't find heart to say what I would!'

'I am – weary and wisht, David; I am. We can get home tomorrow for certain, I hope?'

'We can. And please God we will!' said Mr Heddegan heartily, as if he too were weary of his brief honeymoon. 'I must be into business again on Monday morning at latest.'

They left by the next morning steamer, and in the afternoon took up their residence in their own house at Giant's Town.

The hour that she reached the island it was as if a material weight had been removed from Baptista's shoulders. Her husband attributed the change to the influence of the local breezes after the hot-house atmosphere of the mainland. However that might be, settled here, a few doors from her mother's dwelling, she recovered in no very long time much of her customary bearing, which was never very demonstrative. She accepted her position calmly, and faintly smiled when her neighbours learned to call her Mrs Heddegan, and said she seemed likely to become the leader of fashion in Giant's Town.

Her husband was a man who had made considerably more money by trade than her father had done: and perhaps the greater profusion of surroundings at her command than she had heretofore been mistress of, was not without an effect upon her. One week, two weeks, three weeks passed; and, being pre-eminently a young woman who allowed things to drift, she did nothing whatever either to disclose or conceal traces of her first marriage; or to learn if there existed possibilities – which there undoubtedly did – by which that hasty contract might become revealed to those about her at any unexpected moment.

While yet within the first month of her marriage, and on an evening just before sunset, Baptista was standing within her garden adjoining the house, when she saw passing along the road a personage clad in a greasy black coat and battered tall hat, which, common enough in the slums of a city, had an odd appearance in St Maria's. The tramp, as he seemed to be, marked her at once – bonnetless and unwrapped as she was her features were plainly recognizable – and with an air of friendly surprise came and leant over the wall.

'What! don't you know me?' said he.

She had some dim recollection of his face, but said that she was not acquainted with him.

'Why, your witness to be sure, ma'am. Don't you mind the man that was mending the church-window when you and your intended husband walked up to be made one; and the clerk called me down from the ladder, and I came and did my part by writing my name and occupation?'

Baptista glanced quickly around; her husband was out of earshot. That would have been of less importance but for the fact that the wedding witnessed by this personage had not been the wedding with Mr Heddegan, but the one on the day previous.

'I've had a misfortune since then, that's pulled me under,' continued her friend. 'But don't let me damp yer wedded joy by naming the particulars. Yes, I've seen changes since; though 'tis but a short time ago – let me see, only a month next week, I think; for 'twere the first or second day in August.'

'Yes – that's when it was,' said another man, a sailor, who had come up with a pipe in his mouth, and felt it necessary to join in (Baptista having receded to escape fruther speech). 'For that was the first time I set foot in Giant's Town; and her husband took her to him the same day.'

A dialogue then proceeded between the two men outside the wall, which Baptista could not help hearing.

'Ay, I signed the book that made her one flesh,' repeated the decayed glazier. 'Where's her goodman?'

'About the premises somewhere; but you don't see 'em together much,' replied the sailor in an undertone. 'You see, he's older than she.'

'Older? I should never have thought it from my own observation,' said the glazier. 'He was a remarkably handsome man.'

'Handsome? Well, there he is – we can see for ourselves.'

David Heddegan had, indeed, just shown himself at the upper end of the garden and the glazier, looking in bewilderment from the husband to the wife, saw the latter turn pale.

Now that decayed glazier was a far-seeing and cunning man – too far-seeing and cunning to allow himself to thrive by simple and straightforward means – and he held his peace, till he could read more plainly the meaning of this riddle, merely adding carelessly, 'Well – marriage do alter a man, 'tis true. I should never ha' knowed him!'

He then stared oddly at the disconcerted Baptista, and moving on to where he could again address her, asked her to do him a good turn, since he once had done the same for her. Understanding that he meant money, she handed him some, at which he thanked her, and instantly went away.

VII

She had escaped exposure on this occasion; but the incident had been an awkward one, and should have suggested to Baptista that sooner or later the secret must leak out. As it was, she suspected that at any rate she had not heard the last of the glazier.

In a day or two, when her husband had gone to the old town on the other side of the island, there came a gentle tap at the door, and the worthy witness of her first marriage made his appearance a second time.

'It took me hours to get to the bottom of the mystery – hours!' he said with a gaze of deep confederacy which offended her pride very deeply. 'But thanks to a good intellect I've done it. Now, ma'am, I'm not a man to tell tales, even when a tale would be so good as this. But I'm going back to the mainland again, and a little assistance would be as rain on thirsty ground.'

'I helped you two days ago,' began Baptista.

'Yes – but what was that, my good lady? Not enough to pay my passage to Pen-zephyr. I came over on your account, for I thought there was a mystery somewhere. Now I must go back on my own. Mind this – 'twould be very awkward for you if your old man were to know. He's a queer temper, though he may be fond.'

She knew as well as her visitor how awkward it would be; and the hush-money she paid was heavy that day. She had, however, the satisfaction of watching the man to the steamer, and seeing him diminish out of sight. But Baptista perceived that the system into which she had been led of purchasing silence thus was one fatal to her peace of mind, particularly if it had to be continued.

Hearing no more from the glazier she hoped the difficulty was past. But another week only had gone by, when, as she was pacing the Giant's Walk (the name given to the promenade), she met the same personage in the company of a fat woman carrying a bundle.

'This is the lady, my dear,' he said to his companion. 'This, ma'am, is my wife. We've come to settle in the town for a time, if so be we can find room.'

'That you won't do,' said she. 'Nobody can live here who is not privileged.'

'I am privileged,' said the glazier, 'by my trade.'

Baptista went on, but in the afternoon she received a visit from the man's wife. This honest woman began to depict, in forcible colours, the necessity for keeping up the concealment.

'I will intercede with my husband, ma'am,' she siad. 'He's a true man if rightly managed; and I'll beg him to consider your position. 'Tis very nice house you've got here,' she added, glancing round, 'and well worth a little sacrifice to keep it.'

The unlucky Baptista staved off the danger on this third occasion as she had done on the previous two. But she formed a resolve that, if the attack were once more to be repeated she would face a revelation – worse though that must now be than before she had attempted to purchase silence by bribes. Her tormentors, never believing her capable of acting upon such an intention, came again; but she shut the door in their faces. They retreated, muttering something; but she went to the back of the house, where David Heddegan was.

She looked at him, unconscious of all. The case was serious; she knew that well; and all the more serious in that she liked him better now than she had done at first. Yet, as she herself began to see, the secret was one that was sure to disclose itself. Her name and Charles's stood indelibly written in the registers; and though a month only had passed as yet it was a wonder that his clandestine union with her had not already been discovered by his friends. Thus spurring herself to the inevitable, she spoke to Heddegan.

'David, come indoors. I have something to tell you.'

He hardly regarded her at first. She had discerned that during the last week or two he had seemed preoccupied, as if some private business harassed him. She repeated her request. He replied with a sigh, 'Yes, certainly, mee deer.'

When they had reached the sitting-room and shut the door she repeated, faintly, 'David, I have something to tell you – a sort of tragedy I have concealed. You will hate me for having so far deceived you; but perhaps my telling you voluntarily will make you think a little better of me than you would do otherwise.'

'Tragedy?' he said, awakening to interest. 'Much you can know about tragedies, mee deer, that have been in the world so short a time!'

She saw that he suspected nothing, and it made her task the harder. But on she went steadily. 'It is about something that happened before we were married,' she said.

'Indeed!'

'Not a very long time before – a short time. And it is about a lover,' she faltered.

'I don't much mind that,' he said mildly. 'In truth, I was in hopes 'twas more.'

'In hopes!'

'Well, yes.'

This screwed her up to the necessary effort. 'I met my old sweetheart. He scorned me, chid me, dared me, and I went and married him. We were coming straight here to tell you all what we had done; but he was drowned; and I thought I would say nothing about him: and I married you, David, for the sake of peace and quietness. I've tried to keep it from you, but have found I cannot. There – that's the substance of it, and you can never, never forgive me, I am sure!'

She spoke desperately. But the old man, instead of turning black or blue, or slaying her in his indignation, jumped up from his chair, and began to caper around the room in quite an ecstatic emotion.

'O, happy thing! How well it falls out!' he exclaimed, snapping his fingers over his head. 'Ha-ha – the knot is cut – I see a way out of my trouble – ha-ha!'

She looked at him without uttering a sound, till, as he still continued smiling joyfully, she said, 'O – what do you mean? Is it done to torment me?'

'No – no! O, mee deer, your story helps me out of the most heart-aching quandary a poor man ever found himself in! You see, it is this – *I've* got a tragedy, too; and unless you had had one to tell, I could never have seen my way to tell mine!'

'What is yours – what is it?' she asked, with altogether a new view of things.

'Well – it is a bouncer; mine is a bouncer!' said he, looking on the ground and wiping his eyes.

'Not worse than mine?'

'Well – that depends upon how you look at it. Yours had to do with the past alone; and I don't mind it. You see, we've been married a month, and it don't jar upon me as it would if we'd only been married a day or two. Now mine refers to past, present, and future; so that—'

'Past, present, and future!' she murmured. 'It never occurred to me that *you* had a tragedy too.'

'But I have!' he said, shaking his head. 'In fact, four.'

'Then tell 'em!' cried the young woman.

'I will – I will. But be considerate, I beg 'ee, mee deer. Well – I wasn't a bachelor when I married 'ee any more than you were a spinster. Just as you was a widow-woman, I was a widow-man.'

'Ah!' said she, with some surprise. 'But is that all? – then we are nicely balanced,' she added, relieved.

'No – it is not all. There's the point. I am not only a widower.'

'O, David!'

'I am a widower with four tragedies – that is to say, four strapping girls – the eldest taller than you. Don't 'ee look so struck – dumb-like! It fell out in this way. I knew the poor woman, their mother, in Pen-zephyr for some years; and – to cut a long story short – I privately married her at last, just before she died. I kept the matter secret, but it is getting known among the people here by degrees. I've long felt for the children – that it is my duty to have them here, and do something for them. I have not had courage to break it to 'ee, but I've seen lately that it would soon come to your ears, and that hev worried me.'

'Are they educated?' said the ex-schoolmistress.

'No. I am sorry to say they have been much neglected; in truth, they can hardly read. And so I thought that by marrying a young schoolmistress I should get some one in the house who could teach 'em, and bring 'em into genteel condition, all for nothing. You see, they are growed up too tall to be sent to school.'

'O, mercy!' she almost moaned. 'Four great girls to teach the rudiments to, and have always in the house with me spelling over their books; and I hate teaching, it kills me. I am bitterly punished – I am, I am!'

'You'll get used to 'em, mee deer, and the balance of secrets –

mine against yours – will comfort your heart with a sense of justice. I could send for 'em this week very well – and I will! In faith, I could send this very day. Baptista, you have relieved me of all my difficulty!'

Thus the interview ended, so far as this matter was concerned. Baptista was too stupefied to say more, and when she went away to her room she wept from very mortification at Mr Heddegan's duplicity. Education, the one thing she abhorred; the shame of it to delude a young wife so!

The next meal came round. As they sat, Baptista would not suffer her eyes to turn towards him. He did not attempt to intrude upon her reserve, but every now and then looked under the table and chuckled with satisfaction at the aspect of affairs. 'How very well matched we be!' he said, comfortably.

Next day, when the steamer came in, Baptista saw her husband rush down to meet it; and soon after there appeared at her door four tall, hipless, shoulderless girls, dwindling in height and size from the eldest to the youngest, like a row of Pan pipes; at the head of them standing Heddegan. He smiled pleasantly through the grey fringe of his whiskers and beard, and turning to the girls said, 'Now come forrard, and shake hands properly with your stepmother.'

Thus she made their acquaintance, and he went out, leaving them together. On examination the poor girls turned out to be not only plain-looking, which she could have forgiven, but to have such a lamentably meagre intellectual equipment as to be hopelessly inadequate as companions. Even the eldest, almost her own age, could only read with difficulty words of two syllables; and taste in dress was beyond their comprehension. In the long vista of future years she saw nothing but dreary drudgery at her detested old trade without prospect of reward.

She went about quite despairing during the next few days – an unpromising, unfortunate mood for a woman who had not been married six weeks. From her parents she concealed everything. They had been amongst the few acquaintances of Heddegan who knew nothing of his secret, and were indignant enough when they saw such a ready-made household foisted upon their only child. But she would not support them in their remonstrances.

'No, you don't yet know all,' she said.

Thus Baptista had sense enough to see the retributive fairness of this issue. For some time, whenever conversation arose between her and Heddegan, which was not often, she always said, 'I am miserable, and you know it. Yet I don't wish things to be otherwise.'

But one day when he asked, 'How do you like 'em now?' her answer was unexpected. 'Much better than I did,' she said quietly. 'I may like them very much some day.'

This was the beginning of a serener season for the chastened spirit of Baptista Heddegan. She had, in truth, discovered, underneath the crust of uncouthness and meagre articulation which was due to their Troglodytean existence, that her unwelcomed daughters had natures that were unselfish almost to sublimity. The harsh discipline accorded to their young lives before their mother's wrong had been righted, had operated less to crush them than to lift them above all personal ambition. They considered the world and its contents in a purely objective way, and their own lot seemed only to affect them as that of certain human beings among the rest, whose troubles they knew rather than suffered.

This was such an entirely new way of regarding life to a woman of Baptista's nature, that her attention, from being first arrested by it, became deeply interested. By imperceptible pulses her heart expanded in sympathy with theirs. The sentences of her tragi-comedy, her life, confused till now, became clearer daily. That in humanity, as exemplified by these girls, there was nothing to dislike, but infinitely much to pity, she learnt with the lapse of each week in their company. She grew to like the girls of unpromising exterior, and from liking she got to love them; till they formed an unexpected point of junction between her own and her husband's interests, generating a sterling friendship at least, between a pair in whose existence there had threatened to be neither friendship nor love.

The Withered Arm

Belief in superstition was clearly very widespread in Dorset during Hardy's lifetime and it is not surprising that it features in a number of his novels and short stories – perhaps nowhere quite so effectively as in 'The Withered Arm', first published in *Blackwood's Magazine* in January 1888. When it was later collected in *Wessex Tales*, Hardy made a number of changes based on criticisms that had been advanced that it was weakened by a lack of explanation of the more fantastical elements. To my mind, the original *Blackwood's* version is more powerful than that in the book and consequently it is reprinted hereunder.

Aside from Hardy's knowledge of local folklore, this story is also partly based on an incident from his childhood when his father described to him how a young boy, being hung for being found with a group of men who had set fire to some hay ricks, had weights attached to his feet so that he would die quicker. 'Nothing my father ever said drove the tragedy of life so deeply into my mind,' Hardy remarked later when discussing why he had included this pathetic victim in 'The Withered Arm.' There was also an original of the character, Rhoda Brook, the woman thought to be a sorceress, whose jealousy of her former lover's young bride leads to a terrible finale. Commenting in 1912, Hardy said, 'Since writing this story some years ago I have been reminded by an aged friend who knew 'Rhoda Brook' that, in relating her dream, my forgetfulness has weakened the facts out of which the tale grew. In reality it was while lying down on a hot afternoon that the incubus oppressed her and she flung it off, with the results upon the body of the original as described.' Such a confession does not, let me assure the reader, affect the atmosphere and chill of the story in the slightest!

The Withered Arm

I. A Lorn Milkmaid

It was an eighty-cow dairy, and the troop of milkers, regular and supernumerary, were all at work; for, though the time of year was as yet but early April, the feed lay entirely in water-meadows and the cows were 'in full pail.' The hour was about six in the evening, and three-fourths of the large, red, rectangular animals having been finished off, there was opportunity for a little conversation.

'He brings home his bride tomorrow, I hear. They've come as far as Anglebury today.'

The voice seemed to proceed from the carcass of the cow called Cherry, but the speaker was a milking-woman, whose face was buried in the flank of that motionless beast.

'Has anybody seen her?' said another.

There was a negative response from the first. 'Though they say she's a rosy-cheeked, tisty-tosty little body enough,' she added; and as the milkmaid spoke she turned her face so that she could glance past her cow's tail to the other side of the barton, where a thin faded woman of thirty milked somewhat apart from the rest.

'Years younger than he, they say,' continued the second, with also a glance of reflectiveness in the same direction.

'How old do you call him, then?'

'Thirty or so.'

'More like forty,' broke in an old milkman near, in a long white pinafore or 'wropper,' and with the brim of his hat tied down, so that he looked like a woman. ''A was born before our Great Weir was builded, and I hadn't man's wages when I laved water there.'

The discussion waxed so warm that the purr of the milk-streams became jerky, till a voice from another cow's belly cried with authority, 'Now, then, what the Turk do it matter to us about Farmer Lodge's age, or Farmer Lodge's new mis'ess! I shall have to pay him nine pound a-year for the rent of every one of these milchers, whatever his age or hers. Get on with your work, or 'twill be dark before we have done. The evening is pinking in a'ready.' This speaker was the dairyman himself, by whom the milkmaids and men were employed.

Nothing more was said publicly about Farmer Lodge's wedding, but the first woman murmured under her cow to her next neighbour, ''Tis hard for she,' signifying the thin worn milkmaid aforesaid.

'Oh no,' said the second. 'He hasn't spoken to Rhoda Brook for years.'

When the milking was done they washed their pails and hung them on a many-forked stand made of the peeled limb of an oak-tree, set upright in the earth, and resembling a colossal antlered horn. The majority then dispersed in various directions homeward. The thin woman who had not spoken was joined by a boy of twelve or thereabout, and the twain went away up the field also.

Their course lay apart from that of the others, to a lonely spot high above the water-meads, and not far from the border of Egdon Heath, whose dark countenance was visible in the distance as they drew nigh to their home.

'They've just been saying down in barton that your father brings his young wife home from Anglebury tomorrow,' the woman observed. 'I shall want to send you for a few things to market, and you'll be pretty sure to meet 'em.'

'Yes, mother,' said the boy. 'Is father married, then?'

'Yes. . . . You can give her a look, and tell me what she's like, if you do see her.'

'Yes, mother.'

'If she's dark or fair, and if she's tall – as tall as I. And if she seems like a woman who has ever worked for a living, or one that has been always well off, and has never done anything, and shows marks of the lady on her, as I expect she do.'

'Yes.'

They crept up the hill in the twilight, and entered the cottage. It was thatched, and built of mud-walls, the surface of which had been washed by many rains into channels and depressions that left none of the original flat face visible; while here and there a rafter showed like a bone protruding through the skin.

She was kneeling down in the chimney-corner, before two pieces of turf laid together with the heather inwards, blowing at the red-hot ashes with her breath till the turves flamed. The radiance lit her pale cheek, and made her dark eyes, that had once been handsome, seem handsome anew. 'Yes,' she resumed, 'see if she is dark or fair, and if you can, notice if her hands are white; if not, see if they look as though she had ever done housework, or are milker's hands like mine.'

The boy again promised, inattentively this time, his mother not observing that he was cutting a notch with his pocket-knife in the beech-backed chair.

II. The Young Wife

The road from Anglebury to Stickleford is in general level; but there is one place where a sharp ascent breaks its monotony. Farmers homeward-bound from the former market-town, who trot all the rest of the way, walk their horses up this short incline.

The next evening, while the sun was yet bright, a handsome new gig, with a lemon-coloured body and red wheels, was spinning westward along the level highway at the heels of a powerful mare. The driver was a yeoman in the prime of life, cleanly shaven like an actor, his face being toned to that bluish-vermilion hue which so often graces a thriving farmer's features when returning home after successful dealings in the town. Beside him sat a woman, many years his junior – almost, indeed, a girl. Her face too was fresh in colour, but it was of a totally different quality – soft and evanescent, like the light under a heap of rose-petals.

Few people travelled this way, for it was not a turnpike road; and the long white riband of gravel that stretched before them was empty, save of one small scarce-moving speck, which presently resolved itself into the figure of a boy, who was creeping on at a snail's pace, and continually looking behind him – the heavy bundle he carried being some excuse for, if not the reason of, his dilatoriness. When the bouncing gig-party slowed at the bottom of the incline above mentioned, the pedestrian was only a few yards in front. Supporting the large bundle by putting one hand on his hip, he turned and looked straight at the farmer's wife as though he would read her through and through, pacing along abreast of the horse.

The low sun was full in her face, rendering every feature, shade, and contour distinct, from the curve of her little nostril to the colour of her eyes. The farmer, though he seemed annoyed at the boy's persistent presence, did not order him to get out of the way;

and thus the lad preceded them, his hard gaze never leaving her, till they reached the top of the ascent, when the farmer trotted on with relief in his lineaments – having taken no outward notice of the boy whatever.

'How that poor lad stared at me!' said the young wife.

'Yes, dear; I saw that he did.'

'He is one of the village, I suppose?'

'One of the neighbourhood. I think he lives with his mother a mile or two off.'

'He knows who we are, no doubt?'

'Oh yes. You must expect to be stared at just at first, my pretty Gertrude.'

'I do – though I think the poor boy may have looked at us in the hope we might relieve him of his heavy load, rather than from curiosity.'

'Oh no,' said her husband, offhandedly. 'These country lads will carry a hundredweight once they get it on their backs; besides, his pack had more size than weight in it. Now, then, another mile and I shall be able to show you our house in the distance – if it is not too dark before we get there.' The wheels spun round, and particles flew from their periphery as before, till a white house of ample dimensions revealed itself, with farm-buildings and ricks at the back.

Meanwhile the boy had quickened his pace, and turning up a by-lane some mile and half short of the white farmstead, ascended towards the leaner pastures, and so on to the cottage of his mother.

She had reached home after her day's milking at the outlying dairy, and was washing cabbage at the doorway in the declining light. 'Hold up the net a moment,' she said, without preface, as the boy came up.

He flung down his bundle, held the edge of the cabbage-net, and as she filled its meshes with the dripping leaves she went on, 'Well, did you see her?'

'Yes; quite plain.'

'Is she ladylike?'

'Yes; and more. A lady complete.'

'Is she young?'

'Well, she's growed up, and her ways are quite a woman's.'

'Of course. What colour is her hair and face?'

'Her hair is lightish, and her face like a real live doll's.'

'Her eyes, then, are not dark like mine?'

'No – of a bluish turn, and her mouth is very nice and red; and when she smiles, her teeth show white.'

'Is she tall?' said the woman sharply.

'I couldn't see. She was sitting down.'

'Then do you go to Stickleford church tomorrow morning: she's sure to be there. Go early and notice her walking in, and come home and tell me if she's taller than I.'

'Very well, mother. But why don't you go and see for yourself?'

'*I* go to see her! I wouldn't look up at her if she were to pass my window this instant. She was with Mr Lodge, of course. What did he say or do?'

'Just the same as usual.'

'Took no notice of you?'

'None.'

Next day the mother put a clean shirt on the boy, and started him off for Stickleford church. He reached the ancient little pile when the door was just being opened, and he was the first to enter. Taking his seat by the front, he watched all the parishioners file in. The well-to-do Farmer Lodge came nearly last; and his young wife, who accompanied him, walked up the aisle with the shyness natural to a modest woman who had appeared thus for the first time. As all other eyes were fixed upon her, the youth's stare was not noticed now.

When he reached home his mother said 'Well?' before he had entered the room.

'She is not tall. She is rather short,' he replied.

'Ah!' said his mother, with satisfaction.

'But she's very pretty – very. In fact, she's lovely.' The youthful freshness of the yeoman's wife had evidently made an impression even on the somewhat hard nature of the boy.

'That's all I want to hear,' said his mother quickly. 'Now, spread the table-cloth. The hare you caught is very tender; but mind that nobody catches you. – You've never told me what sort of hands she had.'

'I have never seen 'em. She never took off her gloves.'

'What did she wear this morning?'

'A white bonnet and a silver-coloured gownd. It whewed and whistled so loud when it rubbed against the pews that the lady coloured up more than ever for very shame at the noise, and pulled it in to keep it from touching; but when she pushed into her seat, it whewed more than ever. Mr Lodge, he seemed pleased, and his waistcoat stuck out, and his great golden seals hung like a lord's; but she seemed to wish her noisy gownd anywhere but on her.'

'Not she! However, that will do now.'

These descriptions of the newly married couple were continued from time to time by the boy at his mother's request, after any chance encounter he had had with them. But Rhoda Brook, though she might easily have seen young Mrs Lodge for herself by walking a couple of miles, would never attempt an excursion towards the quarter where the farmhouse lay. Neither did she, at the daily milking in the dairyman's yard on Lodge's outlying second farm, ever speak on the subject of the recent marriage. The dairyman, who rented the cows of Lodge, and knew perfectly the tall milkmaid's history, with manly kindliness always kept the gossip in the cow-barton from annoying Rhoda. But the atmosphere thereabout was full of the subject during the first days of Mrs Lodge's arrival; and from her boy's description and the casual words of the other milkers, Rhoda Brook could raise a mental image of the unconscious Mrs Lodge that was realistic as a photograph.

III. A Vision

One night, two or three weeks after the bridal return, when the boy was gone to bed, Rhoda sat a long time over the turf ashes that she had raked out in front of her to extinguish them. She contemplated so intently the new wife, as presented to her in her mind's eye over the embers, that she forgot the lapse of time. At last, wearied with her day's work, she too retired.

But the figure which had occupied her so much during this and the previous days was not to be banished at night. For the first time Gertrude Lodge visited the supplanted woman in her dreams. Rhoda Brook dreamed – if her assertion that she really saw, before falling asleep, was not to be believed – that the young wife, in the pale silk dress and white bonnet, but with features shockingly distorted, and wrinkled as by age, was sitting upon her chest as she lay. The pressure of Mrs Lodge's person grew heavier; the blue eyes peered cruelly into her face; and then the figure thrust forward its left hand mockingly, so as to make the wedding-ring it wore glitter in Rhoda's eyes. Maddened mentally, and nearly suffocated by pressure, the sleeper struggled; the incubus, still regarding her, withdrew to the foot of the bed, only, however, to come forward by degrees, resume her seat, and flash her left hand as before.

Gasping for breath, Rhoda, in a last desperate effort, swung out her right hand, seized the confronting spectre by its obtrusive left arm, and whirled it backward to the floor, starting up herself as she did so with a low cry.

'Oh, merciful heaven!' she cried, sitting on the edge of the bed in a cold sweat, 'that was not a dream – she was here!'

She could feel her antagonist's arm within her grasp even now – the very flesh and bone of it, as it seemed. She looked on the floor whither she had whirled the spectre, but there was nothing to be seen.

Rhoda Brook slept no more that night, and when she went milking at the next dawn they noticed how pale and haggard she looked. The milk that she drew quivered into the pail; her hand had not calmed even yet, and still retained the feel of the arm. She came home to breakfast as wearily as if it had been supper-time.

'What was that noise in your chimmer, mother, last night?' said her son. 'You fell off the bed, surely?'

'Did you hear anything fall? At what time?'

'Just when the clock struck two.'

She would not explain, and when the meal was done went silently about her household work, the boy assisting her, for he hated going afield on the farms, and she indulged his reluctance. Between eleven and twelve the garden-gate clicked, and she lifted her eyes to the window. At the bottom of the garden, within the gate, stood the woman of her vision. Rhoda seemed transfixed.

'Ah, she said she would come!' exclaimed the boy, also observing her.

'Said so – when? How does she know us?'

'I have seen and spoken to her. I talked to her yesterday.'

'I told you,' said the mother, flushing indignantly, 'never to speak to anybody in that house, or go near the place.'

'I did not speak to her till she spoke to me. And I did not go near the place. I met her in the road.'

'What did you tell her?'

'Nothing. She said, "Are you the poor boy who had to bring the heavy load from market?" And she looked at my boots, and said they would not keep my feet dry if it came on wet, because they were so broken. I told her I lived with my mother, and we had enough to do to keep ourselves, and that's how it was; and she said then, "I'll come and bring you some better boots, and see your mother." She gives away things to other folks in the meads besides us.'

Mrs Lodge was by this time close to the door – not in her silk, as Rhoda had seen her in the bedchamber, but in a morning hat, and gown of common light material, which became her better than silk. On her arm she carried a basket.

The impression remaining from the night's experience was still strong. Brook had almost expected to see the wrinkles, the scorn, and the cruelty on her visitor's face. She would have escaped an interview, had escape been possible. There was, however, no back-door to the cottage, and in an instant the boy had lifted the latch to Mrs Lodge's gentle knock.

'I see I have come to the right house,' said she, glancing at the lad, and smiling. 'But I was not sure till you opened the door.'

The figure and action were those of the phantom; but her voice was so indescribably sweet, her glance so winning, her smile so tender, so unlike that of Rhoda's midnight visitant, that the latter could hardly believe the evidence of her senses. She was truly glad that she had not hidden away in sheer aversion, as she had been inclined to do. In her basket Mrs Lodge brought the pair of boots that she had promised to the boy, and other useful articles.

At these proofs of a kindly feeling towards her and hers, Rhoda's heart reproached her bitterly. This innocent young thing should have her blessing and not her curse. When she left them a light seemed gone from the dwelling. Two days later she came again to know if the boots fitted; and less than a fortnight after that paid Rhoda another call. On this occasion the boy was absent.

'I walk a good deal,' said Mrs Lodge, 'and your house is the nearest outside our own parish. I hope you are well. You don't look quite well.'

Rhoda said she was well enough; and indeed, though the paler of the two, there was more of the strength that endures in her well-defined features and large frame, than in the soft-cheeked young woman before her. The conversation became quite confidential as regarded their powers and weaknesses; and when Mrs Lodge was leaving, Rhoda said, 'I hope you will find this air agree with you, ma'am, and not suffer from the damp of the meads.'

The younger one replied that there was not much doubt of it, her general health being usually good. 'Though, now you remind me,' she added, 'I have one little ailment which puzzles me. It is nothing serious, but I cannot make it out.'

She uncovered her left hand and arm; and their outline confronted Rhoda's gaze as the exact original of the limb she had beheld and seized in her dream. Upon the pink round surface of the arm were faint marks of an unhealthy colour, as if produced by a rough grasp. Rhoda's eyes became riveted on the discolorations; she fancied that she discerned in them the shape of her own four fingers.

'How did it happen?' she said mechanically.

'I cannot tell,' replied Mrs Lodge, shaking her head. 'One night when I was sound asleep, dreaming I was away in some strange place, a pain suddenly shot into my arm there, and was so keen as to awaken me. I must have struck it in the daytime, I suppose, though I don't remember doing so.' She added, laughing, 'I tell my dear husband that it looks just as if he had flown into a rage and struck me there. Oh, I daresay it will soon disappear.'

'Ha, ha! Yes. . . . On what night did it come?'

Mrs Lodge considered, and said it would be a fortnight ago on the morrow. 'When I awoke, I could not remember where I was,' she added, 'till the clock striking two reminded me.'

She had named the night and the hour of Rhoda's spectral encounter, and Brook felt like a guilty thing. The artless disclosure startled her; she could not understand the coincidence; and all the scenery of that ghastly night returned with double vividness to her mind.

'Oh, can it be,' she said to herself, when her visitor had departed, 'that I exercise a malignant power over people against my own will?' She knew that she had been slyly called a witch since her fall; but never having understood why that particular stigma had been attached to her, it had passed disregarded. Could this be the explanation, and had such things as this ever happened before?

IV. A Suggestion

The summer drew on, and Rhoda Brook almost dreaded to meet Mrs Lodge again, notwithstanding that her feeling for the young wife amounted wellnigh to affection. Something in her own individuality seemed to convict Rhoda of crime. Yet a fatality sometimes would direct the steps of the latter to the outskirts of Stickleford whenever she left her house for any other purpose than her daily work; and hence it happened that their next encounter was out of doors. Rhoda could not avoid the subject which had so mystified her, and after the first few words she stammered, 'I hope your – arm is well again, ma'am?' She had perceived with consternation that Gertrude Lodge carried her left arm stiffly.

'No; it is not quite well. Indeed it is no better at all; it is rather worse. It pains me dreadfully sometimes.'

'Perhaps you had better go to a doctor, ma'am.'

She replied that she had already seen a doctor. Her husband had insisted upon her going to one. But the surgeon had not seemed to understand the afflicted limb at all; he had told her to bathe it in hot water, and she had bathed it, but the treatment had done no good.

'Will you let me see it?' said the milkwoman.

Mrs Lodge pushed up her sleeve and disclosed the place, which was a few inches above the wrist. As soon as Rhoda Brook saw it, she could hardly preserve her composure. There was nothing of the nature of a wound, but the arm at that point had a shrivelled look, and the outline of the four fingers appeared more distinct than at the former time. Moreover, they were imprinted in precisely the relative position of her clutch upon the arm in the trance;

the first finger towards Gertrude's wrist, and the fourth towards her elbow.

What the impress resembled seemed to have struck Gertrude herself since their last meeting. 'It looks almost like finger-marks,' she said; adding with a faint laugh, 'my husband says it is as if some witch, or the devil himself, had taken hold of me there, and blasted the flesh.'

Rhoda shivered. 'That's fancy,' she said hurriedly. 'I wouldn't mind it, if I were you.'

'I shouldn't so much mind it,' said the younger, with hesitation, 'if – if I hadn't a notion that it makes my husband – dislike me – no, love me less. Men think so much of personal appearance.'

'Some do – he for one.'

'Yes; and he was very proud of mine, at first.'

'Keep your arm covered from his sight.'

'Ah – he knows the disfigurement is there!' She tried to hide the tears that filled her eyes.

'Well, ma'am, I earnestly hope it will go away soon.'

And so the milkwoman's mind was chained anew to the subject by a horrid sort of spell as she returned home. The sense of having been guilty of an act of malignity increased, affect as she might to ridicule her superstition. In her secret heart Rhoda did not altogether object to a slight diminution of her successor's beauty, by whatever means it had come about; but she did not wish to inflict upon her physical pain. For though this pretty young woman had rendered impossible any reparation which Lodge might have made her for his past conduct, everything like resentment at her unconscious usurpation had quite passed away from the elder's mind.

If the sweet and kindly Gertrude Lodge only knew of the scene in the bed-chamber, what would she think? Not to inform her of it seemed treachery in the presence of her friendliness; but tell she could not of her own accord – neither could she devise a remedy.

She mused upon the matter the greater part of the night; and the next day, after the morning milking, set out to obtain another glimpse of Gertrude Lodge if she could, being held to her by a gruesome fascination. By watching the house from a distance the milkmaid was presently able to discern the farmer's wife in a ride she was taking alone – probably to join her husband in some distant field. Mrs Lodge perceived her, and cantered in her direction.

'Good morning, Rhoda!' she said, when she had come up. 'I was going to call.'

Rhoda noticed that Mrs Lodge held the reins with some difficulty.

'I hope – the bad arm,' said Rhoda.

'They tell me there is possibly one way by which I might be able to find out the cause, and so perhaps the cure, of it,' replied the other anxiously. 'It is by going to some clever man over in Egdon Heath. They did not know if he was still alive – and I cannot remember his name at this moment; but they said that you knew more of his movements than anybody else hereabout, and could tell me if he were still to be consulted. Dear me – what was his name? But you know.'

'Not Conjuror Trendle?' said her thin companion, turning pale.

'Trendle – yes. Is he alive?'

'I believe so,' said Rhoda, more reluctantly.

'Why do you call him conjuror?'

'Well – they say – they used to say he was a – he had powers other folks have not.'

'Oh, how could my people be so superstitious as to recommend a man of that sort! I thought they meant some medical man. I shall think no more of him.'

Rhoda looked relieved, and Mrs Lodge rode on. The milk-woman had inwardly seen, from the moment she heard of her having been mentioned as a reference for this man, that there must exist a sarcastic feeling among the workfolk that a sorceress would know the whereabouts of the exorcist. They suspected her, then. A short time ago this would have given no concern to a woman of her common sense. But she had good reason to be superstitious now; and she had been seized with sudden dread that this Conjuror Trendle might name her as the malignant influence which was blasting the fair person of Gertrude, and so lead her friend to hate her for ever, and to treat her as some fiend in human shape.

But all was not over. Two days after, a shadow intruded into the window-pattern thrown on Rhoda Brook's floor by the afternoon sun. The woman opened the door at once, almost breathlessly.

'Are you alone?' said Gertrude. She seemed to be no less harassed and anxious than Brook herself.

'Yes,' said Rhoda.

'The place on my arm seems worse, and troubles me!' the young farmer's wife went on. 'It is so mysterious! I do hope it will not be a permanent blemish. I have again been thinking of what they said about Conjuror Trendle. I don't really believe in such men, but I should not mind just visiting him, from curiosity – though on no account must my husband know. Is it far to where he lives?'

'Yes – five miles,' said Rhoda, backwardly. 'In the heart of Egdon.'

'Well, I should have to walk. Could not you go with me to show me the way – say tomorrow afternoon?'

'Oh, not I – that is,' the milk-woman murmured, with a start of dismay. Again the dread seized her that something to do with her fierce act in the dream might be revealed, and her character in the eyes of the most useful friend she had ever had be ruined irretrievably.

Mrs Lodge urged, and Rhoda finally assented, though with much misgiving. Sad as the journey would be to her, she could not conscientiously stand in the way of a possible remedy for her patron's strange affliction. It was agreed that, to escape suspicion of their mystic intent, they should meet at the edge of the heath, at the corner of a plantation which was visible from the spot where they now stood.

V. Conjuror Trendle

By the next afternoon, Rhoda would have done anything to escape this inquiry. But she had promised to go. Moreover, there was a horrid fascination at times in becoming instrumental in throwing such possible light on her own character as would reveal her to be something greater in the occult world than she had ever herself suspected.

She started just before the time of day mentioned between them, and half an hour's brisk walking brought her to the south-eastern extension of the Egdon tract of country, where the fir plantation was. A slight figure, cloaked and veiled, was already there. Rhoda recognised, almost with a shudder, that Mrs Lodge bore her left arm in a sling.

They hardly spoke to each other, and immediately set out on their climb into the interior of this solemn country, which stood high above the rich alluvial soil they had left half an hour before. It was a long walk; thick clouds made the atmosphere dark, though it was as yet only early afternoon; and the wind howled dismally over the hills of the heath – not improbably the same heath which had witnessed the agony of the Wessex King Ina, presented to after-ages as Lear. Gertrude Lodge talked most, Rhoda replying with monosyllabic preoccupation. She had a strange dislike to walking on the side of her companion where hung the afflicted arm, moving round to the other when inadvertently near it. Much heather had been brushed by their feet when they descended upon a cart-track, beside which stood the house of the man they sought.

He did not profess his remedial practices openly, or care anything about their continuance, his direct interests being those of a dealer in furze, turf, 'sharp sand' and other local products. Indeed, he affected not to believe largely in his own powers, and when warts that had been shown him for cure miraculously disappeared – which it must be owned they they infallibly did – he would say lightly, 'Oh, I only drink a glass of grog upon 'em – perhaps it's all chance,' and immediately turn the subject.

He was at home when they arrived, having in fact seen them descending into his valley. He was a grey-bearded man, with a reddish face, and he looked singularly at Rhoda the first moment he beheld her. Mrs Lodge told him her errand; and then with words of self-disparagement he examined her arm.

'Medicine can't cure it,' he said, promptly. ''Tis the work of an enemy.'

Rhoda shrank into herself, and drew back.

'An enemy? What enemy?' asked Mrs. Lodge.

He shook his head. 'That's best known to yourself,' he said. 'If you like I can show the person to you, though I shall not myself know who it is. I can do no more; and don't wish to do that.'

She pressed him; on which he told Rhoda to wait outside where she stood, and took Mrs Lodge into the room. It opened immediately from the door; and, as the latter remained ajar, Rhoda Brook could see the proceedings without taking part in them. He brought a tumbler from the dresser, nearly filled it with water, and fetching an egg, prepared it in some private way; after which he broke it on the edge of the glass, so that the white went in and the yolk remained. As it was getting gloomy, he took the glass and its contents to the window, and told Gertrude to watch them closely. They leant over the table together, and the milkwoman could see the opaline hue of the egg fluid changing form as it sank in the water, but she was not near enough to define the shape that it assumed.

'Do you catch the likeness of any face or figure as you look?' demanded the conjuror of the young woman.

She murmured a reply, in tones so low as to be inaudible to Rhoda, and continued to gaze intently into the glass. Rhoda turned, and walked a few steps away.

When Mrs Lodge came out, and her face was met by the light, it appeared exceedingly pale – as pale as Rhoda's – against the sad dun shades of the upland's garniture. Trendle shut the door behind her, and they at once started homeward together. But Rhoda perceived that her companion had quite changed.

'Did he charge much?' she asked, tentatively.

'Oh no – nothing. He would not take a farthing,' said Gertrude.

'And what did you see?' inquired Rhoda.

'Nothing I – care to speak of.' The constraint in her manner was remarkable; her face was so rigid as to wear an oldened aspect, faintly suggestive of the face in Rhoda's bed-chamber.

'Was it you who first proposed coming here?' Mrs Lodge suddenly inquired, after a long pause.

'How very odd, if you did.'

'No. But I am not sorry we have come, all things considered,' she replied. For the first time a sense of triumph possessed her, and she did not altogether deplore that the young thing at her side should learn that their lives had been antagonised by other influences than their own.

The subject was no more alluded to during the long and dreary walk home. But in some way or other a story was whispered about the many-dairied Swenn valley that winter that Mrs Lodge's gradual loss of the use of her left arm was owing to her being 'overlooked' by Rhoda Brook. The latter kept her own counsel about the incubus, but her face grew sadder and thinner; and in the spring she and her boy disappeared from the neighbourhood of Stickleford.

VI. A Second Attempt

Half-a-dozen years passed away, and Mr and Mrs Lodge's married experience sank into prosiness, and worse. The farmer was usually gloomy and silent: the woman whom he had wooed for her grace and beauty was contorted and disfigured in the left limb; moreover, she had brought him no child, which rendered it likely that he would be the last of a family who had occupied that valley for some two hundred years. He thought of Rhoda Brook and her son; and feared this might be a judgment from heaven upon him.

The once blithe-hearted and enlightened Gertrude was changing into an irritable, superstitious woman, whose whole time was given to experimenting upon her ailment with every quack remedy she came across. She was honestly attached to her husband, and was ever secretly hoping against hope to win back his heart again by regaining some at least of her personal beauty. Hence it arose that her closet was lined with bottles, packets, and ointment-pots of every description – nay, bunches of mystic herbs, charms, and books of necromancy, which in her schoolgirl time she would have ridiculed as folly.

'Damned if you won't poison yourself with these apothecary messes and witch mixtures some time or other,' said her husband, when his eye chanced to fall upon the multitudinous array.

She did not reply, but turned her sad soft glance upon him in such heart-swollen reproach that he looked sorry for his words. 'I only meant it for your good, you know, Gertrude,' he added.

'I'll clear out the whole lot, and destroy them,' said she, huskily, 'and attempt such remedies no more!'

'You want somebody to cheer you,' he observed. 'I once thought of adopting a boy; but he is too old now. And he is gone away I don't know where.'

She guessed to whom he alluded; for Rhoda Brook's story had in the course of years become known to her; though not a word had ever passed between her husband and herself on the subject. Neither had she ever spoken to him of her visit to Conjuror Trendle, and of what was revealed to her, or she thought was revealed to her, by that solitary heath-man.

She was now five-and-twenty; but she seemed older. 'Six years of marriage, and only a few months of love,' she sometimes whispered to herself. And then she thought of the apparent cause, and said, with a tragic glance at her withering limb, 'If I could only again be as I was when he first saw me!'

She obediently destroyed her nostrums and charms; but there remained a hankering wish to try something else – some other sort of cure altogether. She had never revisited Trendle since she had been conducted to the house of the solitary by Rhoda against her will; but it now suddenly occurred to Gertrude that she would, in a last desperate effort at deliverance from this seeming curse, again seek out the man, if he yet lived. He was entitled to a certain credence, for the indistinct form he had raised in the glass had undoubtedly resembled the only woman in the world who – as she now knew, though not then – could have a reason for bearing her ill-will. The visit should be paid.

This time she went alone, though she nearly got lost on the heath, and roamed a considerable distance out of her way. Trendle's house was reached at last, however: he was not indoors, and instead of waiting at the cottage she went to where his bent figure was pointed out to her at work a long way off. Trendle remembered her, and laying down the handful of furze-roots which he was gathering and throwing into a heap, he offered to accompany her in her homeward direction, as the distance was considerable and the days were short. So they walked together, his head bowed nearly to the earth, and his form of a colour with it.

'You can send away warts and other excrescences, I know,' she said; 'why can't you send away this?' And the arm was uncovered.

'You think too much of my powers!' said Trendle; 'and I am old and weak now, too. No, no; it is too much for me to attempt in my own person. What have ye tried?'

She named to him some of the hundred medicaments and counter-spells which she had adopted from time to time. He shook his head.

'Some were good enough,' he said, approvingly; 'but not many of them for such as this. This is of the nature of a blight, not of the nature of a wound; and if you ever do throw it off, it will be all at once.'

'If I only could!'

'There is only one chance of doing it known to me. It has never failed in kindred afflictions, – that I can declare. But it is hard to carry out, and especially for a woman.'

'Tell me!' said she.

'You must touch with the limb the neck of a man who's been hanged.'

She started a little at the image he had raised.

'Before he's cold – just after he's cut down,' continued the conjuror, impassively.

'How can that do good?'

'It will turn the blood and change the constitution. But, as I say, to do it is hard. You must get into jail, and wait for him when he's brought off the gallows. Lots have done it, though perhaps not such pretty women as you. I used to send dozens for skin complaints. But that was in former times. The last I sent was in '13 – near twenty years ago.'

He had no more to tell her; and, when he had put her into a straight track homeward, turned and left her, refusing all money as at first.

VII. A Ride

The communication sank deep into Gertrude's mind. Her nature was rather a timid one; and probably of all remedies that the white wizard could have suggested there was not one which would have filled her with so much aversion as this, not to speak of the immense obstacles in the way of its adoption.

Casterbridge, the county-town, was a dozen or fifteen miles off; and though in those days, when men were executed for horse-stealing, arson, and burglary, an assize seldom passed without a hanging, it was not likely that she could get access to the body of the criminal unaided. And the fear of her husband's anger made her reluctant to breathe a word of Trendle's suggestion to him or to anybody about him.

She did nothing for months, and patiently bore her disfigurement as before. But her woman's nature, craving for renewed love, through the medium of renewed beauty (she was but twenty-five), was ever stimulating her to try what, at any rate, could hardly do her any harm. 'What came by a spell will go by a spell surely,' she would say. Whenever her imagination pictured the act she shrank in terror from the possibility of it: then the words of the conjuror, 'It will turn your blood,' were seen to be capable of a scientific no less than a ghastly interpretation; the mastering desire returned, and urged her on again.

There was at this time but one county paper, and that her husband only occasionally borrowed. But old-fashioned days had old-fashioned means, and news was extensively conveyed by word of mouth from market to market or from fair to fair; so that, whenever such an event as an execution was about to take place, few within a radius of twenty miles were ignorant of the coming sight; and, so far as Stickleford was concerned, some enthusiasts had been known to walk all the way to Casterbridge and back in one day, solely to witness the spectacle. The next assizes were in March; and when Gertrude Lodge heard that they had been held, she inquired stealthily at the inn as to the result, as soon as she could find opportunity.

She was, however, too late. The time at which the sentences were to be carried out had arrived, and to make the journey and obtain admission at such short notice required at least her husband's assistance. She dared not tell him, for she had found by delicate experiment that these smouldering village beliefs made him furious if mentioned, partly because he half entertained them himself. It was therefore necessary to wait for another opportunity.

Her determination received a fillip from learning that two epileptic children had attended from this very village of Stickleford many years before with beneficial results, though the experiment had been strongly condemned by the neighbouring clergy. April, May, June passed; and it is no overstatement to say that by the end of the last-named month Gertrude wellnigh longed for the death of a fellow-creature. This time she made earlier inquiries, and was altogether more systematic in her proceedings. Moreover, the season was summer, between the haymaking and the harvest, and in the leisure thus afforded her husband had been holiday-taking away from home.

The assizes were in July, and she went to the inn as before. There was to be one execution – only one, for arson.

Her greatest problem was not how to get to Casterbridge, but what means she should adopt for obtaining admission to the jail. Though access for such purposes had formerly never been denied, the custom had fallen into desuetude; and in contemplating her possible difficulties, she was again almost driven to fall back upon her husband. But, on sounding him about the assizes, he was so uncommunicative, so more than usually cold, that she did not proceed, and decided that whatever she did she would do alone.

Fortune, obdurate hitherto, showed her unexpected favour. On the Thursday before the Saturday fixed for the execution, Lodge remarked to her that he was going away from home for another day or two on business at a fair, and that he was sorry he could not take her with him.

She exhibited on this occasion so much readiness to stay at home that he looked at her in surprise. Time had been when she would have shown deep disappointment at the loss of such a jaunt. However, he lapsed into his usual taciturnity, and on the day named left Stickleford.

It was now her turn. She at first had thought of driving, but on reflection held that driving would not do, since it would necessitate her keeping to the turnpike-road, and so increase by tenfold the risk of her ghastly errand being found out. She decided to ride, and avoid the beaten track, notwithstanding that in her husband's stables there was no animal just at present which by any stretch of imagination could be considered a lady's mount, in spite of his promise before marriage to always keep a mare for her. He had, however, many horses, fine ones of their kind; and among the rest was a serviceable creature, an equine Amazon, with a back as broad as a sofa, on which Gertrude had occasionally taken an airing when unwell. This horse she chose.

On Friday afternoon one of the men brought it round. She was dressed, and before going down looked at her shrivelled arm. 'Ah!' she said to it, 'if it had not been for you this terrible ordeal would have been saved me!'

When strapping up the bundle in which she carried a few articles of clothing, she took occasion to say to the servant, 'I take these in case I should not get back tonight from the person I am going to visit. Don't be alarmed if I am not in by ten, and close up the house as usual. I shall be at home tomorrow for certain.' She meant then to privately tell her husband: the deed accomplished was not like the deed projected. He would almost certainly forgive her.

And then the pretty palpitating Gertrude Lodge went from her husband's homestead in a course directly the opposite of that towards Casterbridge. As soon as she was out of sight she took the first turning to the left, which led into Egdon, and on entering the heath wheeled round, and set out in a course due westerly. A more private way down the county could not be imagined; and as to direction, she had merely to keep her horse's head to a point a little to the right of the sun. She knew that she would light upon a furze-cutter or cottager of some sort from time to time, from whom she might correct her course.

Though the date was comparatively recent, Egdon was much less fragmentary in character than now. The attempts – successful and otherwise – at cultivation on the lower slopes, which intrude and break up the original heath into small detached heaths, had not been carried far: Enclosure Acts had not taken effect, and the banks and fences which now exclude the cattle of those villagers who formerly enjoyed rights of commonage thereon, and the carts of those who had turbary privileges which kept them in firing all the year round, were not erected. Gertrude therefore rode along with no other obstacles than the prickly furze-bushes, the mats of heather, the white water-courses, and the natural steeps and declivities of the ground.

Her horse was sure, if heavy-footed and slow, and though a draught animal, was easy-paced; had it been otherwise, she was not a woman who could have ventured to ride over such a bit of country with a half-dead arm. It was therefore nearly eight o'clock when she drew rein to breathe the mare on the last outlying high point of heath-land towards Casterbridge, previous to leaving Egdon for the cultivated valleys.

She halted before a pond, flanked by the ends of two hedges; a railing ran through the centre of the pond, dividing it in half. Over the railing she saw the low green country; over the green trees the roofs of the town; over the roofs a white flat façade, denoting the entrance to the county jail. On the roof of this front specks were moving about; they seemed to be workmen erecting something. Her flesh crept. She descended slowly, and was soon amid cornfields and pastures. In another half-hour, when it was almost dusk, Gertrude reached the White Hart, the first inn of the town on that side.

Little surprise was excited by her arrival: farmers' wives rode on horseback then more than they do now; though for that matter, Mrs Lodge was not imagined to be a wife at all; the innkeeper supposed her some harum-scarum young woman who had come to attend 'hang-fair' next day. Neither her husband nor herself ever dealt in Casterbridge market, so that she was unknown. While dismounting she beheld a crowd of boys standing at the door of a harness-maker's shop just above the inn, looking inside it with deep interest.

'What is going on there?' she asked of the ostler.

'Making the rope for tomorrow.'

She throbbed responsively, and contracted her arm.

''Tis sold by the inch afterwards,' the man continued. 'I could get ye a bit, miss, for nothing, if you'd like?'

She hastily repudiated any such wish, all the more from a curious creeping feeling that the condemned wretch's destiny was becoming interwoven with her own; and having engaged a room for the night, sat down to think.

Up to this time she had formed but the vaguest notions about her means of obtaining access to the prison. The words of the cunning-man returned to her mind. He had implied that she should use her beauty, impaired though it was, as a pass-key. In her inexperience she knew little about jail functionaries; she had heard of a high sheriff and an under-sheriff, but dimly only. She knew, however, that there must be a hangman, and to the hangman she determined to apply.

VIII. A Water-side Hermit

At this date, and for several years after, there was a hangman to almost every jail. Gertrude found, on inquiry, that the Casterbridge official dwelt in a lonely cottage by a deep slow river flowing under the cliff on which the prison buildings were situate – the stream being the self-same one, though she did not know it, which watered the Stickleford meads lower down in its course.

Having changed her dress, and before she had eaten or drunk – for she could not take her ease till she had ascertained some particulars – Gertrude pursued her way by a path along the water-side to the cottage indicated. Passing thus the outskirts of the jail, she discerned on the level roof over the gateway three rectangular lines against the sky, where the specks had been moving in her distant view; she recognised what the erection was, and passed quickly on. Another hundred yards brought her to the executioner's house, which a boy pointed out. It stood close to the same stream, and was hard by a weir, the waters of which emitted a steady roar.

While she stood hesitating the door opened, and an old man came forth shading a candle with one hand. Locking the door on the outside, he turned to a flight of wooden steps fixed against the end of the cottage, and began to ascend them, this being evidently the staircase to his bedroom. Gertrude hastened forward, but by the time she reached the foot of the ladder he was at the top. She called to him loudly enough to be heard above the roar of the weir; he looked down and said, 'What d'ye want here?'

'To speak to you a minute.'

The candle-light, such as it was, fell upon her imploring, pale, upturned face, and Davies (as the hangman was called) backed down the ladder. 'I was just going to bed,' he said; '"Early to bed and early to rise," but I don't mind stopping a minute for such a one as you. Come into house.' He reopened the door, and preceded her to the room within.

The implements of his daily work, which was that of a jobbing gardener, stood in a corner, and seeing probably that she looked rural, he said, 'If you want me to undertake country work I can't come, for I never leave Casterbridge for gentle nor simple – not I. Though sometimes I make others leave,' he added slyly.

'Yes, yes! That's it! Tomorrow!'

'Ah! I thought so. Well, what's the matter about that? 'Tis no use to come here about the knot – folks do come continually, but I tell 'em one knot is as merciful as another if ye keep it under the ear. Is the unfortunate man a relation; or, I should say, perhaps' (looking at her dress) 'a person who's been in your employ?'

'No. What time is the execution?'

'The same as usual – twelve o'clock, or as soon after as the London mail-coach gets in. We always wait for that, in case of a reprieve.'

'Oh – a reprieve – I hope not!' she said involuntarily.

'Well, – he, he! – as a matter of business, so do I! But still, if ever a young fellow deserved to be let off, this one does; only just turned eighteen, and only present by chance when the rick was fired. Howsomever, there's not much risk of it, as they are obliged to make an example of him, there having been so much destruction of property that way lately.'

'I mean,' she explained, 'that I want to touch him for a charm, a cure of an affliction, by the advice of a man who has proved the virtue of the remedy.'

'Oh yes, miss! Now I understand. I've had such people come in past years. But it didn't strike me that you looked of a sort to require blood-turning. What's the complaint? The wrong kind for this, I'll be bound.'

'My arm.' She reluctantly showed the withered skin.

'Ah! – 'tis all a-scram!' said the hangman, examining it.

'Yes,' said she.

'Well,' he continued with interest, 'that *is* the class o' subject, I'm bound to admit. I like the look of the place; it is truly as suitable for the cure as any I ever saw. 'Twas a knowing man that sent 'ee, whoever he was.'

'You can contrive for me all that's necessary?' she said, breathlessly.

'You should really have gone to the governor of the jail, and your doctor with 'ee, and given your name and address – that's how it used to be done, if I recollect. Still, perhaps, I can manage it for a trifling fee.'

'Oh, thank you! I would rather do it this way, as I should like it kept private.'

'Lover not to know, eh?'

'No – husband.'

'Aha! Very well. I'll get 'ee a touch of the corpse.'

'Where is it now?' she said, shuddering.

'It? – *he*, you mean; he's living yet. Just inside that little small winder up there in the glum.' He signified the jail on the cliff above.

She thought of her husband and her friends. 'Yes,' of course, she said; 'and how am I to proceed?'

He took her to the door. 'Now, do you be waiting at the little wicket in the wall, that you'll find up there in the lane, not later than one o'clock. I will open it from the inside, as I shan't come home to dinner till he's took down. Good night. Be punctual; and if you don't want anybody to know 'ee, wear a veil. Ah – once I had such a daughter as you!'

She went away, and climbed the path above, to assure herself that she would be able to find the wicket next day. Its outline was soon visible to her – a narrow opening in the outer wall of the prison-yard. The steep was so great that, having reached the wicket, she stopped a moment to breathe; and looking back upon the water-side cot, saw the hangman again ascending his outdoor staircase. He entered the loft or chamber to which it led, and in a few minutes extinguished his light.

The town clock struck ten, and she returned to the White Hart as she had come.

IX. A Recounter

It was one o'clock on Saturday. Gertrude Lodge, having been admitted to the jail as above described, was sitting in a waiting-room within the second gate, which stood under a classic archway of ashlar, then comparatively modern, and bearing the inscription, 'COVNTY GAOL: 1793.' This had been the facade she saw from the heath the day before. Near at hand was a passage to the roof on which the gallows stood.

The town was thronged, and the market suspended; but Gertrude had seen scarcely a soul. Having kept her room till the hour of the appointment, she had proceeded to the spot by a way which avoided the open space below the cliff where the spectators had gathered; but she could, even now, hear the multitudinous babble of their voices, out of which rose at intervals the hoarse croak of a single voice, uttering the words, 'Last dying speech and confession!' There had been no reprieve, and the execution was over; but the crowd still waited to see the body taken down.

Soon the persistent girl heard a trampling overhead, then a hand beckoned to her, and, following directions, she went out and crossed the inner paved court beyond the gatehouse, her knees trembling so that she could scarcely walk. One of her arms was out of its sleeve, and only covered by her shawl.

On the spot to which she had now arrived were two trestles, and before she could think of their purpose she heard heavy feet descending stairs somewhere at her back. Turn her head she would not, or could not, and, rigid in this position, she was conscious of a rough coffin passing her shoulder, borne by four men. It was open, and in it lay the body of a young man, wearing the smockfrock of a rustic, and fustian breeches. It had been thrown into the coffin so hastily that the skirt of the smockfrock was hanging over. The burden was temporarily deposited on the trestles.

By this time the young woman's state was such that a grey mist seemed to float before her eyes, on account of which, and the veil she wore, she could scarcely discern anything: it was as though she had half-fainted and could not finish.

'Now,' said a voice close at hand, and she was just conscious that it had been addressed to her.

By a last strenuous effort she advanced, at the same time hearing persons approaching behind her. She bared her poor curst arm; and Davies, taking her hand, held it so that the arm lay across the dead man's neck, upon a line the colour of an unripe blackberry, which surrounded it.

Gertrude shrieked: 'the turn o' the blood,' predicted by the conjuror, had taken place. But at that moment a second shriek rent the air of the enclosure: it was not Gertrude's, and its effect upon her was to make her start round.

Immediately behind her stood Rhoda Brook, her face drawn, and her eyes red with weeping. Behind Rhoda stood her own husband; his countenance lined, his eyes dim, but without a tear.

'D–n you! what are you doing here?' he said, hoarsely.

'Hussy – to come between us and our child now!' cried Rhoda. 'This is the meaning of what Satan showed me in the vision! You are like her at last!' And clutching the bare arm of the younger woman, she pulled her unresistingly back against the wall. Immediately Brook had loosened her hold the fragile young Gertrude slid down against the feet of her husband. When he lifted her up she was unconscious.

The mere sight of the twain had been enough to suggest to her that the dead young man was Rhoda's son. At that time the relatives of an executed convict had the privilege of claiming the body for burial, if they chose to do so; and it was for this purpose that Lodge was awaiting the inquest with Rhoda. He had been summoned by her as soon as the young man was taken in the crime, and at different times since; and he had attended in court during the trial. This was the 'holiday' he had been indulging in of late. The two wretched parents had wished to avoid exposure; and hence had come themselves for the body, a waggon and sheet for its conveyance and covering being in waiting outside.

Gertrude's case was so serious that it was deemed advisable to call to her the surgeon who was at hand. She was taken out of the jail into the town; but she never reached home alive. Her delicate vitality, sapped perhaps by the paralysed arm, collapsed under the double shock that followed the severe strain, physical and mental, to which she had subjected herself during the previous twenty-four hours. Her blood had been 'turned' indeed – too far. Her death took place in the town three days after.

Her husband was never seen in Casterbridge again; once only in the old market-place at Anglebury, which he had so much frequented, and very seldom in public anywhere. Burdened at first with moodiness and remorse, he eventually changed for the better, and appeared as a chastened and serious-minded man. Soon after attending the funeral of his poor young wife, he took steps towards giving up the farms in Stickleford and the adjoining parish, and, having sold every head of his stock, he went away to Port-Bredy, at the other end of the county, living there in solitary lodgings till his death two years later of a painless decline. It was then found that he had bequeathed the whole of his not inconsiderable property to a reformatory for boys, subject to the payment of a small annuity to Rhoda Brook, if she could be found to claim it.

For some time she could not be found; but eventually she reappeared in her old parish, – absolutely refusing, however, to have anything to do with the provision made for her. Her monotonous milking at the dairy was resumed, and followed for many long years, till her form became bent, and her once abundant dark hair white and worn away at the forehead – perhaps by long pressure against the cows. Here, sometimes, those who knew her experiences would stand and observe her, and wonder what sombre thoughts were beating inside that impassive, wrinkled brow, to the rhythm of the alternating milk-streams.

Barbara of the House of Grebe

This next short story may well be the most controversial that Thomas Hardy ever wrote – certainly it was attacked fiercely by a number of critics, the reviewer of *The Spectator*, for example, declaring it to be 'as unnatural as it is disgusting.' T.S. Eliot shared this opinion, writing some years later that it portrayed 'a world of pure Evil' and must have been written 'solely to provide a satisfaction for some morbid emotion.' There is certainly much that is grim about Barbara's story and her revulsion towards her once handsome husband when he returns from Venice hideously disfigured after trying to rescue some people from a fire, but the tale is also firmly based in the Gothic tradition and demonstrates that by the year 1890 when it was published – in the December issue of *The Graphic* – Hardy had become an undisputed master of macabre fiction.

Interestingly, the story was based on a real person, the heiress Barbara Webb, who married the fifth Earl of Shaftesbury in 1786 – although there was little in her family history as terrible as that which befalls the unfortunate Barbara. Her fate and that of her husband and what occurs to her cynical and ruthless suitor are all from Hardy's fertile imagination. In fact, the story was one of a group of ten each dealing with dark family secrets which Hardy wrote about this time and eventually published under the title *A Group of Noble Dames* in 1891. The stories are all told by different narrators and related to an imaginary body known as the Wessex Field and Antiquarian Club. The story of 'Barbara of the House of Grebe' is recounted impassively but with considerable effect by 'The Old Surgeon', a man clearly well versed in the darker side of human nature . . .

Barbara of the House of Grebe

It was apparently an idea, rather than a passion, that inspired Lord Uplandtowers' resolve to win her. Nobody ever knew when he formed it, or whence he got his assurance of success in the face of her manifest dislike of him. Possibly not until after that first important act of her life which I shall presently mention. His matured and cynical doggedness at the age of nineteen, when impulse mostly rules calculation, was remarkable, and might have owed its existence as much to his succession to the earldom and its accompanying local honours in childhood, as to the family character; an elevation which jerked him into maturity, so to speak, without his having known adolescence. He had only reached his twelfth year when his father, the fourth Earl, died, after a course of the Bath waters.

Nevertheless, the family character had a great deal to do with it. Determination was hereditary in the bearers of that escutcheon; sometimes for good, sometimes for evil.

The seats of the two families were about ten miles apart, the way between them lying along the now old, then new, turnpike-road connecting Havenpool and Warborne with the city of Melchester: a road which, though only a branch from what was known as the Great Western Highway, is probably, even at present, as it has been for the last hundred years, one of the finest examples of a macadamized turnpike-track that can be found in England.

The mansion of the Earl, as well as that of his neighbour, Barbara's father, stood back about a mile from the highway, with which each was connected by an ordinary drive and lodge. It was along this particular highway that the young Earl drcve on a certain evening at Christmastide some twenty years before the end of the last century, to attend a ball at Chene Manor, the home of Barbara, and her parents Sir John and Lady Grebe. Sir John's was a baronetcy created a few years before the breaking out of the Civil War, and his lands were even more extensive than those of Lord Uplandtowers himself, comprising this Manor of Chene, another on the coast near, half the Hundred of Cockdene, and well-enclosed lands in several other parishes, notably Warborne and those contiguous. At this time Barbara was barely seventeen, and the ball is the first occasion on which we have any tradition of Lord Uplandtowers attempting tender relations with her; it was early enough, God knows.

An intimate friend – one of the Drenkhards – is said to have dined with him that day, and Lord Uplandtowers had, for a wonder, communicated to his guest the secret design of his heart.

'You'll never get her – sure; you'll never get her!' this friend had said at parting. 'She's not drawn to your lordship by love: and as for thought of a good match, why, there's no more calculation in her than in a bird.'

'We'll see,' said Lord Uplandtowers impassively.

He no doubt thought of his friend's forecast as he travelled along the highway in his chariot; but the sculptural repose of his profile against the vanishing daylight on his right hand would have shown his friend that the Earl's equanimity was undisturbed. He reached the solitary wayside tavern called Lornton Inn – the rendezvous of many a daring poacher for operations in the adjoining forest; and he might have observed, if he had taken the trouble, a strange post-chaise standing in the halting-space before the inn. He duly sped past it, and half-an-hour after through the little town of Warborne. Onward, a mile farther, was the house of his entertainer.

At this date it was an imposing edifice – or, rather, congeries of edifices – as extensive as the residence of the Earl himself, though far less regular. One wing showed extreme antiquity, having huge chimneys, whose substructures projected from the external walls like towers; and a kitchen of vast dimensions, in which (it was said) breakfasts had been cooked for John of Gaunt. Whilst he was yet in the forecourt he could hear the rhythm of French horns and clarionets, the favourite instruments of those days at such entertainments.

Entering the long parlour, in which the dance had just been opened by Lady Grebe with a minuet – it being now seven o'clock, according to the tradition – he was received with a welcome befitting his rank, and looked round for Barbara. She was not dancing, and seemed to be preoccupied – almost, indeed, as though she had been waiting for him. Barbara at this time was a good and pretty girl, who never spoke ill of any one, and hated other pretty women the very least possible. She did not refuse him for the country-dance which followed, and soon after was his partner in a second.

The evening wore on, and the horns and clarionets tootled merrily. Barbara evinced towards her lover neither distinct preference nor aversion; but old eyes would have seen that she pondered something. However, after supper she pleaded a headache, and disappeared. To pass the time of her absence, Lord Uplandtowers went into a little room adjoining the long gallery, where some elderly ones were sitting by the fire – for he had a phlegmatic dislike of dancing for its own sake, – and, lifting the window-curtains, he looked out of the window into the park and wood, dark now as a cavern. Some of the guests appeared to be leaving even so soon as this, two lights showing themselves as turning away from the door and sinking to nothing in the distance.

His hostess put her head into the room to look for partners for the ladies, and Lord Uplandtowers came out. Lady Grebe informed him that Barbara had not returned to the ball-room: she had gone to bed in sheer necessity.

'She has been so excited over the ball all day,' her mother continued, 'that I feared she would be worn out early. . . . But sure, Lord Uplandtowers, you won't be leaving yet?'

He said that it was near twelve o'clock, and that some had already left.

'I protest nobody has gone yet,' said Lady Grebe.

To humour her he stayed till midnight, and then set out. He had made no progress in his suit; but he had assured himself that Barbara gave no other guest the preference, and nearly everybody in the neighbourhood was there.

''Tis only a matter of time,' said the calm young philosopher.

The next morning he lay till near ten o'clock, and he had only just come out upon the head of the staircase when he heard hoofs upon the gravel without; in a few moments the door had been opened, and Sir John Grebe met him in the hall, as he set foot on the lowest stair.

'My lord – where's Barbara – my daughter?'

Even the Earl of Uplandtowers could not repress amazement. 'What's the matter, my dear Sir John,' says he.

The news was startling, indeed. From the Baronet's disjointed explanation Lord Uplandtowers gathered that after his own and the other guests' departure Sir John and Lady Grebe had gone to rest without seeing any more of Barbara; it being understood by them that she had retired to bed when she sent word to say that she could not join the dancers again. Before then she had told her maid that she would dispense with her services for this night; and there was evidence to show that the young lady had never lain down at all, the bed remaining unpressed. Circumstances seemed to prove that the deceitful girl had feigned indisposition to get an excuse for leaving the ball-room, and that she had left the house within ten minutes, presumably during the first dance after supper.

'I saw her go,' said Lord Uplandtowers.

'The devil you did!' says Sir John.

'Yes.' And he mentioned the retreating carriagelights,and how he was assured by Lady Grebe that no guest had departed.

'Surely that was it!' said the father. 'But she's not gone alone, d'ye know!'

'Ah – who is the young man?'

'I can on'y guess. My worst fear is my most likely guess. I'll say no more. I thought – yet I would not believe – it possible that you was the sinner. Would that you had been! But 'tis t'other, 'tis t'other, by G—! I must e'en up, and after 'em!'

'Whom do you suspect?'

Sir John would not give a name, and, stultified rather than agitated, Lord Uplandtowers accompanied him back to Chene. He again asked upon whom were the Baronet's suspicions directed; and the impulsive Sir John was no match for the insistence of Uplandtowers.

He said at length, 'I fear 'tis Edmond Willowes.'

'Who's he?'

'A young fellow of Shottsford-Forum – a widow-woman's son,' the other told him, and explained that Willowes's father, or grandfather, was the last of the old glass-painters in that place, where (as you may know) the art lingered on when it had died out in every other part of England.

'By G— that's bad – mighty bad!' said Lord Uplandtowers, throwing himself back in the chaise in frigid despair.

They dispatched emissaries in all directions; one by the Melchester Road, another by Shottsford-Forum, another coastwards.

But the lovers had a ten-hours' start; and it was apparent that sound judgment had been exercised in choosing as their time of flight the particular night when the movements of a strange carriage would not be noticed, either in the park or on the neighbouring highway, owing to the general press of vehicles. The chaise which had been seen waiting at Lornton Inn was, no doubt, the one they had escaped in; and the pair of heads which had planned so cleverly thus far had probably contrived marriage ere now.

The fears of her parents were realized. A letter sent by special messenger from Barbara, on the evening of that day, briefly informed them that her lover and herself were on the way to London, and before this communication reached her home they would be united as husband and wife. She had taken this extreme step because she loved her dear Edmond as she could love no other man, and because she had seen closing round her the doom of marriage with Lord Uplandtowers, unless she put that threatened fate out of possibility by doing as she had done. She had well considered the step beforehand, and was prepared to live like any other country-townsman's wife if her father repudiated her for her action.

'D— her!' said Lord Uplandtowers, as he drove homeward that night. 'D— her for a fool!' – which shows the kind of love he bore her.

Well; Sir John had already started in pursuit of them as a matter of duty, driving like a wild man to Melchester, and thence by the direct highway to the capital. But he soon saw that he was acting to no purpose; and by and by, discovering that the marriage had actually taken place, he forebore all attempts to unearth them in the City, and returned and sat down with his lady to digest the event as best they could.

To proceed against this Willowes for the abduction of our heiress was, possibly, in their power; yet, when they considered the now unalterable facts, they refrained from violent retribution. Some six weeks passed, during which time Barbara's parents, though they keenly felt her loss, held no communication with the truant, either for reproach or condonation. They continued to think of the disgrace she had brought upon herself; for, though the young man was an honest fellow, and the son of an honest father, the latter had died so early, and his widow had had such struggles to maintain herself, that the son was very imperfectly educated. Moreover, his blood was, as far as they knew, of no distinction whatever, whilst hers, through her mother, was compounded of the best juices of ancient baronial distillation, containing tinctures of Maundeville, and Mohun, and Syward, and Peverell, and Culliford, and Talbot, and Plantagenet, and York, and Lancaster, and God knows what besides, which it was a thousand pities to throw away.

The father and mother sat by the fireplace that was spanned by the four-centred arch bearing the family shields on its haunches, and groaned aloud – the lady more than Sir John.

'To think this should have come upon us in our old age!' said he.

'Speak for yourself!' she snapped through her sobs.

'I am only one-and-forty! . . . Why didn't ye ride faster and overtake 'em!'

In the meantime the young married lovers, caring no more about their blood than about ditch-water, were intensely happy – happy, that is, in the descending scale which, as we all know, Heaven in its wisdom has ordained for such rash cases; that is to say, the first week they were in the seventh heaven, the second in the sixth, the third week temperate, the fourth reflective, and so on; a lover's heart after possession being comparable to the earth in its geologic stages, as described to us sometimes by our worthy President; first a hot coal, then a warm one, then a cooling cinder, then chilly – the simile shall be pursued no further. The long and the short of it was that one day a letter, sealed with their daughter's own little seal, came into Sir John and Lady Grebe's hands; and, on opening it, they found it to contain an appeal from the young couple to Sir John to forgive them for what they had done, and they would fall on their naked knees and be most dutiful children for evermore.

Then Sir John and his lady sat down again by the fireplace with the four-centred arch, and consulted, and re-read the letter. Sir John Grebe, if the truth must be told, loved his daughter's happiness far more, poor man, than he loved his name and lineage; he recalled to his mind all her little ways, gave vent to a sigh; and, by this time acclimatized to the idea of the marriage, said that what was done could not be undone, and that he supposed they must not be too harsh with her. Perhaps Barbara and her husband were in actual need; and how could they let their only child starve?

A slight consolation had come to them in an unexpected manner. They had been credibly informed that an ancestor of plebeian Willowes was once honoured with intermarriage with a scion of the aristocracy who had gone to the dogs. In short, such is the foolishness of distinguished parents, and sometimes of others also, that they wrote that very day to the address Barbara had given them, informing her that she might return home and bring her husband with her; they would not object to see him, would not reproach her, and would endeavour to welcome both, and to discuss with them what could best be arranged for their future.

In three or four days a rather shabby post-chaise drew up at the door of Chene Manor-house, at sound of which the tender-hearted baronet and his wife ran out as if to welcome a prince and princess of the blood. They were overjoyed to see their spoilt child return safe and sound – though she was only Mrs Willowes, wife of Edmond Willowes of nowhere. Barbara burst into penitential tears, and both husband and wife were contrite enough, as well they might be, considering that they had not a guinea to call their own.

When the four had calmed themselves, and not a word of chiding had been uttered to the pair, they discussed the position soberly, young Willowes sitting in the background with great modesty till invited forward by Lady Grebe in no frigid tone.

'How handsome he is!' she said to herself. 'I don't wonder at Barbara's craze for him.'

He was, indeed, one of the handsomest men who ever set his lips on a maid's. A blue coat, murrey waistcoat, and breeches of drab set off a figure that could scarcely be surpassed. He had large dark eyes, anxious now, as they glanced from Barbara to her parents and tenderly back again to her; observing whom, even now in her trepidation, one could see why the *sang froid* of Lord Uplandtowers had been raised to more than lukewarmness. Her fair young face (according to the tale handed down by old women) looked out from under a gray conical hat, trimmed with white ostrich-feathers, and her little toes peeped from a buff petticoat worn under a puce gown. Her features were not regular: they were almost infantine, as you may see from miniatures in possession of the family, her mouth showing much sensitiveness, and one could be sure that her faults would not lie on the side of bad temper unless for urgent reasons.

Well, they discussed their state as became them, and the desire of the young couple to gain the goodwill of those upon whom they were literally dependent for everything induced them to agree to any temporizing measure that was not too irksome. Therefore, having been nearly two months united, they did not oppose Sir John's proposal that he should furnish Edmond Willowes with funds sufficient for him to travel a year on the Continent in the company of a tutor, the young man undertaking to lend himself with the utmost diligence to the tutor's instructions, till he became polished outwardly and inwardly to the degree required in the husband of such a lady as Barbara. He was to apply himself to the study of languages, manners, history, society, ruins, and everything else that came under his eyes, till he should return to take his place without blushing by Barbara's side.

'And by that time,' said worthy Sir John, 'I'll get my little place out at Yewsholt ready for you and Barbara to occupy on your return. The house is small and out of the way; but it will do for a young couple for a while.'

'If 'twere no bigger than a summer-house it would do!' says Barbara.

'If 'twere no bigger than a sedan-chair!' says Willowes. 'And the more lonely the better.'

'We can put up with the loneliness,' said Barbara, with less zest. 'Some friends will come, no doubt.'

All this being laid down, a travelled tutor was called in – a man of many gifts and great experience, – and on a fine morning away tutor and pupil went. A great reason urged against Barbara accompanying her youthful husband was that his attentions to her would naturally be such as to prevent his zealously applying every hour of his time to learning and seeing – an argument of wise prescience, and unanswerable. Regular days for letterwriting were fixed, Barbara and her Edmond exchanged their last kisses at the door, and the chaise swept under the archway into the drive.

He wrote to her from Le Havre, as soon as he reached that port, which was not for seven days, on account of adverse winds; he wrote from Rouen, and from Paris; described to her his sight of the King and Court at Versailles, and the wonderful marble work and mirrors in that palace; wrote next from Lyons; then, after a comparatively long interval, from Turin, narrating his fearful adventures in crossing Mont Cenis on mules, and how he was overtaken with a terrific snowstorm, which had well-nigh been the end of him, and his tutor, and his guides. Then he wrote glowingly of Italy; and Barbara could see the development of her husband's mind reflected in his letters month by month; and she much admired the forethought of her father in suggesting this education for Edmond. Yet she sighed sometimes – her husband being no longer in evidence to fortify her in her choice of him – and timidly dreaded what mortifications might be in store for her by reason of this *mésalliance*. She went out very little; for on the one or two occasions on which she had shown herself to former friends she noticed a distinct difference in their manner, as though they should say, 'Ah, my happy swain's wife; you're caught!'

Edmond's letters were as affectionate as ever; even more affectionate, after a while, than hers were to him. Barbara observed this growing coolness in herself; and like a good and honest lady was horrified and grieved, since her only wish was to act faithfully and uprightly. It troubled her so much that she prayed for a warmer heart, and at last wrote to her husband to beg him, now that he was in the land of Art, to send her his portrait, ever so small, that she might look at it all day and every day, and never for a moment forget his features.

Willowes was nothing loth, and replied that he would do more than she wished: he had made friends with a sculptor in Pisa, who was much interested in him and his history; and he had commissioned this artist to make a bust of himself in marble, which when finished he would send her. What Barbara had wanted was something immediate; but she expressed no objection to the delay; and in his next communication Edmond told her that the sculptor, of his own choice, had decided to increase the bust to a full-length statue, so anxious was he to get a specimen of his skill introduced to the notice of the English aristocracy. It was progressing well, and rapidly.

Meanwhile, Barbara's attention began to be occupied at home with Yewsholt Lodge, the house that her kindhearted father was preparing for her residence when her husband returned. It was a small place on the plan of a large one – a cottage built in the form of a mansion, having a central hall with a wooden gallery running round it, and rooms no bigger than closets to follow this introduction. It stood on a slope so solitary, and surrounded by trees so dense, that the birds who inhabited the boughs sang at strange hours, as if they hardly could distinguish night from day.

During the progress of repairs at this bower Barbara frequently visited it. Though so secluded by the dense growth, it was near the high road, and one day while looking over the fence she saw Lord Uplandtowers riding past. He saluted her courteously, yet with mechanical stiffness, and did not halt. Barbara went home, and continued to pray that she might never cease to love her husband. After that she sickened, and did not come out of doors again for a long time.

The year of education had extended to fourteen months, and the house was in order for Edmond's return to take up his abode there with Barbara, when, instead of the accustomed letter for her, came on to Sir John Grebe in the handwriting of the said tutor, informing him of a terrible catastrophe that had occurred to them at Venice. Mr Willowes and himself had attended the theatre one night during the Carnival of the preceding week, to witness the Italian comedy, when, owing to the carelessness of one of the candle-snuffers, the theatre had caught fire, and been burnt to the ground. Few persons had lost their lives, owing to the superhuman exertions of some of the audience in getting out the senseless sufferers; and, among them all, he who had risked his own life the most heroically was Mr Willowes. In re-entering for the fifth time to save his fellow-creatures some fiery beams had fallen upon him, and he had been given up for lost. He was, however, by the blessing of Providence, recovered, with the life still in him, though he was fearfully burnt; and by almost a miracle he seemed likely to survive, his constitution being wondrously sound. He was, of course, unable to write, but he was receiving the attention of several skilful surgeons. Further report would be made by the next mail or by private hand.

The tutor said nothing in detail of poor Willowes's sufferings, but as soon as the news was broken to Barbara she realized how intense they must have been, and her immediate instinct was to rush to his side, though, on consideration, the journey seemed impossible to her. Her health was by no means what it had been, and to post across Europe at that season of the year, or to traverse the Bay of Biscay in a sailing-craft, was an undertaking that would hardly be justified by the result. But she was anxious to go till, on reading to the end of the letter, her husband's tutor was found to hint very strongly against such a step if it should be contemplated, this being also the opinion of the surgeons. And though Willowes's comrade refrained from giving his reasons, they disclosed themselves plainly enough in the sequel.

The truth was that the worst of the wounds resulting from the fire had occurred to his head and face – that handsome face which had won her heart from her, – and both the tutor and the surgeons knew that for a sensitive young woman to see him before his wounds had healed would cause more misery to her by the shock than happiness to him by her ministrations.

Lady Grebe blurted out what Sir John and Barbara had thought, but had had too much delicacy to express.

'Sure, 'tis mighty hard for you, poor Barbara, that the one little gift he had to justify your rash choice of him – his wonderful good looks – should be taken away like this, to leave 'ee no excuse at all for your conduct in the world's eyes. . . . Well, I wish you'd married t'other – that do I!' And the lady sighed.

'He'll soon get right again,' said her father soothingly.

Such remarks as the above were not often made; but they were frequent enough to cause Barbara an uneasy sense of self-stultification. She determined to hear them no longer; and the house at Yewsholt being ready and furnished, she withdrew thither with her maids, where for the first time she could feel mistress of a home that would be hers and her husband's exclusively, when he came.

After long weeks Willowes had recovered sufficiently to be able to write himself, and slowly and tenderly he enlightened her upon the full extent of his injuries. It was a mercy, he said, that he had not lost his sight entirely; but he was thankful to say that he still retained full vision in one eye, though the other was dark for ever. The sparing manner in which he meted out particulars of his condition told Barbara how appalling had been his experience. He was grateful for her assurance that nothing could change her; but feared she did not fully realize that he was so sadly disfigured as to make it doubtful if she would recognize him. However, in spite of all, his heart was as true to her as it ever had been.

Barbara saw from his anxiety how much lay behind. She replied that she submitted to the decrees of Fate, and would welcome him in any shape as soon as he could come. She told him of the pretty retreat in which she had taken up her abode, pending their joint occupation of it, and did not reveal how much she had sighed over the information that all his good looks were gone. Still less did she say that she felt a certain strangeness in awaiting him, the weeks they had lived together having been so short by comparison with the length of his absence.

Slowly drew on the time when Willowes found himself well enough to come home. He landed at Southampton, and posted thence towards Yewsholt. Barbara arranged to go out to meet him as far as Lornton Inn – the spot between the Forest and the Chase at which he had waited for night on the evening of their elopement. Thither she drove at the appointed hour in a little pony-chaise, presented her by her father on her birthday for her especial use in her new house; which vehicle she sent back on arriving at the inn, the plan agreed upon being that she should perform the return journey with her husband in his hired coach.

There was not much accommodation for a lady at this wayside tavern; but, as it was a fine evening in early summer, she did not mind – walking about outside, and straining her eyes along the highway for the expected one. But each cloud of dust that enlarged in the distance and drew near was found to disclose a conveyance other than his post-chaise. Barbara remained till the appointment was two hours passed, and then began to fear that owing to some adverse wind in the Channel he was not coming that night.

While waiting she was conscious of a curious trepidation that was not entirely solicitude, and did not amount to dread; her tense state of incertitude bordered both on disappointment and on relief. She had lived six or seven weeks with an imperfectly educated yet handsome husband whom now she had not seen for seventeen months, and who was so changed physically by an accident that she was assured she would hardly know him. Can we wonder at her compound state of mind?

But her immediate difficulty was to get away from Lornton Inn, for her situation was becoming embarassing. Like too many of Barbara's actions, this drive had been undertaken without much reflection. Expecting to wait no more than a few minutes for her husband in his post-chaise, and to enter it with him, she had not hesitated to isolate herself by sending back her own little vehicle. She now found that, being so well known in this neighbourhood, her excursion to meet her long-absent husband was exciting great interest. She was conscious that more eyes were watching her from the inn-windows than met her own gaze. Barbara had decided to get home by hiring whatever kind of conveyance the tavern afforded, when, straining her eyes for the last time over the now darkening highway, she perceived yet another dust-cloud drawing near. She paused; a chariot ascended to the inn, and would have passed had not its occupant caught sight of her standing expectantly. The horses were checked on the instant.

'You here – and alone, my dear Mrs Willowes?' said Lord Uplandtowers, whose carriage it was.

She explained what had brought her into this lonely situation; and, as he was going in the direction of her own home, she accepted his offer of a seat beside him. Their conversation was embarrassed and fragmentary at first; but when they had driven a mile or two she was surprised to find herself talking earnestly and warmly to him: her impulsiveness was in truth but the natural consequence of her late existence – a somewhat desolate one by reason of the strange marriage she had made; and there is no more indiscreet mood than that of a woman surprised into talk who has long been imposing upon herself a policy of reserve. Therefore her ingenuous heart rose with a bound into her throat when, in response to his leading questions, or rather hints, she allowed her troubles to leak out of her. Lord Uplandtowers took her quite to her own door, although she had driven three miles out of his way to do so; and in handing her down she heard from him a whisper of stern reproach: 'It need not have been thus if you had listened to me!'

She made no reply, and went indoors. There, as the evening wore away, she regretted more and more that she had been so friendly with Lord Uplandtowers. But he had launched himself upon her so unexpectedly: if she had only foreseen the meeting with him, what a careful line of conduct she would have marked out! Barbara broke into a perspiration of disquiet when she thought of her unreserve, and, in self-chastisement, resolved to sit up till midnight on the bare chance of Edmond's return; directing that supper should be laid for him, improbable as his arrival till the morrow was.

The hours went past, and there was dead silence in and round about Yewsholt Lodge, except for the soughing of the trees; till, when it was near upon midnight, she heard the noise of hoofs and wheels approaching the door. Knowing that it could only be her husband, Barbara instantly went into the hall to meet him. Yet she stood there not without a sensation of faintness, so many were the changes since their parting! And, owing to her casual encounter with Lord Uplandtowers, his voice and image still remained with her, excluding Edmond, her husband, from the inner circle of her impressions.

But she went to the door, and the next moment a figure stepped inside, of which she knew the outline, but little besides. Her husband was attired in a flapping black cloak and slouched hat, appearing altogether as a foreigner, and not as the young English burgess who had left her side. When he came forward into the light of the lamp, she perceived with surprise, and almost with fright, that he wore a mask. At first she had not noticed this – there being nothing in its colour which would lead a casual observer to think he was looking on anything but a real countenance.

He must have seen her start of dismay at the unexpectedness of his appearance, for he said hastily: 'I did not mean to come in to you like this – I thought you would have been in bed. How good you are, dear Barbara!' He put his arm round her, but he did not attempt to kiss her.

'O Edmond – it *is* you? – it must be?' she said, with clasped hands, for though his figure and movement were almost enough to prove it, and the tones were not unlike the old tones, the enunciation was so altered as to seem that of a stranger.

'I am covered like this to hide myself from the curious eyes of the inn-servants and others,' he said, in a low voice. 'I will send back the carriage and join you in a moment.'

'You are quite alone?'

'Quite. My companion stopped at Southampton.'

The wheels of the post-chaise rolled away as she entered the dining-room, where the supper was spread; and presently he rejoined her there. He had removed his cloak and hat, but the mask was still retained; and she could now see that it was of special make, of some flexible material like silk, coloured so as to represent flesh; it joined naturally to the front hair, and was otherwise cleverly executed.

'Barbara – you look ill,' he said, removing his glove, and taking her hand.

'Yes – I have been ill,' said she.

'Is this pretty little house ours?'

'O – yes.' She was hardly conscious of her words, for the hand he had ungloved in order to take hers was contorted, and had one or two of its fingers missing; while through the mask she discerned the twinkle of one eye only.

'I would give anything to kiss you, dearest, now, at this moment!' he continued, with mournful passionateness. 'But I cannot – in this guise. The servants are abed, I suppose?'

'Yes,' said she. 'But I can call them? You will have some supper?'

He said he would have some, but that it was not necessary to call anybody at that hour. Thereupon they approached the table, and sat down, facing each other.

Despite Barbara's scared state of mind, it was forced upon her notice that her husband trembled, as if he feared the impression he was producing, or was about to produce, as much as, or more than, she. He drew nearer, and took her hand again.

'I had this mask made at Venice,' he began, in evident embarrassment. 'My darling Barbara – my dearest wife – do you think you – will mind when I take it off? You will not dislike me – will you?'

'O Edmond, of course I shall not mind,' said she. 'What has happened to you is our misfortune; but I am prepared for it.'

'Are you sure you are prepared?'

'O yes! You are my husband.'

'You really feel quite confident that nothing external can affect you?' he said again, in a voice rendered uncertain by his agitation.

'I think I am – quite,' she answered faintly.

He bent his head. 'I hope, I hope you are,' he whispered.

In the pause which followed, the ticking of the clock in the hall seemed to grow loud; and he turned a little aside to remove the mask. She breathlessly awaited the operation, which was one of some tediousness, watching him one moment, averting her face the next; and when it was done she shut her eyes at the hideous spectacle that was revealed. A quick spasm of horror had passed through her; but though she quailed she forced herself to regard him anew, repressing the cry that would naturally have escaped from her ashy lips. Unable to look at him longer, Barbara sank down on the floor beside her chair, covering her eyes.

'You cannot look at me!' he groaned in a hopeless way. 'I am too terrible an object even for you to bear! I knew it; yet I hoped against it. Oh, this is a bitter fate – curse the skill of those Venetian surgeons who saved me alive! . . . Look up, Barbara,' he continued beseechingly; 'view me completely; say you loathe me, if you do loathe me, and settle the case between us for ever!'

His unhappy wife pulled herself together for a desperate strain. He was her Edmond; he had done her no wrong; he had suffered. A momentary devotion to him helped her, and lifting her eyes as bidden she regarded this human remnant, this *écorché*, a second time. But the sight was too much. She again involuntarily looked aside and shuddered.

'Do you think you can get used to this?' he said. 'Yes or no! Can you bear such a thing of the charnel-house near you? Judge for yourself, Barbara. Your Adonis, your matchless man, has come to this!'

The poor lady stood beside him motionless, save for the restlessness of her eyes. All her natural sentiments of affection and pity were driven clean out of her by a sort of panic; she had just the same sense of dismay and fearfulness that she would have had in the presence of an apparition. She could nohow fancy this to be her chosen one – the man she had loved; he was metamorphosed to a specimen of another species. 'I do not loathe you,' she said with trembling. 'But I am so horrified – so overcome! Let me recover myself. Will you sup now? And while you do so may I go to my room to – regain my old feeling for you? I will try, if I may leave you awhile? Yes, I will try!'

Without waiting for an answer from him, and keeping her gaze carefully averted, the frightened woman crept to the door and out of the room. She heard him sit down to the table, as if to begin supper; though, Heaven knows, his appetite was slight enough after a reception which had confirmed his worst surmises. When Barbara had ascended the stairs and arrived in her chamber she sank down, and buried her face in the coverlet of the bed.

Thus she remained for some time. The bed-chamber was over the dining-room, and presently as she knelt Barbara heard Willowes thrust back his chair, and rise to go into the hall. In five minutes that figure would probably come up the stairs and confront her again; it, – this new and terrible form, that was not her husband's. In the loneliness of this night, with neither maid nor friend beside her, she lost all self-control, and at the first sound of his footstep on the stairs, without so much as flinging a cloak round her, she flew from the room, ran along the gallery to the back staircase, which she descended, and, unlocking the back door, let herself out. She scarcely was aware what she had done till she found herself in the greenhouse, crouching on a flower-stand.

Here she remained, her great timid eyes strained through the glass upon the garden without, and her skirts gathered up, in fear of the field-mice which sometimes came there. Every moment she dreaded to hear footsteps which she ought by law to have longed for, and a voice that should have been as music to her soul. But Edmond Willowes came not that way. The nights were getting short at this season, and soon the dawn appeared, and the first rays of the sun. By daylight she had less fear than in the dark. She thought she could meet him, and accustom herself to the spectacle.

So the much-tried young woman unfastened the door of the hot-house, and went back by the way she had emerged a few hours ago. Her poor husband was probably in bed and asleep, his journey having been long; and she made as little noise as possible in her entry. The house was just as she had left it, and she looked about in the hall for his cloak and hat, but she could not see them; nor did she perceive the small trunk which had been all that he brought with him, his heavier baggage having been left at Southampton for the road-waggon. She summoned courage to mount the stairs; the bedroom-door was open as she had left it. She fearfully peeped round; the bed had not been pressed. Perhaps he had lain down on the dining-room sofa. She descended and entered; he was not there. On the table beside his unsoiled plate lay a note, hastily written on the leaf of a pocket-book. It was something like this:

> 'MY EVER-BELOVED WIFE – *The effect that my forbidding appearance has produced upon you was one which I foresaw as quite possible. I hoped against it, but foolishly so. I was aware that no human love could survive such a catastrophe. I confess I thought yours divine; but, after so long an absence, there could not be left sufficient warmth to overcome the too natural first aversion. It was an experiment, and it has failed. I do not blame you; perhaps, even, it is better so, Good-bye. I leave England for one year. You will see me again at the expiration of that time, if I live. Then I will ascertain your true feeling; and, if it be against me, go away for ever.*
>
> E.W.'

On recovering from her surprise, Barbara's remorse was such that she felt herself absolutely unforgiveable. She should have regarded him as an afflicted being, and not have been this slave to mere eyesight, like a child. To follow him and entreat him to return was her first thought. But on making inquiries she found that nobody had seen him: he had silently disappeared.

More than this, to undo the scene of last night was impossible. Her terror had been too plain, and he was a man unlikely to be coaxed back by her efforts to do her duty. She went and confessed to her parents all that had occurred; which, indeed, soon became known to more persons than those of her own family.

The year passed, and he did not return; and it was doubted if he were alive. Barbara's contrition for her unconquerable repugnance was now such that she longed to build a church-aisle, or erect a monument, and devote herself to deeds of charity for the remainder of her days. To that end she made inquiry of the excellent parson under whom she sat on Sundays, at a vertical distance of twenty feet. But he could only adjust his wig and tap his snuff-box; for such was the lukewarm state of religion in those days, that not an aisle, steeple, porch, east window, Ten-Commandment board, lion-and-unicorn, or brass candlestick, was required anywhere at all in the neighbourhood as a votive offering from a distracted soul – the last century contrasting greatly in this respect with the happy times in which we live, when urgent appeals for contributions to such objects pour in by every morning's post, and nearly all churches have been made to look like new pennies. As the poor lady could not ease her conscience this way, she determined at least to be charitable, and soon had the satisfaction of finding her porch thronged every morning by the raggedest, idlest, most drunken, hypocritical, and worthless tramps of Christendom.

But human hearts are as prone to change as the leaves of the creeper on the wall, and in the course of time, hearing nothing of her husband, Barbara could sit unmoved whilst her mother and friends said in her hearing, 'Well, what has happened is for the best.' She began to think so herself, for even now she could not summon up that lopped and mutilated form without a shiver, though whenever her mind flew back to her early wedded days, and the man who had stood beside her then, a thrill of tenderness moved her, which if quickened by his living presence might have become strong. She was young and inexperienced, and had hardly on his late return grown out of the capricious fancies of girlhood.

But he did not come again, and when she thought of his word that he would return once more, if living, and how unlikely he was to break his word, she gave him up for dead. So did her parents; so also did another person – that man of silence, of irresistible incisiveness, of still countenace, who was as awake as seven sentinels when he seemed to be as sound asleep as the figures on his family monument. Lord Uplandtowers, though not yet thirty, had chuckled like a caustic fogey of threescore when he heard of Barbara's terror and flight at her husband's return, and of the latter's prompt departure. He felt pretty sure, however, that Willowes, despite his hurt feelings, would have reappeared to claim his bright-eyed property if he had been alive at the end of the twelve months.

As there was no husband to live with her, Barbara had relinquished the house prepared for them by her father, and taken up her abode anew at Chene Manor, as in the days of her girlhood. By degrees the episode with Edmond Willowes seemed but a fevered dream, and as the months grew to years Lord Uplandtowers' friendship with the people at Chene – which had somewhat cooled after Barbara's elopement – revived considerably, and he again became a frequent visitor there. He could not make the most trivial alteration or improvement at Knollingwood Hall, where he lived, without riding off to consult with his friend Sir John at Chene; and thus putting himself frequently under her eyes, Barbara grew accustomed to him, and talked to him as freely as to a brother. She even began to look up to him as a person of authority, judgment, and prudence; and though his severity on the bench towards poachers, smugglers, and turnip-stealers was matter of common notoriety, she trusted that much of what was said might be misrepresentation.

Thus they lived on till her husband's absence had stretched to years, and there could be no longer any doubt of his death. A passionless manner of renewing his addresses seemed no longer out of place in Lord Uplandtowers. Barbara did not love him, but hers was essentially one of those sweet-pea or with-wind natures which require a twig of stouter fibre than its own to hang upon and bloom. Now, too, she was older, and admitted to herself that a man whose ancestor had run scores of Saracens through and through in fighting for the site of the Holy Sepulchre was a more desirable husband, socially considered, than one who could only claim with certainty to know that his father and grandfather were respectable burgesses.

Sir John took occasion to inform her that she might legally consider herself a widow; and, in brief, Lord Uplandtowers carried his point with her, and she married him, though he could never get her to own that she loved him as she had loved Willowes. In my childhood I knew an old lady whose mother saw the wedding, and she said that when Lord and Lady Uplandtowers drove away from her father's house in the evening it was in a coach-and-four, and that my lady was dressed in green and silver, and wore the gayest hat and feather that ever were seen; though whether it was that the green did not suit her complexion, or otherwise, the

Countess looked pale, and the reverse of blooming. After their marriage her husband took her to London, and she saw the gaieties of a season there; then they returned to Knollingwood Hall, and thus a year passed away.

Before their marriage her husband had seemed to care but little about her inability to love him passionately. 'Only let me win you,' he had said, 'and I will submit to all that.' But now her lack of warmth seemed to irritate him, and he conducted himself towards her with a resentfulness which led to her passing many hours with him in painful silence. The heir-presumptive to the title was a remote relative, whom Lord Uplandtowers did not exclude from the dislike he entertained towards many persons and things besides, and he had set his mind upon a lineal successor. He blamed her much that there was no promise of this, and asked her what she was good for.

On a particular day in her gloomy life a letter, addressed to her as Mrs Willowes, reached Lady Uplandtowers from an unexpected quarter. A sculptor in Pisa, knowing nothing of her second marriage, informed her that the long-delayed life-size statue of Mr Willowes, which, when her husband left that city, he had been directed to retain till it was sent for, was still in his studio. As his commission had not wholly been paid, and the statue was taking up room he could ill spare, he should be glad to have the debt cleared off, and directions where to forward the figure. Arriving at a time when the Countess was beginning to have little secrets (of a harmless kind, it is true) from her husband, by reason of their growing estrangement, she replied to this letter without saying a word to Lord Uplandtowers, sending off the balance that was owing to the sculptor, and telling him to despatch the statue to her without delay.

It was some weeks before it arrived at Knollingwood Hall, and, by a singular coincidence, during the interval she received the first absolutely conclusive tidings of her Edmond's death. It had taken place years before, in a foreign land, about six months after their parting, and had been induced by the sufferings he had already undergone, coupled with much depression of spirit, which had caused him to succumb to a slight ailment. The news was sent her in a brief and formal letter from some relative of Willowe's in another part of England.

Her grief took the form of passionate pity for his misfortunes, and of reproach to herself for never having been able to conquer her aversion to his latter image by recollection of what Nature had originally made him. The sad spectacle that had gone from earth had never been her Edmond at all to her. O that she could have met him as he was at first! Thus Barbara thought. It was only a few days later that a waggon with two horses, containing an immense packing-case, was seen at breakfast-time both by Barbara and her husband to drive round to the back of the house, and by-and-by they were informed that a case labelled 'Sculpture' had arrived for her ladyship.

'What can that be?' said Lord Uplandtowers.

'It is the statue of poor Edmond, which belongs to me, but has never been sent till now,' she answered.

'Where are you going to put it?' asked he.

'I have not decided,' said the Countess. 'Anywhere, so that it will not annoy you.'

'Oh, it won't annoy me,' says he.

When it had been unpacked in a back room of the house, they went to examine it. The statue was a full-length figure, in the purest Carrara marble, representing Edmond Willowes in all his original beauty, as he had stood at parting from her when about to set out on his travels; a specimen of manhood almost perfect in every line and contour. The work had been carried out with absolute fidelity.

'Phœbus-Apollo, sure,' said the Earl of Uplandtowers, who had never seen Willowes, real or represented, till now.

Barbara did not hear him. She was standing in a sort of trance before the first husband, as if she had no consciousness of the other husband at her side. The mutilated features of Willowes had disappeared from her mind's eye; this perfect being was really the man she had loved, and not that later pitiable figure; in whom love and truth should have seen this image always, but had not done so.

It was not till Lord Uplandtowers said roughly, 'Are you going to stay here all the morning worshipping him?' that she roused herself.

Her husband had not till now the least suspicion that Edmond Willowes originally looked thus, and he thought how deep would have been his jealousy years ago if Willowes had been known to him. Returning to the Hall in the afternoon he found his wife in the gallery, whither the statue had been brought.

She was lost in reverie before it, just as in the morning.

'What are you doing?' he asked.

She started and turned. 'I am looking at my husb – my statue, to see if it is well done,' she stammered. 'Why should I not?'

'There's no reason why,' he said. 'What are you going to do with the monstrous thing? It can't stand here for ever.'

'I don't wish it,' she said. 'I'll find a place.'

In her boudoir there was a deep recess, and while the Earl was absent from home for a few days in the following week, she hired joiners from the village, who under her directions enclosed the recess with a panelled door. Into the tabernacle thus formed she had the statue placed, fastening the door with a lock, the key of which she kept in her pocket.

When her husband returned he missed the statue from the gallery, and, concluding that it had been put away out of deference to his feelings, made no remark. Yet at moments he noticed something on his lady's face which he had never noticed there before. He could not construe it; it was a sort of silent ecstasy, a reserved beatification. What had become of the statue he could not divine, and growing more and more curious, looked about here and there for it till, thinking of her private room, he went towards that spot. After knocking he heard the shutting of a door, and the click of a key; but when he entered his wife was sitting at work, on what was in those days called knotting. Lord Uplandtowers' eye fell upon the newly-painted door where the recess had formerly been.

'You have been carpentering in my absence then, Barbara,' he said carelessly.

'Yes, Uplandtowers.'

'Why did you go putting up such a tasteless enclosure as that – spoiling the handsome arch of the alcove?'

'I wanted more closet-room; and I thought that as this was my own apartment—'

'Of course,' he returned. Lord Uplandtowers knew now where the statue of young Willowes was.

One night, or rather in the smallest hours of the morning, he missed the Countess from his side. Not being a man of nervous imaginings he fell asleep again before he had much considered the matter, and the next morning had forgotten the incident. But a few nights later the same circumstances occurred. This time he fully roused himself; but before he had moved to search for her, she entered the chamber in her dressing-gown, carrying a candle, which she extinguished as she approached, deeming him asleep. He could discover from her breathing that she was strangely moved; but not on this occasion either did he reveal that he had seen her. Presently, when she had lain down, affecting to wake, he asked her some trivial questions. 'Yes, *Edmond*,' she replied absently.

Lord Uplandtowers became convinced that she was in the habit of leaving the chamber in this queer way more frequently than he had observed, and he determined to watch. The next midnight he feigned deep sleep, and shortly after perceived her stealthily rise and let herself out of the room in the dark. He slipped on some clothing and followed. At the farther end of the corridor, where the clash of flint and steel would be out of the hearing of one in the bed-chamber, she struck a light. He stepped aside into an empty room till she had lit a taper and had passed on to her boudoir. In a minute or two he followed. Arrived at the door of the boudoir, he beheld the door of the private recess open, and Barbara within it, standing with her arms clasped tightly round the neck of her Edmond, and her mouth on his. The shawl which she had thrown round her nightclothes had slipped from her shoulders, and her long white robe and pale face lent her the blanched appearance of a second statue embracing the first. Between her kisses, she apostrophized it in a low murmur of infantine tenderness:

'My only love – how could I be so cruel to you, my perfect one – so good and true – I am ever faithful to you, despite my seeming infidelity! I always think of you – dream of you – during the long hours of the day, and in the night-watches! O Edmond, I am always yours!' Such words as these, intermingled with sobs, and streaming tears, and dishevelled hair, testified to an intensity of feeling in his wife which Lord Uplandtowers had not dreamed of her possessing.

'Ha, ha!' says he to himself. 'This is where we evaporate – this is where my hopes of a successor in the title dissolve – ha, ha! This must be seen to, verily!'

Lord Uplandtowers was a subtle man when once he set himself to strategy; though in the present instance he never thought of the simple stratagem of constant tenderness. Nor did he enter the room and surprise his wife as a blunderer would have done, but went back to his chamber as silently as he had left it. When the Countess returned thither, shaken by spent sobs and sighs, he appeared to be soundly sleeping as usual. The next day he began his countermoves by making inquiries as to the whereabouts of the tutor who had travelled with his wife's first husband; this gentleman, he found, was now master of a grammar-school at no great distance from Knollingwood. At the first convenient moment Lord Uplandtowers went thither and obtained an interview with the said gentleman. The schoolmaster was much gratified by a visit from such an influential neighbour, and was ready to communicate anything that his lordship desired to know.

After some general conversation on the school and its progress, the visitor observed that he believed the schoolmaster had once travelled a good deal with the unfortunate Mr Willowes, and had been with him on the occasion of his accident. He, Lord Uplandtowers, was interested in knowing what had really happened at that time, and had often thought of inquiring. And then the Earl not only heard by word of mouth as much as he wished to know, but, their chat becoming more intimate, the schoolmaster drew upon paper a sketch of the disfigured head, explaining with bated breath various details in the representation.

'It was very strange and terrible!' said Lord Uplandtowers, taking the sketch in his hand. 'Neither nose nor ears!'

A poor man in the town nearest to Knollingwood Hall, who combined the art of sign-painting with ingenious mechanical occupations, was sent for by Lord Uplandtowers to come to the Hall on a day in that week when the Countess had gone on a short visit to her parents. His employer made the man understand that the business in which his assistance was demanded was to be considered private, and money insured the observance of this request. The lock of the cupboard was picked, and the ingenious mechanic and painter, assisted by the schoolmaster's sketch, which Lord Uplandtowers had put in his pocket, set to work upon the god-like countenance of the statue under my lord's direction. What the fire had maimed in the original the chisel maimed in the copy. It was a fiendish disfigurement, ruthlessly carried out, and was rendered still more shocking by being tinted to the hues of life, as life had been after the wreck.

Six hours after, when the workman was gone, Lord Uplandtowers looked upon the result, and smiled grimly and said:

'A statue should represent a man as he appeared in life, and that's as he appeared. Ha! ha! But 'tis done to good purpose, and not idly.'

He locked the door of the closet with a skeleton key, and went his way to fetch the Countess home.

That night she slept, but he kept awake. According to the tale, she murmured soft words in her dream; and he knew that the tender converse of her imaginings was held with one whom he had supplanted but in name. At the end of her dream the Countess of Uplandtowers awoke and arose, and then the enactment of former nights was repeated. Her husband remained still and listened. Two strokes sounded from the clock in the pediment without, when, leaving the chamber-door ajar, she passed along the corridor to the other end, where, as usual, she obtained a light. So deep was the silence that he could even from his bed hear her softly blowing the tinder to a glow after striking the steel. She moved on into the boudoir, and he heard, or fancied he heard, the turning of the key in the closet-door. The next moment there came from that direction a loud and prolonged shriek, which resounded to the farthest corners of the house. It was repeated, and there was the noise of a heavy fall.

Lord Uplandtowers sprang out of bed. He hastened along the dark corridor to the door of the boudoir, which stood ajar, and, by the light of the candle within, saw his poor young Countess lying in a heap in her nightdress on the floor of the closet. When he reached her side he found that she had fainted, much to the relief of his fears that matters were worse. He quickly shut up and locked in the hated image which had done the mischief, and lifted his wife in his arms, where in a few instants she opened her eyes. Pressing her face to his without saying a word, he carried her back to her room, endeavouring as he went to disperse her terrors by a laugh in her ear, oddly compounded of causticity, predilection, and brutality.

'Ho – ho – ho!' says he. 'Frightened, dear one, hey? What a baby 'tis! Only a joke, sure, Barbara – a splendid joke! But a baby should not go to closets at midnight to look for the ghost of the dear departed! If it do it must expect to be terrified at his aspect – ho – ho – ho!'

When she was in her bed-chamber, and had quite come to herself, though her nerves were still much shaken, he spoke to her more sternly. 'Now, my lady, answer me: do you love him – eh?'

'No – no!' she faltered, shuddering, with her expanded eyes fixed on her husband. 'He is too terrible – no, no!'

'You are sure?'

'Quite sure!' replied the poor broken-spirited Countess.

But her natural elasticity asserted itself. Next morning he again inquired of her: 'Do you love him now?' She quailed under his gaze, but did not reply.

'That means that you do still, by G—!' he continued.

'It means that I will not tell an untruth, and do not wish to incense my lord,' she answered, with dignity.

'Then suppose we go and have another look at him?' As he spoke, he suddenly took her by the wrist, and turned as if to lead her towards the ghastly closet.

'No – no! Oh – no!' she cried, and her desperate wriggle out of his hand revealed that the fright of the night had left more impression upon her delicate soul than superficially appeared.

'Another dose or two, and she will be cured,' he said to himself.

It was now so generally known that the Earl and Countess were not in accord, that he took no great trouble to disguise his deeds in relation to this matter. During the day he ordered four men with ropes and rollers to attend him in the boudoir. When they arrived, the closet was open, and the upper part of the statue tied up in canvas. He had it taken to the sleeping-chamber. What followed is more or less matter of conjecture. The story, as told to me, goes on to say that, when Lady Uplandtowers retired with him that night, she saw near the foot of the heavy oak four-poster, a tall dark wardrobe, which had not stood there before; but she did not ask what its presence meant.

'I have had a little whim,' he explained when they were in the dark.

'Have you?' says she.

'To erect a little shrine, as it may be called.'

'A little shrine?'

'Yes; to one whom we both equally adore – eh? I'll show you what it contains.'

He pulled a cord which hung covered by the bed-curtains, and the doors of the wardrobe slowly opened, disclosing that the shelves within had been removed throughout, and the interior adapted to receive the ghastly figure, which stood there as it had stood in the boudoir, but with a wax-candle burning on each side of it to throw the cropped and distorted features into relief. She clutched him, uttered a low scream, and buried her head in the bedclothes. 'Oh, take it away – please take it away!' she implored.

'All in good time; namely, when you love me best,' he returned calmly. 'You don't quite yet – eh?'

'I don't know – I think – O Uplandtowers, have mercy – I cannot bear it – O, in pity, take it away!'

'Nonesense; one gets accustomed to anything. Take another gaze.'

In short, he allowed the doors to remain unclosed at the foot of the bed, and the wax-tapers burning; and such was the strange fascination of the grisly exhibition that a morbid curiosity took possession of the Countess as she lay, and, at his repeated request, she did again look out from the coverlet, shuddered, hid her eyes, and looked again, all the while begging him to take it away, or it would drive her out of her senses. But he would not do so as yet, and the wardrobe was not locked till dawn.

The scene was repeated the next night. Firm in enforcing his ferocious correctives, he continued the treatment till the nerves of the poor lady were quivering in agony under the virtuous tortures inflicted by her lord, to bring her truant heart back to faithfulness.

The third night, when the scene had opened as usual, and she lay staring with immense wild eyes at the horrid fascination, on a sudden she gave an unnatural laugh; she laughed more and more, staring at the image, till she literally shrieked with laughter: then there was silence, and he found her to have become insensible. He thought she had fainted, but soon saw that the event was worse: she was in an epileptic fit. He started up, dismayed by the sense that, like many other subtle personages, he had been too exacting for his own interests. Such love as he was capable of, though rather a selfish gloating than a cherishing solicitude, was fanned into life on the instant. He closed the wardrobe with the pulley, clasped her in his arms, took her gently to the window, and did all he could to restore her.

It was a long time before the Countess came to herself, and when she did so, a considerable change seemed to have taken place in her emotions. She flung her arms around him, and with gasps of fear abjectly kissed him many times, at last bursting into tears. She had never wept in this scene before.

'You'll take it away, dearest – you will!' she begged plaintively.

'If you love me.'

'I do – oh, I do!'

'And hate him, and his memory?'

'Yes – yes!'

'Thoroughly?'

'I cannot endure recollection of him?' cried the poor Countess slavishly. 'It fills me with shame – how could I ever be so depraved! I'll never behave badly again, Uplandtowers; and you will never put the hated statue again before my eyes?'

He felt that he could promise with perfect safety. 'Never,' said he.

'And then I'll love you,' she returned eagerly, as if dreading lest the scourge should be applied anew. 'And I'll never, never dream of thinking a single thought that seems like faithlessness to my marriage vow.'

The strange thing now was that this fictitious love wrung from her by terror took on, through mere habit of enactment, a certain quality of reality. A servile mood of attachment to the Earl became distinctly visible in her contemporaneously with an actual dislike for her late husband's memory. The mood of attachment grew and continued when the statue was removed. A permanent revulsion was operant in her, which intensified as time wore on. How fright could have effected such a change of idiosyncracy learned physicians alone can say; but I believe such cases of reactionary instinct are not unknown.

The upshot was that the cure became so permanent as to be itself a new disease. She clung to him so tightly, that she would not willingly be out of his sight for a moment. She would have no sitting-room apart from his, though she could not help starting when he entered suddenly to her. Her eyes were well-nigh always fixed upon him. If he drove out, she wished to go with him; his slightest civilities to other women made her frantically jealous; till at length her very fidelity became a burden to him, absorbing his time, and curtailing his liberty, and causing him to curse and swear. If he ever spoke sharply to her now, she did not revenge herself by flying off to a mental world of her own; all that affection for another, which had provided her with a resource, was now a cold black cinder.

From that time the life of this scared and enervated lady – whose existence might have been developed to so much higher purpose but for the ignoble ambition of her parents and the conventions of the time – was one of obsequious amativeness towards a perverse and cruel man. Little personal events came to her in quick succession – half a dozen, eight, nine, ten such events, – in brief, she bore him no less than eleven children in the eight following years, but half of them came prematurely into the world, or died a few days old; only one, a girl, attained to maturity; she in after years became the wife of the Honourable Mr Beltonleigh, who was created Lord D'Almaine, as may be remembered.

There was no living son and heir. At length, completely worn out in mind and body, Lady Uplandtowers was taken abroad by her husband, to try the effect of a more genial climate upon her wasted frame. But nothing availed to strengthen her, and she died at Florence, a few months after her arrival in Italy.

Contrary to expectation, the Earl of Uplandtowers did not marry again. Such affection as existed in him – strange, hard, brutal as it was – seemed untransferable, and the title, as is known, passed at his death to his nephew. Perhaps it may not be so generally known that, during the enlargement of the Hall for the sixth Earl, while digging in the grounds for the new foundations, the broken fragments of a marble statue were unearthed. They were submitted to various antiquaries, who said that, so far as the damaged pieces would allow them to form an opinion, the statue seemed to be that of a mutilated Roman satyr; or if not, an allegorical figure of Death. Only one or two inhabitants guessed whose statue those fragments had composed.

I should have added that, shortly after the death of the Countess, an excellent sermon was preached by the Dean of Melchester, the subject of which, though names were not mentioned, was unquestionably suggested by the aforesaid events. He dwelt upon the folly of indulgence in sensuous love for a handsome form merely; and showed that the only rational and virtuous growths of that affection were those based upon intrinsic worth. In the case of the tender but somewhat shallow lady whose life I have related, there is no doubt that an infatuation for the person of young Willowes was the chief feeling that induced her to marry him; which was the more deplorable in that his beauty, by all tradition, was the least of his recommendations, every report bearing out the inference that he must have been a man of steadfast nature, bright intelligence, and promising life.

The company thanked the old surgeon for his story, which the rural dean declared to be a far more striking one than anything he could hope to tell. An elderly member of the Club, who was mostly called the Bookworm, said that a woman's natural instinct of fidelity would, indeed, send back her heart to a man after his death in a truly wonderful manner sometimes – if anything occurred to put before her forcibly the original affection between them, and his original aspect in her eyes, – whatever his inferiority may have been, social or otherwise; and then a general conversation ensued upon the power that a woman has of seeing the actual in the representation, the reality in the dream – a power which (according to the sentimental member) men have no faculty of equalling.

THE DOCTOR'S LEGEND

Several experts believe that this next tale was also intended to appear as one of the stories in *A Group of Noble Dames.* Certainly it is related to a gathering of fascinated listeners around a fireside by a narrator simply described as 'The Doctor' – the one common profession surprisingly *not* presently listed among the storytellers in Hardy's collection. And here again the tale has a factual basis in the life of a callous old squire, Joseph Damer of Came House, near Dorchester, whose son married a beautiful sculpturess but later committed suicide – a history that was well-known to Thomas Hardy.

Why the author did not include this tale of the child striken with the terrible 'Death's Head' in his book is an interesting matter for conjecture. The story was certainly published in America on March 26, 1891, in *The Independent* (from which this copy is taken) but made no appearance whatsoever in Britain. It has been claimed that the author was dissatisfied with the tale when he read it in proof, and decided not to offer it to any magazine editor in Britain, though many were now crying out for his work. More likely – in my estimation – because of its basis in fact and the pathetic local tragedy it depicted, Hardy feared the story could well offend the descendants of the Damer family who still lived in the area, and therefore decided against any further publication. And hence 'The Doctor's Legend' has remained a forgotten but nontheless important item of his macabre ouevre for the best part of a century.

THE DOCTOR'S LEGEND

I

'Not more than half a dozen miles from the Wessex coast' (said the doctor) 'is a mansion which appeared newer in the last century than it appears at the present day after years of neglect and occupation by inferior tenants. It was owned by a man of five-and-twenty, than whom a more ambitious personage never surveyed his face in a glass. His name I will not mention out of respect to those of his blood and connections who may remain on earth, if any such there be. In the words of a writer of that time who knew him well, he was 'one whom anything would petrify but nothing would soften'.

'This worthy gentleman was of so elevated and refined a nature that he never gave a penny to women who uttered bad words in their trouble and rage, or who wore dirty aprons in view of his front door. On those misguided ones who did not pull the forelock to him in passing, and call him "your Honour" and "Squire", he turned the shoulder of scorn, especially when he wore his finer ruffles and gold seals.

'Neither his personal nor real estate at this time was large; but the latter he made the most of by jealously guarding it, as of the former by his economies. Yet though his fields and woods were well-watched by his gamekeepers and other dependants, such was his dislike to intrusion that he never ceased to watch the watchers. He stopped footpaths and enclosed lands. He made no exceptions to these sentiments in the case of his own villagers, whose faces were never to be seen in his private grounds except on pressing errands.

'Outside his garden-wall, near the entrance to the park, there lived a poor woman with an only child. This child had been so unfortunate as to trespass upon the Squire's lawn on more than one occasion, in search of flowers; and on this incident, trivial as it was, hung much that was afterwards of concern to the house and lineage of the Squire. It seems that the Squire had sent a message to the little girl's mother concerning the nuisance; nevertheless, only a few days afterwards, he saw the child there again. This unwarrantable impertinence, as the owner and landlord deemed it to be, irritated him exceedingly; and, with his walking cane elevated, he began to pursue the child to teach her by chastisement what she would not learn by exhortation.

'Naturally enough, as soon as the girl saw the Squire in pursuit of her she gave a loud scream, and started off like a hare; but the only entrance to the grounds being on the side which the Squire's position commanded, she could not escape, and endeavoured to elude him by winding, and doubling in her terrified course. Finding her, by reason of her fleetness, not so easy to chastise as he had imagined, her assailant lost his temper – never a very difficult matter – and the more loudly she screamed the more angrily did he pursue. A more untoward interruption to the peace of a beautiful and secluded spot was never seen.

'The race continued, and the Squire, now panting with rage and exertion, drew closer to his victim. To the horrified eyes of the child, when she gazed over her shoulder, his face appeared like a crimson mask set with eyes of fire. The glance sealed her fate in the race. By a sudden start forward he caught hold of her by the skirt of her short frock flying behind. The clutch so terrified the child that, with a louder shriek than ever, she leapt from his grasp, leaving the skirt in his hand. But she did not go far; in a few more moments she fell on the ground in an epileptic fit.

'This strange, and, but for its painfulness, even ludicrous scene, was witnessed by one of the gardeners who had been working near, and the Squire haughtily directed him to take the prostrate and quivering child home; after which he walked off, by no means pleased with himself at the unmanly and undignified part which a violent temper had let him to play.

'The mother of the girl was in great distress when she saw her only child brought home in such a condition; she was still more distressed, when in the course of a day or two, it became doubtful if fright had not deprived the girl entirely of her reason, as well as of her health. In the singular, nervous malady which supervened the child's hair came off and her teeth fell from her gums; till no one could have recognised in the mere scare-crow that she appeared, the happy and laughing youngster of a few weeks before.

'The mother was a woman of very different mettle from her poor child. Impassioned and determined in character, she was not one to provoke with impunity. And her moods were as enduring as they were deep. Seeing what a wreck her darling had become she went on foot to the manor-house, and, contrary to the custom of the villagers, rang at the front door, where she asked to see that ruffian the master of the mansion who had ruined her only child. The Squire sent out reply that he was very sorry for the girl, but that he could not see her mother, accompanying his message by a *solatium* of five shillings.

'In the bitterness of her hate, the woman threw the five-shilling piece through the panes of the dining-room window, and went home to brood again over her idolized child.

'One day a little later, when the girl was well enough to play in the lane, she came in with a bigger girl who took care of her.

'"Death's Head – I be Death's Head – hee, hee!" said the child.

'"What?" said the mother, turning pale.

'The girl in charge explained that the other children had nicknamed her daughter "Death's Head" since she had lost her hair, from her resemblance to a skull.

'When the elder girl was gone the mother carefully regarded the child from the distance. In a moment she saw how cruelly apt the *sobriquet* was. The bald scalp, the hollow cheeks – by reason of the absence of teeth – and the saucer eyes, the cadaverous hue, had, indeed, a startling likeness to that bony relic of mortality.

'At this time the Squire was successfully soliciting in marriage a certain Lady Cicely, the daughter of an ancient and noble house in that county. During the ensuing summer their nuptials were celebrated, and the young wife brought home amid great rejoicing, and ringing of bells, and dancing on the green, followed by a bonfire after dark on the hill. The woman, whose disfigured child was as the apple of her eye to her, saw all this, and the greater the good fortune that fell to the Squire, the more envenomed did she become.

'The newly-wedded lady was much liked by the villagers in general, to whom she was very charitable, intelligently entering into their lives and histories, and endeavouring to relieve their cares. On a particular evening of the ensuing autumn when she had been a wife but a few months, after some parish-visiting, she was returning homeward to dinner on foot, her way to the mansion lying by the churchyard wall. It was barely dusk, but a full harvest moon was shining from the east. At this moment of the Lady Cicely's return it chanced that the widow with her afflicted girl was crossing the churchyard by the footpath from gate to gate. The churchyard was in obscurity, being shaded by the yews. Seeing the lady in the adjoining highway, the woman hastily left the footpath with the child, crossed the graves to the shadow of the wall outside which the lady was passing, and pulled off the child's hood so that the baldness was revealed. Whispering to the child, "Grin at her, my deary!" she held up the little girl as high as she could, which was just sufficient to disclose her face over the coping of the wall to a person on the other side.

'The moonlight fell upon the sepulchral face and head, intensifying the child's daytime aspect till it was only too much like that which had suggested the nickname. The unsuspecting and timid lady – a perfect necrophobist by reason of the care with which everything unpleasant had been kept out of her dainty life – saw the death-like shape, and, shrieking with sudden terror, fell to the ground. The lurking woman with her child disappeared in another direction, and passed through the churchyard gate homeward.

'The Lady Cicely's shriek brought some villagers to the spot. They found her quivering, but not senseless; and she was taken home. There she lay prostrate for some time under the doctor's hands.

II

'It was the following spring, and the time drew near when an infant was to be born to the Squire. Great was the anxiety of all concerned, by reason of the fright and fall from which the Lady Cicely had suffered in the latter part of the preceding year. However, the event which they were all expecting took place, and, to the joy of her friends, no evil consequences seemed to have ensued from the terrifying incident before-mentioned. The child of Lady Cicely was a son and heir.

'Meanwhile the mother of the afflicted child watched these things in silence. Nothing – not even malevolent tricks upon those dear to him – seemed to interrupt the prosperity of the Squire. An uncle of his, a money-lender in some northern city, died childless at this time and left an immense fortune to his nephew the Lady Cicely's husband; who, fortified by this acquisition, now bethought himself of a pedigree as a necessity, so as to be no longer beholden to his wife for all the ancestral credit that his children would possess. By searching in the County history, he happily discovered that one of the Knights who came over with William the Conqueror bore a name which somewhat resembled his own, and from this he constructed an ingenious and creditable genealogical tree; the only rickety point in which occurred at a certain date in the previous century. It was the date whereat it became necessary to show that his great-grandfather (in reality a respectable village tanner) was the indubitable son of a scion of the Knightly family before alluded to, despite the fact that this scion had lived in quite another part of the county. This little artistic junction, however, was satisfactorily manipulated, and the grafting was only to be perceived by the curious.

'His upward progress was uninterrupted. His only son grew to be an interesting lad, though, like his mother, exceedingly timid and impressionable. With his now great wealth, the Squire began to feel that his present modest country-seat was insufficient, and there being at this time an Abbey and its estates in the market by reason of some dispute in the family hitherto its owners, the wealthy gentleman purchased it. The Abbey was of large proportions and stood in a lovely and fertile valley surrounded by many attached estates. It had a situation fit for the home of a prince, still more for that of an Archbishop. This historic spot, with its monkish associations, its fish-ponds, woods, village, abbey-church, and abbots' bones beneath their incised slabs, all passed into the possession of our illustrious self-seeker.

'Meeting his son when the purchase was completed, he smacked the youth on the shoulder.

'"We've estates, and rivers, and hills, and woods, and a beautiful Abbey unrivalled in the whole of Wessex – Ha, ha!" he cried.

'"I don't care about abbeys," said the gentle son. "They are gloomy; this one particularly."

'"Nonsense!" said the father. "And we've a village, and the Abbey church into the bargain."

'"Yes."

'"And dozens of mitred abbots in their stone coffins underground, and tons of monks – all for the same money. . . . Yes, the very dust of those old rascals is mine! Ho, ho!"

'The son turned pale. "Many were holy men," he murmured, "despite the errors in their creed."

'"D—ye, grow up, and get married, and have a wife who'll disabuse you of that ghostly nonsense!" cried the Squire.

'Not more than a year after this, several new peers were created for political reasons with which we have no concern. Among them was the subject of this legend, much to the chagrin of some of his neighbours, who considered that such rapid advancement was too great for his deserts. On this point I express no opinion.

'He now resided at the Abbey, outwardly honoured by all in his vicinity, though perhaps less honoured in their hearts; and many were the visitors from far and near. In due course his son grew to manhood and married a beautiful woman, whose beauty nevertheless was no greater than her taste and accomplishments. She could read Latin and Greek, as well as one or two modern languages; above all she had great skill as a sculptress in marble and other materials.

'The poor widow in the other village seemed to have been blasted out of existence by the success of her long-time enemy. The two could not thrive side by side. She declined and died; her death having, happily, been preceded by that of her child.

'Though the Abbey, with its little cells and quaint turnings, satisfied the curiosity of visitors, it did not satisfy the noble lord (as the Squire had now become). Except the Abbot's Hall, the rooms were miserably small for a baron of his wealth, who expected soon to be an earl, and the parent of a line of earls.

'Moreover the village was close to his very doors – on his very lawn, and he disliked the proximity of its inhabitants, his old craze for seclusion remaining with him still. On Sundays they sat at service in the very Abbey Church which was part of his own residence. Besides, as his son had said, the conventual buildings formed a gloomy dwelling, with its dark corridors, monkish associations, and charnel-like smell.

'So he set to work, and did not spare his thousands. First, he carted the village bodily away to a distance of a mile or more, where he built new, and, it must be added, convenient cottages, and a little barn-like church. The spot on which the old village had stood was now included in his lawn. But the villagers still intruded there, for they came to ring the Abbey-Church bells – a fine peal, which they professed (it is believed truly) to have an immemorial right to chime.

'As the natives persistently came and got drunk in the ringing-loft, the peer determined to put a stop to it. He sold the ring of bells to a founder in a distant city, and to him one day the whole beautiful set of them was conveyed on waggons away from the spot on which they had hung and resounded for so many centuries, and called so many devout souls to prayer. When the villagers saw their dear bells going off in procession, never to return, they stood in their doors and shed tears.

'It was just after this time that the first shadow fell upon the new lord's life. His wife died. Yet the renovation of the residence went on apace. The Abbey was pulled down wing by wing, and a fair mansion built on its site. An additional lawn was planned to extend over the spot where the cloisters had been, and for that purpose the ground was to be lowered and levelled. The flat tombs covering the Abbots were removed one by one, as a necessity of the embellishment, and the bones dug up.

'Of these bones it seemed as if the excavators would never reach the end. It was necessary to dig ditches and pits for them in the plantations, and from their quantity there was not much respect shown to them in wheeling them away.

III

'One morning, when the family were rising from breakfast, a message was brought to my lord that more bones than ever had been found in clearing away the ground for the ball-room, and for the foundations of the new card-parlour. One of the skeletons was that of a mitred abbot – evidently a very holy person. What were they to do with it?

'"Put him into any hole," says my Lord.

'The foreman came a second time. "There is something strange in those bones, my lord," he said; "we remove them by barrow-fuls, and still they seem never to lessen. The more we carry away, the more there are left behind."

'The son looked disturbed, rose from his seat, and went out of the room. Since his mother's death he had been much depressed, and seemed to suffer from nervous debility.

'"Curse the bones," said the peer, angry at the extreme sensitiveness of his son, whose distress and departure he had observed. "More, do ye say? Throw the wormy rubbish into any ditch you can find."

'The servants looked uneasily at each other, for the old Catholicism had not at that time ceased to be the religion of these islands so long as it has now, and much of its superstition and weird fancy still lingered in the minds of the simple folk of this remote nook.

'The son's wife, the bright and accomplished woman aforesaid, to enliven the subject told her father-in-law that she was designing a marble tomb for one of the London churches, and the design was to be a very artistic allegory of Death and the Resurrection; the figure of an Angel on one side, and that of Death on the other (according to the extravagant symbolism of that date, when such designs as this were much in vogue). Might she, the lady asked, have a skull to copy in marble for the head of Death?

'She might have them all, and welcome, her father-in-law said. He would only be too glad.

'She went out to the spot where the new foundations were being dug, and from the heap of bones chose the one of those sad relics which seemed to offer the most perfect model for her chisel.

'"It is the last Abbot's, my lady," said the clerk of the works.

'"It will do," said she; and directed it to be put into a box and sent to the house in London where she and her husband at present resided.

'When she met her husband that day he proposed that they should return to town almost immediately. "This is a gloomy place," said he. "And if ever it comes into my hands I shan't live here much. I've been telling the old man of my debts, too, and he said he won't pay them – be hanged if he will, until he has a grandson at least – So let's be off."

'They returned to town. This young man, the son and heir, though quiet and nervous, was not a very domestic character; he had many friends of both sexes with whom his refined and accomplished wife was unacquainted. Therefore she was thrown much upon her own resources; and her gifts in carving were a real solace to her. She proceeded with her design for the tomb of her acquaintance, and the Abbot's skull having duly arrived, she made use of it as her model as she had planned.

'Her husband being as usual away from home, she worked at her self-imposed task until bed-time – and then retired. When the house had been wrapped in sleep for some hours, the front door was opened, and the absent one entered, a little the worse for liquor – for drinking in those days was one of a nobleman's accomplishments. He ascended the stairs, candle in hand, and feeling uncertain whether his wife had gone to bed or no, entered her studio to look for her. Holding the candle unsteadily above his head, he perceived a heap of modelling clay; behind it a sheeted figure with a death's head above it – this being in fact the draped dummy arrangement that his wife had built up to be ultimately copied in marble for the allegory she had designed to support the mural tablet.

'The sight seemed to overpower the gazer with horror; the candle fell from his hand, and in the darkness he rushed downstairs and out of the house.

'"I've seen it before!" he cried in mad and maudlin accents. "Where? When?"

'At four o'clock the next morning news was brought to the house that my lord's heir had shot himself dead with a pistol at a tavern not far off.

'His reason for the act was absolutely inexplicable to the outer world. The heir to an enormous property and a high title, the husband of a wife as gifted as she was charming; of all the men in English society he seemed to be the least likely to undertake such a desperate deed.

'Only a few persons – his wife not being one of them, though his father was – knew of the sad circumstances in the life of the suicide's mother, the late Lady Cicely, a few months before his birth – in which she was terrified nearly to death by the woman who held up poor little "Death's Head" over the churchyard wall.

'Then people said that in this there was retribution upon the ambitious lord for his wickedness, particularly that of cursing the bones of the holy men of God. I give the superstition for what it is worth. It is enough to add, in this connection, that the old lord died, some say like Herod, of the characteristics he had imputed to the inoffensive human remains. However that may be, in a few years the title was extinct, and now not a relative or scion remains of the family that bore his name.

'A venerable dissenter, a fearless ascetic of the neighbourhood, who had been deprived of his opportunities through some objections taken by the peer, preached a sermon the Sunday after his funeral, and mentioning no names, significantly took as his text Isaiah, XIV, 10–23:

'"Art thou also become weak as we? Art thou become like unto us? Thy pomp is brought down to the grave, and the noise of thy viols: the worm is spread under thee, and the worms cover thee. How art thou fallen from Heaven, O Lucifer, son of the morning! How art thou cut down to the ground, which didst weaken the nations. . . . I will rise up against him, said the Lord of hosts, and cut off from Babylon the name, and remnant, and son, and nephew, saith the Lord."

'Whether as a Christian moralist he was justified in doing this I leave others to judge.'

Here the doctor concluded his story, and the thoughtfulness which it had engendered upon his own features spread over those of his hearers, as they sat with their eyes fixed upon the fire.

THE SUPERSTITIOUS MAN'S STORY

Another Dorset superstition was the inspiration for this next story, which is probably one of the best known of Thomas Hardy's tales of the supernatural. It is the account of a doomed farm labourer, William Privett, who is seen by some of his neighbours entering a church porch on Midsummer Eve, not to reappear – an accepted omen of his impending death. This, in fact, is just one of several supernatural occurrences described during the course of the narrative, the most striking being the sight of a little white moth flying out of Privett's mouth at the moment of his sudden death. As Hardy explained in a letter to the folklorist, Edward Clodd, some years after publishing the tale, 'The association of the miller-moth with the human soul is, or was, until lately, an actual belief down here. It was told me years ago by an old woman.'

'The Superstitious Man's Story' was one of nine stories that Hardy wrote to form a series he called *Wessex Folk* and again first published in America in *Harper's New Monthly Magazine* from March to June 1891. (Two of the striking illustrations at the front of this book are taken from the pages of *Harper's Magazine*). The stories are related by a group of travellers in a carrier van to one of their company, John Lackland, who is returning to his native village after 35 years abroad. The spinner of this intriguing and dramatic tale is the aged registrar who is travelling in the company of his son, a seedsman . . .

THE SUPERSTITIOUS MAN'S STORY

'William, as you may know, was a curious, silent man; you could feel when he came near 'ee; and if he was in the house or anywhere behind your back without your seeing him, there seemed to be something clammy in the air, as if a cellar door was opened close by your elbow. Well, one Sunday, at a time that William was in very good health to all appearance, the bell that was ringing for church went very heavy all of a sudden; the sexton, who told me o't, said he'd not known the bell go so heavy in his hand for years – it was just as if the gudgeons wanted oiling. That was on the Sunday, as I say. During the week after, it chanced that William's wife was staying up late one night to finish her ironing, she doing the washing for Mr and Mrs Hardcome. Her husband had finished his supper and gone to bed as usual some hour or two before. While she ironed she heard him coming down stairs; he stopped to put on his boots at the stair-foot, where he always left them, and then came on into the living-room where she was ironing, passing through it towards the door, this being the only way from the staircase to the outside of the house. No word was said on either side, William not being a man given to much speaking, and his wife being occupied with her work. He went out and closed the door behind him. As her husband had now and then gone out in this way at night before when unwell, or unable to sleep for want of a pipe, she took no particular notice, and continued at her ironing. This she finished shortly after, and as he had not come in she waited awhile for him, putting away the irons and things, and preparing the table for his breakfast in the morning. Still he did not return, but supposing him not far off, and wanting to get to bed

'He went out and closed the door behind him' – an incident from 'The Superstitious Man's Story', *Harper's New Monthly Magazine*, March 1861

herself, tired as she was, she left the door unbarred and went to the stairs, after writing on the back of the door with chalk: *Mind and do the door* (because he was a forgetful man).

'To her great surprise, and I might say alarm, on reaching the foot of the stairs his boots were standing there as they always stood when he had gone to rest; going up to their chamber she found him in bed sleeping as sound as a rock. How he could have got back again without her seeing or hearing him was beyond her comprehension. It could only have been by passing behind her very quietly while she was bumping with the iron. But this notion did not satisfy her: it was surely impossible that she should not have seen him come in through a room so small. She could not unravel the mystery, and felt very queer and uncomfortable about it. However, she would not disturb him to question him then, and went to bed herself.

'He rose and left for his work very early the next morning, before she was awake, and she waited his return to breakfast with much anxiety for an explanation, for thinking over the matter by daylight made it seem only the more startling. When he came in to the meal he said, before she could put her question, "What's the meaning of them words chalked on the door?"

'She told him, and asked him about his going out the night before. William declared that he had never left the bedroom after entering it, having in fact undressed, lain down, and fallen asleep directly, never once waking till the clock struck five, and he rose up to go to his labour.

'Betty Privett was as certain in her own mind that he did go out as she was of her own existence, and was little less certain that he did not return. She felt too disturbed to argue with him, and let the subject drop as though she must have been mistaken. When she was walking down Longpuddle street later in the day she met Jim Weedle's daughter Nancy, and said, "Well, Nancy, you do look sleepy to-day!"

'"Yes, Mrs Privett," says Nancy. "Now don't tell anybody, but I don't mind letting you know what the reason o't is. Last night, being Old Midsummer Eve, some of us went to church porch, and didn't get home till near one."

'"Did ye?" says Mrs Privett. "Old Midsummer yesterday was it? Faith I didn't think whe'r 'twas Midsummer or Michaelmas; I'd too much work to do."

'"Yes. And we were frightened enough, I can tell 'ee, by what we saw."

'"What did ye see?"

'(You may not remember, sir, having gone off to foreign parts so young, that on Midsummer Night it is believed hereabout that the faint shapes of all the folk in the parish who are going to be at death's door within the year can be seen entering the church. Those who get over their illness come out again after a while; those that are doomed to die do not return.)

'"What did you see?" asked William's wife.

'"Well," says Nancy, backwardly – "we needn't tell what we saw, or who we saw."

'"You saw my husband," says Betty Privett, in a quiet way.

'"Well, since you put it so," says Nancy, hanging fire, "we – thought we did see him; but it was darkish, and we was frightened, and of course it might not have been he."

'"Nancy, you needn't mind letting it out, though 'tis kept back in kindness. And he didn't come out of church again: I know it as well as you."

'Nancy did not answer yes or no to that, and no more was said. But three days after, William Privett was mowing with John Chiles in Mr Hardcome's meadow, and in the heat of the day they sat down to eat their bit o' nunch under a tree, and empty their flagon. Afterwards both of 'em fell asleep as they sat. John Chiles was the first to wake, and as he looked towards his fellow-mower he saw one of those great white miller's-souls as we call 'em – that is to say, a miller-moth – come from William's open mouth while he slept, and fly straight away. John thought it odd enough, as William had worked in a mill for several years when he was a boy. He then looked at the sun, and found by the place o't that they had slept a long while, and as William did not wake, John called to him and said it was high time to begin work again. He took no notice, and then John went up and shook him, and found he was dead.

'Now on that very day old Philip Hookhorn was down at Longpuddle Spring dipping up a pitcher of water; and as he turned away, who should he see coming down to the spring on the other side but William, looking very pale and odd. This surprised Philip Hookhorn very much, for years before that time William's little son – his only child – had been drowned in that spring while at play there, and this had so preyed upon William's mind that he'd never been seen near the spring afterwards, and had been known to go half a mile out of his way to avoid the place. On inquiry, it was found that William in body could not have stood by the spring, being in the mead two miles off; and it also came out that the time at which he was seen at the spring was the very time when he died.'

Netty Sargent's Copyhold

'Netty Sargent's Copyhold' is the last of the stories told to John Lackland on his journey to Longpuddle. The teller here is Mr Day, 'the world-ignored old painter' who describes how Netty Sargent secures the ownership of her uncle's house by a clever subterfuge immediately after his death. The setting of this tale is very similar to that in which Hardy himself lived for some years at Higher Bockhampton, and again the author has drawn on an old belief for his plot – for as Ruth Firor has told us, 'The folk-belief that the signature of a person not yet cold in death is valid in law may be a relic of sympathetic magic.'

Curiously, when Hardy came to publish this sequence of stories in Britain in a single volume which he entitled *Life's Little Ironies* (1894), the generic title was changed from *Wessex Folk* – with its hint of folk tales and legends – to *A Few Crusted Characters*. Interestingly, too, we are told that when Mr Day has concluded his tale and the carrier van has safely deposited its passengers in Longpuddle, the figure of John Lackland is observed wandering around the scenes of his youth for a few days, 'and then, ghost-like, it silently disappeared.'

Netty Sargent's Copyhold

'She continued to live with her uncle, in the lonely house by the copse, just as at the time you knew her; a tall spry young woman. Ah, how well one can remember her black hair and dancing eyes at that time, and her sly way of screwing up her mouth when she meant to tease ye! Well, she was hardly out of short frocks before the chaps were after her, and by long and by late she was courted by a young man whom perhaps you did not know – Jasper Cliff was his name – and, though she might have had many a better fellow, he so greatly took her fancy that 'twas Jasper or nobody for her. He was a selfish customer, always thinking less of what he was going to do than of what he was going to gain by his doings. Jasper's eyes might have been fixed upon Netty, but his mind was upon her uncle's house; though he was fond of her in his way – I admit that.

'This house, built by her great-great-grandfather, with its garden and little field, was copyhold – granted upon lives in the old way, and had been so granted for generations. Her uncle's was the last life upon the property; so that at his death, if there was no admittance of new lives, it would all fall into the hands of the lord of the manor. But 'twas easy to admit – a slight "fine," as 'twas called, of a few pounds, was enough to entitle him to a new deed o' grant by the custom of the manor; and the lord could not hinder it.

'Now there could be no better provision for his niece and only relative than a sure house over her head, and Netty's uncle should have seen to the renewal in time, owing to the peculiar custom of forfeiture by the dropping of the last life before the new fine was paid; for the Squire was very anxious to get hold of the house and land; and every Sunday when the old man came into the church and passed the Squire's pew, the Squire would say, "A little weaker in his knees, a little crookeder in his back – and the readmittance not applied for: ha! ha! I shall be able to make a complete clearing of that corner of the manor some day!"

''Twas extraordinary, now we look back upon it, that old Sargent should have been so dilatory; yet some people are like it; and he put off calling at the Squire's agent's office with the fine week after week, saying to himself, "I shall have more time next market-day than I have now." One unfortunate hindrance was that he didn't very well like Jasper Cliff, and as Jasper kept urging Netty, and Netty on that account kept urging her uncle, the old man was inclined to postpone the re-liveing as long as he could, to spite the selfish young lover. At last old Mr Sargent fell ill, and then Jasper could bear it no longer: he produced the fine-money himself, and handed it to Netty, and spoke to her plainly.

'"You and your uncle ought to know better. You should press him more. There's the money. If you let the house and ground slip between ye, I won't marry; hang me if I will! For folks won't deserve a husband that can do such things."

'The worried girl took the money and went home, and told her uncle that it was no house no husband for her. Old Mr Sargent pooh-poohed the money, for the amount was not worth consideration, but he did now bestir himself, for he saw she was bent upon marrying Jasper, and he did not wish to make her unhappy, since she was so determined. It was much to the Squire's annoyance that he found Sargent had moved in the matter at last; but he could not gainsay it, and the documents were prepared (for on this manor the copyholders had writings with their holdings, though on some manors they had none). Old Sargent being now too feeble to go to the agent's house, the deed was to be brought to his house signed, and handed over as a receipt for the money; the counterpart to be signed by Sargent, and sent back to the Squire.

'The agent had promised to call on old Sargent for this purpose at five o'clock, and Netty put the money into her desk to have it close at hand. While doing this she heard a slight cry from her uncle, and turning round, saw that he had fallen forward in his chair. She went and lifted him, but he was unconscious; and unconscious he remained. Neither medicine nor stimulants would bring him to himself. She had been told that he might possibly go off in that way, and it seemed as if the end had come. Before she had started for a doctor his face and extremities grew quite cold and white, and she saw that help would be useless. He was stone-dead.

'Netty's situation rose upon her distracted mind in all its seriousness. The house, garden, and field were lost – by a few hours – and with them a home for herself and her lover. She would not think so meanly of Jasper as to suppose that he would adhere to the resolution declared in a moment of impatience; but she trembled, nevertheless. Why could not her uncle have lived a couple of hours longer, since he had lived so long? It was now past three o'clock; at five the agent was to call, and, if all had gone well, by ten minutes past five the house and holding would have been securely hers for her own and Jasper's lives, these being two of the three proposed to be added by paying the fine. How that wretched old Squire would rejoice at getting the little tenancy into his hands! He did not really require it, but constitutionally hated these tiny copyholds and leaseholds and freeholds, which made islands of independence in the fair, smooth ocean of his estates.

'Then an idea struck into the head of Netty how to accomplish her object in spite of her uncle's negligence. It was a dull December afternoon: and the first step in her scheme – so the story goes, and I see no reason to doubt it –'

'He was stone-dead' – a dramatic illustration for the American publication of 'Netty Sargent's Copyhold' in *Harper's New Monthly Magazine*, June 1891

''Tis true as the light,' affirmed Christopher Twink. 'I was just passing by.'

'The first step in her scheme was to fasten the outer door, to make sure of not being interrupted. Then she set to work by placing her uncle's small, heavy oak table before the fire; then she went to her uncle's corpse, sitting in the chair as he had died – a stuffed arm-chair, on casters, and rather high in the seat, so it was told me – and wheeled the chair, uncle and all, to the table, placing him with his back toward the window, in the attitude of bending over the said oak table, which I knew as a boy as well as I know any piece of furniture in my own house. On the table she laid the large family Bible open before him, and placed his forefinger on the page; and then she opened his eyelids a bit, and put on him his spectacles, so that from behind he appeared for all the world as if he were reading the Scriptures. Then she unfastened the door and sat down, and when it grew dark she lit a candle, and put it on the table beside her uncle's book.

'Folk may well guess how the time passed with her till the agent came, and how, when his knock sounded upon the door, she nearly started out of her skin – at least that's as it was told me. Netty promptly went to the door.

'"I am sorry, sir," she says, under her breath; "my uncle is not so well to-night, and I'm afraid he can't see you."

'"H'm! – that's a pretty tale," says the steward. "So I've come all this way about this trumpery little job for nothing!"

'"O no, sir – I hope not," says Netty. "I suppose the business of granting the new deed can be done just the same?"

'"Done? Certainly not. He must pay the renewal money, and sign the parchment in my presence."

'She looked dubious. "Uncle is so dreadful nervous about law business," says she, "that, as you know, he's put it off and put it off for years; and now today really I've feared it would verily drive him out of his mind. His poor three teeth quite chattered when I said to him that you would be here soon with the parchment writing. He always was afraid of agents, and folks that come for rent, and such-like."

'"Poor old fellow – I'm sorry for him. Well, the thing can't be done unless I see him and witness his signature."

'"Suppose, sir, that you see him sign, and he don't see you looking at him? I'd soothe his nerves by saying you weren't strict about the form of witnessing, and didn't wish to come in. So that it was done in your bare presence it would be sufficient, would it not? As he's such an old, shrinking, shivering man, it would be a great considerateness on your part if that would do?"

'"In my bare presence would do, of course – that's all I come for. But how can I be a witness without his seeing me?"

'"Why, in this way, sir; if you'll oblige me by just stepping here." She conducted him a few yards to the left, till they were opposite the parlour window. The blind had been left up purposely, and the candle-light shone out upon the garden bushes. Within the agent could see, at the other end of the room, the back and side of the old man's head, and his shoulders and arm, sitting with the book and candle before him, and his spectacles on his nose, as she had placed him.

'"He's reading his Bible, as you see, sir," she says, quite in her meekest way.

'"Yes. I thought he was a careless sort of man in matters of religion?"

'"He always was fond of his Bible," Netty assured him. "Though I think he's nodding over it just at this moment. However, that's natural in an old man, and unwell. Now you could stand here and see him sign, couldn't you, sir, as he's such an invalid?"

'"Very well," said the agent, lighting a cigar. "You have ready by you the merely nominal sum you'll have to pay for the admittance, of course?"

'"Yes," said Netty. "I'll bring it out." She fetched the cash, wrapped in paper, and handed it to him, and when he had counted it the steward took from his breast pocket the precious parchments and gave one to her to be signed.

'"Uncle's hand is a little paralyzed," she said. "And what with his being half asleep, too, really I don't know what sort of a signature he'll be able to make."

'"Doesn't matter, so that he signs."

'"Might I hold his hand?"

'"Ay, hold his hand, my young woman – that will be near enough."

'Netty re-entered the house, and the agent continued smoking outside the window. Now came the ticklish part of Netty's performance. The steward saw her put the inkhorn – "horn," says I in my oldfashioned way – the inkstand, before her uncle, and touch his elbow as if to arouse him, and speak to him, and spread out the deed; when she had pointed to show him where to sign she dipped the pen and put it into his hand. To hold his hand she artfully stepped behind him, so that the agent could only see a little bit of his head, and the hand she held; but he saw the old man's hand trace his name on the document. As soon as 'twas done she came out to the steward with the parchment in her hand, and the steward signed as witness by the light from the parlour window. Then he gave her the deed signed by the Squire, and left; and next morning Netty told the neighbours that her uncle was dead in his bed.'

'She must have undressed him and put him there.'

'She must. Oh, that girl had a nerve, I can tell ye! Well, to cut a long story short, that's how she got back the house and field that were, strictly speaking, gone from her; and by getting them, got her a husband.

'Every virtue has its reward, they say. Netty had hers for her ingenious contrivance to gain Jasper. Two years after they were married he took to beating her – not hard, you know; just a smack or two, enough to set her in a temper, and let out to the neighbours what she had done to win him, and how she repented of her pains. When the old Squire was dead, and his son came into the property, this confession of hers began to be whispered about. But Netty was a pretty young woman, and the Squire's son was a pretty young man at that time, and wider-minded than his father, having no objection to little holdings; and he never took any proceedings against her.'

THE FIDDLER OF THE REELS

The central character in this widely praised story, the wizard-like fiddler, Wat Ollamoor, nick-named 'Mop' because of his flowing locks of hair, has been described as an archetypal 'demon lover' whose character and powers haunt the imagination long after the story is finished. Evelyn Hardy goes even further, considering the tale, 'the supreme example in Hardy's work of the malefic power of music, and the only one in which the fiddler, knowing his powers, consciously uses them to destroy his victim.'

'Mop's' magnetic effect on the young and impressionable Caroline Aspent, his seduction of her, and then the cruel trick he plays when he returns to lure their love child away, makes this a story both traditional – because of its hints of witchcraft and mystic powers – as well as modern through its association with the Great Exhibition held in London in 1851. It has been argued that because of this specific reference, Hardy wrote it as a partial link to the World Fair in Chicago which was held in 1893. Certainly it was first submitted to the leading American publication, *Scribner's Magazine*, and appeared in its special 'Exhibition Number' of May 1893, from which this version is taken. We learn, too, that Ollamoor, having secured his child, is believed to have decamped to America and continued his haunting performances there . . .

THE FIDDLER OF THE REELS

'Talking of Exhibitions, World's Fairs, and what not,' said the old gentleman, 'I would not go round the corner to see a dozen of them nowadays. The only exhibition that ever made, or ever will make, any impression upon my imagination was the first of the series, the parent of them all, and now a thing of old times – the Great Exhibition of 1851, in Hyde Park, London. None of the younger generation can realize the sense of novelty it produced in us who were then in our prime. A noun substantive went so far as to become an adjective in honour of the occasion. It was "exhibition" hat, "exhibition" razor-strop, "exhibition" watch; nay, even "exhibition" weather, "exhibition" spirits, sweethearts, babies, wives – for the time.

'For South Wessex, the year formed in many ways an extraordinary chronological frontier or transit-line, at which there occurred what one might call a precipice in Time. As in a geological "fault," we had presented to us a sudden bringing of ancient and modern into absolute contact, such as probably in no other single year since the Conquest was ever witnessed in this part of the country.'

These observations led us onward to talk of the different personages, gentle and simple, who lived and moved within our narrow and peaceful horizon at that time; and of three people in particular, whose queer little history was oddly touched at points by the Exhibition, more concerned with it than that of anybody else who dwelt in those outlying shades of the world, Stickleford, Mellstock, and Egdon. First in prominence among these three came Wat Ollamoor – if that were his real name – whom the seniors in our party had known well.

He was a woman's man, they said, – supremely so – externally little else. To men he was not attractive; perhaps a little repulsive at times. Musician, dandy, and company-man in practice; veterinary surgeon in theory, he lodged awhile in Mellstock village, coming from nobody knew where; though some said his first appearance in this neighbourhood had been as fiddle-player in a show at Greenhill Fair.

Many a worthy villager envied him his power over unsophisticated maidenhood – a power which seemed sometimes to have a touch of the weird and wizardly in it. Personally he was not ill-favoured, though rather un-English, his complexion being a rich olive, his rank hair dark and rather clammy – made still clammier by secret ointments, which, when he came fresh to a party, caused him to smell like 'boys'-love' (southernwood) steeped in lamp-oil. On occasion he wore curls – a double row – running almost horizontally around this head. But as these were sometimes noticeably absent, it was concluded that they were not altogether of Nature's making. By girls whose love for him had turned to hatred he had been nicknamed 'Mop,' from this abundance of hair, which was long enough to rest upon his shoulders; as time passed the name more and more prevailed.

His fiddling possibly had the most to do with the fascination he exercised, for, to speak fairly, it could claim for itself a most peculiar and personal quality, like that in a moving preacher. There were tones in it which bred the immediate conviction that indolence and averseness to systematic application were all that lay between 'Mop' and the career of a second Paganini.

While playing he invariably closed his eyes; using no notes, and, as it were, allowing the violin to wander on at will into the most plaintive passages ever heard by rustic man. There was a certain lingual character in the supplicatory expressions he produced, which would wellnigh have drawn an ache from the heart of a gate-post. He could make any child in the parish, who was at all sensitive to music, burst into tears in a few minutes by simply fiddling one of the old dance-tunes he almost entirely affected – country jigs, reels, and 'Favourite Quick Steps' of the last century – some mutilated remains of which even now reappear as nameless phantoms in new quadrilles and gallops, where they are recognized only by the curious, or by such old-fashioned and far-between people as have been thrown with men like Wat Ollamoor in their early life.

His date was a little later than that of the old Mellstock quire-band which comprised the Dewys, Mail, and the rest – in fact, he did not rise above the horizon thereabout till those well-known musicians were disbanded as ecclesiastical functionaries. In their honest love of thoroughness they despised the new man's style. Theophilus Dewy (Reuben the tranter's younger brother) used to say there was no 'plumness' in it – no bowing, no solidity – it was all fantastical. And probably this was true. Anyhow, Mop had, very obviously, never bowed a note of church-music from his birth; he never once sat in the gallery of Mellstock Church where the others had tuned their venerable psalmody so many hundreds of times; had never, in all likelihood, entered a church at all. All were devil's tunes in his repertory. 'He could no more play the Wold Hundredth to his true time than he could play the brazen serpent,' the tranter would say. (The brazen serpent was supposed in Mellstock to be a musical instrument particularly hard to blow.)

Occasionally Mop could produce the aforesaid moving effect upon the souls of grown-up persons, especially young women of fragile and responsive organization. Such an one was Car'line Aspent. Though she was already engaged to be married before she met him, Car'line, of them all, was the most influenced by Mop Ollamoor's heart-stealing melodies, to her discomfort, nay, positive pain and ultimate injury. She was a pretty, invocating, weak-mouthed girl, whose chief defect as a companion with her sex was a tendency to peevishness now and then. At this time she was not a resident in Mellstock parish where Mop lodged, but lived some miles off at Stickleford, further down the river.

How and where she first made acquaintance with him and his fiddling is not truly known, but the story was that it either began or was developed on one spring evening, when, in passing through Lower Mellstock, she chanced to pause on the bridge near his house to rest herself, and languidly leaned over the parapet. Mop was standing on his door-step, as was his custom, spinning the insidious thread of semi- and demi-semiquavers from the E string of his fiddle for the benefit of passers-by, and laughing as the tears rolled down the cheeks of the little children hanging around him. Car'line pretended to be engrossed with the rippling of the stream under the arches, but in reality she was listening, as he knew. Presently the aching of the heart seized her simultaneously with a wild desire to glide airily in the mazes of an infinite dance. To shake off the fascination she resolved to go on, although it would be necessary to pass him as he played. On stealthily glancing ahead at the performer, she found to her relief that his eyes were closed in abandonment to instrumentation, and she strode on boldly. But when closer her step grew timid, her tread convulsed itself more and more accordantly with the time of the melody, till she very nearly danced along. Gaining another glance at him when immediately opposite, she saw that *one* of his eyes was open, quizzing her as he smiled at her emotional state. Her gait could not divest itself of its compelled capers till she had gone a long way past the house; and Car'line was unable to shake off the strange infatuation for hours.

After that day, whenever there was to be in the neighbourhood a dance to which she could get an invitation, and where Mop Ollamoor was to be the musician, Car'line contrived to be present, though it sometimes involved a walk of several miles; for he did not play so often in Stickleford as elsewhere.

The next evidences of his influence over her were singular enough, and it would require a neurologist to fully explain them. She would be sitting quietly, any evening after dark, in the house of her father, the parish clerk, which stood in the middle of Stickleford village street, this being the highroad between Lower Mellstock and Moreford, five miles eastward. Here, without a moment's warning, and in the midst of a general conversation between her father, sister, and the young man before alluded to, who devotedly wooed her in ignorance of her infatuation, she would start from her seat in the chimney-corner as if she had received a galvanic shock, and spring convulsively towards the ceiling; then she would burst into tears, and it was not till some half-hour had passed that she grew calm as usual. Her father, knowing her hysterical tendencies, was always excessively anxious about this trait in his youngest girl, and feared the attack to be a species of epileptic fit. Not so her sister Julia. Julia had found out what was the cause. At the moment before the jumping, only an exceptionally sensitive ear situated in the chimney-nook could have caught from down the flue the beat of a man's footstep along the highway without. But it was in that footfall, for which she had been waiting, that the origin of Car'line's involuntary springing lay. The pedestrian was Mop Ollamoor, as the girl well knew; but his business that way was not to visit her; he sought another woman whom he spoke of as his Intended, and who lived at Moreford, two miles further on. On one, and only one, occasion did it happen that Car'line could not control her utterance; it was when her sister alone chanced to be present. 'O – O – O –!' she cried. 'He's going to *her*, and not coming to *me*!'

To do the fiddler justice, he had not at first thought greatly of, or spoken much to, this girl of impressionable mould. But he had soon found out her secret, and could not resist a little by-play with her too easily hurt heart, as an interlude between his more serious lovemakings at Moreford. The two became well acquainted, though only by stealth, hardly a soul in Stickleford except her sister, and her lover Ned Hipcroft, being aware of the attachment. Her father disapproved of her coldness to Ned; her sister, too, hoped she might get over this nervous passion for a man of whom so little was known. The ultimate result was that Car'line's manly and simple wooer Edward found his suit becoming practically hopeless. He was a respectable mechanic, in a far sounder position than Mop the nominal horse-doctor; but when, before leaving her, Ned put his flat and final question, would she marry him, then and there, now or never, it was with little expectation of obtaining more than the negative she gave him. Though her father supported him and her sister supported him, he could not play the fiddle so as to draw your soul out of your body like a spider's thread, as Mop did, till you felt as limp as withywind and yearned for something to cling to. Indeed, Hipcroft had not the slightest ear for music; could not sing two notes in tune, much less play them.

The No he had expected and got from her, in spite of a preliminary encouragement, gave Ned a new start in life. It had been uttered in such a tone of sad entreaty that he resolved to persecute her no more; she should not even be distressed by a sight of his form in the distant perspective of the street and lane. He left the place, and his natural course was to London.

The railway to South Wessex was in process of construction, but it was not as yet opened for traffic; and Hipcroft reached the capital by a six days' trudge on foot, as many a better man had done before him. He was one of the last of the artisan class who used that now extinct method of travel to the great centres of labour, so customary then from time immemorial.

In London he lived and worked regularly at his trade. More fortunate than many, his disinterested willingness recommended him from the first. During the ensuing four years he was never out of employment. He neither advanced nor receded in the modern sense; he improved as a workman, but he did not shift one jot in social position. About his love for Car'line he maintained a rigid silence. No doubt he often thought of her; but being always occupied, and having no relations at Stickleford, he held no communication with that part of the country, and showed no desire to return. In his quiet lodging in Lambeth he moved about after working-hours with the facility of a woman, doing his own cooking, attending to his stocking-heels, and shaping himself by degrees to a lifelong bachelorhood. For this conduct one is bound to advance the canonical reason that time could not efface from his heart the image of little Car'line Aspent – and it may be in part true; but there was also the inference that his was a nature not greatly dependent upon the ministrations of the other sex for its comforts.

The fourth year of his residence as a mechanic in London was the year of the Hyde-Park Exhibition already mentioned, and at the construction of this huge glass-house, then unexampled in the world's history, he worked daily. It was an era of great hope and activity among the nations and industries. Though Hipcroft was, in his small way, a central man in the movement, he plodded on with his usual outward placidity. Yet for him, too, the year was destined to have its surprises, for when the bustle of getting the building ready for the opening day was past, the ceremonies had been witnessed, and people were flocking thither from all parts of the globe, he received a letter from Car'line. Till that day the silence of four years between himself and Stickleford had never been broken.

She informed her old lover, in an uncertain penmanship which suggested a trembling hand, of the trouble she had been put to in ascertaining his address, and then broached the subject which had prompted her to write. Four years ago, she said with the greatest delicacy of which she was capable, she had been so foolish as to refuse him. Her wilful wrong-headedness had since been a grief to her many times, and of late particularly. As for Mr Ollamoor, he had been absent almost as long as Ned – she did not know where. She would gladly marry Ned now if he were to ask her again, and be a tender little wife to him till her life's end.

A tide of warm feeling must have surged through Ned Hipcroft's frame on receipt of this news, if we may judge by the issue. Unquestionably he loved her still, even if not to the exclusion of every other happiness. This from his Car'line, she who had been dead to him these many years, alive to him again as of old, was in itself a pleasant, gratifying thing. Ned had grown so resigned to, or satisfied with, his lonely lot, that he probably would not have shown much jubilation at anything. Still, a certain ardour of preoccupation, after his first surprise, revealed how deeply her confession of faith in him had stirred him. Measured and methodical in his ways, he did not answer the letter that day, nor the next, nor the next. He was having 'a good think.' When he did answer it, there was a great deal of sound reasoning mixed in with the unmistakable tenderness of his reply; but the tenderness itself was sufficient to reveal that he was pleased with her straightforward frankness; that the anchorage she had once obtained in his heart was renewable, if it had not been continuously firm.

He told her – and as he wrote his lips twitched humorously over the few gentle words of raillery he indited among the rest of his sentences – that it was all very well for her to come round at this time of day. Why wouldn't she have him when he wanted her? She had no doubt learned that he was not married, but suppose his affections had since been fixed on another? She ought to beg his pardon. Still, he was not the man to forget her. But considering how he had been used, and what he had suffered, she could not quite expect him to go down to Stickleford and fetch her. But if she would come to him, and say she was sorry, as was only fair; why, yes, he would marry her, knowing what a good little woman she was at the core. He added that the request for her to come to him was a less one to make than it would have been when he first left Stickleford, or even a few months ago; for the new railway into South Wessex was now open, and there had just begun to be run wonderfully contrived special trains, called excursion-trains, on account of the Great Exhibition; so that she could come up easily alone.

She said in her reply how good it was of him to treat her so generously, after her hot-and-cold treatment of him; that though she felt frightened at the magnitude of the journey, and was never as yet in a railway-train, having only seen one pass at a distance, she embraced his offer with all her heart; and would, indeed, own to him how sorry she was, and beg his pardon, and try to be a good wife always, and make up for lost time.

The remaining details of when and where were soon settled, Car'line informing him, for her ready identification in the crowd, that she would be wearing 'my new sprigged-laylock cotton gown,' and Ned gaily responding that, having married her the morning after her arrival, he would make a day of it by taking her to the Exhibition. One early summer afternoon, accordingly, he came from his place of work, and hastened towards Waterloo Station to meet her. It was as wet and chilly as an English June day can occasionally be, but as he waited on the platform in the drizzle he glowed inwardly, and seemed to have something to live for again.

The 'excursion-train' – an absolutely new departure in the history of travel – was still a novelty on the Wessex line, and probably everywhere. Crowds of people had flocked to all the stations on the way up to witness the unwonted sight of so long a train's passage, even where they did not take advantage of the opportunity it offered. The seats for the humbler class of travellers in these early experiments in steam-locomotion were open trucks, without any protection whatever from the wind and rain; and damp weather having set in with the afternoon, the unfortunate occupants of these vehicles were, on the train drawing up at the London terminus, found to be in a pitiable condition from their long journey; blue-faced, stiff-necked, sneezing, rain-beaten, chilled to the marrow, many of the men being hatless; in fact, they resembled people who had been out all night in an open boat on a rough sea, rather than inland excursionists for pleasure. The women had in some degree protected themselves by turning up the skirts of their gowns over their heads, but as by this arrangement they were additionally exposed about the hips, they were all more or less in a sorry plight.

In the bustle and crush of alighting forms of both sexes which followed the entry of the huge concatenation into the station, Ned Hipcroft soon discerned the slim little figure his eye was in search of, in the sprigged lilac, as described. She came up to him with a frightened smile – still pretty, though so damp, weather-beaten, and shivering from long exposure to the wind.

'O Ned!' she sputtered, 'I – I—' He clasped her in his arms and kissed her, whereupon she burst into a flood of tears.

'You are wet, my poor dear! I hope you'll not get cold,' he said. And surveying her and her multifarious surrounding packages, he noticed that by the hand she led a toddling child – a little girl of three or so – whose hood was as clammy and tender face as blue as those of the other travellers.

'Who is this – somebody you know?' asked Ned curiously.

'Yes, Ned. She's mine.'

'Yours?'

'Yes – my own.'

'Your own child?'

'Yes!'

'But who's the father?'

'The young man I had after you courted me.'

'Well – as God's in—'

'Ned, I didn't name it in my letter, because, you see, it would have been so hard to explain! I thought that when we met I could tell you how she happened to be born, so much better than in writing! I hope you'll excuse it this once, dear Ned, and not scold me, now I've come so many, many miles!'

'This means Mr Mop Ollamoor, I reckon!' said Hipcroft, gazing palely at them from the distance of the yard or two to which he had withdrawn with a start.

Car'line gasped. 'But he's been gone away for years!' she supplicated. 'And I never had a young man before! And I was so onlucky to be catched the first time he took advantage o' me, though some of the girls down there go on like anything!'

Ned remained in silence, pondering.

'You'll forgive me, dear Ned?' she added, beginning to sob outright. 'I haven't taken 'ee in after all, because – because you can pack us back again, if you want to; though 'tis hundreds o' miles, and so wet, and night a-coming on, and I with no money!'

'What the devil can I do!' Hipcroft groaned.

A more pitiable picture than the pair of helpless creatures

presented was never seen on a rainy day, as they stood on the great, gaunt, puddled platform, a whiff of drizzle blowing under the roof upon them now and then; the pretty attire in which they had started from Stickleford in the early morning bemuddled and sodden, weariness on their faces, and fear of him in their eyes; for the child began to look as if she thought she too had done some wrong, remaining in an appalled silence till the tears rolled down her chubby cheeks.

'What's the matter, my little maid?' said Ned mechanically.

'I do want to go home!' she let out , in tones that told of a bursting heart. 'And my totties be cold, an' I shan't have no bread an' butter no more!'

'I don't know what to say to it all!' declared Ned, his own eye moist as he turned and walked a few steps with his head down; then regarded them again point-blank. From the child escaped troubled breaths and silently welling tears.

'Want some bread and butter, do 'ee?' he said, with factitious hardness.

'Ye–e–s!'

'Well, I dare say I can get 'ee a bit! Naturally, you must want some. And you, too, for that matter, Car'line.'

'I do feel a little hungered. But I can keep it off,' she murmured.

'Folk shouldn't do that,' he said gruffly. . . . 'There, come along!' He caught up the child, as he added, 'You must bide here to-night, anyhow, I s'pose! What can you do otherwise? I'll get 'ee some tea and victuals; and as for this job, I'm sure I don't know what to say! This is the way out.'

They pursued their way, without speaking, to Ned's lodgings, which were not far off. There he dried them and made them comfortable, and prepared tea; they thankfully sat down. The ready-made household of which he suddenly found himself the head imparted a cosy aspect to his room, and a paternal one to himself. Presently he turned to the child and kissed her now blooming cheeks; and, looking wistfully at Car'line, kissed her also.

'I don't see how I can send you back all them miles,' he growled, 'now you've come all the way o' purpose to join me. But you must trust me, Car'line, and show you've real faith in me. Well, do you feel better now, my little woman?'

The child nodded beamingly, her mouth being otherwise occupied.

'I did trust you, Ned, in coming; and I shall always!'

Thus, without any definite agreement to forgive her, he tacitly acquiesced in the fate that Heaven had sent him; and on the day of their marriage (which was not quite so soon as he had expected it could be, on account of the time necessary for banns) he took her to the Exhibition when they came back from church, as he had promised. While standing near a large mirror in one of the courts devoted to furniture, Car'line started, for in the glass appeared the reflection of a form exactly resembling Mop Ollamoor's – so exactly, that it seemed impossible to believe anybody but that artist in person to be the original. On passing round the objects which hemmed in Ned, her, and the child from a direct view, no Mop was to be seen. Whether he were really in London or not at that time was never known; and Car'line always stoutly denied that her readiness to go and meet Ned in town arose from any rumour that Mop had also gone thither; which denial there was no reasonable ground for doubting.

And then the year glided away, and the Exhibition folded itself up and became a thing of the past. The park trees that had been enclosed for six months were again exposed to the winds and storms, and the sod grew green anew. Ned found that Car'line resolved herself into a very good wife and companion, though she had made herself what is called cheap to him; but in that she was like another domestic article, a cheap tea-pot, which often brews better tea than a dear one. One autumn Hipcroft found himself with but little work to do, and a prospect of less for the winter. Both being country born and bred, they fancied they would like to live again in their natural atmosphere. It was accordingly decided between them that they should leave the pent-up London lodging, and that Ned should seek out employment near his native place, his wife and her daughter staying with Car'line's father during the search for occupation and an abode of their own.

Tinglings of pride pervaded Car'line's spasmodic little frame as she journeyed down with Ned to the place she had left two or three years before, in silence and under a cloud. To return to where she had once been despised, a smiling London wife with a distinct London accent, was a triumph which the world did not witness every day.

The train did not stop at the petty roadside station that lay nearest to Stickleford, and the trio went on to Casterbridge. Ned thought it a good opportunity to make a few preliminary inquiries for employment at workshops in the borough where he had been known; and feeling cold from her journey, and it being dry under-foot and only dusk as yet, with a moon on the point of rising, Car'line and her little girl walked on towards Stickleford, leaving Ned to follow at a quicker pace, and pick her up at a certain half-way house, widely known as an inn.

The woman and child pursued the well-remembered way comfortably enough, though they were both becoming wearied. In the course of three miles they had passed Heedless-William's Pond, the familiar landmark by Bloom's End, and were drawing near the Quiet Woman, a lone roadside hostel on the lower verge of the Egdon Heath, since and for many years abolished. In stepping up towards it Car'line heard more voices within than had formerly been customary at such an hour, and she learned that an auction of fat stock had been held near the spot that afternoon. The child would be the better for a rest as well as herself, she thought, and she entered.

The guests and customers overflowed into the passage, and Car'line had no sooner crossed the threshold than a man whom she remembered by sight came forward with a glass and mug in his hands towards a friend leaning against the wall; but, seeing her, very gallantly offered her a drink of the liquor, which was gin-and-beer hot, pouring her out a tumblerful and saying, in a moment or two: 'Surely, 'tis little Car'line Aspent that was – down at Stickleford?'

She assented, and, though she did not exactly want this beverage, she drank it since it was offered, and her entertainer begged her to come in further and sit down. Once within the room she found that all the persons present were seated close against the walls, and there being a chair vacant she did the same. An explanation of their position occurred the next moment. In the opposite corner stood Mop, rosining his bow and looking just the same as ever. The company had cleared the middle of the room for dancing, and they were about to dance again. As she wore a veil to keep off the wind she did not think he had recognized her, or could possibly guess the identity of the child; and to her satisfied surprise she found that she could confront him quite calmly – mistress of herself in the dignity her London life had given her. Before she had quite emptied her glass the dance was called, the dancers formed in two lines, the music sounded, and the figure began.

Then matters changed for Car'line. A tremor quickened itself to life in her, and her hand so shook that she could hardly set down her glass. It was not the dance nor the dancers, but the notes of that old violin which thrilled the London wife, these having still all the witchery that she had so well known of yore, and under which she had used to lose her power of independent will. How it all came back! There was the fiddling figure against the wall; the large, oily, mop-like head of him, and beneath the mop the face with closed eyes.

After the first moments of paralyzed reverie the familiar tune in the familiar rendering made her laugh and shed tears simultaneously. Then a man at the bottom of the dance, whose partner had dropped away, stretched out his hand and beckoned to her to take the place. She did not want to dance; she entreated by signs to be left where she was, but she was entreating of the tune and its player rather than of the dancing man. The saltatory tendency which the fiddler and his cunning instrument had ever been able to start in her was seizing Car'line just as it had done in earlier years, possibly assisted by the gin-and-beer hot. Tired as she was she grasped her little girl by the hand, and plunging in at the bottom of the figure, whirled about with the rest. She found that her companions were mostly people of the neighbouring hamlets and farms – Bloom's End, Mellstock, Lewgate, and elsewhere; and by degrees she was recognized as she convulsively danced on, wishing that Mop would cease and let her heart rest from the aching he caused, and her feet also.

After long and many minutes the dance ended, when she was urged to fortify herself with more gin-and-beer; which she did, feeling very weak and overpowered with hysteric emotion. She refrained from unveiling, to keep Mop in ignorance of her presence, if possible. Several of the guests having left, Car'line hastily wiped her lips and also turned to go; but, according to the account of some who remained, at that very moment a five-handed reel was proposed, in which two or three begged her to join.

She declined on the plea of being tired and having to walk to Stickleford, when Mop began aggressively tweedling 'My Fancy-Lad,' in D major, as the air to which the reel was to be footed. He must have recognized her, though she did not know it, for it was the strain of all seductive strains which she was least able to resist – the one he had played when she was leaning over the bridge at the date of their first acquaintance. Car'line stepped despairingly into the middle of the room with the other four.

Reels were resorted to hereabouts at this time by the more robust spirits, for the reduction of superfluous energy which the ordinary figure-dances were not powerful enough to exhaust. As everybody knows, or does not know, the five reelers stood in the form of a cross, the reel being performed by each line of three alternately, the persons who successively came to the middle place dancing in both directions. Car'line soon found herself in this place, the axis of the whole performance, and could not get out of it, the tune turning into the first part without giving her opportunity. And now she began to suspect that Mop did know her, and was doing this on purpose, though whenever she stole a glance at him his closed eyes betokened obliviousness to everything outside his own brain. She continued to wend her way through the figure of 8 that was formed by her course, the fiddler introducing into his notes the wild and agonizing sweetness of a living voice in one too highly wrought; its pathos running high and running low in endless variation, projecting through her nerves excruciating spasms, a sort of blissful torture. The room swam; the tune was endless; and in about a quarter of an hour the only other woman in the figure dropped out exhausted, and sank panting on a bench.

The reel instantly resolved itself into a four-handed one. Car'line would have given anything to leave off; but she had, or fancied she had, no power, while Mop played such tunes; and thus another ten minutes slipped by, a haze of dust now clouding the candles, the floor being of stone, sanded. Then another dancer fell out – one of the men – and went into the passage in a frantic search for liquor. To turn the figure into a three-handed reel was the work of a second, Mop modulating at the same time into 'The Fairy Dance,' as better suited to the contracted movement, and no less one of those foods of love which, as manufactured by his bow, had always intoxicated her.

In a reel for three there was no rest whatever, and four or five minutes were enough to make her remaining two partners, now thoroughly blown, stamp their last bar, and, like their predecessors, limp off into the next room to get something to drink. Car'line, half-stifled inside her veil, was left dancing alone, the apartment now being empty of everybody save herself, Mop, and their little girl.

She flung up the veil, and cast her eyes upon him, as if imploring him to withdraw himself and his acoustic magnetism from the atmosphere. Mop opened one of his own orbs, as though for the first time, fixed it peeringly upon her, and smiling dreamily, threw into his strains the reserve of expression which he could not afford to waste on a big and noisy dance. Crowds of little chromatic subtleties, capable of drawing tears from a statue, proceeded straightway from the ancient fiddle, as if it were dying of the emotion which had been pent up within it ever since its banishment from some Italian or German city where it first took shape and sound. There was that in the look of Mop's one dark eye which said: 'You cannot leave off, dear, whether you would or no!' and it bred in her a paroxysm of desperation that defied him to tire her down.

She thus continued to dance alone, defiantly as she thought, but in truth slavishly and abjectly, subject to every wave of the melody, and probed by the gimlet-like gaze of her fascinator's open eye; keeping up at the same time a feeble smile in his face, as a feint to signify it was still her own pleasure which led her on. A terrified embarassment as to what she could say to him if she were to leave off, had its unrecognized share in keeping her going. The child, who was beginning to be distressed by the strange situation, came up and whimpered: 'Stop, mother, stop, and let's go home!' as she seized Car'line's hand.

Suddenly Car'line sank staggering to the floor, and rolling over on her face, prone she remained. Mop's fiddle thereupon emitted an elfin shriek of finality; stepping quickly down from the nine-gallon beer-cask which had formed his rostrum, he went to the little girl, who disconsolately bent over her mother.

The guests who had gone into the back room for liquor and change of air, hearing something unusual, trooped back hitherward, where they endeavoured to revive poor, weak Car'line by blowing her with the bellows and opening the window. Ned, her husband, who had been detained in Casterbridge, as aforesaid, came along the road at this juncture, and hearing excited voices through the open casement, and, to his great surprise, the mention of his wife's name, he entered amid the rest upon the scene. Car'line was now in convulsions, weeping violently, and for a long time nothing could be done with her. While he was sending for a cart to take her onward to Stickleford Hipcroft anxiously inquired how it had all happened; and then the assembly explained that a fiddler formerly known in the locality had lately visited his old haunts, and had taken upon himself without invitation to play that evening at the inn and raise a dance.

Ned demanded the fiddler's name, and they said Ollamoor.

'Ah!' exclaimed Ned, looking round him. 'Where is he, and where – where's my little girl?'

Ollamoor had disappeared, and so had the child. Hipcroft was in ordinary a quiet and tractable fellow, but a determination which was to be feared settled in his face now. 'Blast him!' he cried. 'I'll beat his skull in for'n, if I swing for it to-morrow!'

He had rushed to the poker which lay on the hearth, and hastened down the passage, the people following. Outside the house, on the other side of the highway, a mass of dark heath-land rose sullenly upward to its not easily accessible interior, a ravined plateau, whereon jutted into the sky, at the distance of a couple of miles, the firwoods of Mistover backed by the Yalbury coppices – a place of Dantesque gloom at this hour, which would have afforded secure hiding for a battery of artillery, much less a man and a child.

Some other men plunged thitherward with him, and more went along the road. They were gone about twenty minutes altogether, returning without result to the inn. Ned sat down in the settle, and clasped his forehead with his hands.

'Well – what a fool the man is, and hev been all these years, if he thinks the child his, as a' do seem to!' they whispered. 'And everybody else knowing otherwise!'

'No, I don't think 'tis mine!' cried Ned hoarsely, as he looked up from his hands. 'But she *is* mine, all the same! Ha'n't I nussed her?

Ha'n't I fed her and teached her? Ha'n't I played wi'her? O, little Carry – gone with that rogue – gone!'

'You ha'n't lost your mis'ess, anyhow,' they said to console him. 'She's throwed up the sperrits, and she is feeling better, and she's more to 'ee than a child that isn't yours.'

'She isn't! She's not so particular much to me, especially now she's lost the little maid! But Carry's the whole world to me!'

'Well, ver' like you'll find her to-morrow.'

'Ah – but shall I? Yet he *can't* hurt her – surely he can't! Well – how's Car'line now? I am ready. Is the cart here?'

She was lifted into the vehicle, and they sadly lumbered on toward Stickleford. Next day she was calmer; but the fits were still upon her; and her will seemed shattered. For the child she appeared to show singularly little anxiety, though Ned was nearly distracted by his passionate paternal love for a child not his own. It was nevertheless quite expected that the impish Mop would restore the lost one after a freak of a day or two; but time went on, and neither he nor she could be heard of, and Hipcroft murmured that perhaps he was exercising upon her some unholy musical charm, as he had done upon Car'line herself. Weeks passed, and still they could obtain no clue either to the fiddler's whereabouts or to the girl's; and how he could have induced her to go with him remained a mystery.

Then Ned, who had obtained only temporary employment in the neighbourhood, took a sudden hatred towards his native district, and a rumour reaching his ears through the police that a somewhat similar man and child had been seen at a fair near London, he playing a violin, she dancing on stilts, a new interest in the capital took possession of Hipcroft with an intensity which would scarcely allow him time to pack before returning thither. He did not, however, find the lost one, though he made it the entire business of his over-hours to stand about in by-streets in the hope of discovering her, and would start up in the night, saying, 'That rascal's torturing her to maintain him!' To which his wife would answer peevishly, 'Don't 'ee raft yourself so, Ned! You prevent my getting a bit o' rest! He won't hurt her!' and fall asleep again.

That Carry and her father had emigrated to America was the general opinion; Mop, no doubt, finding the girl a highly desirable companion when he had trained her to keep him by her earnings as a dancer. There, for that matter, they may be performing in some capacity now, though he must be an old scamp verging on three-score-and-ten, and she a woman of four-and-forty.

An Imaginative Woman

This is a remarkable story of a woman's inner fantasy life and the extraordinary effect her love for a struggling and ultimately doomed poet she never actually meets has on the child she later bears her vulgar husband. The story of Ella Marchmill, the 'imaginative woman' of the title, is based on a medical hypothesis still debated today about prenatal influences – a theory that clearly caught the interest of Hardy and which he brilliantly intermingled with a similar old folk belief recounted in Dorset that even the physical characteristics of an unborn child could be influenced by the experiences of his mother.

It was Hardy's original intention to call this story 'A Woman of Imagination' while he was writing it in the winter of 1893, but it appeared with the present title when making its debut in print in the revised edition of *Life's Little Ironies* which he issued in 1912. As a matter of record, Hardy returned to this theme again in a grim little poem called 'San Sebastian' in which the narrator, an old soldier, sees a similarity between the eyes of his own daughter and those of a young girl he raped while campaigning in Spain in August 1813.

An Imaginative Woman

When William Marchmill had finished his inquiries for lodgings at the well-known watering-place of Solentsea in Upper Wessex, he returned to the hotel to find his wife. She, with the children, had rambled along the shore, and Marchmill followed in the direction indicated by the military-looking hall-porter.

'By Jove, how far you've gone! I am quite out of breath,' Marchmill said, rather impatiently, when he came up with his wife, who was reading as she walked, the three children being considerably further ahead with the nurse.

Mrs Marchmill started out of the reverie into which the book had thrown her. 'Yes,' she said, 'you've been such a long time. I was tired of staying in that dreary hotel. But I am sorry if you have wanted me, Will?'

'Well, I have had trouble to suit myself. When you see the airy and comfortable rooms heard of, you find they are stuffy and uncomfortable. Will you come and see if what I've fixed on will do? There is not much room, I am afraid; but I can light on nothing better. The town is rather full.'

The pair left the children and nurse to continue their ramble, and went back together.

In age well-balanced, in personal appearance fairly matched, and in domestic requirements conformable, in temper this couple differed, though even here they did not often clash, he being equable, if not lymphatic, and she decidedly nervous and sanguine. It was to their tastes and fancies, those smallest, greatest particulars, that no common denominator could be applied. Marchmill considered his wife's likes and inclinations somewhat silly; she considered his sordid and material. The husband's business was that of a gunmaker in a thriving city northwards, and his soul was in that business always; the lady was best characterized by that superannuated phrase of elegance 'a votary of the muse.' An impressionable, palpitating creature was Ella, shrinking humanely from detailed knowledge of her husband's trade whenever she reflected that everything he manufactured had for its purpose the destruction of life. She could only recover her equanimity by assuring herself that some, at least, of his weapons were sooner or later used for the extermination of horrid vermin and animals almost as cruel to their inferiors in species as human beings were to theirs.

She had never antecedently regarded this occupation of his as any objection to having him for a husband. Indeed, the necessity of getting life-leased at all cost, a cardinal virtue which all good mothers teach, kept her from thinking of it at all till she had closed with William, had passed the honeymoon, and reached the reflecting stage. Then, like a person who has stumbled upon some object in the dark, she wondered what she had got; mentally walked round it, estimated it; whether it were rare or common; contained gold, silver, or lead; were a clog or a pedestal, everything to her or nothing.

She came to some vague conclusions, and since then had kept her heart alive by pitying her proprietor's obtuseness and want of refinement, pitying herself, and letting off her delicate and ethereal emotions in imaginative occupations, day-dreams, and night-sighs, which perhaps would not much have disturbed William if he had known of them.

Her figure was small, elegant, and slight in build, tripping, or rather bounding, in movement. She was dark-eyed, and had that marvellously bright and liquid sparkle in each pupil which characterizes persons of Ella's cast of soul, and is too often a cause of heartache to the possessor's male friends, ultimately sometimes to herself. Her husband was a tall, long-featured man, with a brown beard; he had a pondering regard; and was, it must be added, usually kind and tolerant to her. He spoke in squarely shaped sentences, and was supremely satisfied with a condition of sublunary things which made weapons a necessity.

Husband and wife walked till they had reached the house they were in search of, which stood in a terrace facing the sea, and was fronted by a small garden of wind-proof and salt-proof evergreens, stone steps leading up to the porch. It had its number in the row, but, being rather larger than the rest, was in addition sedulously distinguished as Coburg House by its landlady, though everybody else called it 'Thirteen, New Parade.' The spot was bright and lively now; but in winter it became necessary to place sandbags against the door, and to stuff up the keyhole against the wind and rain, which had worn the paint so thin that the priming and knotting showed through.

The householder, who had been watching for the gentleman's return, met them in the passage, and showed the rooms. She informed them that she was a professional man's widow, left in needy circumstances by the rather sudden death of her husband, and she spoke anxiously of the conveniences of the establishment.

Mrs Marchmill said that she liked the situation and the house; but, it being small, there would not be accomodation enough, unless she could have all the rooms.

The landlady mused with an air of disappointment. She wanted the visitors to be her tenants very badly, she said, with obvious honesty. But unfortunately two of the rooms were occupied permanently by a bachelor gentleman. He did not pay season prices, it was true; but as he kept on his apartments all the year round, and was an extremely nice and interesting young man, who gave no trouble, she did not like to turn him out for a month's 'let,' even at a high figure. 'Perhaps, however,' she added, 'he might offer to go for a time.'

They would not hear of this, and went back to the hotel, intending to proceed to the agent's to inquire further. Hardly had they sat down to tea when the landlady called. Her gentleman, she said, had been so obliging as to offer to give up his rooms for three or four weeks rather than drive the new-comers away.

'It is very kind, but we won't inconvenience him in that way,' said the Marchmills.

'O, it won't inconvenience him, I assure you!' said the landlady eloquently. 'You see, he's a different sort of young man from most – dreamy, solitary, rather melancholy – and he cares more to be here when the south-westerly gales are beating against the door, and the sea washes over the Parade, and there's not a soul in the place, than he does now in the season. He'd just as soon be where, in fact, he's going temporarily, to a little cottage on the Island opposite, for a change.' She hoped therefore that they would come.

The Marchmill family accordingly took possession of the house next day, and it seemed to suit them very well. After luncheon Mr Marchmill strolled out towards the pier, and Mrs Marchmill, having dispatched the children to their outdoor amusements on the sands, settled herself in more completely, examining this and that article, and testing the reflecting powers of the mirror in the wardrobe door.

In the small back sitting-room, which had been the young bachelor's, she found furniture of a more personal nature than in the rest. Shabby books, of correct rather than rare editions, were piled up in a queerly reserved manner in corners, as if the previous occupant had not conceived the possibility that any incoming person of the season's bringing could care to look inside them. The landlady hovered on the threshold to rectify anything that Mrs Marchmill might not find to her satisfaction.

'I'll make this my own little room,' said the latter, 'because the books are here. By the way, the person who has left seems to have a good many. He won't mind my reading some of them, Mrs Hooper, I hope?'

'O dear no, ma'am. Yes, he has a good many. You see, he is in the literary line himself somewhat. He is a poet – yes, really a poet – and he has a little income of his own, which is enough to write verses on, but not enough for cutting a figure, even if he cared to.'

'A poet! O, I did not know that.'

Mrs. Marchmill opened one of the books, and saw the owner's name written on the title-page. 'Dear me!' she continued; 'I know his name very well – Robert Trewe – of course I do; and his writings! And it is *his* rooms we have taken, and *him* we have turned out of his home?'

Ella Marchmill, sitting down alone a few minutes later, thought with interested surprise of Robert Trewe. Her own latter history will best explain that interest. Herself the only daughter of a struggling man of letters, she had during the last year or two taken to writing poems, in an endeavour to find a congenial channel in which to let flow her painfully embayed emotions, whose former limpidity and sparkle seemed departing in the stagnation caused by the routine of a practical household and the gloom of bearing children to a commonplace father. These poems, subscribed with a masculine pseudonym, had appeared in various obscure magazines, and in two cases in rather prominent ones. In the second of the latter the page which bore her effusion at the bottom, in smallish print, bore at the top, in large print, a few verses on the same subject by this very man, Robert Trewe. Both of them had, in fact, been struck by a tragic incident reported in the daily papers, and had used it simultaneously as an inspiration, the editor remarking in a note upon the coincidence, and that the excellence of both poems prompted him to give them together.

After that event Ella, otherwise 'John Ivy,' had watched with much attention the appearance anywhere in print of verse bearing the signature of Robert Trewe, who, with a man's unsusceptibility on the question of sex, had never once thought of passing himself off as a woman. To be sure, Mrs Marchmill had satisfied herself with a sort of reason for doing the contrary in her case; since nobody might believe in her inspiration if they found that the sentiments came from a pushing tradesman's wife, from the mother of three children by a matter-of-fact small-arms manufacturer.

Trewe's verse contrasted with that of the rank and file of recent minor poets in being impassioned rather than ingenious, luxuriant rather than finished. Neither *symboliste* nor *décadent*, he was a pessimist in so far as that character applies to a man who looks at the worst contingencies as well as the best in the human condition. Being little attracted by excellences of form and rhythm apart from content, he sometimes, when feeling outran his artistic speed, perpetrated sonnets in the loosely rhymed Elizabethan fashion, which every right-minded reviewer said he ought not to have done.

With sad and hopeless envy Ella Marchmill had often and often scanned the rival poet's work, so much stronger as it always was than her own feeble lines. She had imitated him, and her inability to touch his level would send her into fits of despondency. Months passed away thus, till she observed from the publishers' list that Trewe had collected his fugitive pieces into a volume, which was duly issued, and was much or little praised according to chance, and had a sale quite sufficient to pay for the printing.

This step onward had suggested to John Ivy the idea of collecting her pieces also, or at any rate of making up a book of her rhymes by adding many in manuscript to the few that had seen the light, for she had been able to get no great number into print. A ruinous charge was made for costs of publication; a few reviews noticed her poor little volume; but nobody talked of it, nobody bought it, and it fell dead in a fortnight – if it had ever been alive.

The author's thoughts were diverted to another groove just then by the discovery that she was going to have a third child, and the collapse of her poetical venture had perhaps less effect upon her mind than it might have done if she had been domestically unoccupied. Her husband had paid the publisher's bill with the doctor's, and there it all had ended for the time. But, though less than a poet of her century, Ella was more than a mere multiplier of her kind, and latterly she had begun to feel the old afflatus once more. And now by an odd conjunction she found herself in the rooms of Robert Trewe.

She thoughtfully rose from her chair and searched the apartment with the interest of a fellow-tradesman. Yes, the volume of his own verse was among the rest. Though quite familiar with its contents, she read it here as if it spoke aloud to her, then called up Mrs Hooper, the landlady, for some trivial service, and inquired again about the young man.

'Well, I'm sure you'd be interested in him, ma'am, if you could see him, only he's so shy that I don't suppose you will.' Mrs Hooper seemed nothing loth to minister to her tenant's curiosity about her predecessor. 'Lived here long? Yes, nearly two years. He keeps on his rooms even when he's not here: the soft air of this place suits his chest, and he likes to be able to come back at any time. He is mostly writing or reading, and doesn't see many people, though, for the matter of that, he is such a good, kind young fellow that folks would only be too glad to be friendly with him if they knew him. You don't meet kindhearted people every day.'

'Ah, he's kind-hearted . . . and good.'

'Yes; he'll oblige me in anything if I ask him.
"Mr. Trewe," I say to him sometimes, "you are rather out of spirits." "Well, I am, Mrs. Hooper," he'll say, "though I don't know how you should find it out." "Why not take a little change?" I ask. Then in a day or two he'll say that he will take a trip to Paris, or Norway, or somewhere; and I assure you he comes back all the better for it.'

'Ah, indeed! His is a sensitive nature, no doubt.'

'Yes. Still he's odd in some things. Once when he had finished a poem of his composition late at night he walked up and down the room rehearsing it; and the floors being so thin – jerry-built houses, you know, though I say it myself – he kept me awake up above him till I wished him further. . . . But we get on very well.'

This was but the beginning of a series of conversations about the rising poet as the days went on. On one of these occasions Mrs Hooper drew Ella's attention to what she had not noticed before:

minute scribblings in pencil on the wall-paper behind the curtains at the head of the bed.

'O! let me look,' said Mrs Marchmill, unable to conceal a rush of tender curiosity as she bent her pretty face close to the wall.

'These,' said Mrs Hooper, with the manner of a woman who knew things, 'are the very beginnings and first thoughts of his verses. He has tried to rub most of them out, but you can read them still. My belief is that he wakes up in the night, you know, with some rhyme in his head, and jots it down there on the wall lest he should forget it by the morning. Some of these very lines you see here I have seen afterwards in print in the magazines. Some are newer; indeed, I have not seen that one before. It must have been done only a few days ago.'

'O yes! . . .'

Ella Marchmill flushed without knowing why, and suddenly wished her companion would go away, now that the information was imparted. An indescribable consciousness of personal interest rather than literary made her anxious to read the inscription alone; and she accordingly waited till she could do so, with a sense that a great store of emotion would be enjoyed in the act.

Perhaps because the sea was choppy outside the Island, Ella's husband found it much pleasanter to go sailing and steaming about without his wife, who was a bad sailor, than with her. He did not disdain to go thus alone on board the steamboats of the cheap-trippers, where there was dancing by moonlight, and where the couples would come suddenly down with a lurch into each other's arms; for, as he blandly told her, the company was too mixed for him to take her amid such scenes. Thus, while this thriving manufacturer got a great deal of change and sea-air out of his sojourn here, the life, external at least, of Ella was monotonous enough, and mainly consisted in passing a certain number of hours each day in bathing and walking up and down a stretch of shore. But the poetic impulse having again waxed strong, she was possessed by an inner flame which left her hardly conscious of what was proceeding around her.

She had read till she knew by heart Trewe's last little volume of verses, and spent a great deal of time in vainly attempting to rival some of them, till, in her failure, she burst into tears. The personal element in the magnetic attraction exercised by this circumambient, unapproachable master of hers was so much stronger than the intellectual and abstract that she could not understand it. To be sure, she was surrounded noon and night by his customary environment, which literally whispered of him to her at every moment; but he was a man she had never seen, and that all that moved her was the instinct to specialize a waiting emotion on the first fit thing that came to hand did not, of course, suggest itself to Ella.

In the natural way of passion under the too practical conditions which civilization has devised for its fruition, her husband's love for her had not survived, except in the form of fitful friendship, any more than, or even so much as, her own for him; and, being a woman of very living ardours, that required sustenance of some sort, they were beginning to feed on this chancing material, which was, indeed, of a quality far better than chance usually offers.

One day the children had been playing hide-and-seek in a closet, whence, in their excitement, they pulled out some clothing. Mrs Hooper explained that it belonged to Mr Trewe, and hung it up in the closet again. Possessed of her fantasy, Ella went later in the afternoon, when nobody was in that part of the house, opened the closet, unhitched one of the articles, a mackintosh, and put it on, with the waterproof cap belonging to it.

'The mantle of Elijah!' she said. 'Would it might inspire me to rival him, glorious genius that he is!'

Her eyes always grew wet when she thought like that, and she turned to look at herself in the glass. *His* heart had beat inside that coat, and *his* brain had worked under that hat at levels of thought she would never reach. The consciousness of her weakness beside him made her feel quite sick. Before she had got the things off her the door opened, and her husband entered the room.

'What the devil –'

She blushed, and removed them.

'I found them in the closet here,' she said, 'and put them on in a freak. What have I else to do? You are always away!'

'Always away? Well . . .'

That evening she had a further talk with the landlady, who might herself have nourished a half-tender regard for the poet, so ready was she to discourse ardently about him.

'You are interested in Mr Trewe, I know, ma'am, she said; 'and he has just sent to say that he is going to call to-morrow afternoon to look up some books of his that he wants, if I'll be in, and he may select them from your room?'

'O yes!'

'You could very well meet Mr Trewe then, if you'd like to be in the way!'

She promised with secret delight, and went to bed musing of him.

Next morning her husband observed: 'I've been thinking of what you said, Ell: that I have gone about a good deal and left you without much to amuse you. Perhaps it's true. Today, as there's not much sea, I'll take you with me on board the yacht.'

For the first time in her experience of such an offer Ella was not glad. But she accepted it for the moment. The time for setting out drew near, and she went to get ready. She stood reflecting. The longing to see the poet she was now distinctly in love with overpowered all other considerations.

'I don't want to go,' she said to herself. 'I can't bear to be away! And I won't go.'

She told her husband that she had changed her mind about wishing to sail. He was indifferent, and went his way.

For the rest of the day the house was quiet, the children having gone out upon the sands. The blinds waved in the sunshine to the soft, steady stroke of the sea beyond the wall; and the notes of the Green Silesian band, a troop of foreign gentlemen hired for the season, had drawn almost all the residents and promenaders away from the vicinity of Coburg House. A knock was audible at the door.

Mrs Marchmill did not hear any servant go to answer it, and she became impatient. The books were in the room where she sat; but nobody came up. She rang the bell.

'There is some person waiting at the door,' she said.

'O no, ma'am! He's gone long ago. I answered it,' the servant replied, and Mrs Hooper came in herself.

'So disappointing!' she said. 'Mr Trewe not coming after all!'

'But I heard him knock, I fancy!'

'No; that was somebody inquiring for lodgings who came to the wrong house. I forgot to tell you that Mr Trewe sent a note just before lunch to say I needn't get any tea for him, as he should not require the books, and wouldn't come to select them.'

Ella was miserable, and for a long time could not even re-read his mournful ballad on 'Severed Lives,' so aching was her erratic little heart, and so tearful her eyes. When the children came in with wet stockings, and ran up to her to tell her of their adventures, she could not feel that she cared about them half as much as usual.

'Mrs Hooper, have you a photograph of – the gentleman who lived here?' She was getting to be curiously shy in mentioning his name.

'Why, yes. It's in the ornamental frame on the mantelpiece in your own bedroom, ma'am.'

'No; the Royal Duke and Duchess are in that.'

'Yes, so they are; but he's behind them. He belongs rightly to that frame, which I bought on purpose; but as he went away he said: "Cover me up from those strangers that are coming, for God's sake. I don't want them staring at me, and I am sure they won't want me staring at them." So I slipped in the Duke and Duchess temporarily in front of him, as they had no frame, and Royalties are more suitable for letting furnished than a private young man. If you take 'em out you'll see him under. Lord, ma'am, he wouldn't mind if he knew it! He didn't think the next tenant would be such an attractive lady as you, or he wouldn't have thought of hiding himself, perhaps.'

'Is he handsome?' she asked timidly.

'*I* call him so. Some, perhaps, wouldn't.'

'Should I?' she asked, with eagerness.

'I think you would, though some would say he's more striking than handsome; a large-eyed thoughtful fellow, you know, with a very electric flash in his eye when he looks round quickly, such as you'd expect a poet to be who doesn't get his living by it.'

'How old is he?'

'Several years older than yourself, ma'am; about thirty-one or two, I think.'

Ella was, as a matter of fact, a few months over thirty herself; but she did not look nearly so much. Though so immature in nature, she was entering on that tract of life in which emotional women begin to suspect that last love may be stronger than first love; and she would soon, alas, enter on the still more melancholy tract when at least the vainer ones of her sex shrink from receiving a male visitor otherwise than with their backs to the window or the blinds half down. She reflected on Mrs Hooper's remark, and said no more about age.

Just then a telegram was brought up. It came from her husband, who had gone down the Channel as far as Budmouth with his friends in the yacht, and would not be able to get back till next day.

After her light dinner Ella idled about the shore with the children till dusk, thinking of the yet uncovered photograph in her room, with a serene sense of something ecstatic to come. For, with the subtle luxuriousness of fancy in which this young woman was an adept, on learning that her husband was to be absent that night she had refrained from incontinently rushing upstairs and opening the pictureframe, preferring to reserve the inspection till she could be alone, and a more romantic tinge be imparted to the occasion by silence, candles, solemn sea and stars outside, than was afforded by the garish afternoon sunlight.

The children had been sent to bed, and Ella soon followed, though it was not yet ten o'clock. To gratify her passionate curiosity she now made her preparations, first getting rid of superfluous garments and putting on her dressing-gown, then arranging a chair in front of the table and reading several pages of Trewe's tenderest utterances. Next she fetched the portrait-frame to the light, opened the back, took out the likeness, and set it up before her.

It was a striking countenance to look upon. The poet wore a luxuriant black moustache and imperial, and a slouched hat which shaded the forehead. The large dark eyes described by the landlady showed an unlimited capacity for misery; they looked out from beneath well-shaped brows as if they were reading the universe in the microcosm of the confronter's face, and were not altogether overjoyed at what the spectacle portended.

Ella murmured in her lowest, richest, tenderest tone: 'And it's *you* who've so cruelly eclipsed me these many times!'

As she gazed long at the portrait she fell into thought, till her eyes filled with tears, and she touched the cardboard with her lips. Then she laughed with a nervous lightness, and wiped her eyes.

She thought how wicked she was, a woman having a husband and three children, to let her mind stray to a stranger in this unconscionable manner. No, he was not a stranger! She knew his thoughts and feelings as well as she knew her own; they were, in fact, the self-same thoughts and feelings as hers, which her husband distinctly lacked; perhaps luckily for himself, considering that he had to provide for family expenses.

'He's nearer my real self, he's more intimate with the real me than Will is, after all, even though I've never seen him,' she said.

She laid his book and picture on the table at the bedside, and when she was reclining on the pillow she re-read those of Robert Trewe's verses which she had marked from time to time as most touching and true. Putting these aside she set up the photograph on its edge upon the coverlet, and contemplated it as she lay. Then she scanned again by the light of the candle the half-obliterated pencillings on the wallpaper beside her head. There they were – phrases, couplets, *bouts-rimés*, beginnings and middles of lines, ideas in the rough, like Shelley's scraps, and the least of them so intense, so sweet, so palpitating, that it seemed as if his very breath, warm and loving, fanned her cheeks from those walls, walls that had surrounded his head times and times as they surrounded her own now. He must often have put up his hand so – with the pencil in it. Yes, the writing was sideways, as it would be if executed by one who extended his arm thus.

These inscribed shapes of the poet's world,

'Forms more real than living man,
Nurslings of immortality,'

were, no doubt, the thoughts and spirit-strivings which had come to him in the dead of night, when he could let himself go and have no fear of the frost of criticism. No doubt they had often been written up hastily by the light of the moon, the rays of the lamp, in the blue-grey dawn, in full daylight perhaps never. And now her hair was dragging where his arm had lain when he secured the fugitive fancies; she was sleeping on a poet's lips, immersed in the very essence of him, permeated by his spirit as by an ether.

While she was dreaming the minutes away thus, a footstep came upon the stairs, and in a moment she heard her husband's heavy step on the landing immediately without.

'Ell, where are you?'

What possessed her she could not have described, but, with an instinctive objection to let her husband know what she had been doing, she slipped the photograph under the pillow just as he flung open the door with the air of a man who had dined not badly.

'O, I beg pardon,' said William Marchmill. 'Have you a headache? I am afraid I have disturbed you.'

'No, I've not got a headache,' said she. 'How is it you've come?'

'Well, we found we could get back in very good time after all, and I didn't want to make another day of it, because of going somewhere else tomorrow.'

'Shall I come down again?'

'O no. I'm as tired as a dog. I've had a good feed, and I shall turn in straight off. I want to get out at six o'clock tomorrow if I can. . . . I shan't disturb you by my getting up; it will be long before you are awake.' And he came forward into the room.

While her eyes followed his movements, Ella softly pushed the photograph further out of sight.

'Sure you're not ill?' he asked, bending over her.

'No, only wicked!'

'Never mind that.' And he stooped and kissed her. 'I wanted to be with you tonight.'

Next morning Marchmill was called at six c'clock; and in waking and yawning she heard him muttering to himself: 'What the deuce is this that's been crackling under me so?' Imagining her asleep he searched round him and withdrew something. Through her half-opened eyes she perceived it to be Mr Trewe.

'Well, I'm damned!' her husband exclaimed.

'What, dear?' said she.

'O, you are awake? Ha! ha!'

'What *do* you mean?'

'Some bloke's photograph – a friend of our landlady's, I suppose. I wonder how it came here; whisked off the mantelpiece by accident perhaps when they were making the bed.'

'I was looking at it yesterday, and it must have dropped in then.'

'O, he's a friend of yours? Bless his picturesque heart!'

Ella's loyalty to the object of her admiration could not endure to hear him ridiculed. 'He's a clever man!' she said, with a tremor in her gentle voice which she herself felt to be absurdly uncalled for. 'He is a rising poet – the gentleman who occupied two of these rooms before we came, though I've never seen him.'

'How do you know, if you've never seen him?'

'Mrs Hooper told me when she showed me the photograph.'

'O, well, I must up and be off. I shall be home rather early. Sorry I can't take you today, dear. Mind the children don't go getting drowned.'

That day Mrs. Marchmill inquired if Mr Trewe were likely to call at any other time.

'Yes,' said Mrs Hooper. 'He's coming this day week to stay with a friend near here till you leave. He'll be sure to call.'

Marchmill did return quite early in the afternoon; and, opening some letters which had arrived in his absence, declared suddenly that he and his family would have to leave a week earlier than they had expected to do – in short, in three days.

'Surely we can stay a week longer?' she pleaded. 'I like it here.'

'I don't. It is getting rather slow.'

'Then you might leave me and the children!'

'How perverse you are, Ell! What's the use? And have to come to fetch you! No: we'll all return together; and we'll make out our time in North Wales or Brighton a little later on. Besides, you've three days longer yet.'

It seemed to be her doom not to meet the man for whose rival talent she had a despairing admiration, and to whose person she was now absolutely attached. Yet she determined to make a last effort; and having gathered from her landlady that Trewe was living in a lonely spot not far from the fashionable town on the Island opposite, she crossed over in the packet from the neighbouring pier the following afternoon.

What a useless journey it was! Ella knew but vaguely where the house stood, and when she fancied she had found it, and ventured to inquire of a pedestrian if he lived there, the answer returned by the man was that he did not know. And if he did live there, how could she call upon him? Some women might have the assurance to do it, but she had not. How crazy he would think her. She might have asked him to call upon her, perhaps; but she had not the courage for that, either. She lingered mournfully about the picturesque seaside eminence till it was time to return to the town and enter the steamer for recrossing, reaching home for dinner without having been greatly missed.

At the last moment, unexpectedly enough, her husband said that he should have no objection to letting her and the children stay on till the end of the week, since she wished to do so, if she felt herself able to get home without him. She concealed the pleasure this extension of time gave her; and Marchmill went off the next morning alone.

But the week passed, and Trewe did not call.

On Saturday morning the remaining members of the Marchmill

family departed from the place which had been productive of so much fervour in her. The dreary, dreary train; the sun shining in moted beams upon the hot cushions; the dusty permanent way; the mean rows of wire – these things were her accompaniment: while out of the window the deep blue sea-levels disappeared from her gaze, and with them her poet's home. Heavy-hearted, she tried to read, and wept instead.

Mr Marchmill was in a thriving way of business, and he and his family lived in a large new house, which stood in rather extensive grounds a few miles outside the midland city wherein he carried on his trade. Ella's life was lonely here, as the suburban life is apt to be, particularly at certain seasons; and she had ample time to indulge her taste for lyric and elegiac composition. She had hardly got back when she encountered a piece by Robert Trewe in the new number of her favourite magazine, which must have been written almost immediately before her visit to Solentsea, for it contained the very couplet she had seen pencilled on the wall-paper by the bed, and Mrs Hooper had declared to be recent. Ella could resist no longer, but seizing a pen impulsively, wrote to him as a brother-poet, using the name of John Ivy, congratulating him in her letter on his triumphant executions in metre and rhythm of thoughts that moved his soul, as compared with her own brow-beaten efforts in the same pathetic trade.

To this address there came a response in a few days, little as she had dared to hope for it – a civil and brief note, in which the young poet stated that, though he was not well acquainted with Mr Ivy's verse, he recalled the name as being one he had seen attached to some very promising pieces; that he was glad to gain Mr. Ivy's acquaintance by letter, and should certainly look with much interest for his productions in the future.

There must have been something juvenile or timid in her own epistle, as one ostensibly coming from a man, she declared to herself; for Trewe quite adopted the tone of an elder and superior in this reply. But what did it matter? He had replied; he had written to her with his own hand from that very room she knew so well, for he was now back again in his quarters.

The correspondence thus begun was continued for two months or more, Ella Marchmill sending him from time to time some that she considered to be the best of her pieces, which he very kindly accepted, though he did not say he sedulously read them, nor did he send her any of his own in return. Ella would have been more hurt at this than she was if she had not known that Trewe laboured under the impression that she was one of his own sex.

Yet the situation was unsatisfactory. A flattering little voice told her that, were he only to see her, matters would be otherwise. No doubt she would have helped on this by making a frank confession of womanhood, to begin with, if something had not happened, to her delight, to render it unnecessary. A friend of her husband's, the editor of the most important newspaper in their city and county, who was dining with them one day, observed during their conversation about the poet that his (the editor's) brother the landscape-painter was a friend of Mr Trewe's, and that the two men were at that very moment in Wales together.

Ella was slightly acquainted with the editor's brother. The next morning down she sat and wrote, inviting him to stay at her house for a short time on his way back, and requesting him to bring with him, if practicable, his companion Mr Trewe, whose acquaintance she was anxious to make. The answer arrived after some few days. Her correspondent and his friend Trewe would have much satisfaction in accepting her invitation on their way southward, which would be on such and such a day in the following week.

Ella was blithe and buoyant. Her scheme had succeeded; her beloved though as yet unseen one was coming. 'Behold, he standeth behind our wall; he looked forth at the windows, showing himself through the lattice,' she thought ecstatically. 'And, lo, the winter is past, the rain is over and gone, the flowers appear on the earth, the time of the singing of birds is come, and the voice of the turtle is heard in our land.'

But it was necessary to consider the details of lodging and feeding him. This she did most solicitously, and awaited the pregnant day and hour.

It was about five in the afternoon when she heard a ring at the door and the editor's brother's voice in the hall. Poetess as she was, or as she thought herself, she had not been too sublime that day to dress with infinite trouble in a fashionable robe of rich material, having a faint resemblance to the *chiton* of the Greeks, a style just then in vogue among ladies of an artistic and romantic turn, which had been obtained by Ella of her Bond Street dressmaker when she was last in London. Her visitor entered the drawing-room. She looked towards his rear; nobody else came through the door. Where, in the name of the God of Love, was Robert Trewe?

'O, I'm sorry,' said the painter, after their introductory words had been spoken. 'Trewe is a curious fellow, you know, Mrs Marchmill. He said he'd come; then he said he couldn't. He's rather dusty. We've been doing a few miles with knapsacks, you know; and he wanted to get on home.'

'He – he's not coming?'

'He's not; and he asked me to make his apologies.'

'When did you p-p-part from him?' she asked, her nether lip starting off quivering so much that it was like a *tremolo*-stop opened in her speech. She longed to run away from this dreadful bore and cry her eyes out.

'Just now, in the turnpike road yonder there.'

'What! he has actually gone past my gates?'

'Yes. When we got to them – handsome gates they are, too, the finest bit of modern wrought-iron work I have seen – when we came to them we stopped, talking there a little while, and then he wished me good-bye and went on. The truth is, he's a little bit depressed just now, and doesn't want to see anybody. He's a very good fellow, and a warm friend, but a little uncertain and gloomy sometimes; he thinks too much of things. His poetry is rather too erotic and passionate, you know, for some tastes; and he has just come in for a terrible slating from the—*Review* that was published yesterday; he saw a copy of it at the station by accident. Perhaps you've read it?'

'No.'

'So much the better. O, it is not worth thinking of; just one of those articles written to order, to please the narrow-minded set of subscribers upon whom the circulation depends. But he's upset by it. He says it is the misrepresentation that hurts him so; that, though he can stand a fair attack, he can't stand lies that he's powerless to refute and stop from spreading. That's just Trewe's weak point. He lives so much by himself that these things affect him much more than they would if he were in the bustle of fashionable or commercial life. So he wouldn't come here, making the excuse that it all looked so new and monied – if you'll pardon –'

'But – he must have known – there was sympathy here! Has he never said anything about getting letters from this address?'

'Yes, yes, he has, from John Ivy – perhaps a relative of yours, he thought, visiting here at the time?'

'Did he – like Ivy, did he say?'

'Well, I don't know that he took any great interest in Ivy.'

'Or in his poems?'

'Or in his poems – so far as I know, that is.'

Robert Trewe took no interest in her house, in her poems, or in their writer. As soon as she could get away she went into the nursery and tried to let off her emotion by unnecessarily kissing the children, till she had a sudden sense of disgust at being reminded how plain-looking they were, like their father.

The obtuse and single-minded landscape-painter never once perceived from her conversation that it was only Trewe she wanted, and not himself. He made the best of his visit, seeming to enjoy the society of Ella's husband, who also took a great fancy to him, and showed him everywhere about the neighbourhood, neither of them noticing Ella's mood.

The painter had been gone only a day or two when, while sitting upstairs alone one morning, she glanced over the London paper just arrived, and read the following paragraph: –

'SUICIDE OF A POET

*'Mr Robert Trewe, who has been favourably known for some years as one of our rising lyrists, committed suicide at his lodgings at Solentsea on Saturday evening last by shooting himself in the right temple with a revolver. Readers hardly need to be reminded that Mr Trewe has recently attracted the attention of a much wider public than had hitherto known him, by his new volume of verse, mostly of an impassioned kind, entitled "Lyrics to a Woman Unknown," which has been already favourably noticed in these pages for the extraordinary gamut of feeling it traverses, and which has been made the subject of a severe, if not ferocious, criticism in the—*Review. *It is supposed, though not certainly known, that the article may have partially conduced to the sad act, as a copy of the review in question was found on his writing-table; and he has been observed to be in a somewhat depressed state of mind since the critique appeared.'*

Then came the report of the inquest, at which the following letter was read, it having been addressed to a friend at a distance: –

'Dear—,—Before these lines reach your hands I shall be delivered from the inconveniences of seeing, hearing, and knowing more of the things around me. I will not trouble you by giving my reasons for the step I

have taken, though I can assure you they were sound and logical. Perhaps had I been blessed with a mother, or a sister, or a female friend of another sort tenderly devoted to me, I might have thought it worth while to continue my present existence. I have long dreamt of such an unattainable creature, as you know; and she, this undiscoverable, elusive one, inspired my last volume; the imaginary woman alone, for, in spite of what has been said in some quarters, there is no real woman behind the title. She has continued to the last unrevealed, unmet, unwon. I think it desirable to mention this in order that no blame may attach to any real woman as having been the cause of my decease by cruel or cavalier treatment of me. Tell my landlady that I am sorry to have caused her this unpleasantness; but my occupancy of the rooms will soon be forgotten. There are ample funds in my name at the bank to pay all expenses.

R. TREWE.'

Ella sat for a while as if stunned, then rushed into the adjoining chamber and flung herself upon her face on the bed.

Her grief and distraction shook her to pieces; and she lay in this frenzy of sorrow for more than an hour. Broken words came every now and then from her quivering lips: 'O, if he had only known of me – known of me – me! . . . O, if I had only once met him – only once; and put my hand upon his hot forehead – kissed him – let him know how I loved him – that I would have suffered shame and scorn, would have lived and died, for him! Perhaps it would have saved his dear life! . . . But no – it was not allowed! God is a jealous God; and that happiness was not for him and me!'

All possibilities were over; the meeting was stultified. Yet it was almost visible to her in her fantasy even now, though it could never be substantiated –

'The hour which might have been, yet might not be,
Which man's and woman's heart conceived and bore,
Yet whereof life was barren.'

She wrote to the landlady at Solentsea in the third person, in as subdued a style as she could command, enclosing a postal order for a sovereign, and informing Mrs Hooper that Mrs Marchmill had seen in the papers the sad account of the poet's death, and having been, as Mrs Hooper was aware, much interested in Mr Trewe during her stay at Coburg House, she would be obliged if Mrs Hooper could obtain a small portion of his hair before his coffin was closed down, and send it her as a memorial of him, as also the photograph that was in the frame.

By the return-post a letter arrived containing what had been requested. Ella wept over the portrait and secured it in her private drawer; the lock of hair she tied with white ribbon and put in her bosom, whence she drew it and kissed it every now and then in some unobserved nook.

'What's the matter?' said her husband, looking up from his newspaper on one of these occasions. 'Crying over something? A lock of hair? Whose is it?'

'He's dead!' she murmured.

'Who?'

'I don't want to tell you, Will, just now, unless you insist!' she said, a sob hanging heavy in her voice.

'O, all right.'

'Do you mind my refusing? I will tell you some day.'

'It doesn't matter in the least, of course.'

He walked away whistling a few bars of no tune in particular; and when he had got down to his factory in the city the subject came into Marchmill's head again.

He, too, was aware that a suicide had taken place recently at the house they had occupied at Solentsea. Having seen the volume of poems in his wife's hand of late, and heard fragments of the landlady's conversation about Trewe when they were her tenants, he all at once said to himself, 'Why of course it's he! . . . How the devil did she get to know him? What sly animals women are!'

Then he placidly dismissed the matter, and went on with his daily affairs. By this time Ella at home had come to a determination. Mrs Hooper, in sending the hair and photograph, had informed her of the day of the funeral; and as the morning and noon wore on an overpowering wish to know where they were laying him took possession of the sympathetic woman. Caring very little now what her husband or any one else might think of her eccentricities, she wrote Marchmill a brief note, stating that she was called away for the afternoon and evening, but would return on the following morning. This she left on his desk, and having given the same information to the servants, went out of the house on foot.

When Mr Marchmill reached home early in the afternoon the servants looked anxious. The nurse took him privately aside, and hinted that her mistress's sadness during the past few days had been such that she feared she had gone out to drown herself. Marchmill reflected. Upon the whole he thought that she had not done that. Without saying whither he was bound he also started off, telling them not to sit up for him. He drove to the railway-station, and took a ticket for Solentsea.

It was dark when he reached the place, though he had come by a fast train, and he knew that if his wife had preceded him thither it could only have been by a slower train, arriving not a great while before his own. The season at Solentsea was now past: the parade was gloomy, and the flys were few and cheap. He asked the way to the Cemetery, and soon reached it. The gate was locked, but the keeper let him in, declaring, however, that there was nobody within the precincts. Although it was not late, the autumnal darkness had now become intense; and he found some difficulty in keeping to the serpentine path which led to the quarter where, as the man had told him, the one or two interments for the day had taken place. He stepped upon the grass, and, stumbling over some pegs, stooped now and then to discern if possible a figure against the sky. He could see none; but lighting on a spot where the soil was trodden, beheld a crouching object beside a newly made grave. She heard him, and sprang up.

'Ell, how silly this is!' he said indignantly. 'Running away from home – I never heard such a thing! Of course I am not jealous of this unfortunate man; but it is too ridiculous that you, a married woman with three children and a fourth coming, should go losing your head like this over a dead lover! . . . Do you know you were locked in? You might not have been able to get out all night.'

She did not answer.

'I hope it didn't go far between you and him, for your own sake.'

'Don't insult me, Will.'

'Mind, I won't have any more of this sort of thing; do you hear?'

'Very well,' she said.

He drew her arm within his own, and conducted her out of the Cemetery. It was impossible to get back that night; and not wishing to be recognized in their present sorry condition he took her to a miserable little coffee-house close to the station, whence they departed early in the morning, travelling almost without speaking, under the sense that it was one of those dreary situations occurring in married life which words could not mend, and reaching their own door at noon.

The months passed, and neither of the twain ever ventured to start a conversation upon this episode. Ella seemed to be only too frequently in a sad and listless mood, which might almost have been called pining. The time was approaching when she would have to undergo the stress of childbirth for a fourth time, and that apparently did not tend to raise her spirits.

'I don't think I shall get over it this time!' she said one day.

'Pooh! what childish foreboding! Why shouldn't it be as well now as ever?'

She shook her head. 'I feel almost sure I am going to die; and I should be glad, if it were not for Nelly, and Frank, and Tiny.'

'And me!'

'You'll soon find somebody to fill my place,' she murmured, with a sad smile. 'And you'll have a perfect right to; I assure you of that.'

'Ell, you are not thinking still about that – poetical friend of yours?'

She neither admitted nor denied the charge. 'I am not going to get over my illness this time,' she reiterated. 'Something tells me I shan't.'

This view of things was rather a bad beginning, as it usually is; and, in fact, six weeks later, in the month of May, she was lying in her room, pulseless and bloodless, with hardly strength enough left to follow up one feeble breath with another, the infant for whose unnecessary life she was slowly parting with her own being fat and well. Just before her death she spoke to Marchmill softly: –

'Will, I want to confess to you the entire circumstances of that – about you know what – that time we visited Solentsea. I can't tell what possessed me – how I could forget you so, my husband! But I had got into a morbid state: I thought you had been unkind; that you had neglected me; that you weren't up to my intellectual level, while he was, and far above it. I wanted a fuller appreciator, perhaps, rather than another lover – '

She could get no further then for very exhaustion; and she went off in sudden collapse a few hours later, without having said anything more to her husband on the subject of her love for the poet. William Marchmill, in truth, like most husbands of several years' standing, was little disturbed by retrospective jealousies, and had not shown the least anxiety to press her for confessions concerning a man dead and gone beyond any power of inconveniencing him more.

But when she had been buried a couple of years it chanced one day that, in turning over some forgotten papers that he wished to destroy before his second wife entered the house, he lighted on a lock of hair in an envelope, with the photograph of the deceased poet, a date being written on the back in his late wife's hand. It was that of the time they spent at Solentsea.

Marchmill looked long and musingly at the hair and portrait, for something struck him. Fetching the little boy who had been the death of his mother, now a noisy toddler, he took him on his knee, held the lock of hair against the child's head, and set up the photograph on the table behind, so that he could closely compare the features each countenance presented. By a known but inexplicable trick of Nature there were undoubtedly strong traces of resemblance to the man Ella had never seen; the dreamy and peculiar expression of the poet's face sat, as the transmitted idea, upon the child's, and the hair was of the same hue.

'I'm damned if I didn't think so!' murmured Marchmill. 'Then she *did* play me false with that fellow at the lodgings! Let me see: the dates – the second week in August . . . the third week in May. . . . Yes . . . yes. . . . Get away, you poor little brat! You are nothing to me!'

The Spectre of the Real

This is the only story Hardy wrote in collaboration with another writer, and though on its publication in *To-Day Magazine* in November 1894 the credit line read, 'By Thomas Hardy and Florence Henniker', according to Michael Millgate in his *Thomas Hardy: A Biography* (1982), 'The story was essentially Hardy's work – compromised not so much by Mrs Henniker's participation as by Hardy's attempts to give that participation a greater substance than the circumstances really allowed.' According to Millgate, Hardy provided the outline for this 'weird tale', as he referred to it, in the autumn of 1893, and after Mrs Henniker had made her contribution such as it was, he 'wrote out the story in its entirety.'

There has been much speculation about Thomas Hardy's relationship with the striking-looking Florence Henniker, the daughter of Lord Houghton, and the wife of a soldier, Major Arthur Henniker. The couple had first met in May 1893 when Hardy was a guest in her brother's house in Dublin. She was already a published novelist (*Sir George*, 1891, and *Foiled*, 1893), and Hardy found her to be a 'charming and intuitive woman'. Later they were to meet at Literary Lunches Florence held in London, and she visited him on a number of occasions in Dorset. If he nursed a secret passion for her – as has been claimed – he did not speak about it, though a number of Hardy's poems about unrequited love are said to refer to her. Despite the fact the two writers continued to correspond from 1893 until just before Florence Henniker's death in 1923, and Hardy offered critical advice on her work, they never wrote another word 'in collaboration'. Following its magazine publication, 'The Spectre of the Real' was later collected in book form in Mrs Henniker's volume, *In Scarlet And Grey*, published in 1896. It has, though, never appeared in any Hardy collection until this one.

The Spectre of the Real

I

A certain March night of this present 'waning age' had settled down upon the woods and the park and the parapets of Ambrose Towers. The harsh stable-clock struck a quarter to ten. Thereupon a girl in light evening attire and wraps came through the entrance-hall, opened the front door and the small wrought-iron gate beyond it which led to the terrace, and stepped into the moonlight. Such a person, such a night, and such a place were unexceptionable materials for a scene in that poetical drama of two which the world has often beheld, which leads up to a contract that causes a slight sinking in the poetry, and a perceptible lack of interest in the play.

She moved so quietly that the alert birds resting in the great cedar-tree never stirred. Gliding across its funereal shadow over a smooth plush of turf, as far as to the Grand Walk whose pebbles shone like the floor-stones of the Apocalyptic City, she paused and looked back at the old brick walls – red in the daytime, sable now – at the shrouded mullions, the silhouette of the tower, though listening rather than seeing seemed her object in coming to the pause. The clammy wings of a bat brushed past her face, startling her and making her shiver a little. The stamping of one or two horses in their stalls surprised her by its distinctness and isolation. The servants' offices were on the other side of the house, and the lady who, with the exception of the girl on the terrace, was its sole occupant, was resting on a sofa behind one of the curtained windows. So Rosalys went on her way unseen, trod the margin of the lake, and plunged into the distant shrubberies.

The clock had reached ten. As the last stroke of the hour rang out a young man scrambled down the sunk fence bordering the pleasure-ground, leapt the iron railing within, and joined the girl who stood awaiting him. In the half-light he could not see how her full underlip trembled, or the fire of joy that kindled in her eyes. But perhaps he guessed from daylight experiences, since he passed his arm round her shoulders with assurance, and kissed her ready mouth many times. Her head still resting against his arm, they walked towards a bench, the rough outlines of which were touched at one end only by the moonrays. At the dark end the pair sat down.

'I cannot come again,' said the girl.

'Oh?' he vaguely returned. 'This is new. What has happened? I thought you said your mother supposed you to be working at your Harmony, and would never imagine our meeting here?' The voice sounded just a trifle hard for a lover's.

'No, she would not. And I still detest deceiving her. I would do it for no one but you, Jim. But what I meant was this: I feel that it can all lead to nothing. Mother is not a bit more worldly than most people, but she naturally does not want her only child to marry a man who has nothing but the pay of an officer in the Line to live upon. At her death (you know she has only a life-interest here) I should have to go away unless my uncle, who succeeds, chose to take me to stay with him. I have no fortune of my own beyond a mere pittance. Two hundred a year.'

Jim's reply was something like a sneer at the absent lady: 'You may as well add to the practical objection the sentimental one – that she wouldn't allow you to change your fine old crusted name for mine, which is merely the older one of the little freeholder turned out of this spot by your ancestor when he came.'

'Dear, dear Jim, don't say those horrid things! As if *I* had ever even thought of that for a moment!'

He shook her hand off impatiently, and walked out into the

moonlight. Certainly, as far as physical outline went, he might have been the direct product of a line of Paladins or hereditary Crusaders. He was tall, straight of limb, with an aquiline nose, and a mouth fitfully scornful. Rosalys sat almost motionless watching him. There was no mistaking the ardour of her feelings; her power over him seemed to be lessened by his consciousness of his influence upon the lower and weaker side of her nature. It gratified him as a man to feel it; and though she was beautiful enough to satisfy the senses of the critical, there was perhaps something of contempt interwoven with his love. His victory had been too easy, too complete.

'Dear Jim, you are not going to be vexed? It really isn't my fault that I can't come out here again! Mother will be downstairs tomorrow, and then she might take it into her head to look at any time into the schoolroom and see how the Harmony gets on.'

'And you are going off to London soon?' said Jim, still speaking gloomily.

'I am afraid so. But couldn't you come there too? I know your leave is not up for a great many weeks?'

He was silent for longer than she had ever known him at these times. Rosalys left her seat on the bench and threw her arms impulsively round him.

'I *can't* go away unless you will come to London when we do, Jim!'

'I will; but on one condition.'

'What condition? You frighten me!'

'That you will marry me when I do join you there.'

The quick breath that heaved in Rosalys ebbed silently, and she leant on the rustic bench with one hand, a trembling being apparent in her garments.

'You really – mean it, Jim, darling?'

He swore that he did; that life was quite unendurable to him as he then experienced it. When she was once his wife, nothing would come between them; but, of course, the marriage need not be known for a time – indeed, must not. He could not take her abroad. The climate of Burmah would be too trying for her; and, besides, they really would not have enough to live upon.

'Couldn't we get on as other people do?' said Rosalys, trying not to cry at these arguments. 'I am so tired of concealment, and I don't like to marry privately! It seems to me, much as I love being with you, that there is a sort of – well – vulgarity in our clandestine meetings as we now enjoy them. Therefore, how should I ever have strength enough to hide the fact of my being your wife, to face my mother day after day with the shadow of this secret between us?'

For all answer Jim kissed her, and stroked her silky, brown curls.

'I suppose I shall end in agreeing with you – I always do!' she said, her mouth quivering. 'Though I *can* be very dogged and obstinate too, Jim! Do you know that all my governesses have said I was the most stubborn child they ever came across? But then, in that case, my temper must be really aroused. You have never seen me as I am when angry. Perhaps, Jim, you would get to hate me?'

She looked at him wistfully with her wet eyes.

'I shall never cease to love you desperately, as I do now!' declared the young man. 'How lovely you look, little Rosalys, with that one moonbeam making your forehead like pure white marble. But time is passing. You must go back, my darling, I'm afraid. And you won't fail me in London? I shall make all the plans. Good-bye – good-bye!'

One clinging, intermittent kiss; and then from the shadow in which he stood Jim watched her light figure passing the lake, and hurrying along in the shelter of the yew hedges towards the great house, asleep under reaching deeps of sky, and the vacant gaze of the round white moon.

II

When clouds are iron-grey above the prim drab houses, and a hard east wind blows flakes of dust, stable-straws, scraps of soiled newspaper, and sharp pieces of grit into the eyes of foot-passengers, a less inviting and romantic dwelling-spot than Belgrave Road can hardly be experienced.

But the Prince's daughter of the Canticles, emerging from her palace to see the vine flourish and the pomegranates bud forth with her Beloved, could not have looked more unconscious of grime than Rosalys Ambrose as she came down the steps of one of the tall houses in the aforesaid respectable place of residence. Her cheeks were hotly pink, her eyes shining, her lips parted. Having once made up her mind, 'qualms of prudence, pride and pelf,' had died within her passionate little heart. After today she would belong absolutely to Jim, be his alone, through all the eternities, as it seemed; and of what account was anything else in the world? The entirely physical character of his affection for her, and perhaps of hers for him, was an unconjectured element herein which might not render less transitory the most transitory of sweet things. Thus hopefully she stepped out of the commonplace home that would, in one sense, be hers no more.

The raw wind whistled up the street, and deepened the colour on her face. She was plainly dressed in grey, and wore a rather thick veil, natural to the dusty day; it could not however conceal the sparkle of her eyes; veils, even thick ones, happily, never do. Hailing a hansom, she told the driver to take her to the corner of the Embankment.

In the midst of her preoccupation she noticed as the cab turned the corner out of Belgrave Road that the bony chestnut-horse went lame. Rosalys was superstitious as well as tenderhearted, and she deemed that some stroke of ill-luck might befall if she drove to be married behind a suffering animal. She alighted and paid off the man, and in her excitement gave him three times his fare. Hurrying forward on foot, she heard her name called, and received a cordial greeting from a tall man with grey whiskers, in whom she recognised Mr Durrant, Jim's father. It occurred to her for a second that he might have discovered the plot and have lain in wait to prevent it. However, he spoke in his usual half-respectful, half-friendly tones, not noticing her frightened face. Mr Durrant was a busy man. Besides holding several very important land-agencies in the county where Rosalys lived, he had business in the City to transact at times. He explained to Miss Ambrose that some urgent affairs he was supervising for a client of his, Lord Parkhurst, had now brought him up to London for a few weeks.

'Lord Parkhurst is away?' she asked, to say something. 'I hear of him sometimes through his uncle Colonel Lacy.'

'Yes. A thorough sailor. Mostly afloat,' Mr Durrant replied. 'Well – we're rather out of the way in Porchester Terrace. Otherwise my wife would be so pleased if you would come to tea, Miss Ambrose! My son Jim, lazy young beggar, is up here now too – going to plays and parties. Well, well, it's natural he should like to amuse himself before he leaves for Burmah, poor boy. Are you looking for a hansom? Yes! Hi!' and he waved his stick.

'Thank you so much,' said Miss Ambrose. 'And I will tell mamma where you and Mrs Durrant are staying.'

She was surprised at her own composure. Her unconscious father-in-law elect helped her into the cab, took off his hat, and walked rapidly away. Rosalys felt her heart stand still when she drew up at the place of meeting. She saw Jim, very blooming, and very well dressed, awaiting her, outwardly calm, at any rate. He jumped into her vehicle, and they drove on City-wards.

'You are only ten minutes late, dearest,' he said. 'Do you know, I was half afraid you might have failed me at the last moment?'

'You don't believe it, Jim!'

'Well, I sometimes think I ought not to expect you to keep engagements with me so honestly as you do. Good, brave little Rosalys!'

They moved on through the press of struggling omnibuses, gigantic vans, covered carts, and foot-passengers who darted at imminent risk of their lives amid the medley of wheels, horses, and shouting drivers. The noise jarred Rosalys' head, and she began to be feverishly anxious.

The church stood in the neighbourhood of a great meat-market, and the pavement was crowded by men in blue linen blouses, their clothes sprinkled with crimson stains. The young girl gave a shiver of disgust.

'How revolting it must be to have a butcher for a husband! They can't have hearts like other men. . . . What a gloomy part of London this is to be married in, Jim!'

'Ah – yes! Everything looks gloomy with the east wind blowing. Now, here we are! Jump out, little woman!'

He handed money to the driver, who went off with the most cursory thoughts of the part that he had played in this little excursion of a palpitating pair into the unknown.

'Jimmy, darling; oughtn't you, or one of us, to have lived here for fifteen days?' she said, as they entered the fine old Norman porch, to which she was quite blind in her preoccupation.

Durrant laughed. 'I have declared that I did,' he answered coolly. 'I hope in the circumstances that it's a forgivable lie. Cheer up, Rosalys; don't all of a sudden look so solemn!'

There were tears in her eyes. The gravity of the step she was about to take had begun to frighten her.

They had some time to wait before the clergyman condescended to come out of the vestry and perform the ceremony which was to unite her to Jim. Two or three other couples were also in the church on the same errand: a haggard woman in a tawdry white bonnet, hanging on to the arm of a short, crimson-faced man, who had evidently been replenishing his inside with gin to nerve himself to the required pitch for the ordeal; a girl with a coarse, hard face, accompanied by a slender youth in shabby black; a tall man of refined aspect, in very poor clothes, whose hollow cough shook his thin shoulders and chest, and told his bride that her happiness, such as it was, would probably last but the briefest space.

Rosalys glanced absently at the beautiful building, with its Norman apse and transverse arches of horse-shoe form, and the massive curves and cushion-capitals that supported the tower-end; the whole impression left by the church being one of singular harmony, loveliness, and above all, repose – which struck even her by its great contrast with her experiences just then. As the clergyman emerged from the vestry a shaft of sunlight smote the altar, touched the quaint tomb where the founder of the building lay in his dreamless sleep, and quivered on the darned clothes of the consumptive bridegroom.

Jim and Rosalys moved forward, and then the light shone for a moment too upon his yellow hair and handsome face. To the woman who loved him it seemed that 'from the crown of his head even to the sole of his foot there was no blemish in him.'

The curate looked sharply at the four couples; angrily, Rosalys fancied, at her. But it was only because the east wind had given him an acute toothache that his gaze was severe, and his reading spiritless.

The four couples having duly contracted their inviolable unities, and slowly gone their ways through the porch, Jim and Rosalys adjourned to a fashionable hotel on the Embankment, where in a room all to themselves they had luncheon, over which Rosalys presided with quite a housewifely air.

'When shall I see you again?' he said, as he put her into a cab two or three hours later on in the afternoon.

'You must arrange all that, Jim. Somehow I feel so depressed, so dreadfully sad now, all of a sudden! Have I been wicked? I don't know!'

Her tone changed, as she met his passionate gaze, and she said very low with a lump in her throat –

'O my dear darling! I care for nothing in the whole wide world, now that I belong to you!'

III

The London weeks went by with all their commonplaces, all their novelties. Mr Durrant, senior, had finished his urgent business, and returned to his square and uninteresting country house. But Jim lingered on in town, although conscious of some subtle change in himself and his view of things. He and Rosalys met whenever it was possible, which was pretty frequently. Often they contrived to do so at hastily arranged luncheons and teas at hotels or restaurants; sometimes, when Mrs Ambrose was suddenly called away, at Jim's own rooms. Sometimes they adventured to queer suburban coffee-houses.

In the lapse of these weeks the twain began somehow to lose a little of their zest for each other's society. Jim himself was aware of it before he had yet discovered that something of the same disappointment was dulling her heart too. On his own side it was the usual lowering of the fire – the slackening of a man's passion for a woman when she becomes his property. On hers it was a more mixed feeling. No doubt her love for Jim had been of but little higher quality than his for her. She had thoroughly abandoned herself to his good looks, his recklessness, his eagerness; and, now that the novelty of wifedom was past, her fervour also began to burn itself down. But beyond, above, this, the concealment of her marriage was repugnant to Rosalys. When the rapture of the early meetings had died away she began to loathe the sordid deceit which these involved; the secretly dispatched letters, the unavoidably brazen lies to her mother, who, if she attached overmuch importance to money and birth, yet loved her daughter in all good faith and simplicity. Then once or twice Jim was late at their interviews. He seemed indifferent and preoccupied. His manner stung Rosalys into impatient utterance at the end of a particular meeting in which this mood was unduly prominent.

'You forget all I have given up for you!' she cried. 'You make a fool of me in allowing me to wait here for you. It is humiliating and vulgar. I hate myself for behaving as I do!'

'The renunciations are not all on your side,' he answered caustically. 'You forget all that the loss of his freedom means to a man!'

Her heart swelled, and she had great difficulty in keeping back her tears. But she took refuge in sullenness.

'Unfortunately we can't undo our folly!' she murmured. 'You will have to make the best of it as well as I. I suppose the awakening to a sense of our idiocy was bound to come sooner or later. But – I didn't think it would come so soon. Jim, look at me! Are you really angry. Don't, for God's sake, go and leave me like this!'

He was walking slowly towards the great iron gate leading out of Kensington Gardens, a dogged cast on his now familiar countenance.

'Don't make a scene in public, for Heaven's sake, Rosalys!'

Feeling that he had spoken too brutally, he suddenly paused and changed.

'I am sorry, little woman, if I was cross! But things have combined to harass me lately. Of course we won't part from one another in anger.'

Jim glanced at her straight profile with its full underlip and firmly curved chin, at the lashes on either lid, and the glossy brown hair twisted in coils under her hat. But the sight of this loveliness, now all his own, failed to arouse the old emotions. He simply contemplated her approvingly from an artistic point of view.

They had reached the gateway, and she placed her hand on his arm.

'Good-bye. When shall we next meet? Today is Tuesday. Shall it be Friday?'

'I am afraid I must go out of London on Thursday for a day or two. I'll write, dear. Let me call a hansom.'

She thanked him in a cold voice again, and with a last hand-shake, and a smile that hovered on sorrow, left him and drove away towards Belgravia.

Once or twice later on they met; the next interview being shorter and sadder perhaps than the last. The one that followed it ended in bitterness.

'This had better be our long good-bye, I suppose?' said she.

'Perhaps it had. . . . You seem to be always looking out for causes of reproach, Rosalys. I don't know what has come over you.'

'It is *you* who have changed!' she cried, with a little stamp. 'And you are by far the most to blame of us two. You forget that I should never have contemplated marriage as a possibility! You have made me lie to my mother, do things of which I am desperately ashamed, and now you don't attempt to disguise your weariness of me!'

It was Jim's turn to lose his temper now. 'You forget that *you* gave me considerable encouragement! Most girls would not have come out again and again to surreptitious meetings with a man who was in love with them – girls brought up as you have been!'

She started as in a spasm. A momentary remorse seized him. He realised that he had been betrayed into speaking as no man of kindly good-feeling could speak. He made a tardy, scarcely gracious apology, and they parted. A few days afterwards he wrote a letter full of penitence for having hurt her, and she answered almost affectionately. But each knew that their short-lived romance was dead as the wind-flowers that had blossomed at its untimely birth.

IV

In August this pair of disappointed people met once more amid their old surroundings. Perhaps their enforced absence from one another gave at first some zest to their reunion. Jim was at times tender, and like his former self; Rosalys, if sad and subdued, less sullen and reproachful than she had been in London.

Mrs Ambrose had fallen into delicate health, and her daughter was in consequence able to dispose of her time outside the house as she wished. The moonlight meetings with Jim were discontinued; but husband and wife went for long strolls sometimes in the remoter nooks of the park, through winding walks in the distant shrubberies, and down paths hidden by high yew hedges from intruding eyes that might look with suspicion on their being together.

On one especially beautiful August day they paced side by side, talking at moments with something of their old tenderness. The sky above the dark-green barriers on either hand was a bottomless deep of blue. The yew-boughs were covered in curious profusion by the handiwork of energetic spiders, who had woven their glistening webs in every variety of barbaric pattern. In shape some resembled hammocks, others purses, others deep bags, in the middle of which a large yellow insect remained motionless and watchful.

'Shall we sit for a little while in the summerhouse?' said Rosalys at last, in flat accents, for a *tête-à-tête* with Jim had long ceased to give her any really strong beats of pleasure. 'I want to talk to you further about plans; how often we had better write, and so on.'

They sat down in an arbour made of rustic logs which overlooked the mere. The woodwork had been left rough within, and dusty spider-webs hung in the crevices; here and there the bark had fallen away in strips; above, on the roof, there were clumps of fungi, looking like tufts of white fur.

'This is a sunless, queer sort of place you have chosen,' he said, looking round critically.

The boughs had grown so thickly in the foreground that the glittering margin of water was hardly perceptible between their interlacing twigs, and no visible hint of a human habitation was given, though the rustic shelter had been originally built with the view of affording a picturesque glimpse of the handsome old brick house, wherein the Ambroses had lived for some three centuries.

'You might have found a more lively scene for what will be, perhaps, our last interview for years,' Jim went on.

'Are you really going so soon?' she asked, passing over the complaint.

'Next week. And my father has made all sorts of arrangements for me. Besides, he is beginning to suspect that you and I are rather too intimate. And your mother knows, somehow or other, that I have been up several times of late. We must be careful.'

'I suppose so,' she answered absently, looking out under the log-roof at a chaffinch swinging himself backwards and forwards on a large bough. A sort of dreary indifference to her surroundings; a sense of being caged and trapped had begun to take possession of Rosalys. The present was full of perplexity, the future objectless. Now and then, when she looked at Jim's lithe figure, and healthy, virile face, she felt that perhaps she might have been able to love him still if only he had cared for her with a remnant of his former passionate devotion. But his indifference was even more palpable than her own. They sat and talked on within the dim arbour for a little while. Then Jim made one of the unfortunate remarks that always galled her to the quick. She rose in anger, answered him with cold sarcasm, and hastened away down the little wood. He followed her, a rather ominous light shining in his eyes.

'Your temper is really growing insufferable, Rosalys!' he cried, and clenched his hand roughly on her arm to detain her.

'How dare you!' said the girl. 'For God's sake leave me, and don't come back again! I rejoice to think that in a few days it will not be in your power to insult me any more!'

'Damn it – I am going to leave you, am I not? I only want to keep you here for a moment to come to some understanding! Indeed, you'll be surprised to find how very much I am going to leave you, when you hear what I mean! My ideas have grown considerably emancipated of late, and therefore I tell you there is no reason on earth why any soul should ever know of that miserable mistake we made in the spring.'

She winced a little; it was an unexpected move; and her eyes lingered uneasily on a copper-coloured butterfly playing a game of hide-and-seek with a little blue companion.

'Who,' he continued, 'is ever going to search the register of that old East-London church? We must philosophically look on the marriage as an awkward fact in our lives, which won't prevent our loving anybody else when we feel inclined. In my opinion this early error will carry one advantage with it – that we shall be unable to extinguish any love we may feel for another person by a sordid matrimonial knot – unless, indeed, after seven years of obliviousness to one another's existence.'

'I'll – try to – emancipate myself likewise,' she said slowly. 'It will be well to forget this tragedy of our lives! And the most tragic part of it is – that we are not even sorry that we don't love each other any more!'

'The truest words you ever spoke!'

'And the surest event that was ever to come, given your nature.'

'And yours!'

She hastened on down the grass walk into the broad gravelled path leading to the house. At the corner stood Mrs Ambrose, who was better, and had come out for a stroll – assuming as an invalid the privilege of wearing a singular scarlet gown, and a hat in which a number of black quills stood startingly erect.

'Ah – Rosy!' she cried. 'Oh, and Mr Durrant? What a colour you have got, child!'

'Yes. Mr Durrant and I have been having a furious political discussion, mamma. I have grown quite hot over it. He is more unreasonable than ever. But when he gets abroad he won't be as he is now. A few years of India will change all that.' And to carry on the idea of her unconcern she turned to whistle to a bold robin that had flitted down from a larch-tree, perched on the yew hedge, and looked inquiringly at her, answering her whistle with his pathetic little pipe.

Durrant had come up behind. 'Yes,' he said cynically. 'One never knows how an enervating country may soften one's brains.'

He bade them a cool good-bye and left. She watched his retreating figure, the figure of the active, the strong, the handsome animal, who had scarcely won the better side of her nature at all. He never turned his head. So this was the end!

The bewildering bitterness of it well-nigh paralysed Rosalys for a few moments. Why had they been allowed – he and she – to love one another with that eager, resistless passion, and then to part with less interest in each other than ordinary friends? She felt ashamed of having ceded herself to him. If her mother had not been beside her she would have screamed out aloud in her exasperating pain.

Mrs Ambrose lifted up her voice. 'What are you looking at, child? . . . My dear, I want a little word with you. Are you sure you are attending? When you pout your lip like that, Rosalys, I always know that you are in a bad frame of mind . . . The vicar has been here; and he has made me a little unhappy.'

'I should have thought he was too stupid to give any one a pang! Why do they put such simpletons into the churches?'

'Well – he says that people are chattering about you and that young Durrant. And I must tell you that – that, from a marrying point of view, he is impossible. You know that. And I don't want him to make up to you. Now, Rosalys, my darling, tell me honestly – I feel I have not looked after you lately as I ought to have done – tell me honestly: Is he in love with you?'

'He is not, mother, to my certain knowledge.'

'Are you with him?'

'No. That I swear.'

V

Seven years and some months had passed since Rosalys spoke as above-written. And never a sound of Jim.

As she had mentally matured under the touch of the gliding seasons, Miss Ambrose had determined to act upon the hint Jim had thrown out to her as to the practical nullity of their marriage contract if they simply kept in different hemispheres without a word. She had never written to him a line; and he had never written a line to her.

He might be dead for all that she knew; he possibly was dead. She had taken no steps to ascertain anything about him, though she had been aware for years that his name was no longer in the Army List. Dead or alive he was completely cut off from the county in which he and she had lived, for his father had died a long time before this, his house and properties had been sold, and not a scion of the house of Durrant remained in that part of England.

Rosalys had readily imbibed his ideas of their mutual independence; and now, after the lapse of all these years, had acted upon them with the surprising literalness of her sex when they act upon advice at all.

Mrs Ambrose, who had distinguished herself in no whit during her fifty years of life saving by the fact of having brought a singularly beautiful girl into the world, had passed quietly out of it. Rosalys's uncle had succeeded his sister-in-law in the possession of the old house with its red tower, and the broad paths and garden-lands; he had been followed by an unsatisfactory son of his, last in the entail, and thus unexpectedly Rosalys Ambrose found herself sole mistress of the spot of her birth.

People marvelled somewhat that she continued to call herself Miss Ambrose. Though a woman now getting on for thirty, she was remarkably attractive both in face and in figure, and could confront the sunlight as well as the moonbeams still. In the manner of women who are yet sure of their charms she was fond of representing herself as much older than she really was. Perhaps she would have been disappointed if her friends had not laughed and contradicted her, and told her that she was still lovely and looked like a young girl. Lord Parkhurst, anyhow, was firmly of that contradictory opinion; and perhaps she cared more for his views than for any one else's at the present time.

That distinguished sailor had been but one of many suitors; but he had stirred her heart as none of the others could do. It was not merely that he was brave, and pleasing, and had returned from a campaign in Egypt with a hero's reputation; but that his chivalrous feelings towards women, originating perhaps in the fact that he knew very little about them, were sufficient to gratify the most exacting of the sex.

His rigid notions of duty and honour, both towards them and from them, made the blood of Rosalys run cold when she thought of a certain little episode of her past life, notwithstanding that, or perhaps because, she loved him dearly.

'He is not the least bit of a flirt, like most sailors,' said Miss Ambrose to her cousin and companion, Miss Jennings, on a particular afternoon in the eighth year of Jim Durrant's obliteration from her life. It was an afternoon with an immense event immediately ahead of it; no less an event than Rosalys's marriage with Lord Parkhurst, which was to take place on the very next day.

The local newspaper had duly announced the coming wedding in proper terms as 'the approaching nuptials of the beautiful and wealthy Miss Ambrose, of Ambrose Towers, with a distinguished naval officer, Lord Parkhurst.' There followed an ornamental account of the future bridegroom's heroic conduct during the late war. 'The handsome face and figure of Lord Parkhurst,' wound up the honest paragraphist, 'are not altogether unknown to us in this vicinity, as he has recently been visiting his uncle, Colonel Lacy, High Sheriff of the county. We wish all prosperity to the happy couple, who have doubtless a brilliant and cloudless future before them.'

This was the way in which her acceptance of Durrant's views had worked themselves out. He had said: 'After seven years of mutual oblivion we can marry again if we choose.'

And she had chosen.

Rosalys almost wished that Lord Parkhurst had been a flirt, or at least had won experience as the victim of one, or many, of those precious creatures, and had not so implicitly trusted her. It would have brought things more nearly to a level.

'A flirt! I should think not,' said Jane Jennings. 'In fact, Rosalys, he is almost alarmingly strict in his ideas. It is a mistake to believe that so many women are angels, as he does. He is too simple. He is bound to be disappointed some day.'

Miss Ambrose sighed nervously. 'Yes,' she said.

'I don't mean by you tomorrow! God forbid!'

'No.'

Miss Ambrose sighed again, and a silence followed, during which, while recalling unutterable things of the past, Rosalys gazed absently out of the window at the lake, that some men were dredging; the mud, left bare by draining down the water, being imprinted with hundreds of little footmarks of plovers feeding there. Eight or nine herons stood further away, one or two composedly fishing, their grey figures reflected with unblurred clearness in the mirror of the pool. Some little water-hens waddled with a fussy gait across the sodden ground in front of them, and a procession of wild geese came through the sky, and passed on till they faded away into a row of black dots.

Suddenly the plovers rose into the air, uttering their customary wails, and dispersing like a group of stars from a rocket; and the herons drew up their flail-like legs, and flapped themselves away.

Something had disturbed them; a carriage sweeping round to the other side of the house.

There's the door-bell!' Rosalys exclaimed, with a start. 'That's he, it must be! Is my hair untidy, Jane? I've been rumpling it awfully, leaning back on the cushions. And do see if my gown is all right at the back – it never did fit well.'

The butler flung open the folding doors, and announced in the voice of a man who felt that it was quite time for this nonsense of calling to be put an end to by the more compact arrangement of the morrow –

'Lord Parkhurst!'

A man of middle size, with a fair and pleasant face, and a short beard, entered the room. His blue eyes smiled rather more than his lips as he took the little hand of his hostess in his own with the air of one verging on proprietorship of the same, and said: 'Now, darling; about what we have to settle before the morning! I have come entirely on business, as you perceive.'

Rosalys tenderly smiled up at him. Miss Jennings left the room, and Rosalys's sailor silently kissed and admired his betrothed, till he continued –

'Ah – my beautiful one! I have nothing to give you in return for the immeasurable gift you are about to bestow on me – excepting such love as no man ever felt before! I almost wish you were not quite so good, and perfect, and innocent as you are! And I wish you were a poorer woman – as poor as I – and had no lovely home such as this. To think you have rejected all other men for such an unworthy fellow as me!'

Rosalys looked away from him along the green vistas of chestnuts and beeches stretching far down outside the windows.

'Oswald – I know how much you care for me; and that is why I – hope you won't be disappointed – after you have taken me tomorrow for good and all! I wonder if I shall hinder and hamper you in your profession? Perhaps you ought to marry a girl much younger than yourself – your nature is so young – not a maturing woman like me.'

For all answer he smiled at her with the confiding, fearless gaze that she loved.

Lord Parkhurst stayed on through a paradisiacal hour till Miss Jennings came to tell them that tea was in the library. Presently they were reminded by the same faithful relative and dependant that on that evening of all evenings they had promised to drive across to the house of Colonel Lacy, Lord Parkhurst's uncle, and one of Rosalys's near neighbours, and dine there quietly with two or three intimate friends.

VI

When Rosalys entered Colonel Lacy's drawing-room before dinner, the eyes of the few guests assembled there were naturally enough fixed upon her.

'By Jove, she's better looking than ever – though she's not more than a year or two under thirty!' whispered young Lacy to a man standing in the shadow behind a high lamp.

The person addressed started, and did not answer for a moment. Then he laughed and said forcedly –

'Yes, wonderfully handsome she certainly is.'

As he spoke his hostess, a fat and genial lady, came blandly towards him.

'Mr Durrant, I'm so sorry we've no lady for you to take in tonight. One or two people have thrown us over. I want to introduce you to Miss Ambrose. Isn't she lovely? Oh, how stupid I am! Of course you grew up in this neighbourhood, and must have known all about her as a girl.'

Jim Durrant it was, in the flesh; once the soldier, now the 'traveller and explorer' of the little-known interior of Asiatic countries, to use the words in which he described himself. His foreign-looking and sun-dried face was rather pale and set as he walked last into the dining-room with young Lacy. He had only arrived on that day at an hotel in the nearest town, where he had been accidentally met and recognised by that young man, and asked to dinner offhand.

Smiling, and apparently unconscious, he sat down on the left side of his hostess, talking calmly to her and across the table to the one or two whom he knew. Rosalys heard his voice as the phantom of a dead sound mingling with the usual trivial words and light laughter of the rest – Lord Parkhurst's conversation about Egyptian finance, and Mrs Lacy's platitudes about the Home Rule question – as if she were living through a curiously incoherent dream.

Suddenly during the progress of dinner Mrs Lacy looked across with a glance of solicitude towards the other end of the table, and said in a low voice –

'I am afraid Miss Ambrose is rather over-strained – as she may naturally be? She looks *so* white and tired. Do you think, Parkhurst, that she finds this room too hot? I will have the window opened at the top.'

'She does look pale,' Lord Parkhurst murmured, and as he spoke glanced anxiously and tenderly towards his betrothed. 'I think, too, she has a little overtaxed herself – she doesn't usually get so white as this.'

Rosalys felt his eyes upon her, looked across at him, and smiled strangely.

When dinner was ended Rosalys still seemed not quite herself, whereupon she was taken in hand by her good and fussy hostess; sal-volatile was brought, and she was given the most comfortable chair and the largest cushions the house afforded. It seemed to Rosalys as if hours had elapsed before the men joined the ladies, and there came that general moving of places like the shuffling of a pack of cards. She heard Jim's voice speaking close to her ear –

'I want to have a word with you.'

'I can't!' she faltered.

'Did you get my letter?'

'No', said she.

'I wonder how that was! Well – I'll be at the door of Ambrose Towers while the stable-clock is striking twelve tonight. Be there to meet me. I'll not detain you long. We must have an understanding.'

'For God's sake how do you come here?'

'I saw in the newspapers that you were going to marry. What could I do otherwise than let you know I was alive?'

'Oh, you might have done it less cruelly!'

'Will you be at the door?'

'I *must*, I suppose! . . . Don't tell him here – before these people! It will be such an agonising disturbance that –'

'Of course I shan't. Be there.'

This was all they could say. Lord Parkhurst came forward, and observing to Durrant 'They are wanting you for bézique,' sat down beside Rosalys.

She had intended to go home early, and went even earlier than she had planned. At half-past ten she found herself in her own hall, not knowing how she had got there, or when she had bidden adieu to Lord Parkhurst, or what she had said to him.

Jim's letter was lying on the table awaiting her.

As soon as she had got upstairs and slipped into her dressing-gown, had dispatched her maid, and ascertained that all the household had retired, she read her husband's note, which briefly informed her that he had led an adventurous life since they had parted, and had come back to see if she were living, when he suddenly heard that she was going to be married. Then Rosalys sat down at her writing-table to begin somehow a letter to Lord Parkhurst. To write that was an imperative duty, before she slept. It need not be said that awful indeed to her was its object – the letting Lord Parkhurst know that she had a husband, and had seen him that day. But she could not shape a single line; and the visioned aspect that she would wear in his eyes as soon as he discovered the truth of her history was so terrible to her that she burst into hysterical sobbing over the paper as she sat.

The clock crept on to twelve before Rosalys had written a word. The labour seemed Herculean – insuperable. Why had she not told him face to face?

Twelve o'clock it was, and nothing done; and controlling herself as women can when they must, she went down to the door. Softly opening it a little way she saw against the iron gate immediately without it the form of her husband, Jim Durrant – upon the whole much the same form she had known eight years ago.

'Here I am,' said he.

'Yes', said she.

'Open this iron thing.'

A momentary feeling of aversion caused her to hesitate.

'Do you hear – do you mean to say – Rosalys!' he began.

'No – no. Of course I will!' She opened the grille and he came up and touched her hand lightly.

'A kiss is not allowed, I suppose,' he observed, with a mock solemnity, 'in view of the fact that you are to be married tomorrow?'

'You know better,' she said, 'Of course I'm not going to commit bigamy! The wedding is not to be.'

'Have you explained it to him?'

'N – no – not yet. I was just writing it when —'

'Ha – you haven't! Good. Woman's way. Shall I give him a friendly call tomorrow morning?'

'Oh, no, no – let me do it!' she implored. I love him so well, and it will break his heart if it is not done gently! O God – if I could only die tonight, while he still believes in me! You don't know what affection I have felt for him!' she continued miserably, not caring what Jim thought. 'He has been my whole world! And he – he believes me to be so good! He has all the old-fashioned ideas of marriage that people of your fast set smile at! He knows nothing of any kind of former acquaintance between you and me. I ought not to have done it – kept him in the dark! I tried not to. But I was so fearfully lonely! And now I've lost him! . . . If I could only have got at that register in that City church, how I would have torn out the leaf!' she added vehemently.

'That's a pleasant remark to make to a husband!'

'Well – that was my feeling; I may as well be honest! I didn't know you were coming back any more; and you yourself suggested that I might be able to re-marry!'

'You'd better do it – I shan't tell. And if anybody else did, the punishment is not heavy nowadays. The judges are beginning to discountenance informers on previous marriages, if the new-assorted couples themselves are satisfied to forget them.'

'Don't insult me so. You've not forgotten how to do that in all these years!'

There was a silence, in which she with passive gloom regarded the familiar scene before her. The inquisitive jays, the pensive wood-doves, that lodged at their ease thereabouts, as if knowing that their proprietor was a gunless woman, all slept calmly, and not a creature was conscious of the presence of these two but a little squirrel they had disturbed in a beech near the shady wall. Durrant remained gazing at her; then he spoke, in a changed and richer voice—

'Rosalys!'

She looked vaguely at his face without answering.

'How pretty you look in this starlight – much as you did when we used to meet here nine or ten years ago!'

'Ah! But—'

' . . . Let me sit down in your hall, or somewhere, Rosalys! I've come a long way today, and I'm tired. And after eight years!'

'I don't know what to say to it – there's no light downstairs! The servants may hear us, too – it is not so very late.'

'We can whisper. And suppose they do? They must know tomorrow.'

She gasped a sigh and preceded him in through the door.

'Yes, they must!' she said.

VII

When they re-appeared the lawn was as silent as when they had left it, though the sleep of things had weakened down to a certain precarious slightness, and round the corner of the house a low line of light showed the dawn.

'Now, good-bye, dear,' said her husband lightly. 'You'll let him know at once?'

'Of course.'

'And send to me directly after?'

'Yes.'

'And now for my walk across the fields to the hotel. These boots are thin, but I know the old way well enough. By Jove, I wonder what Mélanie—'

'Who?'

'Oh – What Mélanie will think, I was going to say. It slipped out. I didn't mean to hurt your feelings at all.'

'Mélanie – who is she?'

'Well – she's a French lady. You know, of course, Rosalys, that I thought you were perhaps dead – and – so this lady passes as Mrs Durrant.'

Rosalys started.

'In fact I found her in the East, and took pity upon her – that's all. Though if it had happened that you had not been living now I have got back, I should have married her at once, of course.'

'Is – she, then, here with you at the hotel?'

'Oh no – I wouldn't bring her on here till I knew how things were.'

'Then where is she?'

'I left her at my rooms in London. Oh, it will be all right – I shall see her safely back to Paris, and make a little provision for her. Nobody in England knows anything of her existence.'

'When – did you part from her?'

'Well, of course, at breakfast-time.'

Rosalys bowed herself against the doorway, and Jim was almost distressed when he saw the distortion of her agonised face.

'Now why should you take on like this! There's nothing in it. People do these things. Living in a prim society here you don't know how the world goes on!'

'Oh, but to think it didn't occur to me that the sort of man—'

Jim, though anxious, seemed to awaken to something humorous in the situation, and vented a momentary chuckle. 'Well, it is rather funny that I should have let it out. But still—'

'Don't make a deep wrong deeper by cruel levity. Go away!'

'You'll be in a better mood tomorrow, mark me; and then I'll tell you all my history. There – I'm gone! *Au revoir*!'

He disappeared under the trees. Rosalys, rousing herself, closed the gate and fastened the door, and sat down in one of the hall chairs, her teeth shut tight, and her little hands clenched. When she had passed this mood, and returned upstairs, she bent again over her writing-table and wept.

But in a few minutes she found herself nerved to an unexpected and passionate vigour of action, and began writing her letter to Lord Parkhurst with great rapidity. Sheet after sheet she filled, and having read them over, she sealed up the letter and placed it on the mantelpiece to be given to a groom and dispatched by hand as soon as the morning was a little further advanced.

With cold feet and a burning head she flung herself upon the bed just as she was, and waited for the day without the power to sleep. When she had lain nearly two hours, and the morning had crept in and she could hear from the direction of the stables that the men were astir, she rang for her maid, and, taking the letter in her hand, stood with it in an attitude of suspense as the woman entered. The latter looked full of intelligence.

'Are any of the men about?' asked Rosalys.

'Yes, ma'am. There have been such an accident in the Meads this past night – about half a mile down the river – and Jones ran up from the lodge to call for help quite early; and Benton and Peters went as soon as they were dressed. A gentleman drowned – yes – it's Mr James Durrant – the son of Mr Durrant who died some years ago. He came home only yesterday, after having been heard nothing of for years and years. He left Mrs Durrant, who they say is a French lady, somewhere in London, but they have telegraphed and found her, and she's coming. They say she's quite distracted. The poor gentleman left the Three Lions last night and went out to dinner, saying he would walk home, as it was a fine night and not very far; and it is supposed he took the old short cut across the moor where there used to be a path when he was a lad at home, crossing the big river by a plank. There is only a rail now, and he must have tried to get across upon it, for it was broken in two, and his body found in the water-weeds just below.'

'Is he – dead?'

'Oh yes. They had a great trouble to get him out. The men have just come from carrying him to the hotel. It will be sad for his poor wife when she gets there.'

'His poor wife – yes.'

'Travelling all the way from London on such an errand!'

Rosalys had allowed the hand in which she held the letter to Lord Parkhurst to drop to her side; she now put it in the pocket of her dressing-gown.

'I was wishing to send somewhere,' she said. 'But I think I shall wait till later.'

The house was astir betimes on account of the wedding, and Rosalys's companion in particular, who was not sad because she was going to live on with the bride. When Miss Jennings saw her cousin's agitation she said she looked ill, and insisted upon sending for the doctor. He, who was the local practitioner, arrived at breakfast-time; very proud to attend such an important lady, who usually got doctored in London. He said that Rosalys was not quite in her ordinary state of health, prescribed a tonic, and declared that she would be all right in an hour or two. He then informed her that he had been suddenly called up that morning about the case of which they had possibly heard – the drowning of Mr Durrant.

'And you could do nothing?'asked Rosalys.

'Oh no. He'd been under water too long for any human aid. Dead and stiff. . . . It was not so very far down from here. . . . Yes, I remember him quite as a boy. But he has had no relations hereabout for years past – old Durrant's property was sold to pay his debts, if you recollect; and nobody expected to see the son again. I think he has lived in the East Indies a good deal. Much better for him if he had not come – poor fellow.'

When the doctor had left, Rosalys went to the window, and remained for some time thinking. There was the lake from which the water had flowed down to the river that had drowned Jim after visiting her last night – as a mere interlude in his life with the Frenchwoman Mélanie. She turned, took from her dressing-gown pocket the renunciatory letter to her intended husband, Lord

Parkhurst, thrust it through the bars of the grate, and watched it till it was entirely consumed.

The wedding had been fixed for an early hour in the afternoon, and as the morning wore on Rosalys felt increasing strength, mental and physical. The doctor's dose had been a powerful one; the image of Mélanie, too, had much to do with her recuperative mood; more still Rosalys's innate qualities, the nerve of the woman who nine years earlier had gone to the city to be married as if it were a mere shopping expedition; most of all, she loved Lord Parkhurst; he was the man among all men she desired. Rosalys allowed things to take their course.

Soon the dressing began; and she sat through it quite calmly. When Lord Parkhurst rode across for a short visit that day he only noticed that she seemed strung-up, nervous, and that the flush of love which mantled her cheek died away to pale rather quickly.

On the way to church the road skirted the low-lying ground where the river was, and about a dozen men were seen in the bright-green meadow, standing beside the deep central stream, and looking intently at a broken rail.

'Who are those men?' said the bride.

'Oh – they are the coroner's jury, I think,' said Miss Jennings, 'come to view the place where the unfortunate Mr Durrant lost his life last night. It was curious that, by the merest accident, he should have been at Mrs Lacy's dinner – since they hardly knew him at all.'

'It was – I saw him there,' said Rosalys.

Ten minutes later she was kneeling against the altar railings, with Lord Parkhurst on her right hand.

The wedding was by no means a gay one, and there were few people invited, Rosalys, for one thing, having hardly any relations. The newly united pair got away from the house very soon after the ceremony. When they drove off there was a group of people round the door, and some among the bystanders asked how far they were going that day.

'To Dover. They cross the Channel tomorrow, I believe.'

Tomorrow came, and those who had gathered together at the wedding went about their usual duties and amusements, Colonel Lacy among the rest. As he and his wife were returning home by the late afternoon train after a short journey up the line, he bought a copy of an evening paper, and glanced at the latest telegrams.

'My good God!' he cried.

'What?' said she, starting towards him.

He tried to read – then handed the paper; and she read for herself –

> 'DOVER. – DEATH OF LORD PARKHURST, R.N.
>
> *'We regret to announce that this distinguished nobleman and heroic naval officer, who arrived with Lady Parkhurst last evening at the Lord Chamberlain Hotel in this town, preparatory to starting on their wedding-tour, entered his dressing-room very early this morning, and shot himself through the head with a revolver. The report was heard shortly after dawn, none of the inmates of the hotel being astir at the time. No reason can be assigned for the rash act.'*

A Committee-Man of 'The Terror'

This dramatic historical tale contains one of the most chilling moments in all Hardy's macabre fiction when the heroine, known alluringly as 'Mademoiselle V—', who is about to elope with the man who had condemned the members of her family to death, sees a procession of their shades – all headless! The story is set at Budmouth (actually Weymouth where Hardy worked as a young architect from 1869–70) during the cessation of the hostilities between France and England in 1802–3, and according to the Hardy expert, Richard Purdy, was based on a letter the author came across from a certain Lady Elizabeth Talbot who described an incident in the Strand, London, when a member of the French Committee of Public Safety was seen by a Parisian lady whose father, mother and brother he had murdered. At this, said the letter, 'she fainted away in the street, and before she recovered enough to speak he had escaped in the crowd.'

Hardy embellished this basic idea as well as changing the location for 'A Committee-Man of "The Terror"' which he offered to *The Illustrated London News* in the autumn of 1896. It later appeared in the issue of November 14, accompanied, sadly, by a number of uninspired illustrations which caused it to be generally unknown for a number of years.

A Committee-Man of 'The Terror'

We had been talking of the Georgian glories of our old-fashioned watering-place, which now, with its substantial russet-red and dun brick buildings in the style of the year eighteen hundred, looks like one side of a Soho or Bloomsbury Street transported to the shore, and draws a smile from the modern tourist who has no eye for solidity of build. The writer, quite a youth, was present merely as a listener. The conversation proceeded from general subjects to particular, until old Mrs H—, whose memory was as perfect at eighty as it had ever been in her life, interested us all by the obvious fidelity with which she repeated a story many times related to her by her mother when our aged friend was a girl – a domestic drama much affecting the life of an acquaintance of her said parent, one Mademoiselle V—, a teacher of French. The incidents occurred in the town during the heyday of its fortunes, at the time of our brief peace with France in 1802 – 3.

'I wrote it down in the shape of a story some years ago, just after my mother's death,' said Mrs H—. 'It is locked up in my desk there now.'

'Read it!' said we.

'No,' said she; 'the light is bad, and I can remember it well enough, word for word, flourishes and all.' We could not be choosers in the circumstances, and she began.

'There are two in it, of course, the man and the woman, and it was on an evening in September that she first got to know him. There had not been such a grand gathering on the Esplanade all the season. His Majesty King George the Third was present, with all the princesses and royal dukes, while upwards of three hundred of the general nobility and other persons of distinction were also in the town at the time. Carriages and other conveyances were arriving every minute from London and elsewhere; and when among the rest a shabby stage-coach came in by a by-route along the coast from Havenpool, and drew up at a second-rate tavern, it attracted comparatively little notice.

'From this dusty vehicle a man alighted, left his small quantity of luggage temporarily at the office, and walked along the street as if to look for lodgings.

'He was about forty-five – possibly fifty – and wore a long coat of faded superfine cloth, with a heavy collar, and a bunched-up neckcloth. He seemed to desire obscurity.

'But the display appeared presently to strike him, and he asked of a rustic he met in the street what was going on; his accent being that of one to whom English pronunciation was difficult.

'The countryman looked at him with a slight surprise, and said, "King Jarge is here and his royal Cwort."

'The stranger inquired if they were going to stay long.

'"Don't know, Sir. Same as they always do, I suppose."

'"How long is that?"

'"Till some time in October. They've come here every zummer since eighty-nine."

'The stranger moved onward down St Thomas Street, and approached the bridge over the harbour backwater, that then, as now, connected the old town with the more modern portion. The spot was swept with the rays of a low sun, which lit up the harbour lengthwise, and shone under the brim of the man's hat and into his eyes as he looked westward. Against the radiance figures were crossing in the opposite direction to his own; among them this lady of my mother's later acquaintance, Mademoiselle V—. She was the daughter of a good old French family, and at that date a pale woman, twenty-eight or thirty years of age, tall and elegant in figure, but plainly dressed and wearing that evening (she said) a small muslin shawl crossed over the bosom in the fashion of the time, and tied behind.

'At sight of his face, which, as she used to tell us, was unusually distinct in the peering sunlight, she could not help giving a little shriek of horror, for a terrible reason connected with her history, and after walking a few steps further, she sank down against the parapet of the bridge in a fainting fit.

'In his preoccupation the foreign gentleman had hardly noticed her, but her strange collapse immediately attracted his attention. He quickly crossed the carriageway, picked her up, and carried her into the first shop adjoining the bridge, explaining that she was a lady who had been taken ill outside.

'She soon revived; but, clearly much puzzled, her helper perceived that she still had a dread of him which was sufficient to hinder her complete recovery of selfcommand. She spoke in a quick and nervous way to the shopkeeper, asking him to call a coach.

'This the shopkeeper did, Mademoiselle V— and the stranger remaining in constrained silence while he was gone. The coach came up, and giving the man the address, she entered it and drove away.

'"Who is that Lady?" said the newly arrived gentleman.

'"She's of your nation, as I should make bold to suppose," said the shopkeeper. And he told the other that she was Mademoiselle V—, governess at General Newbold's, in the same town.

'"You have many foreigners here?" the stranger inquired.

'"Yes, though mostly Hanoverians. But since the peace they are learning French a good deal in genteel society, and French instructors are rather in demand."

'"Yes, I teach it," said the visitor. "I am looking for a tutorship in an academy."

'The information given by the burgess to the Frenchman seemed to explain to the latter nothing of his countrywoman's conduct – which, indeed, was the case – and he left the shop, taking his course again over the bridge and along the south quay to the Old Rooms Inn, where he engaged a bedchamber.

'Thoughts of the woman who had betrayed such agitation at sight of him lingered naturally enough with the newcomer. Though, as I stated, not much less than thirty years of age, Mademoiselle V—, one of his own nation, and of highly refined and delicate appearance, had kindled a singular interest in the middle-aged gentleman's breast, and her large dark eyes, as they had opened and shrunk from him, exhibited a pathetic beauty to which hardly any man could have been insensible.

'The next day, having written some letters, he went out and made known at the office of the town "Guide" and of the newspaper, that a teacher of French and calligraphy had arrived, leaving a card at the bookseller's to the same effect. He then walked on aimlessly, but at length inquired the way to General Newbold's. At the door, without giving his name, he asked to see Mademoiselle V—, and was shown into a little back parlour, where she came to him with a gaze of surprise.

'"My God! Why do you intrude here, Monsieur?" she gasped in French as soon as she saw his face.

'"You were taken ill yesterday. I helped you. You might have been run over if I had not picked you up. It was an act of simple humanity certainly; but I thought I might come to ask if you had recovered?"

'She had turned aside, and had scarcely heard a word of his speech. "I hate you, infamous man!" she said. "I cannot bear your helping me. Go away!"

'"But you are a stranger to me."

'"I know you too well!"

'"You have the advantage then, Mademoiselle. I am a new-comer here. I never have seen you before to my knowledge; and I certainly do not, could not, hate you."

'"Are you not Monsieur B—?"

'He flinched. "I am— in Paris," he said. "But here I am Monsieur G—."

'"That is trivial. You are the man I say you are."

'"How did you know my real name, Mademoiselle?"

'"I saw you in years gone by, when you did not see me. You were formerly Member of the Committee of Public Safety, under the Convention."

'"I was."

'"You guillotined my father, my brother, my uncle – all my family, nearly, and broke my mother's heart. They had done nothing but keep silence. Their sentiments were only guessed. Their headless corpses were thrown indiscriminately into the ditch of the Mousseaux Cemetery, and destroyed with lime."

'He nodded.

'"You left me without a friend, and here I am now, alone in a foreign land."

'"I am sorry for you," said he. "Sorry for the consequence, not for the intent. What I did was a matter of conscience, and, from a point of view indiscernible by you, I did right. I profited not a farthing. But I shall not argue this. You have the satisfaction of seeing me here an exile also, in poverty, betrayed by comrades, as friendless as yourself."

'"It is no satisfaction to me, Monsieur."

"Well, things done cannot be altered. Now to the question: are you quite recovered?"

'"Not from dislike and dread of you – otherwise, yes."

'"Good morning, Mademoiselle."

'"Good morning."

'They did not meet again till one evening at the theatre (which my mother's friend was with great difficulty induced to frequent, to perfect herself in English pronunciation, the idea she entertained at that time being to become a teacher of English in her own country later on). She found him sitting next to her, and it made her pale and restless.

'"You are still afraid of me?"

'"I am. O cannot you understand!"

'He signified the affirmative.

'"I follow the play with difficulty," he said presently.

'"So do I – *now,*" said she.

'He regarded her long, and she was conscious of his look; and while she kept her eyes on the stage they filled with tears. Still she would not move, and the tears ran visibly down her cheek, though the play was a merry one, being no other than Mr Sheridan's comedy of "The Rivals," with Mr S. Kemble as Captain Absolute. He saw her distress, and that her mind was elsewhere; and abruptly rising from his seat at candle-snuffing time he left the theatre.

'Though he lived in the old town, and she in the new, they frequently saw each other at a distance. One of these occasions was when she was on the north side of the harbour, by the ferry, waiting for the boat to take her across. He was standing by Cove Row, on the quay opposite. Instead of entering the boat when it arrived she stepped back from the quay; but looking to see if he remained she beheld him pointing with his finger to the ferry-boat.

'"Enter!" he said, in a voice loud enough to reach her.

'Mademoiselle V— stood still.

'"Enter!" he said, and, as she did not move, he repeated the word a third time.

'She had really been going to cross, and now approached and stepped down into the boat. Though she did not raise her eyes she knew that he was watching her over. At the landing steps she saw from under the brim of her hat a hand stretched down. The steps were steep and slippery.

'"No, Monsieur," she said. "Unless, indeed, you believe in God, and repent of your evil past!"

'"I am sorry you were made to suffer. But I only believe in the god called Reason, and I do not repent. I was the instrument of a national principle. Your friends were not sacrificed for any ends of mine."

'She thereupon withheld her hand, and clambered up unassisted. He went on, ascending the Look-out Hill, and disappearing over the brow. Her way was in the same direction, her errand being to bring home the two young girls under her charge, who had gone to the cliff for an airing. When she joined them at the top she saw his solitary figure at the further edge, standing motionless against the sea. All the while that she remained with her pupils he stood without turning, as if looking at the frigates in the roadstead, but more probably in meditation, unconscious where he was. In leaving the spot one of the children threw away half a sponge-biscuit that she had been eating. Passing near it he stooped, picked it up carefully, and put it in his pocket.

'Mademoiselle V— came homeward, asking herself, "Can he be starving?"

'From that day he was invisible for so long a time that she thought he had gone away altogether. But one evening a note came to her, and she opened it trembling.

> *'I am here ill,' it said, 'and, as you know, alone. There are one or two little things I want done, in case my death should occur, and I should prefer not to ask the people here, if it could be avoided. Have you enough of the gift of charity to come and carry out my wishes before it is too late?'*

'Now so it was that, since seeing him possess himself of the broken cake, she had insensibly begun to feel something that was more than curiosity, though perhaps less than anxiety, about this fellow-countryman of hers; and it was not in her nervous and sensitive heart to resist his appeal. She found his lodging (to which he had removed from the Old Rooms inn for economy) to be a room over a shop, half-way up the steep and narrow street of the old town, to which the fashionable visitors seldom penetrated. With some misgiving she entered the house, and was admitted to the chamber where he lay.

'"You are too good, too good," he murmured. And presently,

"you need not shut the door. You will feel safer, and they will not understand what we say."

'"Are you in want, Monsieur? Can I give you – "

"No, no. I merely want you to do a trifling thing or two that I have not strength enough to do myself. Nobody in the town but you knows who I really am – unless you have told?"

'"I have not told . . . I thought you *might* have acted from principle in those sad days, even—"

'"You are kind to concede that much. However, to the present. I was able to destroy my few papers before I became so weak. . . . But in the drawer there you will find some pieces of linen clothing – only two or three – marked with initials that may be recognized. Will you rip them out with a penknife?"

'She searched as bidden, found the garments, cut out the stitches of the lettering, and replaced the linen as before. A promise to post, in the event of his death, a letter he put in her hand, completed all that he required of her.

'He thanked her. "I think you seem sorry for me," he murmured. "And I am surprised. You are sorry?"

'She evaded the question. "Do you repent and believe?" she asked.

'"No."

'Contrary to her expectations and his own he recovered, though very slowly; and her manner grew more distant thenceforward, though his influence upon her was deeper than she knew. Weeks passed away, and the month of May arrived. One day at this time she met him walking slowly along the beach to the northward.

'"You know the news?" he said.

'"You mean of the rupture between France and England again?"

'"Yes; and the feeling of antagonism is stronger than it was in the last war, owing to Bonaparte's highhanded arrest of the innocent English who were travelling in our country for pleasure. I feel that the war will be long and bitter; and that my wish to live unknown in England will be frustrated. See here."

'He took from his pocket a piece of the single newspaper which circulated in the county in those days, and she read –

> *"The magistrates acting under the Alien Act have been requested to direct a very scrutinizing eye to the Academies in our towns and other places, in which French tutors are employed, and to all of that nationality who profess to be teachers in this country. Many of them are known to be inveterate Enemies and Traitors to the nation among whose people they have found a livelihood and a home."*

'He continued: "I have observed since the declaration of war a marked difference in the conduct of the rougher class of people here towards me. If a great battle were to occur – as it soon will, no doubt – feeling would grow to a pitch that would make it impossible for me, a disguised man of no known occupation, to stay here. With you, whose duties and antecedents are known, it may be less difficult, but still unpleasant. Now I propose this. You have probably seen how my deep sympathy with you has quickened to a warm feeling; and what I say is, will you agree to give me a title to protect you by honouring me with your hand? I am older than you, it is true; but as husband and wife we can leave England together, and make the whole world our country. Though I would propose Quebec, in Canada, as the place which offers the best promise of a home."

'"My God! You surprise me!" said she.

'"But you accept my proposal?"

'"No, no!"

'"And yet I think you will, Mademoiselle, some day!"

'"I think not."

'"I won't distress you further now."

'"Much thanks. . . . I am glad to see you looking better, Monsieur; I mean you are looking better."

'"Ah, yes. I am improving. I walk in the sun every day."

'And almost every day she saw him – sometimes nodding stiffly only, sometimes exchanging formal civilities. "You are not gone yet," she said on one of these occasions.

'"No. At present I don't think of going without you."

'"But you find it uncomfortable here?"

'"Somewhat. So when will have pity on me?"

'She shook her head and went on her way. Yet she was a little moved. "He did it on principle," she would murmur. "He had no animosity towards them, and profited nothing!"

'She wondered how he lived. It was evident that he could not be so poor as she had thought; his pretended poverty might be to escape notice. She could not tell, but she knew that she was dangerously interested in him.

'And he still mended, till his thin, pale face became more full and firm. As he mended she had to meet that request of his, advanced with even stronger insistency.

'The arrival of the King and Court for the season as usual brought matters to a climax for these two lonely exiles and fellow country-people. The King's awkward preference for a part of the coast in such dangerous proximity to France made it necessary that a strict military vigilance should be exercised to guard the royal residents. Half-a-dozen frigates were every night posted in a line across the bay, and two lines of sentinels, one at the water's edge and another behind the Esplanade, occupied the whole sea-front after eight every night. The watering-place was growing an inconvenient residence even for Mademoiselle V— herself, her friendship for this strange French tutor and writing-master who never had any pupils having been observed by many who slightly knew her. The General's wife, whose dependent she was, repeatedly warned her against the acquaintance; while the Hanoverian and other soldiers of the Foreign Legion, who had discovered the nationality of her friend, were more aggressive than the English military gallants who made it their business to notice her.

'In this tense state of affairs her answers became more agitated. "O Heaven, how can I marry you!" she would say.

'"You will; surely you will!" he answered again. "I don't leave without you. And I shall soon be interrogated before the magistrates if I stay here; probably imprisoned. You will come?"

'She felt her defences breaking down. Contrary to all reason and sense of family honour she was, by some abnormal craving, inclining to a tenderness for him that was founded on its opposite.

Sometimes her warm sentiments burnt lower than at others, and then the enormity of her conduct showed itself in more staring hues.

'Shortly after this he came with a resigned look on his face. "It is as I expected," he said. "I have received a hint to go. In good sooth, I am no Bonapartist – I am no enemy to England; but the presence of the King made it impossible for a foreigner with no visible occupation, and who may be a spy, to remain at large in the town. The authorities are civil, but firm. They are no more than reasonable. Good. I must go. You must come also."

'She did not speak. But she nodded assent, her eyes drooping.

'On her way back to the house on the Esplanade she said to herself, " I am glad, I am glad! I could not do otherwise. It is rendering good for evil!" But she knew how she mocked herself in this, and that the moral principle had not operated one jot in her acceptance of him. In truth she had not realized till now the full presence of the emotion which had unconsciously grown up in her for this lonely and severe man, who, in her tradition, was vengeance and irreligion personified. He seemed to absorb her whole nature, and, absorbing, to control it.

'A day or two before the one fixed for the wedding there chanced to come to her a letter from the only acquaintance of her own sex and country she possessed in England, one to whom she had sent intelligence of her approaching marriage, without mentioning with whom. This friend's misfortunes had been somewhat similar to her own, which fact had been one cause of their intimacy; her friend's sister, a nun of the Abbey of Montmartre, having perished on the scaffold at the hands of the same Comité de Salut Public which had numbered Mademoiselle V—'s affianced among its members. The writer had felt her position much again of late, since the renewal of the war, she said; and the letter wound up with a fresh denunciation of the authors of their mutual bereavement and subsequent troubles.

'Coming just then, its contents produced upon Mademoiselle V—the effect of a pail of water upon a somnambulist. What had she been doing in betrothing herself to this man! Was she not making herself a parricide after the event? At this crisis in her feelings her lover called. He beheld her trembling, and, in reply to his question, she told him of her scruples with impulsive candour.

'She had not intended to do this, but his attitude of tender command coerced her into frankness. Thereupon he exhibited an agitation never before apparent in him. He said, "But all that is past. You are the symbol of Charity, and we are pledged to let bygones be."

'His words soothed her for the moment, but she was sadly silent, and he went away.

'That night she saw (as she firmly believed to the end of her life) a divinely sent vision. A procession of her lost relatives – father, brother, uncle, cousin – seemed to cross her chamber between her bed and the window, and when she endeavoured to trace their features she perceived them to be headless, and that she had recognized them by their familiar clothes only. In the morning she could not shake off the effects of this appearance on her nerves. All that day she saw nothing of her wooer, he being occupied in making arrangements for their departure. It grew towards evening – the marriage eve; but, in spite of his reassuring visit, her sense of family duty waxed stronger now that she was left alone. Yet, she asked herself, how could she, alone and unprotected, go at this eleventh hour and reassert to an affianced husband that she could not and would not marry him while admitting at the same time that she loved him? The situation dismayed her. She had relinquished her post as governess, and was staying temporarily in a room near the coachoffice, where she expected him to call in the morning to carry out the business of their union and departure.

'Wisely or foolishly, Mademoiselle V— came to a resolution: that her only safety lay in flight. His contiguity influenced her too sensibly; she could not reason. So packing up her few possessions and placing on the table the small sum she owed, she went out privately, secured a last available seat in the London coach, and, almost before she had fully weighed her action, she was rolling out of the town in the dusk of the September evening.

'Having taken this startling step she began to reflect upon her reasons. He had been one of that tragic Committee the sound of whose name was a horror to the civilized world; yet he had been only *one* of several members, and, it seemed, not the most active. He had marked down names on principle, had felt no personal enmity against his victims, and had enriched himself not a sou out of the office he had held. Nothing could change the past. Meanwhile he loved her, and her heart inclined to as much of him as she could detach from that past. Why not, as he had suggested, bury memories, and inaugurate a new era by this union? In other words, why not indulge her tenderness, since its nullification could do no good.

'Thus she held self-communion in her seat in the coach, passing through Casterbridge, and Shottsford, and on to the White Hart at Melchester, at which place the whole fabric of her recent intentions crumbled down. Better be staunch having got so far; let things take their course, and marry boldly the man who had so impressed her. How great he was; how small was she! And she had presumed to judge him! Abandoning her place in the coach with the precipitancy that had characterized her taking it, she waited till the vehicle had driven off, something in the departing shapes of the outside passengers against the starlit sky giving her a start, as she afterwards remembered. Presently the down coach, "The Morning Herald," entered the city, and she hastily obtained a place on the top.

'"I'll be firm – I'll be his – if it cost me my immortal soul!" she said. And with troubled breathings she journeyed back over the road she had just traced.

'She reached our royal watering-place by the time the day broke, and her first aim was to get back to the hired room in which her last few days had been spent. When the landlady appeared at the door in response to Mademoiselle V—'s nervous summons, she explained her sudden departure and return as best she could; and no objection being offered to her re-engagement of the room for one day longer she ascended to the chamber and sat down panting. She was back once more, and her wild tergiversations were a secret from him whom alone they concerned.

'A sealed letter was on the mantelpiece. "Yes, it is directed to you, Mademoiselle," said the woman who had followed her. "But we were wondering what to do with it. A town messenger brought it after you had gone last night."

'When the landlady had left, Mademoiselle V— opened the letter and read –

> "MY DEAR AND HONOURED FRIEND. – *You have been throughout our acquaintance absolutely candid concerning your misgivings. But I have been reserved concerning mine. That is the difference between us. You probably have not guessed that every qualm you have felt on the subject of our marriage has been paralleled in my heart to the full. Thus it happened that your involuntary outburst of remorse yesterday, though mechanically deprecated by me in your presence, was a last item in my own doubts on the wisdom of our union, giving them a force that I could no longer withstand. I came home; and, on reflection, much as I honour and adore you, I decide to set you free.*
>
> *"As one whose life has been devoted, and I may say sacrificed, to the cause of Liberty, I cannot allow your judgment (probably a permanent one) to be fettered beyond release by a feeling which may be transient only.*
>
> *"It would be no less than excruciating to both that I should announce this decision to you by word of mouth. I have therefore taken the less painful course of writing. Before you receive this I shall have left the town by the evening coach for London, on reaching which city my movements will be revealed to none.*
>
> *"Regard me, Mademoiselle, as dead, and accept my renewed assurances of respect, remembrance, and affection."*

'When she had recovered from her shock of surprise and grief, she remembered that at the starting of the coach out of Melchester before dawn, the shape of a figure among the outside passengers against the starlit sky had caused her a momentary start, from its resemblance to that of her friend. Knowing nothing of each other's intentions, and screened from each other by the darkness, they had left the town by the same conveyance. "He, the greater, persevered; I, the smaller, returned!" she said.

'Recovering from her stupor, Mademoiselle V— bethought herself again of her employer, Mrs Newbold, whom recent events had estranged. To that lady she went with a full heart, and explained everything. Mrs Newbold kept to herself her opinion of the episode, and reinstalled the deserted bride in her old position as governess to the family.

'A governess she remained to the end of her days. After the final peace with France she became acquainted with my mother, to whom by degrees she imparted these experiences of hers. As her hair grew white, and her features pinched, Mademoiselle V— would wonder what nook of the world contained her lover, if he lived, and if by any chance she might see him again. But when, some time in the 'twenties, death came to her, at no great age, that outline against the stars of the morning remained as the last glimpse she ever obtained of her family's foe and her once affianced husband.'

THE GRAVE BY THE HANDPOST

Once again in this story, partly set on Christmas Eve and intended for Christmas-time publication, Hardy fell back an old superstition – though a gruesome one, by any standards! The old belief which forms the basis of the tale concerns vampires, and the custom of burying anyone who had committed suicide at a crossroads and driving a six-foot wooden stake through their heart. Such people who had taken their own lives, it was believed, could not rest easy and would return to prey on the living unless restrained in this manner. It was only as late as 1830 that the custom was abolished by law. Ruth Firor both admires and is chilled by this tale. 'It introduces us to a new kind of ghost,' she has written, 'which it does not introduce in person, but indirectly – the malicious, dangerous physical ghost of the suicide buried at the crossroads with a stake through his body. The story is as gruesome as anything in Hardy.'

The background villages of the story, Broad Sidlinch and Chalk-Newton, with their violently opposing attitudes towards suicides, were again based on real places that Hardy knew: Sydling St Nicholas and Maiden Newton, both between seven and eight miles north west of Dorchester. 'The Grave by the Handpost' with its vivid portrait of the people of these two communities was first published in the *St James's Budget* of December 1897 – complete with the perhaps deliberately restrained sub-title, 'A Christmas Reminiscence'!

THE GRAVE BY THE HANDPOST

I never pass through Chalk-Newton without turning to regard the neighbouring upland, at a point where a lane crosses the lone straight highway dividing this from the next parish; a sight which does not fail to recall the event that once happened there; and, though it may seem superfluous, at this date, to disinter more memories of village history, the whispers of that spot may claim to be preserved.

It was on a dark, yet mild and exceptionally dry evening at Christmas-time (according to the testimony of William Dewy of Mellstock, Michael Mail, and others), that the choir of Chalk-Newton – a large parish situate about halfway between the towns of Ivell and Casterbridge, and now a railway station – left their homes just before midnight to repeat their annual harmonies under the windows of the local population. The band of instrumentalists and singers was one of the largest in the county; and, unlike the smaller and finer Mellstock string-band, which eschewed all but the catgut, it included brass and reed performers at full Sunday services, and reached all across the west gallery.

On this night there were two or three violins, two 'cellos, a tenor viol, double bass, hautboy, clarionets, serpent, and seven singers. It was, however, not the choir's labours, but what its members chanced to witness, that particularly marked the occasion.

They had pursued their rounds for many years without meeting with any incident of an unusual kind, but tonight, according to the assertions of several, there prevailed, to begin with, an exceptionally solemn and thoughtful mood among two or three of the oldest in the band, as if they were thinking they might be joined by the phantoms of dead friends who had been of their number in earlier years, and now were mute in the churchyard under flattening mounds – friends who had shown greater zest for melody in their time than was shown in this; or that some past voice of a semi-transparent figure might quaver from some bedroom-window its acknowledgment of their nocturnal greeting, instead of a familiar living neighbour. Whether this were fact or fancy, the younger members of the choir met together with their customary thoughtlessness and buoyancy. When they had gathered by the stone stump of the cross in the middle of the village, near the White Horse Inn, which they made their starting-point, some one observed that they were full early, that it was not yet twelve o'clock. The local waits of those days mostly refrained from sounding a note before Christmas morning had astronomically arrived, and not caring to return to their beer, they decided to begin with some outlying cottages in Sidlinch Lane, where the people had no clocks, and would not know whether it were night or morning. In that direction they accordingly went; and as they ascended to higher ground their attention was attracted by a light beyond the houses, quite at the top of the lane.

The road from Chalk-Newton to Broad Sidlinch is about two miles long, and in the middle of its course, where it passes over the ridge dividing the two villages, it crosses at right angles, as has been stated, the lonely monotonous old highway known as Long Ash Lane, which runs, straight as a surveyor's line, many miles north and south of this spot, on the foundation of a Roman road, and has often been mentioned in these narratives. Though now quite deserted and grass-grown, at the beginning of the century it was well kept and frequented by traffic. The glimmering light appeared to come from the precise point where the roads intersected.

'I think I know what that mid mean!' one of the group remarked.

They stood a few moments, discussing the probability of the light having origin in an event of which rumours had reached them, and resolved to go up the hill.

Approaching the high land their conjectures were strengthened. Long Ash Lane cut athwart them, right and left; and they saw that at the junction of the four ways, under the handpost, a grave was dug, into which, as the choir drew nigh, a corpse had just been thrown by the four Sidlinch men employed for the purpose. The cart and horse which had brought the body thither stood silently by.

The singers and musicians from Chalk-Newton halted, and looked on while the gravediggers shovelled in and trod down the earth, till, the hole being filled, the latter threw their spades into the cart, and prepared to depart.

'Who mid ye be a-burying there?' asked Lot Swanhills in a raised voice. 'Not the sergeant?'

The Sidlinch men had been so deeply engrossed in their task that they had not noticed the lanterns of the Chalk-Newton choir till now.

'What – be you the Newton carol-singers?' returned the representatives of Sidlinch.

'Ay, sure. Can it be that it is old Sergeant Holway you've a-buried there?'

''Tis so. You've heard about it, then?'

The choir knew no particulars – only that he had shot himself in his apple-closet on the previous Sunday. 'Nobody seem'th to know what 'a did it for, 'a b'lieve? Leastwise, we don't know at Chalk-Newton,' continued Lot.

'O yes. It all came out at the inquest.'

The singers drew close, and the Sidlinch men, pausing to rest after their labours, told the story. 'It was all owing to that son of his, poor old man. It broke his heart.'

'But the son is a soldier, surely; now with his regiment in the East Indies?'

'Ay. And it have been rough with the army over there lately. 'Twas a pity his father persuaded him to go. But Luke shouldn't have twyted the sergeant o't, since 'a did it for the best.'

The circumstances, in brief, were these: The sergeant who had come to this lamentable end, father of the young soldier who had gone with his regiment to the East, had been singularly comfortable in his military experiences, these having ended long before the outbreak of the great war with France. On his discharge, after duly serving his time, he had returned to his native village, and married, and taken kindly to domestic life. But the war in which England next involved herself had cost him many frettings that age and infirmity prevented him from being ever again an active unit of the army. When his only son grew to young manhood, and the question arose of his going out in life, the lad expressed his wish to be a mechanic. But his father advised enthusiastically for the army.

'Trade is coming to nothing in these days,' he said. 'And if the war with the French lasts, as it will, trade will be still worse. The army, Luke – that's the thing for 'ee. 'Twas the making of me, and 'twill be the making of you. I hadn't half such a chance as you'll have in these splendid hotter times.'

Luke demurred, for he was a home-keeping, peace-loving youth. But, putting respectful trust in his father's judgment, he at length gave way, and enlisted in the —d Foot. In the course of a few weeks he was sent out to India to his regiment, which had distinguished itself in the East under General Wellesley.

But Luke was unlucky. News came home indirectly that he lay

sick out there; and then on one recent day when his father was out walking, the old man had received tidings that a letter awaited him at Casterbridge. The sergeant sent a special messenger the whole nine miles, and the letter was paid for and brought home; but though, as he had guessed, it came from Luke, its contents were of an unexpected tenor.

The letter had been written during a time of deep depression. Luke said that his life was a burden and a slavery, and bitterly reproached his father for advising him to embark on a career for which he felt unsuited. He found himself suffering fatigues and illnesses without gaining glory, and engaged in a cause which he did not understand or appreciate. If it had not been for his father's bad advice he, Luke, would now have been working comfortably at a trade in the village that he had never wished to leave.

After reading the letter the sergeant advanced a few steps till he was quite out of sight of everybody, and then sat down on the bank by the wayside.

When he arose half-an-hour later he looked withered and broken, and from that day his natural spirits left him. Wounded to the quick by his son's sarcastic stings, he indulged in liquor more and more frequently. His wife had died some years before this date, and the sergeant lived alone in the house which had been hers. One morning in the December under notice the report of a gun had been heard on his premises, and on entering the neighbours found him in a dying state. He had shot himself with an old firelock that he used for scaring birds; and from what he had said the day before, and the arrangements he had made for his decease, there was no doubt that his end had been deliberately planned, as a consequence of the despondency into which he had been thrown by his son's letter. The coroner's jury returned a verdict of *felo-de-se*.

'Here's his son's letter,' said one of the Sidlinch men. ''Twas found in his father's pocket. You can see by the state o't how many times he read it over. Howsomever, the Lord's will be done, since it must, whether or no.'

The grave was filled up and levelled, no mound being shaped over it. The Sidlinch men then bade the Chalk-Newton choir good-night, and departed with the cart in which they had brought the sergeant's body to the hill. When their tread had died away from the ear, and the wind swept over the isolated grave with its customary siffle of indifference, Lot Swanhills turned and spoke to old Richard Toller, the hautboy player.

''Tis hard upon a man, and he a wold sojer, to serve en so, Richard. Not that the sergeant was ever in a battle bigger than would go into a half-acre paddock, that's true. Still, his soul ought to hae as good a chance as another man's, all the same, hey?'

Richard replied that he was quite of the same opinion. 'What d'ye say to lifting up a carrel over his grave, as 'tis Christmas, and no hurry to begin down in parish, and 'twouldn't take up ten minutes, and not a soul up here to say us nay, or know anything about it?'

Lot nodded assent. 'The man ought to hae his chances,' he repeated.

'Ye may as well spet upon his grave, for all the good we shall do en by what we lift up, now he's got so far,' said Notton, the clarionet man and professed sceptic of the choir. 'But I'm agreed if the rest be.'

They thereupon placed themselves in a semicircle by the newly-stirred earth, and roused the dull air with the well-known Number Sixteen of their collection, which Lot gave out as being the one he thought best suited to the occasion and the mood: –

He comes´ the pri´-soners to´ re-lease´,
In Sa´-tan's bon´-dage held´.

'Jown it – we've never played to a dead man afore,' said Ezra Cattstock, when, having concluded the last verse, they stood reflecting for a breath or two. 'But it do seem more merciful than to go away and leave en, as they t'other fellers have done.'

'Now backalong to Newton, and by the time we get overright the pa'son's 'twill be half after twelve,' said the leader.

They had not, however, done more than gather up their instruments when the wind brought to their notice the noise of a vehicle rapidly driven up the same lane from Sidlinch which the gravediggers had lately retraced. To avoid being run over when moving on, they waited till the benighted traveller, whoever he might be, should pass them where they stood in the wider area of the Cross.

In half a minute the light of the lanters fell upon a hired fly, drawn by a steaming and jaded horse. It reached the handpost, when a voice from the inside cried, 'Stop here!' The driver pulled rein. The carriage door was opened from within, and there leapt out a private soldier in the uniform of some line regiment. He looked around, and was apparently surprised to see the musicians standing there.

'Have you buried a man here?' he asked.

'No. We bain't Sidlinch folk, thank God; we be Newton choir. Though a man is just buried here, that's true; and we've raised a carrel over the poor mortal's natomy. What – do my eyes see before me young Luke Holway, that went wi' his regiment to the East Indies, or do I see his spirit straight from the battlefield? Be you the son that wrote the letter —'

'Don't – don't ask me. The funeral is over, then?'

'There wer no funeral, in a Christen manner of speaking. But's buried, sure enough. You must have met the men going back in the empty cart.'

'Like a dog in a ditch, and all through me!'

He remained silent, looking at the grave, and they could not help pitying him. 'My friends,' he said, 'I understand better now. You have, I suppose, in neighbourly charity, sung peace to his soul? I thank you, from my heart, for your kind pity. Yes; I am Sergeant Holway's miserable son – I'm the son who has brought about his father's death, as truly as if I had done it with my own hand!'

'No, no. Don't ye take on so, young man. He'd been naturally low for a good while, off and on, so we hear.'

'We were out in the East when I wrote to him. Everything had seemed to go wrong with mc. Just after my letter had gone we were ordered home. That's how it is you see me here. As soon as we got into barracks at Casterbridge I heard o' this –. . . . Damn me! I'll dare to follow my father, and make away with myself, too. It is the only thing left to do!'

'Don't ye be rash, Luke Holway, I say again; but try to make amends by your future life. And maybe your father will smile a smile down from heaven upon 'ee for 't.'

He shook his head. 'I don't know about that!' he answered bitterly.

'Try and be worthy of your father at his best. 'Tis not too late.'

'D'ye think not? I fancy it is! . . . Well, I'll turn it over. Thank you for your good counsel. I'll live for one thing, at any rate. I'll move father's body to a decent Christian churchyard, if I do it with my own hands. I can't save his life, but I can give him an honourable grave. He shan't lie in this accursed place!'

'Ay, as our pa'son says, 'tis a barbarous custom they keep up at Sidlinch, and ought to be done away wi'. The man a' old soldier, too. You see, our pa'son is not like yours at Sidlinch.'

'He says it is barbarous, does he? So it is!' cried the soldier. 'Now hearken, my friends.' Then he proceeded to inquire if they would increase his indebtedness to them by undertaking the removal, privately, of the body of the suicide to the churchyard, not of Sidlinch, a parish he now hated, but of Chalk-Newton. He would give them all he possessed to do it.

Lot asked Ezra Cattstock what he thought of it.

Cattstock, the 'cello player, who was also the sexton, demurred, and advised the young soldier to sound the rector about it first. 'Mid be he would object, and yet 'a midn't. The pa'son o' Sidlinch is a hard man, I own ye, and 'a said if folk will kill theirselves in hot blood they must take the consequences. But ours don't think like that at all, and might allow it.'

'What's his name?'

'The honourable and reverent Mr Oldham, brother to Lord Wessex. But you needn't be afeard o' en on that account. He'll talk to 'ee like a common man, if so be you haven't had enough drink to gie 'ee bad breath.'

'O, the same as formerly. I'll ask him. Thank you. And that duty done – '

'What then?'

'There's war in Spain. I hear our next move is there. I'll try to show myself to be what my father wished me. I don't suppose I shall – but I'll try in my feeble way. That much I swear – here over his body. So help me God.'

Luke smacked his palm against the white handpost with such force that it shook. 'Yes, there's war in Spain; and another chance for me to be worthy of father.'

So the matter ended that night. That the private acted in one thing as he had vowed to do soon became apparent, for during the Christmas week the rector came into the churchyard when Cattstock was there, and asked him to find a spot that would be suitable for the purpose of such an interment, adding that he had slightly known the late sergeant, and was not aware of any law which forbade him to assent to the removal, the letter of the rule having been observed. But as he did not wish to seem moved by opposition to his neighbour at Sidlinch, he had stipulated that the act of charity should be carried out at night, and as privately as possible, and that the grave should be in an obscure part of the enclosure. 'You had better see the young man about it at once,' added the rector.

But before Ezra had done anything Luke came down to his house. His furlough had been cut short, owing to new developments of the war in the Peninsula, and being obliged to go back to his regiment immediately, he was compelled to leave the exhumation and reinterment to his friends. Everything was paid for, and he implored them all to see it carried out forthwith.

With this the soldier left. The next day Ezra, on thinking the matter over, again went across to the rectory, struck with sudden misgiving. He had remembered that the sergeant had been buried without a coffin, and he was not sure that a stake had not been driven through him. The business would be more troublesome than they had at first supposed.

'Yes, indeed!' murmured the rector. 'I am afraid it is not feasible after all.'

The next event was the arrival of a headstone by carrier from the nearest town; to be left at Mr Ezra Cattstock's; all expenses paid. The sexton and the carrier deposited the stone in the former's outhouse; and Ezra, left alone, put on his spectacles and read the brief and simple inscription: –

HERE LYETH THE BODY OF SAMUEL HOLWAY, LATE SERGEANT IN HIS MAJESTY'S – D REGIMENT OF FOOT, WHO DEPARTED THIS LIFE DECEMBER THE 20TH, 180–. ERECTED BY L. H.

'I AM NOT WORTHY TO BE CALLED THY SON.'

Ezra again called at the riverside rectory. 'The stone is come, sir. But I'm afeard we can't do it nohow.'

'I should like to oblige him,' said the gentlemanly old incumbent. 'And I would forgo all fees willingly. Still, if you and the others don't think you can carry it out, I am in doubt what to say.'

'Well, sir; I've made inquiry of a Sidlinch woman as to his burial, and what I thought seems true. They buried en wi' a new six-foot hurdle-saul drough's body, from the sheep-pen up in North Ewelease, though they won't own to it now. And the question is, Is the moving worth while, considering the awkwardness?'

'Have you heard anything more of the young man?'

Ezra had only heard that he had embarked that week for Spain with the rest of the regiment. 'And if he's as desperate as 'a seemed, we shall never see him here in England again.'

'It is an awkward case,' said the rector.

Ezra talked it over with the choir; one of whom suggested that the stone might be erected at the cross-roads. This was regarded as impracticable. Another said that it might be set up in the churchyard without removing the body; but this was seen to be dishonest. So nothing was done.

The headstone remained in Ezra's outhouse till, growing tired of seeing it there, he put it away among the bushes at the bottom of his garden. The subject was sometimes revived among them, but it always ended with: 'Considering how 'a was buried, we can hardly make a job o't.'

There was always the consciousness that Luke would never come back, an impression strengthened by the disasters which were rumoured to have befallen the army in Spain. This tended to make their inertness permanent. The headstone grew green as it lay on its back under Ezra's bushes; then a tree by the river was blown down, and, falling across the stone, cracked it in three pieces. Ultimately the pieces became buried in the leaves and mould.

Luke had not been born a Chalk-Newton man, and he had no relations left in Sidlinch, so that no tidings of him reached either village throughout the war. But after Waterloo and the fall of Napoleon there arrived at Sidlinch one day an English sergeant-major covered with stripes and, as it turned out, rich in glory. Foreign service had so totally changed Luke Holway that it was not until he told his name that the inhabitants recognized him as the sergeant's only son.

He had served with unswerving effectiveness through the Peninsular campaigns under Wellington; had fought at Busaco, Fuentes d'Onoro, Ciudad Rodrigo, Badajoz, Salamanca, Vittoria, Quatre Bras, and Waterloo; and had now returned to enjoy a more than earned pension and repose in his native district.

He hardly stayed in Sidlinch longer than to take a meal on his arrival. The same evening he started on foot over the hill to Chalk-Newton, passing the handpost, and saying as he glanced at the spot, 'Thank God: he's not there!' Nightfall was approaching when he reached the latter village; but he made straight for the churchyard. On his entering it there remained light enough to discern the headstones by, and these he narrowly scanned. But though he searched the front part by the road, and the back part by the river, what he sought he could not find – the grave of Sergeant Holway, and a memorial bearing the inscription: 'I AM NOT WORTHY TO BE CALLED THY SON.'

He left the churchyard and made inquiries. The honourable and reverend old rector was dead, and so were many of the choir; but by degrees the sergeant-major learnt that his father still lay at the cross-roads in Long Ash Lane.

Luke pursued his way moodily homewards, to do which, in the natural course, he would be compelled to repass the spot, there being no other road between the two villages. But he could not now go by that place, vociferous with reproaches in his father's tones; and he got over the hedge and wandered deviously through the ploughed fields to avoid the scene. Through many a fight and fatigue Luke had been sustained by the thought that he was restoring the family honour and making noble amends. Yet his father lay still in degradation. It was rather a sentiment than a fact that his father's body had been made to suffer for his own misdeeds; but to his super-sensitiveness it seemed that his efforts to retrieve his character and to propitiate the shade of the insulted one had ended in failure.

He endeavoured, however, to shake off his lethargy, and, not liking the associations of Sidlinch, hired a small cottage at Chalk-Newton which had long been empty. Here he lived alone, becoming quite a hermit, and allowing no woman to enter the house.

The Christmas after taking up his abode herein he was sitting in the chimney-corner by himself, when he heard faint notes in the distance, and soon a melody burst forth immediately outside his own window. It came from the carol-singers, as usual; and though many of the old hands, Ezra and Lot included, had gone to their rest, the same old carols were still played out of the same old books. There resounded through the sergeant-major's window-shutters the familiar lines that the deceased choir had rendered over his father's grave: –

He comes´ the pri´-soners to´ re-lease´,
In Sa´-tan's bon´-dage held´.

When they had finished they went on to another house, leaving him to silence and loneliness as before.

The candle wanted snuffing, but he did not snuff it, and he sat on till it had burnt down into the socket and made waves of shadow on the ceiling.

The Christmas cheerfulness of next morning was broken at breakfast-time by tragic intelligence which went down the village like wind. Sergeant-Major Holway had been found shot through the head by his own hand at the cross-roads in Long Ash Lane where his father lay buried.

On the table in the cottage he had left a piece of paper, on which he had written his wish that he might be buried at the Cross beside his father. But the paper was accidentally swept to the floor, and overlooked till after his funeral, which took place in the ordinary way in the churchyard.

A CHANGED MAN

In the closing year of the nineteenth century, Thomas Hardy wrote what was to prove his last supernatural short story – as well as being his last piece of fiction of any kind. The attacks of the critics on his novels *Tess of the D'Urbervilles* (1891) and *Jude the Obscure* (1896) had made him despair of the prose form, and instead he turned his attention to what had always been his first love, poetry. Until his death in 1928, all the remainder of his work to be in verse.

'A Changed Man' can be seen in hindsight as almost a perfect finale to Hardy's contributions to the macabre genre. Not only does it seem to echo some of his earliest stories like 'The Three Strangers', but there is also a mixture of the Gothic and the kind of rural folklore from which he borrowed so freely all his life. The inspiration for this tale of a group of Hussars who are relentlessly followed by the ghost of a cholera victim was actually the Reverend Henry Moule, the vicar of Fordington (and the father of Hardy's great friend, Horace Moule) who had become a hero preventing the spread of this terrible disease during its outbreaks in 1849 and 1854. Although completed before the dawn of the new century, 'A Changed Man' was not published until the April issue of *The Sphere* magazine where it was sombrely illustrated. That it pleased Hardy is beyond doubt, for when it was later collected with his remaining short fiction in 1913, not only did it provide the book with its title, but the author himself unequivocally declared it to be 'the best of these tales'. One could only wish that he had been encouraged enough to have written more in the genre to which he had brought such style and imagination instead of thereafter lapsing into the silence which was never to be broken.

A CHANGED MAN

I

The person who, next to the actors themselves, chanced to know most of their story, lived just below 'Top o' Town' (as the spot was called) in an old substantially-built house, distinguished among its neighbours by having an oriel window on the first floor, whence could be obtained a raking view of the High Street, west and east, the former including Laura's dwelling, the end of the Town Avenue hard by (in which were played the odd pranks hereafter to be mentioned), the Port-Bredy road rising westwards, and the turning that led to the cavalry barracks where the Captain was quartered. Looking eastward down the town from the same favoured gazebo, the long perspective of houses declined and dwindled till they merged in the highway across the moor. The white riband of road disappeared over Grey's Bridge a quarter of a mile off, to plunge into innumerable rustic windings, shy shades, and solitary undulations up hill and down dale for one hundred and twenty miles till it exhibited itself at Hyde Park Corner as a smooth bland surface in touch with a busy and fashionable world.

To the barracks aforesaid had recently arrived the —th Hussars, a regiment new to the locality. Almost before any acquaintance with its members had been made by the townspeople, a report spread that they were a 'crack' body of men, and had brought a splendid band. For some reason or other the town had not been used as the headquarters of cavalry for many years, the various troops stationed there having consisted of casual detachments only; so that it was with a sense of honour that everybody – even the small furniture-broker from whom the married troopers hired tables and chairs – received the news of their crack quality.

In those days the Hussar regiments still wore over the left shoulder that attractive attachment, or frilled half-coat, hanging loosely behind like the wounded wing of a bird, which was called the pelisse, though it was known among the troopers themselves as a 'sling-jacket.' It added amazingly to their picturesqueness in women's eyes, and , indeed, in the eyes of men also.

The burgher who lived in the house with the oriel window sat during a great many hours of the day in that projection, for he was an invalid, and time hung heavily on his hands unless he maintained a constant interest in proceedings without. Not more than a week after the arrival of the Hussars his ears were assailed by the shout of one schoolboy to another in the street below.

'Have 'ee heard this about the Hussars? They are haunted! Yes – a ghost troubles 'em; he has followed 'em about the world for years.'

A haunted regiment: that was a new idea for either invalid or stalwart. The listener in the oriel came to the conclusion that there were some lively characters among the —th Hussars.

He made Captain Maumbry's acquaintance in an informal manner at an afternoon tea to which he went in a wheeled chair – one of the very rare outings that the state of his health permitted. Maumbry showed himself to be a handsome man of twenty-eight or thirty, with an attractive hint of wickedness in his manner that was sure to make him adorable with good young women. The large dark eyes that lit his pale face expressed this wickedness strongly, though such was the adaptability of their rays that one could think they might have expressed sadness or seriousness just as readily, if he had had a mind for such.

An old and deaf lady who was present asked Captain Maumbry bluntly: 'What's this we hear about you? They say your regiment is haunted.'

The Captain's face assumed an aspect of grave, even sad, concern. 'Yes,' he replied, 'it is too true.'

Some younger ladies smiled till they saw how serious he looked, when they looked serious likewise.

'Really?' said the old lady.

'Yes. We naturally don't wish to say much about it.'

'No, no; of course not. But – how haunted?'

'Well; the – *thing*, as I'll call it, follows us. In country quarters or town, abroad or at home, it's just the same.'

'How do you account for it?'

'H'm' Maumbry lowered his voice. 'Some crime committed by certain of our regiment in past years, we suppose.'

'Dear me. . . . How very horrid, and singular!'

'But, as I said, we don't speak of it much.'

'No . . . no.'

When the Hussar was gone, a young lady, disclosing a long-suppressed interest, asked if the ghost had been seen by any of the town.

The lawyer's son, who always had the latest borough news, said that, though it was seldom seen by any one but the Hussars themselves, more than one townsman and woman had already set eyes on it, to his or her terror. The phantom mostly appeared very late at night, under the dense trees of the town-avenue nearest the barracks. It was about ten feet high; its teeth chattered with a dry naked sound, as if they were those of a skeleton; and its hip-bones could be heard grating in their sockets.

During the darkest weeks of winter several timid persons were seriously frightened by the object answering to this cheerful description, and the police began to look into the matter. Whereupon the appearances grew less frequent, and some of the Boys of the regiment thankfully stated that they had not been so free from ghostly visitation for years as they had become since their arrival in Casterbridge.

This playing at ghosts was the most innocent of the amusements indulged in by the choice young spirits who inhabited the lichened, red-brick building at the top of the town bearing 'W.D.' and a broad arrow on its quoins. Far more serious escapades – levities relating to love, wine, cards, betting – were talked of, with no doubt more or less of exaggeration. That the Hussars, Captain Maumbry included, were the cause of bitter tears to several young women of the town and country is unquestionably true, despite the fact that the gaieties of the young men wore a more staring colour in this old-fashioned place than they would have done in a large and modern city.

II

Regularly once a week they rode out in marching order.

Returning up the town on one of these occasions, the romantic pelisse flapping behind each horseman's shoulder in the soft south-west wind, Captain Maumbry glanced up at the oriel. A mutual nod was exchanged between him and the person who sat there reading. The reader and a friend in the room with him followed the troop with their eyes all the way up the street, till, when the soldiers were opposite the house in which Laura lived, that young lady became discernible in the balcony.

'They are engaged to be married, I hear,' said the friend.

'Who – Maumbry and Laura? Never – so soon?'

'Yes.'

'He'll never marry. Several girls have been mentioned in connection with his name. I am sorry for Laura.'

'Oh, but you needn't be. They are excellently matched.'

'She's only one more.'

'She's one more, and more still. She had regularly caught him. She is a born player of the game of hearts, and she knew how to beat him in his own practices. If there is one woman in the town who has any chance of holding her own and marrying him, she is that woman.'

This was true, as it turned out. By natural proclivity Laura had from the first entered heart and soul into military romance as exhibited in the plots and characters of those living exponents of it who came under her notice. From her earliest young womanhood civilians, however promising, had no chance of winning her interest if the meanest warrior were within the horizon. It may be that the position of her uncle's house (which was her home) at the corner of West Street nearest the barracks, the daily passing of the troops, the constant blowing of trumpet-calls a furlong from her windows, coupled with the fact that she knew nothing of the inner realities of military life, and hence idealized it, had also helped her mind's original bias for thinking men-at-arms the only ones worthy of a woman's heart.

Captain Maumbry was a typical prize; one whom all surrounding maidens had coveted, ached for, angled for, wept for, had by her judicious management become subdued to her purpose; and in addition to the pleasure of marrying the man she loved, Laura had the joy of feeling herself hated by the mothers of all the marriageable girls of the neighbourhood.

The man in the oriel went to the wedding; not as a guest, for at this time he was but slightly acquainted with the parties; but mainly because the church was close to his house; partly, too, for a reason which moved many others to be spectators of the ceremony; a subconsciousness that, though the couple might be happy in their experiences, there was sufficient possibility of their being otherwise to colour the musings of an onlooker with a pleasing pathos of conjecture. He could on occasion do a pretty stroke of rhyming in those days, and he beguiled the time of waiting by pencilling on a blank page of his prayer-book a few lines which, though kept private then, may be given here: –

AT A HASTY WEDDING

(Triolet)

If hours be years the twain are blest,
For now they solace swift desire
By lifelong ties that tether zest
If hours be years. The twain are blest
Do eastern suns slope never west,
Nor pallid ashes follow fire.
If hours be years the twain are blest
For now they solace swift desire.

As if, however, to falsify all prophecies, the couple seemed to find in marriage the secret of perpetuating the intoxication of a courtship which, on Maumbry's side at least, had opened without serious intent. During the winter following they were the most popular pair in and about Casterbridge – nay in South Wessex itself. No smart dinner in the country houses of the younger and gayer families within driving distance of the borough was complete without their lively presence; Mrs Maumbry was the blithest of the whirling figures at the county ball; and when followed that inevitable incident of garrison-town life, an amateur dramatic entertainment, it was just the same. The acting was for the benefit of such and such an excellent charity – nobody cared what, provided the play were played – and both Captain Maumbry and his wife were in the piece, having been in fact, by mutual consent, the originators of the performance. And so with laughter, and thoughtlessness, and movement, all went merrily. There was a little backwardness in the bill-paying of the couple; but in justice to them it must be added that sooner or later all owings were paid.

III

At the chapel-of-ease attended by the troops, there arose above the edge of the pulpit one Sunday an unknown face. This was the face of a new curate. He placed upon the desk, not the familiar sermon book, but merely a Bible. The person who tells these things was not present at that service, but he soon learnt that the young curate was nothing less than a great surprise to his congregation; a mixed one always, for though the Hussars occupied the body of the building, its nooks and corners were crammed with civilians, whom up to the present, even the least uncharitable would have described as being attracted thither less by the services than by the soldiery.

Now there arose a second reason for squeezing into an already overcrowded church. The persuasive and gentle eloquence of Mr Sainway operated like a charm upon those accustomed only to the higher and dryer styles of preaching, and for a time the other churches of the town were thinned of their sitters.

At this point in the nineteenth century the sermon was the sole reason for churchgoing amongst a vast body of religious people. The liturgy was a formal preliminary, which, like the Royal proclamation in a court of assize, had to be got through before the real interest began; and on reaching home the question was simply: Who preached, and how did he handle his subject? Even had an archbishop officiated in the service proper nobody would have cared much about what was said or sung. People who had formerly attended in the morning only began to go in the evening, and even to the special addresses in the afternoon.

One day when Captain Maumbry entered his wife's drawing-room, filled with hired furniture, she thought he was somebody else, for he had not come upstairs humming the most catching air afloat in musical circles or in his usual careless way.

'What's the matter, Jack?' she said without looking up from a note she was writing.

'Well – not much, that I know.'

'O, but there is,' she murmured as she wrote.

'Why – this cursed new lath in a sheet – I mean the new parson! He wants us to stop the band-playing on Sunday afternoons.'

Laura looked up aghast.

'Why, it is the one thing that enables the few rational beings hereabouts to keep alive from Saturday to Monday!'

'He says all the town flock to the music and don't come to the service, and that the pieces played are profane, or mundane, or inane, or something – not what ought to be played on Sunday. Of course 'tis Lautmann who settles those things.'

Lautmann was the bandmaster.

The barrack-green on Sunday afternoons had, indeed, become the promenade of a great many townspeople cheerfully inclined, many even of those who attended in the morning at Mr Sainway's service; and little boys who ought to have been listening to the curate's afternoon lecture were too often seen rolling upon the grass and making faces behind the more dignified listeners.

Laura heard no more about the matter, however, for two or three weeks, when suddenly remembering it she asked her husband if any further objections had been raised.

'O – Mr Sainway. I forgot to tell you. I've made his acquaintance. He is not a bad sort of man.'

Laura asked if either Maumbry or some others of the officers did not give the presumptuous curate a good setting down for his interference.

'O well – we've forgotten that. He's a stunning preacher, they tell me.'

The acquaintance developed apparently, for the Captain said to her a little later on, 'There's a good deal in Sainway's argument about having no band on Sunday afternoons. After all, it is close to his church. But he doesn't press his objections unduly.'

'I am surprised to hear you defend him!'

'It was only a passing thought of mine. We naturally don't wish to offend the inhabitants of the town if they don't like it.'

'But they do.'

The invalid in the oriel never clearly gathered the details of progress in this conflict of lay and clerical opinion; but so it was that, to the disappointment of musicians, the grief of out-walking lovers, and the regret of the junior population of the town and country round, the band-playing on Sunday afternoons ceased in Casterbridge barrack-square.

By this time the Maumbrys had frequently listened to the preaching of the gentle if narrow-minded curate; for these light-natured, hit-or-miss, rackety people went to church like others for respectability's sake. None so orthodox as your unmitigated worldling. A more remarkable event was the sight to the man in the window of Captain Maumbry and Mr Sainway walking down the High Street in earnest conversation. On his mentioning this fact to a caller he was assured that it was a matter of common talk that they were always together.

The observer would soon have learnt this with his own eyes if he had not been told. They began to pass together nearly every day. Hitherto Mrs Maumbry, in fashionable walking clothes, had usually been her husband's companion; but this was less frequent now. The close and singular friendship between the two men went on for nearly a year, when Mr Sainway was presented to a living in a densely-populated town in the midland counties. He bade the parishioners of his old place a reluctant farewell and departed, the touching sermon he preached on the occasion being published by the local printer. Everybody was sorry to lose him; and it was with genuine grief that his Casterbridge congregation learnt later on that soon after his induction to his benefice, during some bitter weather, he had fallen seriously ill of inflammation of the lungs, of which he eventually died.

We now get below the surface of things. Of all who had known the dead curate, none grieved for him like the man who on his first arrival had called him a 'lath in a sheet' Mrs Maumbry had never greatly sympathized with the impressive parson; indeed, she had been secretly glad that he had gone away to better himself. He had considerably diminished the pleasures of a woman by whom the joys of earth and good company had been appreciated to the full. Sorry for her husband in his loss of a friend who had been none of hers, she was yet quite unprepared for the sequel.

'There is something that I have wanted to tell you lately, dear.' he said one morning at breakfast with hesitation. 'Have you guessed what it is?'

She had guessed nothing.

'That I think of retiring from the army.'

'What!'

'I have thought more and more of Sainway since his death, and of what he used to say to me so earnestly. And I feel certain I shall be right in obeying a call within me to give up this fighting trade and enter the Church.'

'What – be a parson?'

'Yes.'

'But what should *I* do?'

'Be a parson's wife.'

'Never!' she affirmed.

'But how can you help it?'

'I'll run away rather!' she said vehemently.

'No, you mustn't,' Maumbry replied, in the tone he used when his mind was made up. 'You'll get accustomed to the idea, for I am constrained to carry it out, though it is against my worldly interests. I am forced on by a Hand outside me to tread in the steps of Sainway.'

'Jack,' she asked, with calm pallor and round eyes; 'do you mean to say seriously that you are arranging to be a curate instead of a soldier?'

'I might say a curate *is* a soldier – of the church militant; but I don't want to offend you with doctrine. I distinctly say, yes.'

Late one evening, a little time onward, he caught her sitting by the dim firelight in her room. She did not know he had entered; and he found her weeping. 'What are you crying about, poor dearest?' he said.

She started. 'Because of what you have told me!'

The Captain grew very unhappy; but he was undeterred.

In due time the town learnt, to its intense surprise, that Captain

Maumbry had retired from the —th Hussars and gone to Fountall Theological College to prepare for the ministry.

IV

'O, the pity of it! Such a dashing soldier – so popular – such an acquisition to the town – the soul of social life here! And now! . . . One should not speak ill of the dead, but that dreadful Mr Sainway – it was too cruel of him!'

This is a summary of what was said when Captain, now the Reverend, John Maumbry was enabled by circumstances to indulge his heart's desire of returning to the scene of his former exploits in the capacity of a minister of the Gospel. A low-lying district of the town, which at that date was crowded with impoverished cottagers, was crying for a curate, and Mr Maumbry generously offered himself as one willing to undertake labours that were certain to produce little result, and no thanks, credit, or emolument.

Let the truth be told about him as a clergyman; he proved to be anything but a brilliant success. Painstaking, single-minded, deeply in earnest as all could see, his delivery was laboured, his sermons were dull to listen to, and alas, too, too long. Even the dispassionate judges who sat by the hour in the bar-parlour of the White Hart – an inn standing at the dividing line between the poor quarter aforesaid and the fashionable quarter of Maumbry's former triumphs, and hence affording a position of strict impartiality – agreed in substance with the young ladies to the westward, though their views were somewhat more tersely expressed: 'Surely, God A'mighty spwiled a good sojer to make a bad pa'son when He shifted Cap'n Ma'mbry into a sarpless!'

The latter knew that such things were said, but he pursued his daily labours in and out of the hovels wiht serene unconcern.

It was about this time that the invalid in the oriel became more than a mere bowing acquaintance of Mrs Maumbry's. She had returned to the town with her husband, and was living with him in a little house in the centre of his circle of ministration, when by some means she became one of the invalid's visitors. After a general conversation while sitting in his room with a friend of both, an incident led up to the matter that still rankled deeply in her soul. Her face was now paler and thinner than it had been; even more attractive, her disappointments having inscribed themselves as meek thoughtfulness on a look that was once a little frivolous. The two ladies had called to be allowed to use the window for observing the departure of the Hussars, who were leaving for barracks much nearer to London.

The troopers turned the corner of Barrack Road into the top of High Street, headed by their band playing 'The girl I left behind me' (which was formerly always the tune for such times, though it is now nearly disused). They came and passed the oriel, where an officer or two, looking up and discovering Mrs Maumbry, saluted her, whose eyes filled with tears as the notes of the band waned away. Before the little group had recovered from that sense of the romantic which such spectacles impart, Mr Maumbry came along the pavement. He probably had bidden his former brethren-in-arms a farewell at the top of the street, for he walked from that direction in his rather shabby clerical clothes, and with a basket on his arm which seemed to hold some purchases he had been making for his poorer parishioners. Unlike the soldiers he went along quite unconscious of his appearance or of the scene around.

The contrast was too much for Laura. With lips that now quivered, she asked the invalid what he thought of the change that had come to her.

It was difficult to answer, and with a wilfulness that was too strong in her she repeated the question.

'Do you think,' she added, 'that a woman's husband has a right to do such a thing, even if he does feel a certain call to it?'

Her listener sympathized too largely with both of them to be anything but unsatisfactory in his reply. Laura gazed longingly out of the window towards the thin dusty line of Hussars, now smalling towards the Mellstock Ridge. 'I,' she said, 'who should have been in their van on the way to London, am doomed to fester in a hole in Durnover Lane!'

Many events had passed and many rumours had been current concerning her before the invalid saw her again after her leave-taking that day.

V

Casterbridge had known many military and civil episodes; many happy times, and times less happy; and now came the time of her visitation. The scourge of cholera had been laid on the suffering country, and the low-lying purlieus of this ancient borough had more than their share of the infliction. Mixen Lane, in the Durnover quarter, and in Maumbry's parish, was where the blow fell most heavily. Yet there was a certain mercy in its choice of a date, for Maumbry was the man for such an hour.

The spread of the epidemic was so rapid that many left the town and took lodgings in the villages and farms. Mr Maumbry's house was close to the most infected street, and he himself was occupied morn, noon, and night in endeavours to stamp out the plague and in alleviating the sufferings of the victims. So, as a matter of ordinary precaution, he decided to isolate his wife somewhere away from him for a while.

She suggested a village by the sea, near Budmouth Regis, and lodgings were obtained for her at Creston, a spot divided from the Casterbridge valley by a high ridge that gave it quite another atmosphere, though it lay no more than six miles off.

Thither she went. While she was rusticating in this place of safety, and her husband was slaving in the slums, she struck up an acquaintance with a lieutenant in the—st Foot, a Mr Vannicock, who was stationed with his regiment at the Budmouth infantry barracks. As Laura frequently sat on the shelving beach, watching each thin wave slide up to her, and hearing, without heeding, its gnaw at the pebbles in its retreat, he often took a walk that way.

The acquaintance grew and ripened. Her situation, her history, her beauty, her age – a year or two above his own – all tended to make an impression on the young man's heart, and a reckless flirtation was soon in blithe progress upon that lonely shore.

It was said by her detractors afterwards that she had chosen her lodging to be near this gentleman, but there is reason to believe that she had never seen him till her arrival there. Just now Casterbridge was so deeply occupied with its own sad affairs – a daily burying of the dead and destruction of contaminated clothes and bedding – that it had little inclination to promulgate such gossip as may have reached its ears on the pair. Nobody long considered Laura in the tragic cloud which overhung all.

Meanwhile, on the Budmouth side of the hill the very mood of men was in contrast. The visitation there had been slight and much earlier, and normal occupations and pastimes had been resumed. Mr Maumbry had arranged to see Laura twice a week in the open air, that she might run no risk from him; and, having heard nothing of the faint rumour, he met her as usual one dry and windy afternoon on the summit of the dividing hill, near where the high road from town to town crosses the old Ridge-way at right angles.

He waved his hand, and smiled as she approached, shouting to her: 'We will keep this wall between us, dear.' (Walls formed the field-fences here.) 'You musn't be endangered. It won't be for long, with God's help!'

'I will do as you tell me, Jack. But you are running too much risk yourself, aren't you? I get little news of you; but I fancy you are.'

'Not more than others.'

Thus somewhat formally they talked, an insulating wind beating the wall between them like a mill-weir.

'But you wanted to ask me something?' he added.

'Yes. You know we are trying in Budmouth to raise some money for your sufferers; and the way we have thought of is by a dramatic performance. They want me to take a part.'

His face saddened. 'I have known so much of that sort of thing, and all that accompanies it! I wish you had thought of some other way.'

She said lightly that she was afraid it was all settled. 'You object to my taking a part, then? Of course –'

He told her that he did not like to say he positively objected. He wished they had chosen an oratorio, or lecture, or anything more in keeping with the necessity it was to relieve.

'But,' said she impatiently, 'people won't come to oratorios or lectures! They will crowd to comedies and farces.'

'Well, I cannot dictate to Budmouth how it shall earn the money it is going to give us. Who is getting up this performance?'

'The boys of the—st.'

'Ah, yes; our old game!' replied Mr Maumbry. 'The grief of Casterbridge is the excuse for their frivolity. Candidly, dear Laura, I wish you wouldn't play in it. But I don't forbid you to. I leave the whole to your judgment.'

The interview ended, and they went their ways northward and southward. Time disclosed to all concerned that Mrs Maumbry played in the comedy as the heroine, the lover's part being taken by Mr Vannicock.

VI

Thus was helped on an event which the conduct of the mutually-attracted ones had been generating for some time.

It is unnecessary to give details. The—st Foot left for Bristol, and this precipitated their action. After a week of hesitation she agreed to leave her home at Creston and meet Vannicock on the ridge hard by, and to accompany him to Bath, where he had secured lodgings for her, so that she would be only about a dozen miles from his quarters.

Accordingly, on the evening chosen, she laid on her dressing-table a note for her husband, running thus: –

> *DEAR JACK – I am unable to endure this life any longer, and I have resolved to put an end to it. I told you I should run away if you persisted in being a clergyman, and now I am doing it. One cannot help one's nature. I have resolved to throw in my lot with Mr Vannicock, and I hope rather than expect you will forgive me. – L.*

Then, with hardly a scrap of luggage, she went, ascending to the ridge in the dusk of early evening. Almost on the very spot where her husband had stood at their last tryst she beheld the outline of Vannicock, who had come all the way from Bristol to fetch her.

'I don't like meeting here – it is so unlucky!' she cried to him. 'For God's sake let us have a place of our own. Go back to the milestone, and I'll come on.'

He went back to the milestone that stands on the north slope of the ridge, where the old and new roads diverge, and she joined him there.

She was taciturn and sorrowful when he asked her why she would not meet him on the top. At last she inquired how they were going to travel.

He explained that he proposed to walk to Mellstock Hill, on the other side of Casterbridge, where a fly was waiting to take them by a cross-cut into the Ivell Road, and onward to that town. The Bristol railway was open to Ivell.

This plan they followed, and walked briskly through the dull gloom till they neared Casterbridge, which place they avoided by turning to the right at the Roman Amphitheatre and bearing round to Durnover Cross. Thence the way was solitary and open across the moor to the hill whereon the Ivell fly awaited them.

'I have noticed for some time,' she said, 'a lurid glare over the Durnover end of the town. It seems to come from somewhere about Mixen Lane.'

'The lamps,' he suggested.

'There's not a lamp as big as a rushlight in the whole lane. It is where the cholera is worst.'

By Standfast Corner, a little beyond the Cross, they suddenly obtained an end view of the lane. Large bonfires were burning in the middle of the way, with a view to purifying the air; and from the wretched tenements with which the lane was lined in those days persons were bringing out bedding and clothing. Some was thrown into the fires, the rest placed in wheelbarrows and wheeled into the moor directly in the track of the fugitives.

They followed on, and came up to where a vast copper was set in the open air. Here the linen was boiled and disinfected. By the light of the lanterns Laura discovered that her husband was standing by the copper, and that it was he who unloaded the barrow and immersed its contents. The night was so calm and muggy that the conversation by the copper reached her ears.

'Are there many more loads tonight?'

'There's the clothes o' they that died this afternoon, sir. But that might bide till tomorrow, for you must be tired out.'

'We'll do it at once, for I can't ask anybody else to undertake it. Overturn that load on the grass and fetch the rest.'

The man did so and went off with the barrow. Maumbry paused for a moment to wipe his face, and resumed his homely drudgery amid this squalid and reeking scene, pressing down and stirring the contents of the copper with what looked like an old rolling-pin. The steam therefrom, laden with death, travelled in a low trail across the meadow.

Laura spoke suddenly: 'I won't go tonight after all. He is so tired, and I must help him. I didn't know things were so bad as this!'

Vannicock's arm dropped from her waist, where it had been resting as they walked. 'Will you leave?' she asked.

'I will if you say I must. But I'd rather help too.' There was no expostulation in his tone.

Laura had gone forward. 'Jack,' she said. 'I am come to help!'

The weary curate turned and held up the lantern. 'O – what, is it you, Laura?' he asked in surprise. 'Why did you come into this? You had better go back – the risk is great.'

'But I want to help you, Jack. Please let me help! I didn't come by myself – Mr Vannicock kept me company. He will make himself useful too, if he's not gone on. Mr Vannicock!'

The young lieutenant came forward reluctantly. Mr Maumbry spoke formally to him, adding as he resumed his labour, 'I thought the—st Foot had gone to Bristol.'

'We have. But I have run down again for a few things.'

The two newcomers began to assist, Vannicock placing on the ground the small bag containing Laura's toilet articles that he had been carrying. The barrow-man soon returned with another load, and all continued work for nearly a half-hour, when a coachman came out from the shadows to the north.

'Beg pardon, sir,' he whispered to Vannicock, 'but I've waited so long on Mellstock hill that at last I drove down to the turnpike; and seeing the light here, I ran on to find out what had happened.'

Lieutenant Vannicock told him to wait a few minutes, and the last barrow-load was got through. Mr Maumbry stretched himself and breathed heavily, saying, 'There; we can do no more.'

As if from the relaxation of effort he seemed to be seized with violent pain. He pressed his hands to his sides and bent forward.

'Ah! I think it has got hold of me at last,' he said with difficulty. 'I must try to get home. Let Mr Vannicock take you back, Laura.'

He walked a few steps, they helping him, but was obliged to sink down on the grass.

'I am – afraid – you'll have to send for a hurdle, or shutter, or something,' he went on feebly, 'or try to get me into the barrow.'

But Vannicock had called to the driver of the fly, and they waited until it was brought on from the turn-pike hard by. Mr Maumbry was placed therein. Laura entered with him, and they drove to his humble residence near the Cross, where he was got upstairs.

Vannicock stood outside by the empty fly awhile, but Laura did not reappear. He thereupon entered the fly and told the driver to take him back to Ivell.

VII

Mr Maumbry had over-exerted himself in the relief of the suffering poor, and fell a victim – one of the last – to the pestilence which had carried off so many. Two days later he lay in his coffin.

Laura was in the room below. A servant brought in some letters, and she glanced them over. One was the note from herself to Maumbry, informing him that she was unable to endure life with him any longer and was about to elope with Vannicock. Having read the letter she took it upstairs to where the dead man was, and slipped it into his coffin. The next day she buried him.

She was now free.

She shut up his house at Durnover Cross and returned to her lodgings at Creston. Soon she had a letter from Vannicock, and six weeks after her husband's death her lover came to see her.

'I forgot to give you back this – that night,' he said presently, handing her the little bag she had taken as her whole luggage when leaving.

Laura received it and absently shook it out. There fell upon the carpet her brush, comb, slippers, nightdress, and other simple necessaries for a journey. They had an intolerably ghastly look now, and she tried to cover them.

'I can now,' he said, 'ask you to belong to me legally – when a proper interval has gone – instead of as we meant.'

There was languor in his utterance, hinting at a possibility that it was perfunctorily made. Laura picked up her articles, answering that he certainly could so ask her – she was free. Yet not her expression either could be called an ardent reponse. Then she blinked more and more quickly and put her handkerchief to her face. She was weeping violently.

He did not move or try to comfort her in any way. What had come between them? No living person. They had been lovers. There was now no material obstacle whatever to their union. But there was the insistent shadow of that unconscious one; the thin figure of him, moving to and fro in front of the ghastly furnace in the gloom of Durnover Moor.

Yet Vannicock called upon Laura when he was in the neighbourhood, which was not often; but in two years, as if on purpose to further the marriage which everybody was expecting, the—st Foot returned to Budmouth Regis.

Thereupon the two could not help encountering each other at times. But whether because the obstacle had been the source of the love, or from a sense of error, and because Mrs Maumbry bore a less attractive look as a widow than before, their feelings seemed to decline from their former incandescence to a mere tepid civility. What domestic issues supervened in Vannicock's further story the man in the oriel never knew; but Mrs Maumbry lived and died a widow.

A Christmas Ghost-Story

Although after the year 1899, Thomas Hardy wrote no more novels and short stories, he did continue to utilize his interest in the supernatural in his poetry as a scan through the pages of his various collections will quickly demonstrate. Titles like 'The Dead Man Walking', 'The Vampirine Fair', 'The Phantom Horsewoman', 'Haunting Fingers' and 'I Travel As A Phantom Now' bear eloquent witness to his fascination with the weird and the mysterious throughout the remainder of his life.

Even as a poet, Hardy could not avoid controversy, however, and 'A Christmas Ghost Story' which he contributed to the *Westminster Gazette* of December 23, 1899 resulted in a stinging attack on the sentiment of the poem in the leader column of the *Daily Chronicle* on Christmas Day. Despite the writer's admission that the poem was 'a fine conception,' the paper concluded, 'We fear that the soldier is Mr Hardy's soldier and not one of the Dublin Fusiliers who cried amidst the storm of bullets at Tugela, 'Let us make a name for ourselves!' Hardy instantly took up his pen to defend his work, and the Editor of the *Chronicle*, in printing his reply, had the good grace to admit he could not find fault with the poet's argument. 'Mr Hardy's dead soldier,' he added in a footnote to the letter, 'is rightly admitted to the best company of Christmas ghosts, and we feel the pathetic beauty of the conception, whatever we may think of its metaphysics.'

For those readers who may not be familiar ith 'A Christmas Ghost-Story' and even less familiar with Thomas Hardy's defense of his unique ghost, I have appended both of them here as they seem to me to provide a most suitable conclusion to this collection.

A Christmas Ghost-Story

South of the Line, inland from far Durban,
A mouldering soldier lies – your countryman.
Awry and doubled up are his gray bones,
And on the breeze his puzzled phantom moans
Nightly to clear Canopus: 'I would know
By whom and when the All-Earth-gladdening Law
Of Peace, brought in by that Man Crucified,
Was ruled to be inept, and set aside?
And what of logic or of truth appears
In tacking 'Anno Domini' to the years?

Near twenty-hundred liveried thus have hied,
But tarries yet the Cause for which He died.'

Christmas-eve 1899.

A CHRISTMAS GHOST-STORY

[To the Editor of the *Daily Chronicle*:]

Sir, – In your interesting leading article of this morning, on Christmas Day, you appear to demur to the character of the soldier's phantom in my few lines entitled 'A Christmas Ghost Story' (printed in the *Westminster Gazette* for Dec 23), as scarcely exhibiting the primary quality of, say, a Dublin Fusilier, which is assumed to be physical courage; the said phantom being plaintive, embittered, and sad at the prevalence of war during a nominal Æra of peace. But surely there is artistic propriety – and, if I may say so, moral and religious propriety – in making him, or it, feel thus, especially in a poem intended for Christmas Day. One's modern fancy of a disembodied spirit – unless intentionally humorous – is that of an entity which has passed into a tenuous, impartial, sexless, fitful form of existence, to which bodily courage is a contradiction in terms. Having no physical frame to defend or sacrifice, how can he show either courage or fear? His views are no longer local; nations are all one to him; his country is not bounded by seas, but is co-extensive with the globe itself, if it does not even include all the inhabited planets of the sky. He has put off the substance, and has put on, in part at any rate, the essence of the Universe.

If we go back to the ancient fancy on this subject, and look into the works of great imaginative writers, they seem to construct their soldier-shades much on the same principle – often with a stronger infusion of emotion, and less of sturdiness. The Homeric ghost of Patroclus was plaintively anxious about his funeral rites, and Virgil's military ghosts – though some of them certainly were cheerful, and eager for war news – were as a body tremulous and pensive. The prophet Samuel, a man of great will and energy when on earth, was 'disquieted' and obviously apprehensive when he was raised by the Witch of Endor at the request of Saul. Morever, the authors of these Latin, Greek, and Hebrew fantasies were ignorant of the teaching of Christmas Day, that which alone moved the humble Natal shade to speak at all.

In Christian times Dante makes the chief Farinata exhibit a fine scornfulness, but even his Caesar, Hector, Æneas, Saladin, and heroes of that stamp, have, if I am not mistaken, an aspect neither sad nor joyful, and only reach the level of serenity. Hamlet's father, impliedly martial in life, was not particularly brave as a spectre. In short, and speaking generally, these creatures of the imagination are uncertain, fleeting, and quivering, like winds, mists, gossamer-webs, and fallen autumn leaves; they are sad, pensive, and frequently feel more or less sorrow for the acts of their corporeal years.

Thus I venture to think that the phantom of a slain soldier, neither British nor Boer, but a composite, typical phantom, may consistently be made to regret on or about Christmas Eve (when even the beasts of the field kneel, according to a tradition of my childhood) the battles of his life and war in general, although he may have shouted in the admirable ardor and pride of his flesh-time, as he is said to have done: 'Let us make a name for ourselves!'

Your obedient servant,

Dec. 25. THOMAS HARDY.